The Inspector Banks series is . . .

"EXCELLENT."—*Mostly Murder*

"JUSTLY ACCLAIMED."—*Publishers Weekly*

"SUPERIOR."—*New York Times Book Review*

Wednesday's Child

Nominated for the Edgar Award for Best Novel

"TAUT . . . [A] DRAMATIC AND POIGNANT ENDING . . . the characters are so believable you find yourself wondering what they're doing after Robinson stops writing."
—*San Jose Mercury News*

"SEAMLESS PLOTTING . . . Alan Banks—and Robinson—get better and better."
—*Hartford Courant*

"IF YOU HAVE NOT READ ANYTHING BY PETER ROBINSON, I would strongly recommend picking up *Wednesday's Child* . . . Robinson keeps us in suspense until, literally, the very last sentence. A great story."
—*Mostly Murder*

"ROBINSON ALWAYS DELIVERS AN EXCELLENT STORY, and this is one of his better ones."
—*Chattanooga Times*

continued on the next page . . .

Past Reason Hated

MORE MYSTERIES FROM THE
BERKLEY PUBLISHING GROUP . . .

THE HERON CARVIC MISS SEETON MYSTERIES: Retired art teacher Miss Seeton steps in where Scotland Yard stumbles. "A most beguiling protagonist!"
—*New York Times*

by Heron Carvic
MISS SEETON SINGS
MISS SEETON DRAWS THE LINE
WITCH MISS SEETON
PICTURE MISS SEETON
ODDS ON MISS SEETON

by Hampton Charles
ADVANTAGE MISS SEETON
MISS SEETON AT THE HELM
MISS SEETON, BY APPOINTMENT

by Hamilton Crane
HANDS UP, MISS SEETON
MISS SEETON CRACKS THE CASE
MISS SEETON PAINTS THE TOWN
MISS SEETON BY MOONLIGHT
MISS SEETON ROCKS THE CRADLE
MISS SEETON GOES TO BAT
MISS SEETON PLANTS SUSPICION
STARRING MISS SEETON
MISS SEETON UNDERCOVER
MISS SEETON RULES
SOLD TO MISS SEETON

KATE SHUGAK MYSTERIES: A former D.A. solves crimes in the far Alaska north . . .

by Dana Stabenow
A COLD DAY FOR MURDER
DEAD IN THE WATER
A FATAL THAW

A COLD-BLOODED BUSINESS
PLAY WITH FIRE

INSPECTOR BANKS MYSTERIES: Award-winning British detective fiction at its finest . . . "Robinson's novels are habit-forming!"—*West Coast Review of Books*

by Peter Robinson
THE HANGING VALLEY
WEDNESDAY'S CHILD

PAST REASON HATED
FINAL ACCOUNT

CASS JAMESON MYSTERIES: Lawyer Cass Jameson seeks justice in the criminal courts of New York City in this highly acclaimed series . . . "A witty, gritty heroine." —*New York Post*

by Carolyn Wheat
FRESH KILLS
MEAN STREAK

DEAD MAN'S THOUGHTS

SCOTLAND YARD MYSTERIES: Featuring Detective Superintendent Duncan Kincaid and his partner, Sergeant Gemma James . . . "Charming!"
—*New York Times Book Review*

by Deborah Crombie
A SHARE IN DEATH
LEAVE THE GRAVE GREEN

ALL SHALL BE WELL

JACK McMORROW MYSTERIES: The highly acclaimed series set in a Maine mill town and starring a newspaperman with a knack for crime solving . . . "Gerry Boyle is the genuine article." —Robert B. Parker

by Gerry Boyle
DEADLINE

BLOODLINE

FINAL ACCOUNT

AN INSPECTOR BANKS MYSTERY

PETER ROBINSON

BERKLEY PRIME CRIME, NEW YORK

This book is a work of fiction. Names, characters, places, and incidents either are the product of the author's imagination or are used fictitiously, and any resemblance to actual persons, living or dead, events or locales is entirely coincidental.

FINAL ACCOUNT

A Berkley Prime Crime Book / published by arrangement with the author

PRINTING HISTORY
Originally published in Canada in 1994
Berkley Prime Crime hardcover edition / September 1995
Berkley Prime Crime mass market edition / July 1996

The Putnam Berkley World Wide Web site address is
http://www.berkley.com

ISBN: 0-425-15382-7

Berkley Prime Crime Books are published
by The Berkley Publishing Group,
200 Madison Avenue, New York, NY 10016.
The name BERKLEY PRIME CRIME and the BERKLEY PRIME CRIME
design are trademarks belonging to Berkley Publishing Corporation.

PRINTED IN THE UNITED STATES OF AMERICA

10 9 8 7 6 5 4 3 2 1

For Sheila

ACKNOWLEDGMENTS

My thanks are long overdue to Cynthia Good, my editor from the beginning of the series. I must also thank my agent, Dominick Abel, for his advice and encouragement. This book in particular could not have been completed without the help of many people, all generous with their time and expertise. My thanks go especially to Keith Wright of Nottingham CID, both detective and novelist; Douglas Lucas, Director of the Centre for Forensic Sciences, Toronto; Mario Possamai for his book *Money on the Run*; Ken McFarland, Chartered Accountant; John Picton, journalist; and to Rick Blechta for putting me right about violists. Any errors are entirely my own and were made purely in the interests of dramatic fiction.

Dry bones that dream are bitter.
They dream and darken our sun.

W. B. YEATS
The Dreaming of the Bones

: 1

The uniformed constable lifted the tape and waved Detective Chief Inspector Banks through the gate at two forty-seven in the morning.

Banks's headlights danced over the scene as he drove into the bumpy farmyard and came to a halt. To his left stood the squat, solid house itself, with its walls of thick limestone and mossy, flagstone roof. Lights shone in both the upstairs and downstairs windows. To his right, a high stone wall buttressed a copse that straggled up the daleside, where the trees became lost in darkness. Straight ahead stood the barn.

A group of officers had gathered around the open doors, inside which a ball of light seemed to be moving. They looked like the cast of a fifties sci-fi film gazing in awe on an alien spaceship or life-form.

When Banks arrived, they parted in silence to let him through. As he entered, he noticed one young PC leaning against the outside wall dribbling vomit on his size twelves. Inside, the scene looked like a film set.

Peter Darby, the police photographer, was busy video-taping, and the source of the light was attached to the top of his camera. It created an eerie chiaroscuro and sudden, sickening illuminations as it swept around the barn's interior. All he needed, Banks thought, was for someone to yell "Action!" and the place would suddenly be full of sound and motion.

But no amount of yelling would breathe life back into the grotesque shape on the floor, by which a whey-faced young police surgeon, Dr. Burns, squatted with a black notebook in his hand.

At first, the position of the body reminded Banks of a parody of Moslem prayer: the kneeling man bent forward from the waist, arms stretched out in front, bum in the air, forehead touching the ground, perhaps facing Mecca. His fists were clenched in the dirt, and Banks noticed the glint of a gold cufflink, initialled "KAR," as Darby's light flashed on it.

But there was no forehead to touch the ground. Above the charcoal suit jacket, the blood-soaked collar of the man's shirt protruded about an inch, and after that came nothing but a dark, coagulated mass of bone and tissue spread out on the dirt like an oil stain: a shotgun wound, by the look of it. Patches of blood, bone and brain matter stuck to the whitewashed stone walls in abstract-expressionist patterns. Darby's roving light caught what looked like a fragment of skull sprouting a tuft of fair hair beside a rusty hoe.

Banks felt the bile rise in his throat. He could still smell the gunpowder, reminiscent of a childhood bonfire night, mixed with the stink of urine and feces and the rancid raw meat smell of sudden violent death.

"What time did the call come in?" he asked the PC beside him.

"One thirty-eight, sir. PC Carstairs from Relton was first on the scene. He's still puking up out front."

Banks nodded. "Do we know who the victim was?"

"DC Gay checked his wallet, sir. Name's Keith Roth-well. That's the name of the bloke who lived here, all right." He pointed over to the house. "Arkbeck Farm, it's called."

"A farmer?"

"Nay, sir. Accountant. Some sort of businessman, any-road."

One of the constables found a light switch and turned on the bare bulb, which became a foundation for the brighter light of Darby's video camera. Most regions didn't use video because it was hard to get good enough quality, but Peter Darby was a hardware junkie, forever experimenting.

Banks turned his attention back to the scene. The place looked as if it had once been a large stone Yorkshire barn, with double doors and a hayloft, called a "field house" in those parts. Originally, it would have been used to keep the cows inside between November and May, and to store fodder, but Rothwell seemed to have converted it into a garage.

To Banks's right, a silver-grey BMW, parked at a slight angle, took up about half the space. Beyond the car, against the far wall, a number of metal shelf units held all the tools and potions one would associate with car care: anti-freeze, wax polish, oily rags, screwdrivers, spanners. Rothwell had retained the rural look in the other half of the garage. He had even hung old farm implements on the whitewashed stone wall: a mucking rake, a hay knife, a draining scoop and a Tom spade, among others, all suitably rusted.

As he stood there, Banks tried to picture what might have happened. The victim had clearly been kneeling, perhaps praying or pleading for his life. It certainly didn't look as if he had tried to escape. Why had he submitted so easily? Not much choice, probably, Banks thought. You usually don't argue when someone is pointing a shotgun at you. But still . . . would a man simply kneel there, brace himself and wait for his executioner to pull the trigger?

Banks turned and left the barn. Outside, he met Detective Sergeant Philip Richmond and Detective Constable Susan Gay coming from around the back.

"Nothing there, sir, far as I can tell," said Richmond, a large torch in his hand. Susan, beside him, looked pale in the glow from the barn entrance.

"All right?" Banks asked her.

"I'm okay now, sir. I was sick, though."

Richmond looked the same as ever. His sang-froid was legendary around the place, so much so that Banks sometimes wondered if he had any feelings at all or whether he had come to resemble one of those computers he spent most of his time with.

"Anyone know what happened?" Banks asked.

"PC Carstairs had a quick word with the victim's wife when he first got here," said Susan. "All she could tell him was that a couple of men were waiting when she got home and they took her husband outside and shot him." She shrugged. "Then she became hysterical. I believe she's under sedation now, sir. I fished his wallet from his pocket, anyway," she went on, holding up a plastic bag. "Says his name's—"

"Yes, I know," said Banks. "Have we got an Exhibits Officer yet?"

"No, sir," Susan answered, then both she and Phil Richmond looked away. Exhibits Officer was one of the least popular jobs in an investigation. It meant keeping track of every piece of possible evidence and preserving a record of continuity. It usually went to whoever was in the dog-house at the time.

"Get young Farnley on the job, then," Banks said. PC Farnley hadn't offended anyone or cocked up a case, but he lacked imagination and had a general reputation around the station as a crashing golf bore.

Clearly relieved, Richmond and Susan wandered off towards the Scene-of-Crime team, who had just pulled into the farmyard in a large van. As they piled out in their white boiler suits, they looked like a team of government scientists sent to examine the alien landing-spot. Pretty soon, Banks thought, if they weren't all careful, there would be a giant spider or a huge gooey blob rolling around the Yorkshire Dales gobbling up everyone in sight.

The night was cool and still, the air moist, tinged with a hint of manure. Banks still felt half-asleep, despite the shock of what he had seen in the garage. Maybe he was dreaming. No. He thought of Sandra, warm at home in bed, and sighed.

Detective Superintendent Gristhorpe's arrival at about

three-thirty brought him out of his reverie. Gristhorpe limped over from his car. He wore an old donkey-jacket over his shirt, and he clearly hadn't bothered to shave or comb his unruly thatch of grey hair.

"Bloody hell, Alan," he said by way of greeting, "tha looks like Columbo."

There's the pot calling the kettle black, Banks thought. Still, the super was right. He had thrown on an old raincoat over his shirt and trousers because he knew the night would be chilly.

After Banks had explained what he had found out so far, Gristhorpe took a quick look in the barn, questioned PC Carstairs, the first officer at the scene, then rejoined Banks, his usually ruddy, pock-marked face a little paler. "Let's go in the house, shall we, Alan?" he said. "I hear PC Weaver's brewing up. He should be able to give us some background."

They walked across the dirt yard. Above them, the stars shone cold and bright like chips of ice on black velvet.

The farmhouse was cosy and warm inside, a welcome change from the cool night and the gruesome scene in the barn. It had been renovated according to the yuppie idea of the real rustic look, with exposed beams and rough stone walls in an open, split-level living-room, all earthy browns and greens. The remains of a log fire glowed in the stone hearth, and beside it stood a pair of antique andirons and a matching rack holding poker and tongs.

In front of the fire, Banks noticed two hard-backed chairs facing one another. One of them had fallen over, or had been pushed on its side. Beside both of them lay coils of rope. One of the chair seats looked wet.

Banks and Gristhorpe walked through into the ultra-modern kitchen, which looked like something from a colour supplement, where PC Weaver was pouring boiling water into a large red teapot.

"Nearly ready, sir," he said, when he saw the CID officers. "I'll just let it mash a couple of minutes."

The kitchen walls were done in bright red and white patterned tiles, and every available inch of space had been used to wedge fitted microwave, oven, fridge, dishwasher, cupboards and the like. It also boasted a central island unit, complete with tall pine stools. Banks and Gristhorpe sat down.

"How's his wife?" Gristhorpe asked.

"There's a wife and daughter here, sir," said Weaver. "The doctor's seen them. They're both unharmed, but they're suffering from shock. Hardly surprising when you consider they found the body. They're upstairs with WPC Smithies. Apparently there's also a son rambling around America somewhere."

"Who was this Rothwell bloke?" Banks asked. "He must have had a bob or two. Anything missing?"

"We don't know yet, sir," Weaver said. He looked around the bright kitchen. "But I see what you mean. He was some sort of financial whiz-kid, I think. These new-fangled kitchens don't come cheap, I can tell you. The wife's got in the habit of leaving the *Mail on Sunday* supplement open at some design or another. Her way of dropping hints, like, and about as subtle as a blow on the head with a hammer. The price of them makes me cringe. I tell her the one we've got is perfectly all right, but she—"

As he talked, Weaver began to pour the tea into the row of cups and mugs he had arranged. But after filling the second one, he stopped and stared at the door. Banks and Gristhorpe followed his gaze and saw a young girl standing there, her slight figure framed in the doorway. She rubbed her eyes and stretched.

"Hello," she said. "Are you the detectives? I'd like to talk to you. My name's Alison Rothwell and someone just killed my father."

2

She was about fifteen, Banks guessed, but she made no attempt to make herself look older, as many teenagers do. She wore a baggy, grey sweatshirt advertising an American football team, and a blue tracksuit bottom with a white stripe down each side. Apart from the bruiselike pouches under her light blue eyes, her complexion was pale. Her mousy blonde hair was parted in the centre and hung in uncombed strands over her shoulders. Her mouth, with its pale, thin lips, was too small for her oval face.

"Can I have some tea, please?" she asked. Banks noticed she had a slight lisp.

PC Weaver looked for direction. "Go ahead, lad," Gristhorpe told him. "Give the lass some tea." Then he turned to Alison Rothwell. "Are you sure you wouldn't rather be upstairs with your mum, love?"

Alison shook her head. "Mum'll be all right. She's asleep and there's a policewoman sitting by her. I can't sleep. It keeps going round in my mind, what happened. I want to tell you about it now. Can I?"

"Of course." Gristhorpe asked PC Weaver to stay and take notes. He introduced Banks and himself, then pulled out a stool for her. Alison gave them a sad, shy smile and sat down, holding the mug of tea to her chest with both hands as if she needed its heat. Gristhorpe indicated subtly that Banks should do the questioning.

"Are you sure you feel up to this?" Banks asked her first.

Alison nodded. "I think so."

"Would you like to tell us what happened, then?"

Alison took a deep breath. Her eyes focused on something Banks couldn't see.

"It was just after dark," she began. "About ten o'clock, quarter past or thereabouts. I was reading. I thought I heard a sound out in the yard."

"What kind of sound?" Banks asked.

"I . . . I don't know. Just as if someone was out there. A thud, like someone bumping into something or something falling on the ground."

"Carry on."

Alison hugged her cup even closer. "At first I didn't pay it any mind. I carried on reading, then I heard another sound, a sort of scraping, maybe ten minutes later."

"Then what did you do?" Banks asked.

"I turned the yard light on and looked out of the window, but I couldn't see anything."

"Did you have the television on, some music?"

"No. That's why I could hear the sounds outside so clearly. Usually it's so quiet and peaceful up here. All you can hear at night is the wind through the trees, and sometimes a lost sheep baa-ing, or a curlew up on the moors."

"Weren't you scared being by yourself?"

"No. I like it. Even when I heard the noise I just thought it might be a stray dog or a sheep or something."

"Where were your parents at this time?"

"They were out. It's their wedding anniversary. Their twenty-first. They went out to dinner in Eastvale."

"You didn't want to go with them?"

"No. Well . . . I mean, it was *their* anniversary, wasn't it?" She turned up her nose. "Besides, I don't like fancy restaurants. And I don't like Italian food. Anyway, it's not as if it was *Home Alone* or something. I *am* nearly sixteen, you know. And it was my choice. I'd rather stay home and read. I don't mind being by myself."

Perhaps, Banks guessed, they hadn't invited her. "Carry on," he said. "After you turned the yard light on, what did you do?"

"When I couldn't see anything, I just sort of brushed it off. Then I heard another noise, like a stone or something, hitting the wall. I was fed up of being disturbed by then, so I decided to go out and see what it was."

"You still weren't frightened?"

"A bit, maybe, by then. But not *really* scared. I still thought it was probably an animal or something like that, maybe a fox. We get them sometimes."

"Then what happened?"

"I opened the front door, and as soon as I stepped out, someone grabbed me and dragged me back inside and tied me to the chair. Then they put a rag in my mouth and put tape over it. I couldn't swallow properly. It was all dry and it tasted of salt and oil."

Banks noticed her knuckles had turned white around the mug. He worried she would crush it. "How many of them were there, Alison?" he asked.

"Two."

"Do you remember anything about them?"

She shook her head. "They were both dressed all in black, except one of them had white trainers on. The other had some sort of suede slip-ons, brown I think."

"You didn't see their faces?"

Alison hooked her feet over the crossbar. "No, they had balaclavas on, black ones. But they weren't like the ones you'd buy to keep you warm. They were just made of cotton or some other thin material. They had little slits for the eyes and slits just under the nose so they could breathe."

Banks noticed that she had turned paler. "Are you all right, Alison?" he asked. "Do you want to stop now and rest?"

Alison shook her head. Her teeth were clenched. "No. I'll be all right. Just let me . . ." She sipped some tea and seemed to relax a little.

"How tall were they?" Banks asked.

"One was about as big as you." She looked at Banks, who at only five foot nine was quite small for a policeman—just over regulation height, in fact. "But he was fatter. Not really fat, but just not, you know, wiry . . . like you. The other was a few inches taller, maybe six foot, and quite thin."

"You're doing really well, Alison," Banks said. "Was

there anything else about them?''

"No. I can't remember.''

"Did either of them speak?''

"When he dragged me back inside, the smaller one said, 'Keep quiet and do as you're told and we won't hurt you.' ''

"Did you notice his accent?''

"Not really. It sounded ordinary. I mean, not foreign or anything.''

"Local?''

"Yorkshire, yes. But not Dales. Maybe Leeds or something. You know how it sounds different, more citi- fied?''

"Good. You're doing just fine. What happened next?''

"They tied me to the chair with some rope and just sat and watched television. First the news was on, then some horrible American film about a psycho slashing women. They seemed to like that. One of them kept laughing when a woman got killed, as if it was funny.''

"You heard them laugh?''

"Just one of them, the tall one. The other one told him to shut up. He sounded like he was in charge.''

"The smaller one?''

"Yes.''

"That's all he said: 'Shut up'?''

"Yes.''

"Was there anything unusual about the taller man's laugh?''

"I . . . I don't . . . I can't remember.'' Alison wiped a tear from her eye with the sleeve of her sweatshirt. "It was just a laugh, that's all.''

"It's all right. Don't worry about it. Did they harm you in any way?''

Alison reddened and looked down into her half-empty mug. "The smaller one came over to me when I was tied up, and he put his hand on my breast. But the other one made him stop. It was the only time he said anything.''

"How did he make him stop? What did he do?''

"He just said not to, that it wasn't part of the deal."

"Did he use those exact words, Alison? Did he say, 'It's not part of the deal'?"

"Yes. I think so. I mean, I'm not completely sure, but it was something like that. The smaller man didn't seem to like it, being told what to do by the other, but he left me alone after that."

"Did you see any kind of weapon?" Banks asked.

"Yes. The kind of gun that farmers have, with two barrels. A shotgun."

"Who had it?"

"The smaller man, the one in charge."

"Did you hear a car at any time?"

"No. Only when Mum and Dad came home. I mean, I heard cars go by on the road sometimes, you know, the one that goes through Relton and right over the moors into the next dale. But I didn't hear anyone coming or going along our driveway."

"What happened when your parents came home?"

Alison paused and swirled the tea in the bottom of her mug as if she were trying to see into her future. "It must have been about half past eleven or later. The men waited behind the door and the tall one grabbed Mum while the other put his gun to Dad's neck. I tried to scream and warn them, honest I did, but the rag in my mouth ... I just couldn't make a sound. . . ." She ran her sleeve across her eyes again and sniffled. Banks gestured to PC Weaver, who found a box of tissues on the window-sill and brought them over.

"Thank you," Alison said. "I'm sorry."

"You don't have to go on if you don't want," Banks said. "It can wait till tomorrow."

"No. I've started. I want to. Besides, there's not much more to tell. They tied Mum up the same as me and we sat there facing each other. Then they went outside with Dad. Then we heard the bang."

"How long between the time they went out and the
shot?"

Alison shook her head dreamily. She held the mug up
close to her throat. The sleeves of her sweatshirt had
slipped down, and Banks could see the raw, red lines where
the rope had cut into her flesh. "I don't know. It seemed
like a long time. But all I can remember is we just sat
looking at each other, Mum and me, and we didn't know
what was happening. I remember a night-bird calling
somewhere. Not a curlew. I don't know what it was. And
it seemed like forever, like time just stretched out and Mum
and I got really scared now looking at one another not
knowing what was going on. Then we heard the explosion
and . . . and it was like it all snapped and I saw something
die in Mum's eyes, it was so, so . . ." Alison dropped the
mug, which clipped the corner of the table then fell and
spilled without breaking on the floor. The sobs seemed to
start deep inside her, then she began to shake and wail.

Banks went over and put his arms around her, and she
clung onto him for dear life, sobbing against his chest.

3

"It looks like his office," Banks said, when Gristhorpe
turned on the light in the last upstairs room.

Two large desks formed an L-shape. On one of them
stood a computer and a laser printer, and on a small table
next to them stood a fax machine with a basket attached at
the front for collecting the cut-off sheets. At the back of
the computer desk, a hutch stood against the wall. The com-
partments were full of boxes of disks and software manuals,
mostly for word processing, spreadsheets and accounting
programmes, along with some for standard utilities.

The other desk stood in front of the window, which
framed a view of the farmyard. Scene-of-Crime Officers
were still going about their business down there taking samples of just about everything in sight, measuring distances,

trying to get casts of footprints, sifting soil. In the barn, their bright arc lamps had replaced Darby's roving light.

This was the desk where Rothwell dealt with handwritten correspondence and phone calls, Banks guessed. There was a blotter, which looked new—no handy wrong-way-around clues scrawled there—a jam-jar full of pens and pencils, a blank scratch-pad, an electronic adding machine of the kind that produces a printed tape of its calculations, and an appointment calendar open at the day of the murder, 12th May.

The only things written there were "Dr. Hunter" beside the 10:00 a.m. slot, "Make dinner reservation: Mario's, 8:30 p.m." Below that, and written in capitals all across the afternoon, "FLOWERS?" Banks had noticed a vase full of fresh flowers in the living-room. An anniversary present? Sad when touching gestures like that outlive the giver. He thought of Sandra again, and suddenly he wanted very much to be near her, to bridge the distance that had grown between them, to hold her and feel her warmth. He shivered.

"All right, Alan?" Gristhorpe asked.

"Fine. Someone just walked over my grave."

"Look at all this." Gristhorpe pointed to the two metal filing cabinets and the heavy-duty shelves that took up the room's only long, unbroken wall. "Business records, by the looks of it. Someone's going to have to sift through it." He looked towards the computer and grimaced. "We'd better get Phil to have a look at this lot tomorrow," he said. "I wouldn't trust myself to turn the bloody thing on without blowing it up."

Banks grinned. He was aware of Gristhorpe's Luddite attitude towards computers. He quite liked them, himself. Of course, he had only the most rudimentary skills and never seemed to be able to do anything right, but Phil Richmond, "Phil the Hacker" as he was known around the station, ought to be able to tell them a thing or two about Rothwell's system.

Finding nothing else of immediate interest in the office, they walked out to the rear of the house, which faced north, and stood in the back garden, the hems of their trousers damp with dew. It was after five now, close to dawn. A pale sun was slowly rising in the east behind a veil of thin cloud that had appeared over the last couple of hours, mauve on the horizon, but giving the rest of the sky a light grey wash and the landscape the look of a water-colour. A few birds sang, and occasionally the sound of a farm vehicle starting up broke the silence. The air smelled moist and fresh.

It was certainly a *garden* they stood in, and not just a backyard. Someone—Rothwell? His wife?—had planted rows of vegetables—beans, cabbage, lettuce, all neatly marked—a small area of herbs and a strawberry patch. At the far end, beyond a dry-stone wall, the land fell away steeply to a beck that coursed down the daleside until it fed into the River Swain at Fortford.

The village of Fortford, about a mile down the hillside, was just waking up. Below the exposed foundations of the Roman fort on its knoll to the east, the cottages with their flagstone roofs huddled around the green and the square-towered church. Already, smoke drifted from some of the chimneys as farm labourers and shopkeepers prepared themselves for the coming day. Country folk were early risers.

The whitewashed front of the sixteenth-century Rose and Crown glowed pink in the early light. Even in there, someone would soon be in the kitchen, making bacon and eggs for the paying guests, especially for the ramblers, who liked to be off early. At the thought of food, his stomach rumbled. He knew Ian Falkland, the landlord of the Rose and Crown, and thought it might not be a bad idea to have a chat with him about Keith Rothwell. Though he was an expatriate Londoner, like Banks, Ian knew most of the local dalesfolk, and, given his line of work, he picked up a fair amount of gossip.

Finally, Banks turned to Gristhorpe and broke the silence. "They certainly seemed to know what was what, didn't they?" he said. "I don't imagine it was a lucky guess that the girl was in the house alone."

"You're thinking along the same lines as I am, aren't you, Alan?" said Gristhorpe. "An execution. A hit. Call it what you will."

Banks nodded. "I can't see any other lines to think along yet. Everything points to it. The way they came in and waited, the position of the body, the coolness, the professionalism of it all. Even the way one of them said touching the girl wasn't part of the deal. It was all planned. Yes, I think it was an execution. It certainly wasn't a robbery or a random killing. They hadn't been through the house, as far as we could tell. Everything seems in order. And if it was a robbery, they'd no need to kill him, especially that way. The question is why? Why should anyone want to execute an accountant?"

"Hmm," said Gristhorpe. "Unhappy client, maybe? Someone he turned in to the Inland Revenue?" Nearby, a peewit sensed their closeness to its ground nest and started buzzing them, piping its high-pitched call. "One of the things we have to do is find out how *honest* an accountant our Mr. Rothwell was," Gristhorpe went on. "But let's not speculate too much yet, Alan. We don't know if there's anything missing, for a start. Rothwell might have had a million in gold bullion hidden away in his garage for all we know. But you're right about the execution angle. And that means we could be dealing with something very big, big enough to contract a murder for."

"Sir?"

At that moment, one of the SOC officers came into the garden through the back door.

Gristhorpe turned. "Yes?"

"We've found something, sir. In the garage. I think you'd both better come and have a look for yourselves."

4

They followed the officer back to the brightly lit garage. Rothwell's body had, mercifully, been taken to the morgue, where Dr. Glendenning, the Home Office pathologist, would get to work on it as soon as he could. Two men from the SOC team stood by the barn door. One was holding something with a pair of tweezers and the other was peering at it closely.

"What is it?" Banks asked.

"It's wadding, sir. From the shotgun," said the SOCO with the tweezers. "You see, sir, you can buy commercially made shotgun cartridges, but you can also reload the shells at home. Plenty of farmers and recreational shooters do it. Saves money."

"Is that what this bloke did?" Banks asked.

"Looks like it, sir."

"To save money? Typical Yorkshireman. Like a Scotsman stripped of his generosity."

"Cheeky southern bastard," said Gristhorpe, then turned to the SOCO. "Go on, lad."

"Well, sir, I don't know how much you know about shotguns, but they take cartridges, not bullets."

Banks knew that much, at least, and he suspected that Gristhorpe, from Dales farming stock, knew a heck of a lot more. But they usually found it best to let the SOCOs show off a bit.

"We're listening," said Gristhorpe.

Emboldened by that, the officer went on. "A shotgun shell's made up of a primer, a charge of gunpowder and the pellets, or shot. There's no slug and there's no rifling in the barrel, so you can't get any characteristic markings to trace back to the weapon. Except from the shell, of course, which bears the imprint of the firing and loading mechanisms. But we don't have a shell. What we do have is this." He held up the wadding. "Commercial wadding is usually made of either paper or plastic, and you can sometimes trace the shell's manufacturer through it. But this isn't commercial.''

''What exactly is it?'' asked Banks, reaching out.

The SOCO passed him the tweezers and said, ''Don't know for certain yet, but it looks like something from a colour magazine. And luckily, it's not too badly burned inside, only charred around the edges. It's tightly packed, but we'll get it unfolded and straightened out when we get it to the lab, then maybe we'll be able to tell you the name, date and page number.''

''Then all we'll have to do is check the list of subscribers,'' said Banks, ''and it'll lead us straight to our killer. Dream on.''

The SOCO laughed. ''We're not miracle workers, sir.''

''Has anyone got a magnifying glass?'' Banks asked the assembly at large. ''And I don't want any bloody cracks about Sherlock Holmes.''

One of the SOCOs passed him a glass, the rectangular kind that came with the tiny-print, two-volume edition of the *Oxford English Dictionary*. Banks held up the wadding and examined it through the glass.

What he saw was an irregularly shaped wad of crumpled paper, no more than about an inch across at its widest point. At first he couldn't make out anything but the blackened edge of the wadded paper but it certainly looked as if it were from some kind of magazine. He looked more closely, turning the wadding this way and that, holding it closer and further, then finally the disembodied shapes coalesced into something recognizable. ''Bloody hell,'' he muttered letting his arm fall slowly to his side.

''What is it, Alan?'' Gristhorpe asked.

Banks handed him the glass. ''You'd better have a look for yourself,'' he said. ''You won't believe me.''

Banks stood back and watched Gristhorpe scrutinize the wadding, knowing that it would be only a matter of moments before he noticed, as Banks had done, part of a pink tongue licking a dribble of semen from the tip of an erect penis.

2

1

Traditional police wisdom has it that if a case doesn't yield leads in the first twenty-four hours, then everyone is in for a long, tough haul. In practice, of course, the period doesn't always turn out to be twenty-four hours; it can be twenty-three, nine, fourteen, or even forty-eight. That's the problem: when do you scale down your efforts? The answer, Banks reminded himself as he dragged his weary bones into the "Boardroom" of Eastvale Divisional Police Headquarters at ten o'clock that morning, is that you don't.

The Suzy Lamplugh case was a good example. It started as a missing-persons report. One lunch-time, a young woman left the estate agent's office in Fulham, where she worked, and disappeared. Only after over a year's intensive detective work, which resulted in more than six hundred sworn statements, thousands of interviews, 26,000 index cards and nobody knew how many man-hours, was the investigation wound down. Suzy Lamplugh was never found, either alive or dead.

By the time Banks arrived at the station, Superintendent Gristhorpe had appointed Phil Richmond Office Manager and asked him to set up the Murder Room, where all information regarding the Keith Rothwell case would be carefully indexed, cross-referenced and filed. At first, Gristhorpe thought it should be established in Fortford or Relton, close to the scene, but later decided that they had better facilities at the Eastvale station. It was only about seven miles from Fortford, anyway.

Richmond was also the only one among them who had

training in the use of the HOLMES computer system—acronym for the Home Office Major Enquiry System, with a superfluous "L" for effect. HOLMES wasn't without its problems, especially as not all the country's police forces used the same computer languages. Still, if no developments occurred before long, Richmond's skill might prove useful.

Gristhorpe had also given a brief press conference first thing in the morning. The sooner photographs of Keith Rothwell and descriptions of the killers, balaclavas and all, were sitting beside the public's breakfast plates or flashing on their TV screens, the sooner information would start to come in. The news was too late for that morning's papers, but it would make local radio and television, the *Yorkshire Evening Post*, and tomorrow's national dailies.

Of course, Gristhorpe had given hardly any details about the murder itself. At first, he had even resisted the idea of releasing Rothwell's name. After all, there had been no formal identification, and they didn't have his fingerprints on file for comparison. On the other hand, there was little doubt as to what had happened, and they were hardly going to drag Alison or her mother along to the mortuary to identify the remains.

Gristhorpe had also been in touch with the anti-terrorist squad at Scotland Yard. Yorkshire was far from a stranger to IRA action. People still remembered the M62 bomb in 1974, when a coach carrying British servicemen and their families was blown up, killing eleven and wounding fourteen. Many even claimed to have heard the explosion from as far away as Leeds and Bradford. More recently, two policemen had been shot by IRA members during a routine traffic check on the A1.

The anti-terrorist squad would be able to tell Gristhorpe whether Rothwell had any connections, however tenuous, that would make him a target. As an accountant, he could, for example, have been handling money for a terrorist group. In addition, forensic information and details of the *modus operandi* would be made known to the squad, who would see if the information matched anything on file.

While Gristhorpe handled the news media and Richmond set up the Murder Room, Banks and Susan Gay had conducted a breakfast-time house-to-house of Relton and Fortford—including a visit to the Rose and Crown and a generous breakfast from Ian Falkland—trying to find out a bit about Rothwell, and whether anyone had seen or heard anything unusual on the night of the murder.

Gristhorpe, Richmond and Susan Gay were already in the room when Banks arrived and poured himself a large black coffee. The conference room was nicknamed the "Boardroom" because of its well-polished, heavy oval table and ten stiff-backed chairs, not to mention the coarse-textured burgundy wallpaper, which gave the room a constant aura of semi-darkness, and the large oil painting (in ornate gilt frame) of one of Eastvale's most successful nineteenth-century wool merchants, looking decidedly sober and stiff in his tight-fitting suit and starched collar.

"Right," said Gristhorpe, "time to get up to date. Alan?"

Banks slipped a few sheets of paper from his briefcase and rubbed his eyes. "Not much so far, I'm afraid. Rothwell was trained as an accountant. At least we've got that much confirmed. Some of the locals in Relton and Fortford knew him, but not well. Apparently, he was a quiet sort of bloke. Kept to himself."

"Who did he work for?"

"Self-employed. We got this from Ian Falkland, landlord of the Rose and Crown in Fortford. He said Rothwell used to drop by now and then for a quick jar before dinner. Never had more than a couple of halves. Well-liked, quiet, decent sort of chap. Anyway, he used to work for Hatchard and Pratt, the Eastvale firm, until he started his own business. Falkland used him for the pub's accounts. I gather Rothwell saved him a bob or two from the Inland Revenue." Banks scratched the small scar by his right eye.

"There's a bit more to it than that, though," he went on. "Falkland got the impression that Rothwell owned a few businesses as well, and that accountancy was becoming more of a sideline for him. We couldn't get any more than that, but we'll be having a close look at his office today."

Gristhorpe nodded.

"And that's about it," Banks said. "The Rothwell family had been living at Arkbeck Farm for almost five years. They used to live in Eastvale." He looked at his watch. "I'm going out to Arkbeck Farm again after this meeting. I'm hoping Mrs. Rothwell will have recovered enough to tell us something about what happened."

"Good. Any leads on the two men?"

"Not yet, but Susan spoke to someone who thinks he saw a car."

Gristhorpe looked at Susan.

"That's right, sir," she said. "It was around sunset last night, before it got completely dark. A retired schoolteacher from Fortford was coming back home after visiting his daughter in Pateley Bridge. He said he liked to take the lonely roads over the moors."

"Where did he see this car?"

"At the edge of the moors above Relton, sir. It was parked in a turn-off, just a dip by the side of the road. I think it used to be an old drover's track, but it's not used any more, and only the bit by the road is clear. The rest has been taken over by moorland. Anyway, sir, the thing is that the way the road curves in a wide semi-circle around the farm, this spot would only be about a quarter of a mile away on foot. Remember that copse opposite the farmhouse? Well, it's the same one that straggles up the daleside as far as this turn-off. It would provide excellent cover if someone wanted to get to the farm without being seen, and Alison wouldn't have heard the car approaching if it had been parked way up on the road."

"Sounds promising," said Gristhorpe. "Did the witness notice anything about the car?"

"Yes, sir. He said it looked like an old Escort. It was a light colour. For some reason he thought pale blue. And there was either rust or mud or grass around the lower chassis."

"It's hardly the bloody stretch-limousine you associate with hit men, is it?" Gristhorpe said.

"More of a Yorkshire version," said Banks.

Gristhorpe laughed. "Aye. Better follow it up, then, Susan. Get a description of the car out. I don't suppose your retired schoolteacher happened to see two men dressed in black carrying a shotgun, did he?"

Susan grinned. "No, sir."

"Rothwell didn't do any farming himself, did he?" Gristhorpe asked Banks.

"No. Only that vegetable patch we saw at the back. He rented out the rest of his land to neighbouring farmers. There's a fellow I know farms up near Relton I want to talk to. Pat Clifford. He should know if there were any problems in that area."

"Good," said Gristhorpe. "As you know, a lot of locals don't like newcomers buying up empty farms and not using them properly."

Gristhorpe, Banks knew, had lived in the farmhouse above Lyndgarth all his life. Perhaps he had even been born there. He had sold off most of the land after his parents died and kept only enough for a small garden and for his chief off-duty indulgences: a dry-stone wall he worked on periodically, which went nowhere and fenced nothing in.

"Anyway," Gristhorpe went on, "there's been some bad feeling. I can't see a local farmer hiring a couple of killers—people like to take care of their own around these parts—but stranger things have happened. And remember: shotguns are common as cow-clap around farms. Anything on that wadding yet?"

Banks shook his head. "The lab's still working on it. I've already asked West Yorkshire to make a few enquiries at the kind of places that sell that sort of magazine. I talked to Ken Blackstone at Millgarth in Leeds. He's a DI there and an old mate.''

"Good," said Gristhorpe, then turned to Richmond. "Phil, why don't you go up to Arkbeck Farm with Alan and have a look at Rothwell's computer before you get bogged down managing the office?"

"Yes, sir. Do you think we should have it brought in after I've had a quick look?"

Gristhorpe nodded. "Aye, good idea." He scratched his pock-marked cheek. "Look, Phil, I know you're supposed to be leaving us for the Yard at the end of the week, but—"

"It's all right, sir," Richmond said. "I understand. I'll stick around as long as you need me."

"Good lad. Susan, did you find anything interesting in the appointment book?"

Susan Gay shook her head. "Not yet, sir. He had a doctor's appointment for yesterday morning with Dr. Hunter. I called the office and it appears he kept it. Routine physical. No problems. I'm working my way through. He didn't write much down—or maybe he kept it on computer—but there's a few names to check out, mostly local businesses. I must say, though, sir, he didn't exactly have a full appointment book. There are plenty of empty days."

"Maybe he didn't need the money. Maybe he could afford to pick and choose. Have a word with someone at his old firm, Hatchard and Pratt. They're just on Market Street. They might be able to tell us something about his background." Gristhorpe looked at his watch. "Okay, we've all got plenty to do, better get to it."

2

"I'm afraid my mother's still in bed," Alison told Banks at Arkbeck Farm. "I told her you were here . . ." She shrugged.

That was odd, Banks thought. Surely a mother would want to comfort her daughter and protect her from prying policemen? "Have you remembered anything else?" he asked.

Alison Rothwell looked worn out and worried to death. She wore her hair, unwashed and a little greasy, tied back, emphasizing her broad forehead, a plain white T-shirt and stonewashed designer jeans. She sat with her legs tucked under her, and as she talked, she fiddled with a ring on the little finger of her right hand. "I don't know," she said. The lisp made her sound like a little girl.

They sat in a small, cheerful room at the back of the house with ivory-painted walls and Wedgwood blue upholstery. A bookcase stood against one wall, mostly full of paperbacks, their spines a riot of orange, green and black. Against the wall opposite stood an upright piano with a highly lacquered cherry-wood finish. On top of it stood an untidy pile of sheet music. WPC Smithies, who had stayed with the Rothwells, sat discreetly in a corner, notebook open. Phil Richmond was upstairs in Keith Rothwell's study, clicking away on the computer.

The large bay window, open about a foot to let in the birdsongs and fresh air, looked out over Fortford and the dale beyond. It was a familiar enough view to Banks. He had seen it from "Maggie's Farm" on the other side of Relton, and from the house of a man called Adam Harkness on the valley bottom. The sight never failed to impress, though, even on a dull day like today, with the grey-brown ruins of Devraulx Abbey poking through the trees of its grounds, the village of Lyndgarth clustered around its lop-sided green and, towering over the patchwork of pale green fields and dry-stone walls that rose steeply to the heights, the forbidding line of Aldington Edge, a long limestone scar streaked with fissures from top to bottom like gleaming skeleton's teeth.

"I know it's painful to remember," Banks went on, "but we need all the help we can get if we're to catch these men."

"I know. I'm sorry."

"Do you remember hearing any sounds between the time they went outside and when you heard the bang?"

Alison frowned. "I don't think so."

"No sounds of a struggle, or screaming?"

"No. It was all so quiet. That's what I remember."

"No talking?"

"I didn't hear any."

"And you don't know how long they were out there before the explosion?"

"No. I was scared and I was worried. Mum was sitting facing me. I could see how frightened she was, but I couldn't do anything. I just felt so powerless."

"When it was all over, did you hear any sounds then?"

"I don't think so."

"Try to remember. Did you hear what direction they went off in?"

"No."

"Any sounds of a car?"

She paused. "I think I heard a car door shut, but I can't be sure. I mean, I didn't hear it drive away, but I think I kept sort of drifting in and out. I think I heard a sound like the slam of a car door in the distance."

"Do you know which direction it came from?"

"Further up the daleside, I think. Relton way."

"Good. Now, can you remember anything else about the men?"

"One of them, the one who touched me. I've been think-ing about it. He had big brown eyes, a sort of light hazel colour, and watery. There's a word for it. Like a dog."

"Spaniel?"

"Yes. That's it. Spaniel eyes. Or puppy dog. He had puppy-dog eyes. But they're usually . . . you know, they usually make you feel sorry for the person, but these didn't. They were cruel."

"Did either of the men say anything else?"

"No."

"Did they go anywhere else in the house? Any other rooms?"

"No."

"Did you see them take anything at all?"

Alison shook her head.

"When your father saw them and later went outside with them, how did he seem?"

"What do you mean?"

"Was he surprised?"

"When he first came in and they grabbed him, yes."

"But after?"

"I . . . I don't know. He didn't do anything or say anything. He just stood there."

"Do you think he recognized the men?"

"How could he? They were all covered up."

"Did he seem surprised after the immediate shock had worn off?"

"I don't think he did, no. Just . . . resigned."

"Was he expecting them?"

"I . . . I don't know. I don't think so."

"Do you think he knew them, knew why they were there?"

"How could he?"

She spoke with such disbelief that Banks wondered if she had noticed that her father really *wasn't* so shocked or surprised and it confused her. "Do you think he knew what was happening?" he pressed. "Why it was happening?"

"Maybe. No. I don't know. He couldn't possibly, could he?" She screwed up her eyes. "I can't see it that clearly. I don't want to see it clearly."

"All right, Alison. It's all right. I'm sorry, but I have to ask."

"I know. I don't mean to be a cry-baby." She rubbed her bare arm over her eyes.

"You're being very brave. Just one more question about what happened and then we'll move on. Okay?"

"Okay."

"Did your father go quietly or did they have to force him?"

"No, he just walked out with them. He didn't say anything."

"Did he look frightened?"

"He didn't look anything." She reddened. "And he didn't *do* anything. He just left Mum and me all tied up and let them take him and . . . and kill him like an animal."

"All right, Alison, calm down. How did you get free from the chair after they'd gone?"

Alison sniffled and blew her nose. "It was a long time," she said finally. "Hours maybe. Some of the time I just sat there, but not really there, if you know what I mean. I think Mum had fainted. They'd really tied us tight and I couldn't feel my hands properly."

As she spoke, she rubbed at her wrists, still ringed by the burn-marks. "In the end, I tipped my chair and crawled over near the table where my mother's sewing basket was. I knew there were scissors in there. I had to rub my hands for a long time, so they could feel properly, and I don't know how . . . but in the end I cut the rope, then I untied Mum." She shifted her position. "I'm worried about Mum. She's not herself. She doesn't want to eat. What's going to happen to her?"

"I'm all right, Alison, dear. There's no need to worry."

The voice came from the doorway, and Banks turned for his first glance of Mrs. Rothwell. She was a tall woman with short grey hair and fine-boned, angular features, the small nose perhaps just a little too sharply chiselled. There seemed an unusually wide space, Banks thought, between her nose and her thin upper lip, which gave her tilted head a haughty, imperious aspect. Banks could see where Alison got her small mouth from.

Her chestnut-brown eyes looked dull. Tranquillizers prescribed by Dr. Burns, Banks guessed. They would help to explain her listless movements, too. Her skin was pale, as if drained of blood, though Banks could tell she had put some make-up on. In fact, she had made a great effort to look her best. She wore black silk slacks over her thin, boyish hips, and a cable-knit jumper in a rainbow pattern, which looked to Banks's untutored eye like an exclusive design. At least he had never seen one like it before. Even in her sedated grief, there was something controlled, commanding and attention-demanding about her, a kind of tightly reined-in power.

She sat down in the other armchair, crossed her legs and clasped her hands on her lap. Banks noticed the chunky rings on her fingers: diamond clusters, a large ruby and a broad gold wedding band.

Banks introduced himself and expressed his condolences. She inclined her head slightly in acceptance.

"I'm afraid I have some difficult questions for you, Mrs. Rothwell," he said.

"Not about last night," she said, one bejewelled hand going to her throat. "I can't talk about it. I feel faint, my voice goes and I just can't talk."

"Mummy," said Alison. "I've told him about . . . about that. Haven't I?" And she looked at Banks as if daring him to disagree.

"Yes," he said. "Actually, it wasn't that I wanted to ask about specifically. It's just that we need more information on your husband's movements and activities. Can you help?"

She nodded. "I'm sorry, Chief Inspector. I'm not usually such a mess." She touched her hair. "I must look dreadful."

Banks murmured a compliment. "Did your husband have any enemies that you knew of?" he asked.

"No. None at all. But then he didn't bore me with the details of his business. I really had no idea what kind of people he dealt with." Her accent, Banks noticed, was Eastvale filtered through elocution lessons. *Elocution lessons.* He hadn't thought people took those in this day and age.

"So he never brought his business home, so to speak?"

"No."

"Did he travel much?"

"Do you mean abroad?"

"Anywhere."

"Well, he did go abroad now and then, on business, and of course, we'd holiday in Mexico, Hawaii or Bermuda. He also travelled a lot locally in the course of business. He was away a lot."

"Where did he go?"

"Oh, all over. Leeds, Manchester, Liverpool, Birmingham, Bristol. Sometimes to London, Europe. He had a very important job. He was a brilliant financial analyst, much in demand. He could pick and choose his clients, could Keith, he didn't have to take just any old thing that came along."

"You mentioned financial analysis. What exactly did he do?"

She picked at the wool on her sleeve with long, bony fingers. "As I said, he didn't tell me much about work, not about the details, anyway. He qualified as a chartered accountant, of course, but that was only part of it. He had a genius for figures. He advised people what to do with their money, helped businesses out of difficulties. I suppose he was a kind of trouble-shooter, if you like. A very exclusive one. He didn't need any new clients and people only found out about him by word of mouth."

That all sounded sufficiently vague to be suspicious to Banks. On the other hand, what did *he* do? Investigate crimes, yes. But to do so, he chatted with locals over a pint, interviewed bereaved relatives, pored over fingerprints and blood samples. It would all sound rather nebulous and aimless to an outsider.

"And you never met any of his business associates?"

"We had people for dinner occasionally, but we never talked business."

"Maybe, if you have a moment later, you could make a list of those you entertained most frequently?"

She raised her eyebrows. "If you want."

"Now, Mrs. Rothwell," Banks said, wishing he could have a cigarette in what was obviously a non-smoking household, "this next question may strike you as rather indelicate, but were there any problems in the family?"

"Of course not. We're a happy family. Aren't we, Alison?"

Alison looked at Banks. "Yes, Mother," she said.

Banks turned back to Mrs. Rothwell. "Had your husband been behaving at all unusually recently?" he asked. "Had you noticed any changes in him?"

She frowned. "He *had* been a bit edgy, tense, a bit more preoccupied and secretive than usual. I mean, he was always quiet, but he'd been even more so."

"For how long?"

She shrugged. "Two or three weeks."

"But he never told you what was wrong?"

"No."

"Did you ask?"

"My husband didn't appreciate people prying into his private business affairs, Chief Inspector."

"Not even his wife?"

"I assumed that if and when he wanted to tell me, he would do so."

"What did you talk about over dinner yesterday?"

She shrugged. "Just the usual things. The children, the house extension we wanted to have done . . . I don't know, really. What do you talk about when you're out for dinner with *your* wife?"

Good question, Banks thought. It had been so long since he and Sandra had gone out to dinner together that he couldn't remember what they talked about. "Did you have any idea what he might have been worried about?" he asked.

"No. I suppose it was one of the usual business problems. Keith really cared about his clients."

"What business problems? I thought he didn't talk to you about business."

"He didn't, Chief Inspector. Please don't twist what I say. He just made the occasional offhand comment. You know, maybe he'd read something in the *Financial Times* or something and make a comment. I never understood what he meant. Anyway, I think one of the companies he was trying to help was sinking fast. Things like that always upset him."

"Do you know which company?"

"No. It'll be on his computer. He put everything on that computer." Suddenly, Mrs. Rothwell put the back of one ringed hand to her forehead in what seemed to Banks a gesture from a nineteenth-century melodrama. Her forehead looked clammy. "I'm afraid I can't talk any more," she whispered. "I feel a bit faint and dizzy. I . . . Alison."

Alison helped her up and they left the room. Banks glanced over at WPC Smithies. "Have you picked up anything at all from them?" he asked.

"Sorry, sir," she said. "Nothing. I'll tell you one thing, though, they're a weird pair. It's an odd family. I think they're both retreating from reality, in their own ways, trying to deny what happened, or how it happened. But you can see that for yourself."

"Yes."

Banks listened to a clock tick on the mantelpiece. It was one of those timepieces with all its brass and silver innards showing inside a glass dome.

A couple of minutes later, Alison came back. "I'm sorry," she said. "Mummy's still weak and in shock. The doctor gave her some pills."

"That's understandable, Alison," said Banks. "I'd almost finished, anyway. Just one last question. Do you know where your brother is? We'll have to get in touch with him."

Alison picked up a postcard from the top of the piano, gave it to Banks and sat down again.

The card showed the San Francisco Golden Gate Bridge,

which looked orange to Banks. He flipped it over. Post-marked two weeks ago, it read,

Dear Ali,
    Love California, and San Francisco is a great city, but it's time to move on. I'm even getting used to driving on the wrong side of the road! This sight-seeing's a tiring business so I'm off to Florida for a couple of weeks just lying in the sun. Ah, what bliss! Also to check out the motion picture conservatory in Sarasota. I'm driving down the coast highway and fly-ing to Tampa from LA on Sunday. More news when I get there. Love to Mum,

                                                              Tom

"How long has he been gone?"
"Six weeks. Just over. He left on March 31st."
"What does he do? What was that about a motion picture conservatory?"
Alison gave a brief smile. "He wants to work in films. He worked in a video shop and saved up. He's hoping to go to film college in America and learn how to become a director."
"How old is he?"
"Twenty-one."
Banks stood up. "All right, Alison," he said. "Thanks very much for all your help. WPC Smithies will be staying here for a while, so if you need anyone . . . And I'll ask the doctor to pay your mother another visit."
"Thank you. Please don't worry about us."
Banks looked in on Richmond, who sat bathed in the bluish glow of Rothwell's monitor, oblivious to the world, then went out to his car and lit a cigarette. He rolled the window down and listened to the birds as he smoked. Birds aside, it was bloody quiet up here. How, he wondered, could a teenager like Alison stand the isolation? As WPC Smithies had said, the Rothwells were an odd family.

As he drove along the bumpy track to the Relton road, he slipped in a tape of Dr. John playing solo New Orleans piano music. He had developed a craving for piano music—*any* kind of piano music—recently. He was even thinking of taking piano lessons; he wanted to learn how to play *everything*—classical, jazz, blues. The only thing that held him back was that he felt too old to embark on such a venture. His forty-first birthday was coming up in a couple of weeks.

In Relton, a couple of old ladies holding shopping baskets stood chatting outside the butcher's shop, probably about the murder.

Banks thought again about Alison Rothwell and her mother as he pulled up outside the Black Sheep. What were they holding back? And what was it that bothered him? No matter what Mrs. Rothwell and Alison had said, there was something wrong in that family, and he had a hunch that Tom Rothwell might know what it was. The sooner they contacted him the better.

3

Laurence Pratt delved deep in his bottom drawer and pulled out a bottle of Courvoisier VSOP and two snifters.

"I'm sorry," he apologized to DC Susan Gay, who sat opposite him at the broad teak desk. "It's not that I'm a secret tippler. I keep it for emergencies, and I'm afraid what you've just told me most definitely constitutes one. You'll join me?"

"No, thank you."

"Not on duty?"

"Sometimes," Susan said. "But not today."

"Very well." He poured himself a generous measure, swirled it and took a sip. A little colour came back to his cheeks. "Ah . . . that's better."

"If we could get back to Mr. Rothwell, sir?"

"Yes. Yes, of course. But you must understand Miss, Miss . . . ?"

"Gay, sir. DC Gay."

She saw the inadvertent smile flash across his face. People often smiled like that when she introduced herself. "Gay" had been a perfectly good name when she was a kid—her nickname for a while had been "Happy" Gay—but now its meaning was no longer the same. One clever bugger had actually asked, "Did you say AC or DC Gay?" She comforted herself with the thought that he was doing three to five in Strangeways thanks largely to her court evidence.

"Yes," he went on, a frown quickly displacing the smile. "I'd heard about Keith's death, of course, on the radio this lunch-time, but they didn't say *how* it happened. That's a bit of a shock, to be honest. You see, I knew Keith quite well. I'm only about three years older than he, and we worked here together for some years."

"He left the firm five years ago, is that right?"

"About right. A big move like that takes quite a bit of planning, quite a bit of organizing. There were client files to be transferred, that sort of thing. And he had the house to think of, too."

"He was a partner?"

"Yes. My father, Jeremiah Pratt, was one of the founders of the firm. He's retired now."

"I understand the family used to live in Eastvale, is that right?"

"Yes. Quite a nice house out towards the York round-about. Catterick Street."

"Why did they move?"

"Mary always fancied living in the country. I don't know why. She wasn't any kind of nature girl. I think perhaps she wanted to play Lady of the Manor."

"Oh? Why's that?"

Pratt shrugged. "Just her nature."

"What about her husband?"

"Keith didn't mind. I should imagine he liked the soli-
tude. I don't mean he was exactly anti-social, but he was
never a great mixer, not lately, anyway. He travelled a lot,
too."

Pratt was in his mid-forties, Susan guessed, which did
indeed make him just a few years older than Keith Rothwell. Quite good-looking, with a strong jaw and grey eyes,
he wore his white shirt with the sleeves rolled up and his
mauve and green tie clipped with what looked like a silver
American dollar sign. His hairline was receding and what
hair remained was grey at the temples. He wore black-
framed glasses, which sat about halfway down his nose.

"Did you ever visit him there?"

"Yes. My wife and I dined with the Rothwells on several
occasions."

"Were you friends?"

Pratt took another sip of Cognac, put his hand out and
waggled it from side to side. "Hmm. Somewhere between
friends and colleagues, I'd say."

"Why did he leave Hatchard and Pratt?"

Pratt broke eye contact and looked into the liquid he
swirled in his snifter. "Ambition, maybe? Straightforward
accountancy bored him. He was fond of abstractions, very
good with figures. He certainly had a flair for financial management. Very creative."

"Does that imply fraudulent?"

Pratt looked up at her. She couldn't read his expression.
"I resent that implication," he said.

"Was there any bad feeling?"

"I don't know what you mean."

"When he left the firm. Had there been any arguments,
any problems?"

"Good lord, this was five years ago!"

"Even so."

Pratt adopted a stiffer tone. "No, of course there hadn't.
Everything was perfectly amicable. We were sorry to lose
him, of course, but . . ."

"He wasn't fired or anything?"

"No."

"Did he take any clients with him?"

Pratt shuffled in his chair. "There will always be clients who feel they owe their loyalty to an individual member of the firm rather than to the firm as a whole."

"Are you sure this didn't cause bad feeling?"

"No, of course not. While it's unprofessional to solicit clients and woo them away, most firms *do* accept that they will lose some business whenever a popular member leaves to set up on his own. Say, for example, you visit a particular dentist in a group practice. You feel comfortable with him. He understands how you feel about dentists, you feel safe with him. If he left and set up on his own, would you go with him or stay and take your chances?"

Susan smiled. "I see what you mean. Do you think you could provide me with a list of names of the clients he took?"

Pratt chewed his lower lip for a moment, as if debating the ethics of such a request, then said, "I don't see why not. You could find out from his records anyway."

"Thank you. He must have made a fair bit of money somehow," Susan said. "How did he do it?"

Pratt, who if truth be told, Susan thought, suppressing a giggle, might not be entirely happy about *his* name, either, made a steeple of his hairy hands. "The same way we all do, I assume," he said. "Hard work. Good investments. Excellent service. Arkbeck Farm was in pretty poor shape when they bought it, you know. It didn't cost a fortune, and he'd no trouble arranging a fair mortgage. He put a lot into that house over the years."

Susan looked at her notes and frowned as if she were having trouble reading or understanding them. "I understand Mr. Rothwell actually owned a number of businesses. Do you know anything about this?"

Pratt shook his head. "Not really. I understand he was

interested in property development. As I said, Keith was an astute businessman.''

"Did Mrs. Rothwell work?''

"Mary? Good heavens, no! Well, not in the sense that she went out and made money. Mary was a housewife all the way. Well, perhaps 'house manager' or 'lady of leisure' would be a more appropriate term, as she didn't actually do the work herself. Except for the garden. You must have seen Arkbeck, how clean it is, how well appointed?''

"I'm afraid I had other things on my mind when I was there, sir,'' Susan said, "but I know what you mean.''

Pratt nodded. "For Mary,'' he went on, "everything centred around the home, the family and the immediate community. Everything had to be just so, to look just right, and it had to be *seen* to look that way. I imagine she was a hard taskmaster, or should that be taskmistress? Of course, she didn't spend *all* her time in the house. There were the Women's Institute, the Church committees, the good works and the charities. Mary kept very busy, I can assure you.''

"Good works? Charities?'' There was something positively Victorian about this. Susan pictured an earnest woman striding from hovel to hovel in a flurry of garments, long dress trailing in the mud, distributing alms to the peasants and preaching self-improvement.

"Yes. She collected for a number of good causes. You know, the RSPCA, NSPCC, cancer, heart foundation and the like. Nothing political—I mean, no ban the bomb or anything—and nothing controversial, like AIDS research. Just the basics. She was the boss's daughter, after all. She had certain Conservative standards to keep up.''

"The boss's daughter?''

"Yes, didn't you know? Her maiden name was Mary Hatchard. She was old man Hatchard's daughter. He's dead now, of course.''

"So Keith Rothwell married the boss's daugher,'' Susan mused aloud. "I don't suppose that did his career any harm?''

"No, it didn't. But that was more good luck than good management, if you ask me. Keith didn't just marry the boss's daughter, he got her pregnant first, with Tom, as it turns out, *then* he married her."

"How did that go over?"

Pratt paused and picked up a paper-clip. "Not very well at first. Old man Hatchard was mad as hell. He kept the lid on it pretty well, of course, and after he'd had time to consider it, I think he was glad to get her off his hands. He could hardly have her married to a mere junior, though, so Keith came up pretty quickly through the ranks to full partner."

Pratt twisted the paper-clip. He seemed to be enjoying this game, Susan thought. He was holding back, toying with her. She had a sense that if she didn't ask exactly the right questions, she wouldn't get the answers she needed. The problem was, she didn't know what the right questions were.

They sat in his office over Winston's Tobacconists, looking out on North Market Street, and Susan could hear the muted traffic sounds through the double-glazing. "Look," Pratt went on, "I realize I'm the one being questioned, but could you tell me how Mary is? And Alison? I do regard myself as something of a friend of the family, and if there's anything I can do . . ."

"Thank you, sir. I'll make sure they know. Can you think of any reason anyone might have for killing Mr. Rothwell?"

"No, I can't. Not in the way you described."

"What do you mean?"

"Well, I suppose I could imagine a burglar, say, perhaps killing someone who got in the way. You read about it in the papers, especially these days. Or an accident, some kids joyriding. But this . . . ? It sounds like an assassination to me."

"When was the last time you saw him?"

"About a month ago. No, earlier. In March, I think.

Shortly after St. Patrick's day. The wife and I went for dinner. Mary's a splendid cook.''

"Did they entertain frequently?"

"Not that I know of. They had occasional small dinner parties, maximum six people. Keith didn't like socializing much, but Mary loved to show off the house, especially if she'd acquired a new piece of furniture or something. So they compromised. Last time it was the kitchen we had to admire. They used to have a country-style one, Aga and all, but someone started poking fun at 'Aga-louts' in the papers, so Mary got annoyed and went for the modern look.''

"I see. What about the son, Tom? What do you know of him?"

"Tom? He's travelling in America, I understand. Good for him. Nothing like travel when you're young, before you get too tied down. Tom was always a cheerful and polite kid as far as I was concerned.''

"No trouble?"

"Not in any real sense, no. I mean, he wasn't into drugs or any of that weird stuff. At worst I'd say he was a bit uncertain about what he wanted to do with his life, and his father was perhaps just a little impatient.''

"In what way?"

"He wanted Tom to go into business or law. Something solid and respectable like that.''

"And Tom?"

"Tom's the artsy type. But he's a bright lad. With his personality he could go almost anywhere. He just doesn't know where yet. After he left school, he drifted a bit. Still is doing, it seems.''

"Would you say there was friction between them?"

"You can't be suggesting—"

"I'm not suggesting anything." Susan leaned back in the chair. "Look, Mr. Pratt, as far as we know Tom Rothwell is somewhere in the USA. We're trying to find him, but it could take time. The reason I'm asking you all these questions is because we need to know *everything* about Keith Rothwell.''

''Yes, of course. I'm sorry. But what with the shock of Keith's death and you asking about Tom . . .''

Susan leaned forward again. ''Is there any reason,'' she asked, ''why you should think I was putting forward Tom as a suspect?''

''Stop trying to read between the lines. There's nothing written there. It was just the way you were asking about him, that's all. Tom and his father had the usual father-son arguments, but nothing more.''

''Where did Tom get the money for a trip to America?''

''What? I don't know. Saved up, I suppose.''

''You say you last saw Keith Rothwell in March?''

''Yes.''

''Have you spoken with him at all since then?''

''No.''

''Did he seem in any way different from usual then? Worried about anything? Nervous?''

''No, not that I can remember. It was a perfectly normal evening. Mary cooked duck *à l'orange*. Tom dropped in briefly, all excited about his trip. Alison stayed in her room.''

''Did she usually do that?''

''Alison's a sweet child, but she's a real loner, very secretive. Takes after her father. She's a bit of a bookworm, too.''

''What did you talk about that evening?''

''Oh, I can't remember. The usual stuff. Politics. Europe. The economy. Holiday plans.''

''Who else was there?''

''Just us, this time.''

''And Mr. Rothwell said nothing that caused you any concern?''

''No. He was quiet.''

''Unusually so?''

''He was usually quiet.''

"Secretive?"

Pratt swivelled his chair and gazed out of the window at the upper storey of the Victorian community centre. Susan followed his gaze. She was surprised to see a number of gargoyles there she had never noticed before.

When he spoke again, Pratt still didn't look at Susan. She could see him only in profile. "I've always felt that about him, yes," he said. "That's why I hesitated to call him a *close* friend. There was always something in reserve." He turned to face Susan again and placed his hands, palms down, on the desk. "Oh, years ago we'd let loose once in while, go get blind drunk and not give a damn. Sometimes we'd go fishing together. But over time, Keith sort of reined himself in, cut himself off. I don't really know how to explain this. It was just a feeling. Keith was a very private person . . . well, lots of people are . . . But the thing was, I had no idea what he lived for."

"Did he suffer from depression? Did you think—"

Pratt waved a hand. "No. No, you're getting me wrong. He wasn't suicidal. That's not what I meant."

"Can you try and explain?"

"I'll try. It's hard, though. I mean, I'd be hard pushed to say what I live for, too. There's the wife and kids, of course, my pride and joy. And we like to go hang-gliding over Semerwater on suitable weekends. I collect antiques, I love cricket, and we like to explore new places on our holidays. See what I mean? None of that's what I actually *live for*, but it's all part of it." He took off his glasses and rubbed the back of his hand over his eyes and the bridge of his nose, then put them back on again. "I know, I'm getting too philosophical. But I told you it was hard to explain."

Susan smiled. "I'm still listening."

"Well, all those are just *things*, aren't they? Possessions or activities. Things we do, things we care about. But there's something behind them all that ties them all together into *my* life, who I am, what I am. With Keith, you never

knew. He was a cipher. For example, I'm sure he loved his
family, but he never really showed it or spoke much about
it. I don't know what really *mattered* to him. He never
talked about hobbies or anything like that. I don't know
what he did in his spare time. It's more than being private
or secretive, it's as if there was a dimension *missing*, a man
with a hole in the middle.'' He scratched his temple. ''This
is ridiculous. Please forgive me. Keith was a perfectly nice
bloke. Wouldn't hurt a fly. But you never really knew what
gripped him about life, what his *dream* was. I mean, mine's
a villa in Portugal, but a dream doesn't have to be a thing,
does it? I don't know . . . maybe he valued abstractions too
much.''

He paused, as if he had run out of breath and ideas.
Susan didn't really know what to jot down, but she finally
settled for ''dimension missing . . . interests and concerns
elusive.'' It would do. She had a good memory for conversations and could recount verbatim most of what Pratt
had said, if Banks wished to hear it.

''Let's get back to Mr. Rothwell's work with your firm.
Is there anything you can tell me about his . . . style . . .
shall we say, his business practices?''

''You want to know if Keith was a crook, don't you?''

She did, of course, though that wasn't why she was asking. Still, she thought, never look a gift horse in the mouth.
She gave him a ''you caught me at it'' smile. ''Well, was
he?''

''Of course not.''

''Oh, come on, Mr. Pratt. Surely in your business you
must sail a little close to the wind at times?''

''I resent that remark, especially coming from a policeman.''

Susan let that one slip by. ''*Touché*,'' she said. Pratt
seemed pleased enough with himself. Let him feel he's winning, she thought, then he'll tell you anyway, just to show
he holds the power to do so. She was still sure he was
holding something back. ''But seriously, Mr. Pratt,'' she

went on, "I'm not just playing games, bandying insults. If there was anything at all unusual in Mr. Rothwell's business dealings, I hardly need tell you it could have a bearing on his murder."

"Hmm." Pratt swirled the rest of the brandy and tossed it back. He put the snifter in his "Out" tray, no doubt for the secretary to take and wash. "I stand by what I said," he went on. "Keith Rothwell never did anything truly *illegal* that I knew of. Certainly nothing that could be relevant to his death."

"But . . . ?"

He sighed. "Well, maybe I wasn't *entirely* truthful earlier. I suppose I'd better tell you about it, hadn't I? You're bound to find out somehow."

Susan turned her page. "I'm listening," she said.

: 3

1

The Black Sheep was the closest Swainsdale had to a well-kept secret. Most tourists were put off by the pub's external shabbiness. Those who prided themselves on not judging a book by its cover would, more often than not, pop their heads around the door, see the even shabbier interior and leave.

The renowned surliness of the landlord, Larry Grafton, kept them away in droves, too. There was a rumour that Larry had once refused to serve an American tourist with a Glenmorangie and ginger, objecting to the utter lack of taste that led her to ask for such a concoction. Banks believed it.

Larry was Dales born and bred, not one of the new landlords up from London. So many were recent immigrants these days, like Ian Falkland in the Rose and Crown. That was a tourist pub if ever there was one, Banks thought, probably selling more lager and lime, pork scratchings and microwaved curries than anything else.

The Black Sheep didn't advertise its pub grub, but anyone who knew about it could get as thick and fresh a ham and piccalilli sandwich as ever they'd want from Elsie, Larry's wife. And on some days, if her arthritis hadn't been bothering her too much and she felt like cooking, she could do you a fry-up so good you could feel your arteries hardening as you ate.

As usual, the public bar was empty apart from one table of old men playing dominoes and a couple of young farmhands reading the sports news in the *Daily Mirror*.

As Banks had expected, Pat Clifford also stood propping
up the bar. Pat was a hard, stout man with a round head,
stubble for hair and a rough, red face burned by the sun
and whipped by the wind and rain for fifty years.

"Hello, stranger," said Pat, as Banks stood next to him.
"Long time, no see."

Banks apologized for his absence and brought up the
subject of Keith Rothwell.

"So tha only comes when tha wants summat, is that it?"
Pat said. But he said it with a smile, and over the years
Banks had learned that Yorkshire folk often take the sting
out of their criticisms that way. They put a sting in their
compliments, too, on those rare occasions they get around
to giving any.

In this case, Banks guessed that Pat wasn't mortally offended at his protracted absence; he only wanted to make
a point of it, let Banks know his feelings, and then get on
with things. Banks acknowledged his culpability with a
mild protest about the pressures of work, as expected, then
listened to a minute or so of Pat's complaining about how
the elderly and isolated were neglected by all and sundry.

When Pat's glass was empty, an event which occurred
with alarming immediacy at the end of the diatribe, Banks's
offer to buy him another was grudgingly accepted. Pat took
a couple of sips, put the glass down on the bar and wiped
his lips with the back of his grimy hand.

"He came in once or twice, did Mr. Rothwell. Local,
like. Nobody objected."

"How often?"

"Once a week, mebbe. Sometimes twice. Larry—?"
And he asked the landlord the same question. Larry, who
hardly had a charabanc full of thirsty customers to serve,
came over and stood with them. He still treated Banks with
a certain amount of disdain—after all, Banks was a southerner *and* a copper—but he showed respect, too.

Banks had never tried *too* hard to fit in, to pretend he
was one of the crowd like some of the other incomers. He

knew there was nothing annoyed a Dalesman so much as pretentiousness, airs and graces, and that there was nothing more contemptible or condescending than a southerner appropriating Dales speech and ways, playing the expert on a place he had only just come to. Banks kept his distance, kept his counsel, and in return he was accorded that particular Yorkshire brand of grudging acceptance.

"Just at lunch-times, like," Larry said. "Never saw him of an evening. He'd come in for one of Elsie's sandwiches and always drink half a pint. Just one half, mind you."

"Did he talk much?"

Larry drifted off to dry some glasses and Pat picked up the threads. "Nay. He weren't much of a chatterbox, weren't Mr. Rothwell. Bit of a dry stick, if you ask me."

"What do you mean? Was he stuck-up?"

"No-o. Just had nowt to talk abaht, that's all." He tapped the side of his nose. "If you listen as much as I do," he said, "you soon find out what interests people. There's not much when it comes down to it, tha knows." He started counting on the stubby fingers that stuck out of his cut-off gloves. "Telly, that's number one. Sport—number two. And sex. That's number three. After that there's nobbut money and weather left."

Banks smiled. "What about politics?" he asked.

Pat pulled a face. "Only when them daft buggers in t'Common Market 'ave been up to summat with their Common Agricultural Policy." Then he grinned, showing stained, crooked teeth. "Aye, I suppose that's often enough these days," he admitted, counting it off. "Politics. Number four."

"And what did Mr. Rothwell talk about when he was here?" Banks asked.

"Nowt. That's what I'm telling thee, lad. Oh, I s'pose seeing as he was an accountant, he was interested in money, but he kept that to himself. He'd be standing there, all right, just where you are, munching on his sandwich, supping his half-pint, and nodding in all the right places, but he never had owt to say. It seemed to me as if he were really somewhere else. And he didn't know 'Neighbours' from 'Coronation Street,' if you ask me—or Leeds United from Northampton.''

"There's not a lot of difference as far as their performances go over the last few weeks, if you ask me, Pat.''

Pat grunted.

"So you didn't really know Keith Rothwell?'' Banks asked.

"No. Nobody did.''

"That's right, Mr. Banks,'' added Larry as he stood by them to pull a pint. "He said he came for the company, what with working alone at home and all that, but I reckon as he came to get away from that there wife of his.'' Then he was gone, bearing the pint.

Banks turned to Pat. "What did he mean?''

"Ah, take no notice of him,'' Pat said with a dismissive wave in Grafton's direction. "Mebbe he was a bit henpecked, at that. It must be hard working at home when the wife's around all the time. Never get a minute's peace, you wouldn't. But Larry's lass, Cathy, did for Mrs. Rothwell now and again, like, and she says she were a bit of an interfering mistress, if you know what I mean. Standing over young Cathy while she worked and saying that weren't done right, or that needed a bit more elbow grease. I nobbut met Mrs. Rothwell once or twice, but my Grace speaks well of her, and that's enough for me.''

Banks thought he might have a word with Larry's lass, Cathy. He noticed Pat's empty glass. "Another?''

"Oh, aye. Thank you very much.'' Banks bought him a pint, but decided to forgo a second himself, much as the idea appealed. "There were one time, when I comes to think on it,'' Pat said, "that Mr. Rothwell seemed a bit odd.''

"When was this?''

"Abaht two or three weeks ago. He came in one lunchtime, as usual, like, but he must have had a couple of pints, not 'alves. Anyroad, he got quite chatty, told a couple of jokes, and we all had a good chuckle, didn't we, Larry?"

"Aye," shouted Larry from down the bar.

That sounded odd to Banks. According to Mrs. Rothwell, her husband had been tense and edgy over the past three weeks. If he could chat and laugh at the Black Sheep, then maybe the problem had been at home. "Is that all?" he asked.

"*All?* Well, it were summat for us to see him enjoying himself for once. I'd say that were enough, wouldn't you?"

"Did he say anything unusual?"

"No. He just acted like an ordinary person. An ordinary *happy* person."

"As if he'd received some good news or something?"

"He didn't say owt about that."

Banks gave up and moved on. "I know there's been a bit of ill feeling among the hill-farmers about incomers lately," he said. "Did any of it spill over to Mr. Rothwell?"

Pat sniffed. "You wouldn't understand, Mr. Banks," he said softly, offering an unfiltered cigarette. Banks refused it and lit a Silk Cut. "It's not that there's any ill feeling, as such. We just don't know where we stand, how to plan for the future. One day the government says this, the next day it's something else. Agricultural Policy . . . Europe . . . grugh." He spat on the floor to show his feelings. Either nobody noticed or the practice was perfectly welcome in the Black Sheep, another reason why people stayed away. "It needs years of experience to do it right, does hill-farming," Pat went on. "Continuity, passed on from father to son. When too many farms fall to weekenders and holiday-makers, pasture gets abused, walls get neglected. Live and let live, that's what I say. But we want some respect and some understanding. And right now we're not getting any."

"But what about the incomers?"

"Aye, hold thy horses, lad, I'm getting to them. We're

not bloody park-keepers, tha knows. We don't graft for hours on end in all t'weather God sends keeping stone walls in good repair because we think they look picturesque, tha knows. They're to keep old Harry Cobb's sheep off my pasture and to make sure there's no hanky-panky between his breed and mine.''

Banks nodded. ''Fair enough, Pat. But how deep did the feeling go? Keith Rothwell bought that farm five years ago, or thereabouts. I've seen what he's done to it, and it's not a farm any more.''

''Aye, well at least Mr. Rothwell's a Swainsdale lad, even if he did come from Eastvale. Nay, there were no problems. He sold off his land—I got some of it, and so did Frank Rowbottom. If you're thinking me or Frank did it, then . . .''

''No, nothing like that,'' Banks said. ''I just wanted to get a sense of how Rothwell fitted in with the local scene, if he did.''

''Well, he did and he didn't,'' said Pat. ''He was here and he wasn't, and that's all I can tell thee. He could tell a joke well enough when he put his mind to it, though.'' Pat chuckled at the memory.

As puzzled as he was before, Banks said goodbye and went outside. On the way back, he slipped in a cassette of Busoni's Bach transcriptions. The precise, ordered music had no influence on the chaos of his thoughts.

2

Back in his office, Banks first glanced at Dr. Glendenning's post-mortem notes. Generally, there was no such thing as a *preliminary* post-mortem report, but Dr. Glendenning usually condescended to send over the main points in lay-man's language as quickly as possible. He also liked to appear at the scene, but this time he had been staying overnight with friends in Harrogate.

There was nothing in the notes that Banks hadn't expected. Rothwell hadn't been poisoned before he was shot; the stomach contents revealed only pasta and red wine. Dr. Glendenning gave cause of death as a shotgun wound to the occipital region, the back of head, most likely a contact wound given the massive damage to bone and tissue. He also noted that it was lucky they already knew who the victim was, as there wasn't enough connected bone or tissue left to reconstruct the face, and though the tooth fragments could probably be collected and analyzed, it would take a bloody long time. The blood group was "O," which matched that supplied by Rothwell's doctor, as well as that of about half the population.

Rothwell had most likely been killed in the place and position they found him, Dr. Glendenning pointed out, because what blood remained had collected as purplish hypostasis around the upper chest and the ragged edges of the neck. He estimated time of death between eleven and one the previous night.

A cadaveric spasm had caused Rothwell to grab and hold onto a handful of dust at the moment of death, and Banks thought of the T.S. Eliot quotation, "I will show you fear in a handful of dust," which he had come across as the title of an Evelyn Waugh novel.

Rothwell had been in generally good shape, Dr. Glendenning said, and the only evidence of any ill health was an appendix scar. Rothwell's doctor, Dr. Hunter, was able to verify that Rothwell had had his appendix removed just over three years ago.

When Banks had finished, he phoned Sandra to say he didn't know when he would be home. She said that didn't surprise her. Then he went over to the window and looked down on the cobbled market square, most of which was covered by parked cars. The gold hands against the blue face of the church clock stood at a quarter to four.

Banks lit a cigarette and watched the local merchants taking deliveries and the tourists snapping pictures of the ancient market cross and the Norman church front. It was fine enough weather out there, sports jacket warm, but the grey wash that had come at dawn still obscured the sunshine. On Banks's *Dalesman* calendar, the May photograph showed a field of brilliant pink and purple flowers below Great Shunner Fell in Swaledale. So far, the real May had been struggling against showers and cool temperatures.

Sitting at his rattly metal desk, Banks next opened the envelope of Rothwell's pocket contents and spread them out in front of him.

There were a few business cards in a leather slip-case, describing Rothwell as a "Financial Consultant." In his wallet were three credit cards, including an American Express Gold; the receipt from Mario's on the night of his anniversary dinner; receipts from Austick's bookshop, a computer supplies shop and two restaurants, all from Leeds, and all dated the previous week; and photos of Alison and Mary Rothwell. Happy families indeed. In cash, Rothwell had a hundred and five pounds in his wallet, in new twenties and one crumpled old fiver.

Other pockets revealed a handkerchief, good quality silk and monogrammed "KAR," like the cufflinks on the body, BMW keys, house keys, a small pack of Rennies, two buttons, a gold Cross fountain pen, an empty leather-bound notebook, and—horror of horrors—a packet of ten Benson and Hedges, six of which had been smoked.

Banks felt a surge of respect for the late Keith Rothwell. But perhaps the cigarettes helped to explain something, too. Banks was certain that Mary Rothwell would never have permitted her husband to pollute the house with his filthy habit. Smoking, then, could be the main reason he liked to sneak off to the Black Sheep or the Rose and Crown every now and then. It certainly wasn't drinking. A secret smoker, then? Or did she know? He found no gold lighter, only a sulphurous old box of Pilot matches; and Rothwell was the kind of person who put his spent matches back in the box facing the opposite direction from the live ones.

It was almost six when the phone rang: Vic Manson calling from the forensic lab. Vic spent almost as much time with the Scene-of-Crime team from North Yorkshire Head-quarters, in Northallerton, as he did at the lab, and though Banks knew Vic was a fingerprints expert, he sometimes wasn't sure exactly what he did or where he really worked.

"What have you got for us?" Banks asked.

"Hold your horses."

"Social call, is it, then?"

"Not exactly."

"Then what?"

"The wadding, for a start."

"What about it?"

"We managed to get some more of the paper unfolded. It wasn't too badly burned inside. Anyway, the document analysts say it's good magazine quality, probably German. No prints. Nothing but blurs. It's not your common-or-garden girlie magazine, but it's not hard-core perversion either. The fullest picture we could get seemed to be a shaved vagina with a finger touching the clitoris. Bright red nail varnish. The fingernail, that is."

"That must be the other side of what I saw," said Banks. "Does it help?"

"It might do. Apparently there are people who have a fetish about shaved vaginas. It's something to go on, anyway."

Banks sighed. "Or maybe our killer's just got a warped sense of humour. We can check with the PNC, anyway, see if there's been any similar incidents. What about the weapon?"

"Twelve-gauge, double-barrel. Judging by the amount of shot we've collected, the bastard who did it must have used both of them."

"Anything from the house?"

"No prints, if that's what you mean. They wore gloves. And there was nothing special about the rope they used to tie up the wife and daughter, either. By the way, remember one of the chairs was wet, the one overturned by the table?"

"Yes."

"It was urine. The poor lass must have been so scared she pissed herself."

Banks swallowed. That was Alison's chair. She was the one who had eventually made her way to the sewing basket and toppled her chair. "Any footprints?" he asked.

"We're still working on it, but don't hold your breath. The ground had pretty much dried out after last week's rain."

"Okay, Vic, thanks for calling. Keep at it and keep me informed, okay?"

"Will do."

After he had hung up, Banks lit another cigarette and walked over to the window again. Most of the tourists were getting in their cars, removing the crook-locks and driving home. The cobbles, cross and church front looked slate grey in the dull afternoon light. At the far side of the square, the El Toro coffee bar and Joplin's newsagent's seemed to be doing good business.

Banks thought of Alison, who had shown so much courage in telling them about what had happened at Arkbeck Farm. Someone had scared her so much she had sat in her own urine, probably for hours. The idea of her indignity and humiliation made him angry. He vowed he would find whoever was responsible for doing that to her and make damn sure they suffered.

3

The Queen's Arms was always busy at six o'clock on a Friday, and it was only through good luck and quick reflexes that Banks and Susan Gay managed to grab a copper-topped table by the window when a party of cashiers from the NatWest Bank gathered their things and left.

As happened so often in the Dales, the weather had

changed dramatically over a very short period. A light breeze had sprung up and blown away the clouds. Now, the early evening sunlight glowed through the red and amber panes and shot bright rays though the clear ones, lighting on a foaming glass of ale and highlighting the smoke swirling in the air.

The sunlight and smoke reminded Banks of the effect the projection camera created at the cinema when smoking was allowed there. As kids, he and his friends used to put their money together for a packet of five Woodbines, then go to the morning matinee at the Palace: a Three Stooges short, a Buck Rogers or Flash Gordon serial, and a black-and-white western, maybe a Hopalong Cassidy. Slumped down in their seats, they would smoke "wild woodies" until they felt sick. He smiled at the memory and reached for a Silk Cut.

Conversation and laughter ebbed and flowed all around them, and the general mood was ebullient. After all, it was the weekend. For most people in the pub, there would be no work until Monday morning. They could go off shopping to York or Leeds, wallpaper the bedroom, visit Aunt Maisie in Skipton, or just lounge around and watch football or racing on telly. It was Cup Final day tomorrow, Banks remembered. Fat chance he'd get of watching it.

The best he could hope was that he would get home before too late tonight and spend some time with Sandra. It was the ideal opportunity for a bit of bridge-building. Tracy was away in France on a school exchange, and Brian was at Portsmouth Polytechnic, so they had the house to themselves for once. He would be too late for a shared dinner, but maybe a nice bottle of claret, a few Chopin "Nocturnes," candlelight . . . then, who knew what might follow?

It was a nice fantasy. But right now he was waiting for Gristhorpe and Richmond, here to combine the pleasure of a pint and a steak-and-kidney pud with the business of swopping notes and fishing for leads at an informal meeting.

Once in a while, through the laughter and the arguments, Banks heard the Rothwell case mentioned. "Did you hear about that terrible murder up near Relton . . . ?" "Hear about that bloke got shot out in the dale? I heard they blew his head right off his shoulders . . ." By now, of course, everyone had had a chance to read the *Yorkshire Evening Post*, and people were only too willing to embroider on the scant details the newspaper gave. Rumour and fantasy were rife. What Gristhorpe hadn't told the media so far was that Rothwell had been executed "gangland" style, and that the weapon used was a shotgun.

The best the press could manage so far was "LOCAL BUSINESSMAN MURDERED. . . . Not more than a mile above the peaceful Swainsdale village of Fortford, a mild-mannered accountant was shot to death in his own garage in the early hours of this morning. . . ." There followed an appeal for information about "two men in black" and a photograph of Keith Rothwell, looking exactly like a mild-mannered accountant, with his thinning fair hair combed back, showing the slight widow's peak, his high forehead, slightly prissy lips and the wire-rimmed glasses. The glasses, Banks knew, had been found shattered to pieces along with the other wreckage of Rothwell's skull.

Banks waved to Gristhorpe and Richmond, who nudged their way through the crowd to join them at the table. While he was on his feet, Richmond went to get a round of drinks and put in the food orders.

"At least we don't have to worry about civilians over-hearing classified information," Gristhorpe said as he sat down and scraped his stool forward along the worn stone flagging. "I can hardly even hear myself think."

When Richmond got back with the tray of drinks, Gristhorpe said, "Right, Phil, tell us what you found."

They huddled close around the table. Richmond took a sip of his St. Clements. "There are several items that have been either encrypted or assigned passwords," he said. "Some are complete directories, and one's just a document file in a directory. He's called it 'LETTER.' "

"Can you get access?" Gristhorpe asked.

"Not easily, no, sir. Not unless you type the password at the prompt. Believe me, I've tried every trick and all I've got for my pains is gibberish."

"All right." Gristhorpe coughed and waved away Banks's smoke with an exaggerated gesture. "Let's assume he had some special reason for keeping these items secret. That means we're definitely interested. You said you couldn't gain access easily, but is there a way?"

Richmond cleared his throat. "Well, yes there is. Actually, there are two ways."

"Come on, then, lad. Don't keep us in suspense."

"We could bring an expert. I mean a *real* expert, like someone who writes the programmes."

"Aye, and the other option?"

"Well, it's not much known, for obvious reasons, but I went to a seminar once and the lecturer told me something that struck me as very odd."

"What?"

"Well, there's a company that sells by-pass programmes for various software security systems."

"That would probably be cheaper and quicker, wouldn't it?" said Gristhorpe. "Can you get hold of a copy?"

"Yes, sir. But it's not cheap. Actually, it's quite expensive."

"How much?"

"About two hundred quid."

Gristhorpe whistled between his teeth, then he said, "We don't have a lot of choice, do we? Go ahead, order one."

"I already have done, sir."

"And?"

"They're based in Akron, Ohio, but they told me there's a distributor in Taunton, Devon, who has some in stock. It could take a while to get it up here."

"Tell the buggers to send it by courier, then. We might as well be hung for a sheep as a lamb. Lord knows what the DCC will have to say come accounting time."

"Maybe if it helps us solve the case," Banks chipped in, "he'll increase our budget."

Gristhorpe laughed. "In a pig's arse, he will. Go on, Phil."

"That's all, really," said Richmond. "In the meantime, I'll keep trying and see what I can do. People sometimes write their passwords down in case they forget them. If Rothwell did, the only problem is finding out *where* and in what form."

"Interesting," Banks said. "I've got one of those plastic cards, the ones you use to get money at the hole in the wall. I keep the number written in my address book disguised as part of a telephone number in case I forget it."

"Exactly," said Richmond.

"Short of trying every name and number in Rothwell's address book," Gristhorpe said, "is there any quick way of doing this?"

"I don't think so, sir," Richmond said. "But often the password is a name the user has strong affinities with."

" 'Rosebud'?" Banks suggested.

"Right," said Richmond. "That sort of thing. Maybe something from his childhood."

" 'Woodbines,' " said Banks. "Sorry, Phil, just thinking out loud."

"But it could be anything. The name of a family member, for example. Or a random arrangement of letters, spaces, numbers and punctuation marks. It doesn't have to make any sense at all."

"Bloody hell." Gristhorpe ran his hand through his unruly thatch of grey hair.

"All I can say is leave it with me, sir. I'll do what I can. And I'll ask the software distributor to put a rush on it."

"All right. Susan? Anything from Hatchard and Pratt."

Susan leaned forward to make herself heard. Just as she

was about to start, Cyril called out their food number, and Richmond and Banks went through to bring back the trays. After a few mouthfuls, Susan started again. "Yes," she said, dabbing at the side of her mouth with a napkin. "As it turns out, Rothwell was asked to leave the firm."

"Asked to leave?" Gristhorpe echoed. "Does that mean fired?"

"Not exactly, sir. He was a partner. You can't just fire partners. He was also married to the boss's daughter. Mary Rothwell's maiden name is Hatchard. He was asked to resign. They didn't want a fuss."

"Interesting," said Gristhorpe. "What was it all about, then?"

Susan ate another mouthful of her Cornish pasty, then washed it down with a sip of Britvic orange and pushed her plate aside. "Laurence Pratt was reluctant to tell me about it," she said, "but I think he knew he'd be in more trouble if we found out some other way. It seems Rothwell was caught padding the time sheets. It's not a rare fiddle, according to Pratt. And he doesn't regard it as strictly illegal, but it *is* unethical, and it's bad luck for anyone who gets caught. Rothwell got off lucky."

"What happened?" asked Gristhorpe.

"This was about five years ago. Rothwell was doing a lot of work for a large company. Pratt wouldn't tell me who it was, but I don't think that really matters. The point is that Pratt's father was looking over the billings and noticed that Rothwell had doubled up on his hours here and there, at times he couldn't have been working on their account because he'd been on another job, or out of town."

"What did he do? Isn't there some regulatory board he should have been reported to?"

"Yes, sir, there is. But, remember, Rothwell was married to Hatchard's daughter, Mary. They'd been together nearly sixteen years by then, had two kids. Old man Hatchard would hardly want his son-in-law struck off and his family name dragged through the mud, which is probably what would have happened if Rothwell had been reported. I also got the impression that it might have been Mary's demands that set Rothwell padding his accounts in the first place. Nothing was directly stated, you understand, sir, just hinted. Imagine the headlines: 'Accountant fired for padding books to keep boss's daughter in the manner to which she was accustomed.' Hardly bears thinking about, does it? Anyway, Laurence Pratt and Rothwell were quite close friends then, so Pratt interceded and stuck up for him. Rothwell was lucky. He had a lot going for him. And there's another reason they didn't want a hue and cry.''

''Which is?''

''Confidence and confidentiality, sir. If it got out to the large company that Rothwell was fiddling, then it would put the partnership in an awkward position. Much better they don't find out and Rothwell simply decides to move on. Keep it in the family. They'd never question the bills, or miss the money.''

''I see.'' Gristhorpe rubbed his whiskery chin.

''It's something that could have led to a motive, isn't it, sir? Greed, dishonesty.''

''Aye,'' said Gristhorpe. ''It is that. Which makes me think even more that these secret files might prove interesting reading.'' He tapped the table-top. ''Good work, Susan. Let's make Rothwell's business affairs a major line of enquiry. I'll get in touch with the Fraud Squad. I've heard from the anti-terrorist squad, by the way, and they've come up with nothing so far. They want to be kept up to date, of course, but I think we can rule out Rothwell dealing arms or money to the IRA. Anything to add, Alan?''

''I think we should follow up on the wadding. There could be a porn connection.''

''Rothwell in the porn business?''

''It's possible. After all, he had plenty of money, didn't he? He must have got it from somewhere. I'm not suggesting he was a front player, one who got his hands dirty. Maybe he just made some investments or handled finances.

Take the lid off that can of worms—video nasties, prostitution and the like—and it wouldn't surprise me to find
murder. Perhaps the wadding was a kind of signature, a
symbol.''

''It sounds a bit too fanciful to me,'' said Gristhorpe,
''but I take your point. It's all tied together, anyway, isn't
it? If he was in the porn business, then that makes porn
part of his business affairs. We'll follow up on it.''

''DS Hatchley's coming back on Monday,'' said Banks.
''I think he'd be a good man for the job. Remember he
spent a while working on the Vice Squad for West Yorkshire? Besides, he'd enjoy it.''

Gristhorpe snorted. ''I suppose he would. But keep him
on a tight leash. He's like a bloody bull in a china shop.''

Banks grinned. He knew that Gristhorpe and Hatchley
didn't get along. Jim Hatchley was a big, bluff, burly,
boozy, roast-beef sort of Yorkshireman, a rugby prop forward until cigarettes and drink took their toll. More at home
playing darts in the public bar than chatting in the lounge,
he was the kind of person everyone underestimated, and
that often worked to the advantage of the Eastvale CID.
And he also had a valuable, county-wide network of low-
life, quasi-criminal informers that nobody had been able to
penetrate.

''The Rothwells are an interesting family,'' Banks went
on after a sip of Theakston's. ''Mrs. Rothwell assured me
everything was fine and dandy on the domestic front, but
methought the lady did protest too much. I wonder how
much communication there really was between them all.
It's nothing I can put my finger on, but there's something
bothering me. I think the son, Tom, might have something
to do with it.''

''I got that impression, too,'' said Susan. ''It all looks
fine on the surface, but I'd like to know what life at Arkbeck Farm was like. After I'd talked to Laurence Pratt, I
got to thinking that if Tom was the reason Keith and Mary
Rothwell had to get married, and Rothwell was unhappy in

his marriage, then he might blame Tom. Irrational, of course, but things happen like that."

"I'd leave the psychology to Jenny Fuller," said Gristhorpe.

Susan reddened.

"Susan's right," said Banks. "The sooner we find Tom Rothwell, the better."

Gristhorpe shrugged. "It's up to the Florida police now. We've passed on all the information we've got. Come on, Alan, surely you don't think the wife and daughter had anything to do with it?"

"It would be hard to believe, wouldn't it? On the other hand, we've only *their* word for what happened. Nobody else saw the two men in black. What if Alison and her mother *did* want rid of Rothwell for some reason?"

"Next you'll be telling me the wife and daughter were making porno films for Rothwell. You talked to Alison. You could see the lass was upset."

"Alison might not have had anything to do with it."

"You mean Mrs. Rothwell? Wasn't she in shock?"

"So I'm told. I didn't get to see her until late this morning. That gave her plenty of time to compose herself, work up an act."

"But the SOC team went through the place as thoroughly as they usually do, hayloft and all. They couldn't find any traces of a weapon."

"I'm not saying she shot him."

"What then? She hired a couple of killers to do it for her?"

"I don't know. She could certainly afford it. I suppose I'm playing devil's advocate, trying to look at it from all angles. I still maintain they're an odd family. Alison was genuinely terrified, I know that. But there's something not quite right about them all, and I'd like to know what that is. I knew when I drove away from Arkbeck Farm that something I'd seen there was bothering me, nagging away, but I didn't know what it was until a short while ago."

"And?" asked Gristhorpe.

"It was Tom's postcard from California. It was addressed to Alison—he called her Ali—and at the end he wrote, 'Love to Mum.' There was no mention of his father."

"Hmm," said Gristhorpe. "It doesn't have to mean anything."

"Maybe not. But that's not all. When I looked through Rothwell's wallet a while back, I found photos of Mary and Alison, but none of Tom. Not one."

: 4

1

A night's sleep is supposed to refresh you, not make you feel as if you're recovering from a bloody anaesthetic, thought Banks miserably on Saturday morning.

Never a morning person at the best of times, he sat over his second cup of black coffee and a slice of whole wheat toast and Seville marmalade, newspaper propped up in front of him, trying to muster enough energy to get going. As a background to the radio traffic reports, he could hear Sandra having a shower upstairs. Banks hated the contraption—he always seemed to get a lukewarm dribble rather than a hot shower—but Sandra and Tracy swore by it. Banks preferred a long, hot bath with a little quiet background music and a good book.

After catching up with paperwork, he hadn't got home until almost eleven the previous night. He wished Sandra had been angry that they'd had to miss the claret, the Chopin and the candlelight, but she hadn't seemed to care. He didn't know whether she was pretending or she *really* didn't care. In fact, she said she'd just got back from a reception at the community centre herself. It was getting to be par for the course. They had seen so little of one another lately that they were fast becoming strangers. It seemed to Banks that what had been a strength in their relationship— their natural independence—was quickly becoming a threat.

And while Sandra had slept like a log, Banks had tossed and turned all night beside her, worried about the Rothwell case, with only brief, fitful periods of sleep full of shifting images: the pornographic wadding, the headless corpse. Now it was eight-thirty the next morning, and his eyes felt like sandpaper, his brain stuffed with cotton wool.

The national dailies and radio news carried stories on the Keith Rothwell killing—sandwiched between a bloodthirsty put-down of riots on a Caribbean island, where another dictator was nearing the end of his reign of terror, and a male Member of Parliament caught *in flagrante* with a sixteen-year-old rent-boy on Clapham Common. It probably wouldn't even have made the papers if it had happened somewhere a bit more up-market, like Hampstead Heath, Banks thought.

The Rothwell murder would be on television too, no doubt, amidst all the speculation on that afternoon's Cup Final, but Banks had never been able to bring himself to turn the thing on during daylight hours.

Now, hints were appearing in the media that the killing was more than a run-of-the-mill domestic disagreement or a burglary gone wrong. According to the radio, Scotland Yard, Interpol and the FBI had been called in. That, Banks reflected, was a slight exaggeration. The Americans had been asked to help trace Tom Rothwell, though as far as Banks knew it was the Florida State Police, not the FBI. Interpol was something the reporters always threw in for good measure, these days, and Scotland Yard was an outright lie.

Banks scanned the *Yorkshire Post* and *The Independent* reports to see if either newspaper knew more than the police. Sometimes they did, and it could be damned embarrassing all round. Not this time, though. To them, Rothwell was as much the "quiet, unassuming local accountant and businessman" as he was to the rest of the world.

"More coffee?"

Banks looked up to see Sandra standing at the machine in her navy-blue bathrobe, wet hair hanging over the terrycloth at her shoulders. He hadn't heard her come down.

"Please." He held his cup out.

Sandra poured, then put some bread in the toaster and picked up the *Yorkshire Post*. After she had read about Rothwell, she whistled. "Is this what kept you out so late last night?"

"Hmm," murmured Banks.

The toast popped up. Sandra put the paper down and went to see to it. "I've met her a couple of times, you know," she said over her shoulder, buttering toast.

Banks folded *The Independent* and looked at Sandra's profile. When it was wet, her hair looked darker, of course, but one of the things Banks found attractive about her was the contrast between her blonde hair and black eyebrows. This time, when he looked at her, he felt an ache deep inside. "Who?" he asked.

"Mrs. Rothwell. Mary Rothwell."

"How on earth did you come across her?"

"At the gallery."

Sandra ran the local gallery in the Eastvale community centre, where she organized art and photography exhibitions.

"I didn't know she was the artistic type."

"She's not really. I think for her it was just the thing to do. Women's Institute sort of stuff, you know, organize cultural outings." Sandra sat down with her toast and wrinkled her nose.

Banks laughed, sensing a definite thaw in the cold war. "Snob."

"What! Me?" She hit him lightly with the folded newspaper.

"Anyway," Banks said, "the poor woman's on tranquilizers. Both she and her daughter saw Rothwell's body before they called us, and you can take my word for it, that's enough to give anyone the heebie-jeebies."

"How's the daughter?"

"Alison? Not quite so bad, at least not on the surface." Banks shrugged. "More resilient, maybe, or she could just be repressing it more. Tina Smithies says she's worried

they're both losing touch." He looked at his watch. "I'd
better go."

Sandra followed him to the door and leaned against the
bannister. She nibbled her toast as she watched him put on
his light grey sports jacket and pick up his briefcase. "I
can't say I know her well enough to get any kind of impression," she said, holding her dressing-gown at the collar
when Banks opened the door, "but I did sense that she's
the kind who . . . well, she puts on a few airs and graces.
Not so much as to be a complete pseud, but you can tell
there's a touch of the Lady Muck about her. Imperious.
And she likes people to know she's not short of a bob or
two. You know, she flashes her rings, jewellery, stuff like
that. She also struck me as being a very *cold* woman, I
don't know why. All sharp edges, like a drawer full of
kitchen knives."

Banks leaned against the door jamb. "It's a bloody
strange family altogether," he said.

Sandra shrugged. "Just thought I'd put in my two
penn'orth. I don't suppose you know when you'll be
back?"

"No. Sorry, got to dash." Banks risked a quick kiss on
the lips. They tasted of strawberry jam.

"Can you leave me the car, today?" Sandra called after
him. "There's a water-colour exhibition I want to see in
Ripon. One of our locals is exhibiting. I don't know when
I'll be back, either."

"Okay," said Banks, wincing at the barb. He could always sign a car out of the pool if he needed one. It wouldn't
have a cassette deck, but then this was hardly the best of
all possible worlds, was it? At least it should have a radio.
He set off determined, after a miserable night, not to let
things get him down.

It was a beautiful morning. Calendar weather. May, as
he knew it, had finally arrived. The sky was a cloudless
blue, apart from a few high milky swirls, and even this
early in the morning the temperature seemed to have risen

a few notches since yesterday. Banks wouldn't be surprised if it were shirtsleeves weather before the day was out.

As he walked, he plugged in his earphones and switched on the Walkman in his briefcase. The tape started at the jazzy "Forlane" section of Ravel's *Le Tombeau de Couperin*. Not bad for a walk to work on a fine spring morning.

It was only about a mile to the station along Market Street, and Banks liked the way the townscape changed almost yard by yard as he walked. At his end of town, the road was broad, and the area was much like the outer part of any town centre: the main road with its garage, supermarket, school, zebra crossings and roundabouts, surrounded by residential streets of tall Victorian houses, most of them converted to student flats, all with names like Mafeking Avenue, Sebastopol Terrace, Crimea Close and Waterloo Road, and a strong smell of petrol and diesel fumes pervading the air.

But the closer Market Street got to the actual marketplace, the more it narrowed and turned into a tourist attraction with its overhanging first-floor bays, where people could almost shake hands with someone across the street; the magnifying-glass windows of twee souvenir shops; an expensive walkers' gear shop with orange Gore-tex clothing hanging by the doorway and a stand of walking-sticks out on the pavement; a Waterstone's Bookshop, the street's most recent addition; the mingled aromas from Hambleton's Tea and Coffee Emporium and Farleigh's bakery across the street; an Oddbins wine shop; the Golden Grill cafe; and a newsagent's with a rack of newspapers out front, some of them folded over at Rothwell's grainy photograph, and a display of local guides and Ordnance Survey maps in the window. This narrow part of Market Street was always jammed with honking traffic, too—mostly visitors and delivery vans.

Halfway through the "Menuet" section, Banks arrived at the station, a three-storey, Tudor-fronted building facing the market square. First he called in at the Murder Room and talked to Phil Richmond. The Florida State Police had tracked down the car rental company Tom Rothwell had used at Tampa airport. At least it was a start. Now the police had a licence number to look for among the millions of cars parked at the thousands of Florida hotels, motels and beach clubs.

The PNC reported nothing doing on the use of pornographic wadding at other crime scenes.

Gristhorpe was in a meeting with Inspector Macmillan of the Fraud Squad, and Susan Gay was in her hutch phoning around the list of Rothwell's clients Laurence Pratt had given her. Banks poured a coffee and went to his office.

He opened his window and sniffed the air, then lit a cigarette and stood looking down on the early tourists in their bright anoraks and cagoules milling about the cobbled square. It was ten past nine on a Saturday morning, market-day in Eastvale, and the vendors at their canvas-covered stalls, like the old wild-west wagon trains, hawked everything from flat caps and multi-pocketed fishing jackets to burglar alarms, spark plugs and non-stick ovenware. The cheese van was there, as usual, and Banks thought he might nip out and buy a wedge of Coverdale or Wensleydale Blue if he got the chance. If.

Banks mulled over what Sandra had told him about Mary Rothwell. So far, he had an impression of her as an ostentatious and overbearing woman who put too much value on appearances, and of Keith Rothwell as an unassuming, yet sly and greedy, man, easily prey to temptation. Greed, as Susan Gay had remarked, is often a way of making dangerous enemies, and a habit of secrecy is a damn good way of making things difficult for the police. But did the greed originate in Rothwell himself, or had he felt pushed into it by the demands of his wife?

There had certainly been hints in what both Ian Falkland and Larry Grafton had said that Rothwell had been something of a henpecked husband, escaping to the pub for a half-pint and a quiet smoke whenever he could.

In Banks's experience, such people often developed rich and secret fantasy lives, which sometimes imposed on reality with messy and unpredictable results. Keith Rothwell had supplied his wife and children with all the conveniences and many of the luxuries they wanted. What did he get out of it? What did he have going for himself? Nobody seemed to know or care what made him tick.

Banks moved away from the window and stubbed out his cigarette. There was at least one thing he could do right now, he thought, reaching for a pen and notepad. "WANTED," he wrote, "male Caucasian, about five feet nine, slight paunch, large wet brown eyes, commonly described as 'spaniel' or 'puppy dog' eyes, fondness for shotguns, can't keep his hands off young girls and probably has a taste for pornography of the shaved pussy variety." He could just imagine the laughter and the nudge-nudges in police stations around the country as that went out over the PNC.

Just as he was about to start working on a revised version, the phone rang and Sergeant Rowe put him through to a distraught woman asking for the ubiquitous "someone in charge."

"Can I help you?" Banks asked her.

"They said they'd put me through to someone in charge. Are you in charge?"

"Depends what you mean," said Banks. "In charge of what? What's it about?"

"The man in the paper this morning, the one who was killed."

Suddenly Banks pricked up his ears. Was he mistaken, or was she sobbing as she spoke? "Yes," he said. "Go on."

"I knew him."

"You knew Keith Rothwell?"

"No, no—" She sobbed again then came back on the line. "You've got it wrong. That's not his name. His name is Robert. Robert Calvert. That's who he is. You've got it all wrong. Is Robert really dead?"

The back of his neck tingling, Banks gripped his pen tight between his fingers. "I think we'd better have a talk, love," he said. "The sooner, the better. Would you like to give me your name and address?"

2

Susan Gay drove the unmarked police Fiesta to Leeds, with Banks beside her tapping his fingers on his knees. It wasn't because of her driving. Ordinarily, he would enjoy such a trip and take his time if there were no rush, but today he was anxious to interview the woman who had phoned, Pamela Jeffreys.

He wasn't smoking, either, and that also made him jittery. He refrained in deference to Susan, though she magnanimously said it was okay if he opened the windows. There wasn't much worse, in his experience, than trying to enjoy a cigarette in a car next to a non-smoker with a force nine gale blowing all around you, no matter how good the weather.

As Banks had hoped, though the car had no cassette player, it did have a radio, and he was able to lose himself in a Poulenc chamber concert on Radio Three as he considered the implications of what he had just heard.

"How are we going to play this, sir?" Susan asked as she turned onto the Inner Ring Road and went into the yellow-lit tunnel.

Banks dragged himself out of a passage in the "Sextet" where a sense of sadness seemed to pervade the levity of the woodwinds. "By ear," he said.

They had already called DI Ken Blackstone, out of courtesy for intruding on his patch, and Ken had found nothing on Pamela Jeffreys in records. Hardly surprising, Banks thought, as there was no reason to suppose she was a criminal. He glanced out of the window and saw they were crossing the bridge over the River Aire and the Leeds-

Liverpool Canal. The dirty, sluggish water looked especially vile in the bright sunlight.

"Do we tell her anything?" Susan asked.

"If she's read the papers, she'll know almost as much about Keith Rothwell's life as we do. Whether she'll believe it or not is another matter."

"What do you think it's all about?"

"I haven't a clue. We'll soon find out."

Susan negotiated the large roundabout on Wellington Road. Above them, the dark, medieval fortress of Armley Jail loomed on its hill. Susan veered right at the junction with Tong Road, passed the disused Crown bingo hall, the medical centre and the New Wortley Cemetery and headed towards Armley. It was an area of waste ground and boarded-up shopfronts, with the high black spire of St. Bartholomew's visible above the decay. She slowed to look at the street names, found Wesley Road, turned right, then right again and looked for the address Pamela Jeffreys had given.

"This is it, sir," she said finally, pulling into a street of terraced back-to-backs, nicely done up, each with a postage-stamp lawn behind a privet hedge, some with new frosted-glass or wood-panel doors and dormer windows. "Number twenty, twenty-four . . . Here it is." She pulled up outside number twenty-eight.

The row of houses stood across the street from some allotments behind a low stone wall, where a number of retired or unemployed men worked their patches, stopping now and then to chat. Someone had rested a transistor radio on the wall, and Banks could hear the preamble to the Cup Final commentary. Not far down the street was an old chapel which, according to the sign, had been converted into a Sikh temple. They walked down the path to number twenty-eight and rang the doorbell.

The woman who opened the door had clearly been crying, but it didn't mar her looks one bit, Banks thought. Perhaps the whites of her almond eyes were a little too red and the glossy blue-black hair could have done with a good brushing, but there was no denying that she was a woman of exceptional beauty.

Northern Indian, Banks guessed, or perhaps from Bangladesh or Pakistan, she had skin the colour of burnished gold, with high cheekbones, full, finely drawn lips and a figure that wouldn't be out of place in *Playboy*, revealed to great advantage by skin-tight ice-blue jeans and a jade-green T-shirt tucked in at her narrow waist. Around her neck, she wore a necklace of many-coloured glass beads. She also wore a gold stud in her left nostril. She looked to be in her mid-twenties.

Her fingers, Banks noticed as she raised her hand to push the door shut, were long and tapered, with clear nails cut very short. A spiral gold bracelet slipped down her slim wrist over her forearm. On the other wrist, she wore a simple Timex with a black plastic strap. She had only one ring, and that was a gold band on the middle finger of her right hand. Light down covered her bare brown arms.

The living-room was arranged for comfort. A small three-piece suite with burgundy velour upholstery formed a semicircle around a thick glass coffee-table in front of the fireplace, which may once have housed a real coal fire but now was given over to an electric one with three elements and a fake flaming-coals effect. On the coffee-table, the new Mary Wesley paperback lay open face down beside a copy of the *Radio Times* and an earthenware mug half full of milky tea.

A few family photographs in gilt frames stood on the mantelpiece. On the wall above the fire hung a print of Ganesh, the elephant god in a brightly coloured primitive style. In the corner by the front window stood a television with a video on a shelf underneath. The only other furniture in the room was a mini stereo system and several racks of compact discs, a glass-fronted cabinet of crystalware and a small bookcase mostly full of modern fiction and books about music.

But it was the far end of the room that caught Banks's interest, for there stood a music stand with some sheet music on it, and beside that, on a chair, lay what he first took to be an oversized violin, but quickly recognized as a viola.

The woman sat on the sofa, curling her legs up beside her, and Banks and Susan took the armchairs.

"Are you a musician?" Banks asked.

"Yes," she said.

"Professional?"

"Uh-huh. I'm with the Northern Philharmonia, and I do a bit of chamber work on the side. Why?"

"Just curious." Banks was impressed. The English Northern Philharmonia played for Opera North, among other things, and was widely regarded as one of the best opera orchestras in the country. He had been to see Opera North's superb production of *La Bohème* recently and must have heard Pamela Jeffreys play.

"Ms. Jeffreys," he began, after a brief silence. "I must admit that your phone call has us a bit confused."

"Not half as much as that rubbish in the newspaper has *me* confused." She had no Indian accent at all, just West Yorkshire with a cultured, university edge.

Banks slipped a recent good-quality photograph of Keith Rothwell from his briefcase and passed it to her. "Is this the man we're talking about?"

"Yes. I think this is Robert, though he looks a bit stiff here." She handed it back. "There's a mistake, isn't there? It must be someone who looks just like him, that's it."

"What exactly was your relationship?"

She fiddled with her necklace. "We're friends. Maybe we were more than that at one time, but now we're just friends."

"Were you lovers?"

"Yes. For a while."

"For how long?"

"Three or four months."

"Until when?"

"Six months ago."

"So you've known him for about ten months altogether?"

"Yes."

"How did you meet?"

"In a pub. The Boulevard, on Westgate actually. I was with some friends. Robert was by himself. We just got talking, like you do."

"Have you seen him since you stopped being lovers?"

"Yes. I told you. We remained friends. We don't see each other as often, of course, but we still go out every now and then, purely Platonic. I like Robert. He's good fun to be with, even when we stopped being lovers. Look, what's all this in—"

"When did you last see him, Ms. Jeffreys?"

"Pamela. Please call me Pamela. Let me see . . . it must have been a month or more ago. Look, is this some mistake, or what?"

"We don't know yet, Pamela," Susan Gay said. "We really don't, love. You'll help us best get it sorted out if you answer Chief Inspector Banks's questions."

Pamela nodded.

"Was there anything unusual about Mr. . . . about Robert the last time you saw him?" Banks asked.

"No."

"He didn't say anything, tell you about anything that was worrying him?"

"No. Robert never seemed to worry about anything. Except he hated being called Bob."

"So there was nothing at all different about him?"

"Well, I wouldn't say that."

"Oh?"

"It's just a guess, like."

"What was it?"

"I think he'd met someone else. Another woman. I think he was in love."

Banks swallowed, hardly able to believe what he was

hearing. This couldn't be dull, dry, mild-mannered Keith Rothwell. Surely Rothwell wasn't the kind of man to have a wife and children in Swainsdale and a beautiful girlfriend like Pamela Jeffreys in Leeds, whom he could simply dump for yet *another* woman?

"Don't get me wrong," Pamela went on. "I'm not bitter or anything. We had a good time, and it was never anything more. We didn't lie to each other. Neither of us wanted to get too involved. And one thing Robert doesn't do is mess you around. That's why we can still be friends. But he made it clear it was over between us—at least in *that* way—and I got the impression it was because he'd found someone else."

"Did you ever see this woman?"

"No."

"Did he ever speak of her?"

"No. I just *knew*. A woman can tell about these things, that's all."

"Did you ask him about her?"

"I broached the subject once or twice."

"What happened?"

"He changed it." She smiled. "He has a way."

"How often did you see each other?"

"When we were going out?"

"Yes."

"Just once or twice a week. Mostly late in the week, weekends sometimes. He travels a lot on business. Anyway, he's usually at home every week at some time, at least for a day or two."

"What's his business?"

"Dunno. That's another thing he never said much about. I can't say I was really that interested, either. I mean, it's boring, isn't it, talking about business. I liked going out with Robert because he was fun. He could leave his work at home."

"Did he smoke?"

"What an odd question. Yes, as a matter of fact. Not much, though."

"What brand?"

"Benson and Hedges. I don't mind people smoking."

Encouraged, Banks slipped his Silk Cut out of his pocket. Pamela smiled and brought him a glass ashtray. "What was he like?" Banks asked. "What kind of things did you used to do together?"

Pamela looked at Banks with a glint of naughty humour in her eyes and raised her eyebrows. Banks felt himself flush. "I mean where did you used to go?" he said quickly.

"Yeah, I know. Hmmm . . . Well, we'd go out for dinner about once a week. Brasserie 44—you know, down by the river—or La Grillade, until it moved. He likes good food. Let's see . . . sometimes we'd go to concerts at the Town Hall, if I wasn't playing, of course, but he's not very fond of classical music, to be honest. Prefers that dreadful trad jazz. And sometimes we'd just stay in, order a pizza or a curry and watch telly if there was something good on. Or rent a video. He likes oldies. *Casablanca*, *The Maltese Falcon*, that kind of thing. So do I. Let me see . . . we'd go to Napoleon's every once in a while—"

"Napoleon's?"

"Yeah. You know, the casino. And he took me to the races a couple of times—once at Pontefract and once at Doncaster. That's about it, really. Oh, and we went dancing now and then. Quite fleet on his feet is Robert."

Banks coughed and stubbed out his cigarette. "Dancing? The casino?"

"Yes. He loves a flutter, does Robert. It worried me sometimes the way he'd go through a hundred or more some nights." She shrugged. "But it wasn't my place to say, was it? I mean it wasn't as if we were *married* or anything, or even living together. And he seemed to have plenty of money. Not that that's what interested me about him." She pulled at her necklace again. "Can't you tell me what's going on, Chief Inspector? It's not the same person that was murdered, is it? I was so upset when I saw the paper this morning. Tell me it's a case of mistaken identity."

Banks shook his head. "I don't know. Maybe he had a double. Did he ever say anything about being married?"

"No, never."

"Did he have an appendix scar?"

This time, Pamela blushed. "Yes," she said. "Yes, he did. But so do lots of other people. I had mine out when I was sixteen."

"When you spent time together," Banks said, "did he always come here, to your house? Didn't you ever visit him at his hotel?"

She frowned. "Hotel? What hotel?"

"The one he stayed at when he was in town, I assume. Did you always meet here?"

"Of course not. Sometimes he came here, certainly. I've nothing to be ashamed of, and I don't care what the neighbours say. Bloody racists, some of them. You know, my mum and dad came over to Shipley to work in the woollen mills in 1952. *Nineteen fifty-two*. They even changed their name from Jaffrey to Jeffreys because it sounded more English. Can you believe it? I was born here, brought up here, went to school and university here, and some of them still call me a bleeding Paki." She shrugged. "What can you do? Anyway, you were saying?"

"I was asking why you never saw him at his hotel."

"Oh, that's easy. I don't know what you're talking about. You see, it *can't* be the same person, can it? That proves it." She leaned forward quickly and clapped her hands. The bracelet spiralled. "You see, Robert didn't stay at any hotel. Sometimes he came here, yes, but not always. Other times I went to his place. His flat. He's got a flat in Headingley."

3

Banks turned the Yale key in the lock and the three of them stood on the threshold of Robert Calvert's Headingley flat. It was in the nice part of Headingley, more West Park, Banks noted, not the scruffy part around Hyde Park that was honeycombed with student bedsits.

It hadn't been easy getting in. Pamela Jeffreys didn't have a key, so they had to ask one of the tenants in the building to direct them to the agency that handled rentals. Naturally, it was closed at four o'clock on a Saturday afternoon, so then they had to get hold of one of the staff at home and arrange for her to come in, grumbling all the way, open up the office and give them a spare key.

And no, she told them, she had never met Robert Calvert. The man was a model tenant; he paid his rent on time, and that was all that mattered. One of the secretaries probably handed him the key, but he'd had the place about eighteen months and turnover in secretaries was pretty high. However, if Banks wanted to come back on Monday morning. . . . Still, Banks reflected as they stood at the front door, all in all it had taken only about an hour and a half from the first time they had heard of the place, so that wasn't bad going.

"Better not touch anything," Banks said as they stood in the hallway. "Which is the living-room?" he asked Pamela.

"That one, on the left."

The door was ajar and Banks nudged it open with his elbow. The bottom of the door rubbed over the fitted beige carpet. Susan Gay and Pamela walked in behind him.

"There's only this room, a bedroom, kitchen and bathroom," Pamela said. "It's not very big, but it's cosy."

The living-room was certainly not the kind of place Banks could imagine Mary Rothwell caring much for. Equipped with all the usual stuff—TV, video, stereo, a few jazz compact discs, books, armchairs, gas fireplace—it smelled of stale smoke and had that comfortable, lived-in feel Banks had never sensed at Arkbeck Farm. Perhaps it was something to do with the old magazines—mostly jazz and racing—strewn over the scratched coffee-table, the overflowing ashtray, the worn upholstery on the armchair by the fire, or the framed photographs of a younger-looking Rothwell on the mantelpiece. On the wall hung a framed print of Monet's "Waterloo Bridge, Grey Day."

They went into the bedroom and found the same mess. The bed was unmade, and discarded socks, underpants and shirts lay on the floor beside it.

There was also a small desk against one wall, on which stood a jar of pens and pencils, a roll of Sellotape and a stapler, in addition to several sheets of paper, some of them scrawled all over with numbers. "Is this the kind of thing you're looking for?" Pamela asked.

Carefully, Banks opened the drawer and found a wallet. Without disturbing anything, he could see, through the transparent plastic holder inside, credit cards in the name of Robert Calvert. He put it back.

A couple of suits hung in the wardrobe, along with shirts, ties, casual jackets and trousers. Banks felt in the pockets and found nothing but pennies, sales slips, a couple of felt-tip pens, matches, betting slips and some fluff.

As wood doesn't usually yield fingerprints, he didn't have to be too careful opening cupboards and drawers. Calvert's dresser contained the usual jumble of jeans, jumpers, socks and underwear. A packet of condoms lay forlornly next to a passport and a selection of Dutch, French, Greek and Swiss small change in the drawer of the bedside table. The passport was in the name of Robert Calvert. There were no entry or exit stamps, but then there wouldn't be if he did most of his travelling in Europe, as the coins seemed to indicate. On the bedside table was a shaded reading lamp and a copy of *The Economist*.

The kitchen was certainly compact, and by the sparsity of the fridge's contents, it looked as if Calvert did most of his eating out. A small wine-rack stood on the counter. Banks checked the contents: a white Burgundy, Veuve Clicquot Champagne, a Rioja.

Calvert's bathroom was clean and tidy. His medicine cabinet revealed only the barest of essentials: paracetamol tablets, Aspro, Milk of Magnesia, Alka Seltzer, Fisherman's Friend, Elastoplast, cotton swabs, hydrogen peroxide, Old Spice deodorant and shaving cream, a packet of orange disposable razors, toothbrush and a half-used tube of Colgate. Calvert had squeezed it in the middle, Banks noticed, not from bottom to top. Could this be the same man who returned his used matches to the box?

"Come on," Banks said. "We'd better use a call-box. I don't want to risk smudging any prints there may be on the telephone."

"What's going on?" Pamela asked as they walked down the street.

"I'm sorry," Susan said to her. "We really don't know. We're not just putting you off. We're as confused as you are. If we can find some of Robert's fingerprints in the flat, then we can check them against our files and find out once and for all if it's the same man."

"But it just *can't* be," Pamela said. "I'm sure of it."

A pub on the main road advertised a beer garden at the back, and as they were all thirsty, Banks suggested he might as well make the call from there.

He phoned the station and Phil Richmond said he would arrange to get Vic Manson to the flat as soon as possible.

That done, he ordered the drinks and discovered from the barman that Arsenal had won the FA Cup. Good for them, Banks thought. When he had lived in London, he had been an Arsenal supporter, though he always had a soft spot for Peterborough United, his home-town team, struggling as they were near the bottom of the First Division.

The beer garden was quiet. They sat at a heavy wooden bench beside a bowling green and sipped their drinks. Two old men in white were playing on the green, and occasion-

ally the clack of the bowls disturbed the silence. Banks and
Susan shared salted roast peanuts and cheese-and-onion
crisps, as neither had eaten since breakfast. The sun felt
warm on the back of Banks's neck.

"You can go home whenever you want," Banks told
Pamela as she took off the tan suede jacket she had put on
to go out. "We have to stay here, but we'll pay for a taxi.
I'm sorry we had to ruin your day for you."

Pamela squinted in the sun, reached into her bag and
pulled out a pair of large pink-rimmed sunglasses. "It's all
right," she said, picking up her gin and tonic. "I know it
wasn't Robert they were talking about in the paper. Who
was this man, this Keith Rothwell?"

"He was an accountant who got murdered," Banks told
her. "We can't really say much more than that. Did you
ever hear the name before?"

Pamela shook her head. "The papers said he was married."

"Yes."

"Robert didn't act like a married man."

"What do you mean?"

"Guilt. Secrecy. Fleeting visits. Furtive phone calls. The
usual stuff. There was none of that with Robert. We went
about quite openly. He wasn't tied down. He was a
dreamer. Besides, you just *know*." She took her glasses off
and squinted at Banks. "I'll bet you're married, aren't
you?"

"Yes," said Banks, and saw, he hoped, a hint of disappointment in her eyes.

"Told you." She put her sunglasses on again.

Banks noticed Susan grinning behind her glass of lem-
onade. He gave her a dirty look. A clack of bowls came
from the green and one of the old men did a little dance of
victory.

"So, you see," Pamela went on. "It can't be the same
man. If I'm sure of one thing, it's that Robert Calvert definitely wasn't a married man with a family."

Banks picked up his pint and raised it in a toast. "I hope you're right," he said, looking at her brave smile and remembering the scene in Rothwell's garage only two nights ago. "I sincerely hope you're right."

: 5

1

There was always something sad about an empty farmyard, Banks thought as he got out of the car in front of Arkbeck Farm again. There should be chickens squawking all over the place, the occasional wandering cow, maybe a barking sheepdog or two.

He thought of the nest egg he had held at his Uncle Len's farm in Gloucestershire on childhood family visits. They used it to encourage hens to lay, he remembered, and when his Aunt Chloe had handed it to him in the coop, it had still felt warm. Banks also remembered the smells of hay and cow dung, the shiny metal milk churns sitting by the roadside waiting to be picked up.

As he rang the doorbell, he doubted that the Rothwells felt the same way about empty farmyards. The place seemed to suit Alison's introspective nature; her father had no doubt appreciated the seclusion and the protection from prying eyes and questions it offered; and Mary Rothwell . . . well, Banks could hardly imagine her mucking out the byre or feeding the pigs. He couldn't imagine her handing a child a warm porcelain egg, either.

''Do come in,'' Mary Rothwell said, opening the door. Banks followed her to the split-level living-room. Today she wore a white shirt that buttoned on the ''man's'' side and a loose grey skirt that reached her ankles. Alison lay sprawled on the sofa reading.

On the way to Arkbeck Farm, he had considered what to say to them regarding his talk with Pamela Jeffreys in Leeds, but he hadn't come up with any clear plan. Vic

Manson hadn't got back to him yet about the prints, so he still couldn't be absolutely certain that Robert Calvert and Keith Rothwell were the same person. Best play it by ear, he decided.

"How are you doing?" he asked Mary Rothwell.

"Could be worse," she replied. He noticed her eyes were baggy under the make-up. "I haven't been sleeping well, despite the pills, and I'm a mass of nerves, but if I keep myself busy, time passes. I have the funeral to organize. Please, sit down."

Banks had come partly to explain that a van was on its way to pick up Keith Rothwell's computer disks and business files and spirit them off to the Fraud Squad's headquarters in Northallerton, where a team of suits would pore over them for months, maybe years, costing the taxpayers millions. He didn't put it like that, of course. Just as he had finished explaining, he heard the van pull up out front.

He went to the front door and directed the men to Rothwell's office, then returned to the living-room, shutting the door firmly behind him. It was dark in the room, and a little chilly, despite the fine weather outside. "They shouldn't bother us," he said. "Perhaps a little music?"

Mary Rothwell nodded and turned on the radio. Engelbert Humperdinck came on, singing "Release Me." Banks often regretted that humans hadn't been born with the capacity to close their ears as they did their eyes. He did his best, anyway, and reflected that it was all in a good cause, blanking out the sounds of Keith Rothwell's office being dismantled and carried away.

"Have you found Tom?" Mary Rothwell said, sitting down. She sat at the edge of the armchair, Banks noticed, and twisted her hands in her lap, a mass of gold and precious stones. She seemed so stiff he wished someone would give her a massage. Her skin, he felt, would be brittle as lacquered hair to the touch.

Banks explained that they had tracked down the car rental agency he had used and that it wouldn't be long before someone spotted the car.

"He should be home," she said. "We need him. There's the funeral . . . all the arrangements. . . ."

"We're doing our best, Mrs. Rothwell."

"Of course. I didn't mean to imply anything."

"It's all right. Are you up to answering a few more questions?"

"I suppose so. As long as you don't want to talk about what I went through the other night. I couldn't bear that." Her eyes moved in the direction of the garage and Banks could see the fear and horror flood into them.

"No, not that." She would have to talk about it sometime, Banks almost told her, but not now, not yet. "It's Mr. Rothwell I want to talk about. We need a better idea of how he spent his time."

"Well, it's hard to say, really," she began. "When he was here, he was up in his office most of the time. I could hear him clicking away on the computer."

"Did you ever hear him on the phone?"

"He had his own line up there. I didn't listen in, if that's what you mean."

"No, I didn't mean that. But sometimes you just can't help overhearing something, anything."

"No. He always kept the door shut. I could hear his voice, like I could hear the keyboard, but it was muffled, even if I was passing by the office."

"So you never knew who he was talking to or what he was saying?"

"No."

"Did he have many calls in the days leading up to his death?"

"Not so much as I noticed. No more than usual. I could always hear it ring, you see, even from downstairs." She stood up. "Would you like a cup of tea? I can—"

"Not at the moment, thank you," Banks said. He didn't want her crossing the path of the removal team. For one thing, it would upset and distract her, and for another she would start telling them off about trailing dirt in and out.

She walked over to the fireplace, straightened a porcelain figurine, then came and sat down in the same position. Alison went on reading her book. It was *Villette*, by Charlotte Brontë, Banks noticed. Surely a bit heavy for a fifteen-year-old?

"I understand your husband would drop in at the Black Sheep or the Rose and Crown now and then?" Banks asked.

"Yes. He wasn't much of a drinker, but he liked to get out of the house for an hour or so. You do when you work at home, don't you? You get to feel all cooped up. He'd usually walk there and back. It was good exercise. Businessmen often don't exercise enough, do they, living such sedentary lives, but Keith believed in keeping in good shape. He swam regularly, too, in Eastvale, and he would sometimes go for long runs." She started picking pieces of imaginary lint from her skirt. Banks heard a thud from the staircase, and this time he couldn't stop her from dashing to the door and yanking it open.

"Watch what you're doing, you clumsy little man!" she said. "Just look at this. You've gouged a hole in my wall. The plaster's fallen off. You'll have to pay for that, you know. I'll be talking to your superior." She popped her head back around the door and said, "I'll make that tea now, shall I?" then disappeared into the kitchen.

Banks, still sitting, noticed Alison look up and raise her eyes. "She's been like this since yesterday," she said. "Can't sit still. It's even worse than usual."

"She's upset," Banks said. "It's her way of dealing with it."

"Or *not* dealing with it. I saw him too, you know. Do you think I can forget so easily?"

"You've got to talk to each other," Banks said. He noticed the book was shaking in her hands and she was making an effort to keep it still.

"If Tom doesn't come home soon, I'm going to run

away,'' she said. ''I can't stand it any longer. She's always going on about something or other and running about like a headless chi—'' She put her hand to her mouth. ''My God, what a thing to say. I'm awful, aren't I? Oh, I hope Tom comes back soon. He must or I'll go mad. We'll both go mad.''

A bit melodramatic, Banks thought, but perhaps to be expected from a young girl on a steady diet of Charlotte Brontë.

Mary Rothwell came in bearing a tea tray and wearing a brave smile. Alison picked up her book again and lapsed into moody silence while her mother poured the tea into delicate china cups with hand-painted roses on the sides and gold around the rims. Banks always felt clumsy and nervous drinking from such fine china; he was afraid he would drop the cup or break off the flimsy handle while lifting it to his mouth.

''Why are they taking all Keith's files anyway?'' Mary Rothwell asked.

''We're beginning to think that your husband might have been involved in some shady financial dealings,'' Banks explained. ''And they could have something to do with his murder.''

''Shady?'' She said it as Lady Bracknell said, ''A handbag?''

''He might not have known what he was involved in,'' Banks lied. ''It's just a line of enquiry we have to follow.''

''I can assure you that my husband was as honest as the day is long.''

''Mrs. Rothwell, can you tell me *anything* about what your husband did when he was travelling on business?''

''How would I know? I wasn't there.''

''Which hotels did he stay in? You must have phoned him.''

''No. He phoned me occasionally. He told me it was better that way for his tax expenses.'' She shrugged. ''Well, *he* was the businessman. I've already told you he travelled all over the place.''

''You never went with him?''

''No, of course not. I have an aversion to lengthy car rides. Besides, they were business trips. One doesn't take one's spouse on business trips.''

''So you've no idea what he got up to in Leeds or wherever?''

She put down her cup. ''Are you implying something, Chief Inspector? Keith didn't 'get up to' anything.''

Banks was dying for a cigarette. He finished the weak tea and put his cup and saucer down gently on the coffee-table. ''Do you know if your husband was much of a gambler?'' he asked.

''Gambler?'' She laughed. ''Good heavens, no. Keith never even bet on the Grand National, and most people do that, don't they? No, money for my husband was too hard earned to be frittered away like that. Keith had a poor childhood, you know, and one learns the value of money quite early on.''

''What sort of childhood?''

''His father was a small shopkeeper, and they suffered terribly when the supermarkets started to become popular. He eventually went bankrupt. Keith didn't like to talk about it.''

Banks remembered the cigarettes he had found among the contents of Rothwell's pockets. ''Did you know that your husband smoked?'' he asked.

''One minor weakness,'' Mary Rothwell said, turning up her nose. ''It's a smelly and unpleasant habit, as well as a possibly fatal one. I certainly wouldn't let him do it in the house, and I was always trying to persuade him to stop.''

I'll bet you were, Banks thought. ''Have you ever heard of a woman called Pamela Jeffreys?'' he asked.

Mary Rothwell frowned. For the first time, she sat back in the chair and gripped its arms with both hands. ''No. Why?'' Banks saw suspicion and apprehension in her eyes.

Outside, the van door closed and the engine revved up. Banks noticed Mrs. Rothwell glance towards the window. "They're finished," he said. "What about Robert Calvert? Does the name mean anything to you?"

She shook her head. "No, nothing. Look, what's this all about? Are these the people you think killed Keith? Are these the ones who got him involved in this criminal scheme you were talking about?"

Banks sighed. "I don't know," he said. "Maybe, but I don't know."

"Why don't you go and arrest *them* instead of bothering us?"

Banks didn't think he was likely to get anything else out of Mary Rothwell, or out of Alison. He stood up. "I'm sorry we had to bother you," he said. "We'll be in touch as soon as we track down your son. And please let us know if you hear from him first. Don't worry, I'll see myself out." And he left.

Maybe she hadn't heard of Pamela Jeffreys, he thought as he got in the car, but he was certain that she suspected her husband might have been seeing another woman. It was there in her eyes, in the whiteness of her knuckles.

He slipped a Thelonious Monk tape in the deck and set off for his next appointment. As the edgy, repetitive figure at the opening of "Raise Four" almost pushed his ears to the limits of endurance, he wondered how long Mary Rothwell would be able to maintain her thinly-lacquered surface before the cracks started to show.

2

"Well, now, if it ain't Mr. Banks again," said Larry Grafton when Banks walked into the Black Sheep that lunchtime with *The Sunday Times* folded under his arm. "Twice in one week. We are honoured. What can we do for you this time?"

"You could start with a pint of best bitter and follow it

with a plate of your Elsie's delightful roast beef and York-shire pud. And you could cut the bloody sarcasm.''

Grafton laughed and started pulling. Elsie's Sunday lunches were another well-kept secret, and only a privileged few got to taste them. Banks didn't fool himself that he was an accepted member of the élite; he knew damn well that publicans liked to keep on the good side of the law.

''And,'' he said, when Larry handed him his pint, ''I'd like a word with your Cathy, if I might.''

''About the Rothwells, is it?''

''Yes.''

''Aye. Well she's just having her dinner. I'll send her through when she's done.''

''Thanks.''

Banks took his drink and sat by the tiled fireplace. Before he sat, he glanced at the collection of butterflies pinned to a board in a glass case on the wall. The pub wasn't as busy as most on a Sunday lunch-time. Of course, there was no sandwich-board outside advertising ''Traditional Sunday Lunch.''

Banks's roast beef and Yorkshires came, as good as ever. Not for the first time, he reflected that Elsie's was the only roast beef in Yorkshire, apart from Sandra's, that was pink in the middle. As he ate, he propped the paper against a bottle of HP sauce and began to read an analysis of the growing political unrest on an obscure Caribbean island, feeling an irrational rage grow in him as he read. Christ, how he loathed these tinpot dictators, the ones who stuffed their maws with the best of everything while their subjects starved, who tortured and murdered anyone who dared to complain.

Just as he had picked up the books supplement, he no-ticed a tourist couple walk in and look around. They went to the bar and the man asked Larry Grafton what food he offered.

''Nowt,'' said Grafton. ''We don't do food.''

The man looked towards Banks. ''But he's got some.''

"Last plate."

The man looked at his watch. "But it's only twelve-thirty."

Grafton shrugged.

"Besides, you said you don't do food. You're contradicting yourself. You heard him, didn't you, darling?"

His wife said nothing; she just stood there looking embarrassed. He had the kind of upper-class accent that expects immediate subservience, but he obviously didn't know there could be nothing more calculated to get right up a Yorkshireman's nose.

"Look," said Grafton, "does tha want a drink or doesn't tha?"

"We want food," the man said.

His wife tugged at his sleeve. "Come on, darling," she whispered just in Banks's range of hearing. "Don't cause a fuss. Let's go. There are plenty of other pubs."

"But I—" The man glared petulantly at Grafton, who stared back stone-faced, then followed his wife's advice.

"Really," Banks heard him say on his way out, "you'd think these people didn't want to make an honest living. They're supposed to be in the service industry."

Larry Grafton winked at Banks and ambled off to serve one of the locals. Banks reflected that maybe the tourist was right. What the hell was wrong with Larry Grafton? Nowt so queer as folk, he decided, and went back to his roast beef. A couple of minutes later, when he had just finished, Cathy Grafton came from the back and joined him. He folded up his newspaper, pushed his empty plate aside and lit a cigarette.

Cathy was a plump girl of about sixteen with a fringe and a blotchy complexion, as if she had been sitting too close to the fire too long. She also had the longest, curliest and most beautiful eyelashes Banks had ever seen.

"Dad says you want to talk to me," she said, wedging herself into a chair. Her accent was thick, and Banks had to listen closely to understand everything she said, even though he had been in Swainsdale for four years.

"You helped Mary Rothwell do the housework at Arkbeck Farm, didn't you?"

"Aye. I do for a few folk around here. I know I should be paying more mind to school, like, but Mum says we need t'money."

Banks smiled. Not surprising, given the way Grafton scared business away. "What was it like, working at Arkbeck?" he asked.

Cathy frowned. "What do you mean?"

"Did you like working there?"

"It were all reet."

"How about Mary Rothwell? Did you get along well with her?"

Cathy wouldn't meet his eyes. She shifted in her chair and looked down at the scored table.

"Cathy?"

"I heard. It's just I was always told not to speak ill."

"Of the dead? Mary Rothwell isn't dead."

"No. Of me employer."

"Am I to take it that you *didn't* get along, then?"

"Take it as you will, Mr. Banks."

"Cathy, this could be very important. Mr. Rothwell was killed, you know."

"Aye, I know. It's got nowt to do with *her*, though, does it?"

"We still need to know all we can about the family."

Cathy contemplated the table for a while longer. More locals came in. One or two looked in Banks's direction, nudged their friends and raised their eyebrows. "She were just bossy, that's all," Cathy said at last.

"Mary Rothwell was?"

"Aye. She'd stand over you while you were working, with her arms folded, like this, and tell you you'd missed a bit or you weren't polishing hard enough. I used to hate doing for her. Will I still have to, do you think?"

"I don't know," Banks said. "What about Alison?"

"What about her?"

"You're about the same age, surely you must have had things in common, things to talk about. Pop stars and the like."

Cathy emitted a loud snort. "Little Miss La-di-da," she sneered, then shook her head. "No, I can't say as we did. She always had her nose stuck in a book."

"You never chatted with her?"

"No. Every time she saw me she turned up her nose. Stuck-up little madam."

"How did the family members get along with one another?"

"I weren't there often enough to notice. Not when they was all together, like."

"But you must have some idea, from your observations?"

"They didn't say much. It were a quiet house. He were in his office, when he were at home, like, and I were never allowed up there."

"Who cleaned it?"

"Dunno. Maybe he did it himself. I know he didn't like people to go in. Look, Mr. Banks, I've got to get back and help me mum. Is there anything else?"

"Did you notice any changes in the family recently? Did they behave any differently?"

"Not so far as I could tell."

"What about Tom, the son? Did you know him?"

"He were t'best of the lot," Cathy said without hesitation. "Always had a smile and a good-morning for you." She blushed.

"He's been away for a while now. Did you notice any changes before he left?"

"They used to argue."

"Who did?"

"Him and his father."

"What about?"

"How would I know? I didn't listen. Sometimes you couldn't help but hear."

"Hear what?"

"Just their voices, when they were shouting, like."

"Did you ever hear what they were arguing about?"

"Once t'door were open a bit, and I heard his dad mention a name then say something like, 'I'm disappointed in you.' He said 'shame,' too."

"What was a shame?"

"No. Just the word. I just heard the word 'shame,' that's all. I could tell Mr. Rothwell were very angry, but he sounded cold, you know."

"Did he say why he was disappointed?"

She shook her head.

"What was the name he mentioned?"

"Sounded like Aston or Afton or summat like that."

"Did you hear what Tom said back?"

"He said, 'You're a right one to talk about being disappointed in *me*.'"

"Did you hear anything more?"

"No." The chair scraped along the stone flags as she stood up. "I've got to go, really. Me mum'll kill me." And she hurried back behind the bar with surprising agility.

3

"Vic Manson matched prints from the Calvert flat with the ones from the body," Gristhorpe explained back at the station later that afternoon. "There were a couple of other sets, too, mostly smudged, not on file."

It was hot, and Banks was standing by the open window of his office. Gristhorpe sat with his feet up on the desk.

"So Rothwell was Calvert and Calvert was Rothwell," Banks said.

"It certainly looks that way, aye."

Banks leaned against the window frame and shook his head. "I still can't believe it. All right, so we know Rothwell had a secretive side to his nature, and he was greedy, or desperate for cash, to the point of dishonesty once. But this Calvert sounds to me like some sort of playboy. If you could have heard Pamela Jeffreys. Casinos, races, dancing . . . bloody hell. And you should have seen her, the one he chucked over.''

''So you've told me already, two or three times at least,'' Gristhorpe said with a smile. ''A proper bobby-dazzler by the sound of her. I'll take your word for it.''

''Well, she dazzled this bobby, anyway,'' said Banks, sitting opposite Gristhorpe. He sighed. ''I suppose we just have to accept it: Rothwell led a double life. Like Alec Guinness in that film about the ship's captain.''

''*The Captain's Paradise*?''

''That's the one. The question we have to ask ourselves now is what, if anything, does that fact have to do with his murder?''

''Has the girlfriend dazzled you so much you haven't considered she might have a part to play?''

''The thought's crossed my mind once or twice, yes. I just can't see how. Apparently Roth . . . Calvert found *another* woman five or six months ago. Pamela Jeffreys seemed to think he'd fallen in love. It's her we need to find, but she hasn't come forward yet.''

''There's always jealousy as a motive, then.''

''I don't think so. It's *possible*, though. Maybe Mary Rothwell found out about him and arranged a hit.''

''I was thinking more about this Pamela Jeffreys.''

''Couldn't afford it. She's a classical musician. Besides, she didn't really strike me as the jealous type. She said Calvert was just fun to be with. They never made any commitments.''

''She could be lying.''

''I suppose so.''

''And don't forget the possible porn connection. If Rothwell was mixed up with beautiful women, even under another identity, who knows?''

Banks couldn't believe it, but he didn't bother protesting to Gristhorpe. "I'll have to talk to her again anyway," he said.

"Poor you."

"What did the Fraud Squad have to say?"

Gristhorpe scratched his hooked nose. "Funny lot, aren't they?" he said. "I spent a good part of this morning with DI Macmillan. Used to be in banking. Boring little bugger, but you should have seen his eyes light up when he heard about the locked files. Anyway, they've had a quick look at the stuff from Arkbeck Farm, and Macmillan and I had another chat about an hour ago. They haven't much to go on, yet, of course, and they're as anxious as young Phil for that by-pass software, but Macmillan's even more excited now."

"Where has the software got to, by the way?"

"On its way, according to Phil. Apparently they were out of stock but they managed to scrounge around."

"Sorry. What did Macmillan have to say?"

"Well, he said he won't know anything for certain until they manage to open some of those locked directories. He thinks that's where the really interesting stuff is. But even some of the written documents in the filing cabinets gave him enough to suspect Rothwell was heavily into money-laundering or abetting tax evasion. Apparently, there was a fair bit of cryptic correspondence with foreign banks: Liechtenstein, Netherlands Antilles, Jersey, Switzerland, the Cayman Islands, among others. Dead giveaway, Macmillan said."

"Tax havens," said Banks. "Isn't that what they are?"

Gristhorpe held up a finger. "Aha! That was my first thought, too. But they're only tax havens because they have strict secrecy policies and a very flexible attitude towards whom they take on as their clients."

"In other words," offered Banks, "if you want to deposit a lot of money with them, they'll take it, no questions asked?"

"That's about it, aye. Within the law, of course. They do insist that they verify the money's source is legal. When it comes down to it, though, banks are basically run on greed, aren't they?"

"I won't argue with that. So Keith Rothwell was putting a lot of money in foreign banks?"

"Macmillan thought he might have been acting for a third party. He could hardly have made that much money himself. It's a very complicated business. As I said, either he was involved in aiding and abetting some pretty serious tax evasion, or he was part of a money-laundering scheme. There are still more questions than answers."

"Did Macmillan tell you how this money-laundering business works?" Banks asked.

"Aye, a bit. According to him, it's basically simple. It's only in the application it gets complicated. What happens is that somebody gets hold of a lot of money illegally, and he wants it to look legal so he can live off it without raising any suspicions." Gristhorpe paused.

"Go on," Banks urged.

Gristhorpe ran his hand through his hair. "Well, that's about it, really. I told you it was basically simple. Macmillan said it would take forever to explain all the technicalities of doing it. As far as legal money is concerned, he said, you can either earn it, borrow it or receive it as a gift. When you've laundered your dirty money, it has to look like it came to you one of those ways."

"I assume we're talking about drug money here," Banks said. "Or the profits from some sort of organized crime— prostitution, pornography, loan sharks?"

Gristhorpe nodded. "You know as well as I do, Alan, that the top cats in the drug trade pull in enormous wads of cash every day. You can't just walk into a showroom and buy a Rolls in cash without raising a few eyebrows, and the last thing you want is any attention from the police or the Inland Revenue."

Banks walked over to the window again and lit a cigarette. Most of the cars were gone from the cobbled square now and the hush of an early Sunday evening had fallen over the town. A young woman in jeans and a red T-shirt struck a pose by the ancient market cross as her male companion took a photograph, then they got into a blue Nissan Micra and drove off.

"What's in it for the launderer?" Banks asked.

"According to Macmillan, he'd get maybe four per cent for laundering the safer sort of funds and up to ten per cent for seriously dirty money."

"Per cent of what?"

"Depends," said Gristhorpe. "On a cursory glance, Macmillan estimated between four and six million quid. He said that was conservative."

"Over how long?"

"That's four to six a year, Alan."

"Jesus Christ!"

"Money worth murdering for, isn't it? In addition to Rothwell's legitimate earnings as a financial consultant, if he were in this money-laundering racket he also stood to earn, let's say five per cent of five million a year, to make it easy. How much is that?"

"Quarter of a million quid."

"Aye, my arithmetic was never among the best. Well, no wonder the bugger could afford a BMW and a new kitchen." He rubbed his hands together. "And that's about it. Macmillan said they'll start putting a financial profile together first thing in the morning: bank accounts, credit cards, building societies, Inland Revenue, loans, investments, the lot. He said they shouldn't have any trouble getting a warrant from the judge, given the circumstances. He's also getting in touch with the Yard. This is big, Alan."

"What about Calvert?" Banks asked.

"Well, they'll have to cover him too, now, won't they?"

A sharp knock at the door was immediately followed by Phil Richmond holding a small package. "I've got it," he

said, an excited light in his eyes. ''The by-pass software.
Give me a few minutes to study the manual and we'll see
what we can do.''

They all followed him to the computer room, once a
cupboard for storing cleaning materials, and stood around
tensely in the cramped space while he booted up and con-
sulted the instructions. All Rothwell's computer gear and
records were with the Fraud Squad, but Richmond had
made back-up disks of the relevant files.

Susan Gay popped her head around the door and, finding
no room left inside, stood in the doorway. Banks watched
as Richmond went through a series of commands. Dialogue
boxes appeared and disappeared; drive lights flashed on and
off; the machine buzzed and hummed. Banks noticed Gristhorpe chewing on his thumbnail.

''Got it,'' Richmond said. Then a locked file called
SUMMARY.924 came to the screen:

Halcyon Props.	16/9/92	82062	C.I.	Ibk.	GCA
Mercury Exps.	18/9/92	49876	Jsy.Cbk	PA	
Jupiter Pds.	23/9/92	47650	Lst.	Zbk	SA
Marryat Dvpts.	4/10/92	76980	N.A. Kbk	PA	
	(end 1st shpt)				
Neptune Hlds	6/11/92	65734	Jsy.Cbk	SPA	
City Ents	13/11/92	32450	Sw.	Nbk	LRA
Harbour Trst.	21/11/92	23443	BVI.Hbk	DTFA	
Sunland Props	29/11/92	85443	B.	Gbk	RDA

''What the hell is all that about?'' Banks asked.

''It looks like financial records for the last quarter of
1992,'' Gristhorpe said. ''Companies, banks, dates, maybe
numbered accounts. Keep going, Phil. Try that 'LETTER'
file you mentioned.''

Richmond highlighted the locked file, tapped at the keyboard again, and the file appeared unscrambled, for all to
see.

It was a letter, dated 1st May and addressed to a Mr.

Daniel Clegg, Solicitor, of Park Square, Leeds, and on first glance, it seemed innocuous enough:

> Dear Mr. Clegg,
> In the light of certain information that has recently come to my attention, I regret that we must terminate our association.
>
> Yours faithfully,
Keith Rothwell

"That's it?" Gristhorpe asked. "Are you sure you didn't lose anything?"

Richmond returned to the keyboard to check, then shook his head. "No, sir. That's it."

Banks backed towards the door. "Interesting," he said. "I wonder what 'information' that was?" He looked at Gristhorpe, who said, "Get it printed out, will you, Phil, before it disappears into the bloody ether."

: 6

1

In Park Square on that fine Monday morning in May, with the pink and white blossoms still on the trees, Banks could easily have imagined himself a Regency dandy out for a stroll while composing a satire upon the Prince's latest folly.

Opposite the Town Hall and the Court Centre, but hidden behind Westgate, Park Square is one of the few examples of elegant, late eighteenth-century Leeds remaining. Unlike most of the fashionable West End squares, it survived Benjamin Gott's Bean Ing Mills, an enormous steam-powered woollen factory which literally smoked out the middle-classes and sent them scurrying north to the fresher air of Headingley, Chapel Allerton and Roundhay, away from the soot and smoke carried over the town on the prevailing westerly winds.

Banks faced the terrace of nicely restored two- and three-storey Georgian houses, built of red brick and yellow sandstone, with their black iron railings, Queen Anne pediments and classical-style doorways with columns and entablatures. Very impressive, he thought, finding the right house. As expected, it was just the kind of place to have several polished brass nameplates beside the door, one of which read "Daniel Clegg, Solicitor."

A list on the wall inside the open front door told him that the office he wanted was on the first floor. He walked up, saw the name on the frosted-glass door, then knocked and entered.

He found himself in a dim anteroom that smelled vaguely

of paint, where a woman sat behind a desk sorting through a stack of letters. When he came in, he noticed a look of fear flash through her eyes, quickly replaced by one of suspicion. "Can I help you?" she asked, as if she didn't really want to.

She was about thirty, Banks guessed, with curly brown hair, a thin, olive-complexioned face and a rather long nose. Her pale green eyes were pink around the rims. She wore a loose fawn cardigan over her white blouse, despite the heat. Banks introduced himself and showed his card. "I'd like to see Mr. Clegg," he said. "Is he around?"

"He's not here."

"Do you know when he'll be back?"

"No." It sounded like "dough."

"Do you know where he is?"

"No."

"What's your name?"

"Elizabeth. Elizabeth Moorhead. I'm Mr. Clegg's secretary. Everyone calls me Betty." She took a crumpled paper tissue from the sleeve of her cardigan and blew her nose. "Cold," she said. "Godda cold. In May. Can you believe it? I hate summer colds."

"I'd like to see Mr. Clegg, Betty," Banks said again. "Is there a problem?"

"I should say so."

"Can I help?"

She drew back a bit, as if still deciding whether to trust him. "What do you want him for?"

Banks hesitated for a moment, then told her. At least he would get some kind of reaction. "I wanted to ask a few questions about Keith Rothwell."

Her brow wrinkled in a frown. "Mr. Rothwell? Yes, of course. Poor Mr. Rothwell. He and Mr. Clegg had some business together now and then. I read about him in the papers. It was terrible what happened."

"Did you know him well?"

"Mr. Rothwell? No, not at all, not really. But he'd been

here, in this office. I mean, I knew him to say hello to.''

"When did you see him last?''

"Just last week, it was. Tuesday or Wednesday, I think. He was standing right there where you are now. Isn't it terrible?''

Banks agreed that it was. "Can you try and remember which day it was? It could be important.''

She muttered to herself about appointments and flipped through a heavy book on her desk. Finally, she said, "It was Wednesday, just before I finished for the day at five. Mr. Rothwell didn't have an appointment, but I remember because it was just after Mr. Hoskins left a client. Mr. Rothwell had to wait out here a few moments and we chatted about how lovely the gardens are at this time of year.''

"That's all you talked about?''

"Yes.''

"Then what?''

"Then Mr. Clegg came out and they went off.''

"Do you know where?''

"No, but I think they went for a drink. They had business to discuss.''

So Rothwell had visited Clegg in Leeds the day before his murder, almost two weeks after the letter ending their association. Why? It certainly hadn't been noted in his appointment book. "How did Mr. Rothwell seem?'' he asked.

"No different from usual.''

"And Mr. Clegg?''

"Fine. Why are you asking?''

"Did you notice any tension between them?''

"No.''

"Has anything odd been happening around here lately? Has Mr. Clegg received any strange messages, for example?''

"No-o.'' Some hesitation there. He would get back to it later.

Banks glanced around the small, tidy anteroom. "Does everything go through you? Mail, phone calls?''

"Most things, yes. But Mr. Clegg has a private line, too."

"I see. How did he react to the news of Mr. Rothwell's death?"

She studied Banks closely, then appeared to decide to trust him. She sighed and rested her hands on the desk, palms down. "That's just the problem," she said. "I don't know. I haven't seen him since. He's not here. I mean, he's not just out of the office right now, but he's disappeared. Into thin air."

"Disappeared? Have you told the local police?"

She shook her head. "I wouldn't want to look a fool."

"Has he done anything like this before?"

"No. Never. But if he *has* just gone off . . . you know. With a woman or something . . . I mean he *could* have, couldn't he?"

"When did you last see him?"

"Last Thursday. He left the office about half past five and that was the last I saw of him. He didn't come in to work on Friday morning."

"Have you tried to call him at home?"

"Yes, but all I got was the answering machine."

"Did he say anything about a business trip?" Banks asked.

"No. And he usually tells me if he's going to be away for any length of time."

"Do you know what kind of business relationship Mr. Clegg had with Keith Rothwell?"

"No. I'm only his secretary. Mr. Clegg didn't take me into his confidence. All I know is that Mr. Rothwell came to the office now and then and sometimes they'd go out to lunch together, or for drinks after work. I knew Mr. Rothwell was an accountant, so I supposed it would be something to do with tax. Mr. Clegg specializes in tax law, you see. I'm sorry I can't be of more help."

"Maybe you can be. It seems a bit of a coincidence, doesn't it, Mr. Rothwell getting killed and Mr. Clegg disappearing around the same time?''

She shrugged. ''I didn't hear about Mr. Rothwell's death until Saturday. I just never thought . . .''

''Have you ever heard of someone called Robert Calvert?''

''No.''

''Are you sure? Did Mr. Clegg never mention the name?''

''No. He wasn't a client. I'm sure I'd remember.''

''Why didn't you get in touch with the police when you realized Mr. Clegg had disappeared and you heard about Mr. Rothwell's murder?''

''Why should I? Mr. Clegg had a lot of clients. He knew a lot of businessmen.''

''But they don't usually get murdered.''

She sneezed. ''No. As I said, it's tragic what happened, but I don't see how as it connects with Mr. Clegg.''

''Maybe it does, and maybe it doesn't,'' Banks said. ''But don't you think that's for us to decide?''

''I don't know what you mean.'' She reached for the tissue again. This time it disintegrated when she blew her nose. She dropped it in the waste-paper bin and took a fresh one from the box on her desk.

Banks regarded her closely. He didn't think she was lying or evading the issue; she simply didn't understand what he was getting at. He sometimes expected everyone to view the world with the same suspicious mind and jaundiced eye as he did. Besides, she didn't know about the letter Rothwell had left in the locked file.

He sat on the edge of the desk. ''Right, Betty, let's go back a bit. When I came in, you were frightened. Why?''

She paused for a moment, then said, ''I thought you might be one of them again.''

''One of whom?''

''On Saturday morning I was here doing some filing and two men came in and started asking questions about Mr. Clegg. They weren't very nice.''

"Is that what you were thinking of when I asked you earlier if anything odd had been going on?"

"Yes."

"Why didn't you tell me then?"

"It . . . I . . . I didn't connect it. You've got me all confused."

"All right, Betty, take it easy. Did they hurt you?"

"Of course not. Or I certainly *would* have called the police. You see, sometimes in this business you get people who are . . . well, less than polite. They get upset about money and sometimes they don't care who they take it out on."

"And these men were just rude?"

"Yes. Well, just a bit brusque, really. Nothing unusual. I mean, I'm only a secretary, right? I'm not important. They can afford to be short with me."

"So what bothered you? Why does it stick in your mind? Why were you frightened? Did they threaten you?"

"Not in so many words. But I got the impression that they were testing me to see what I knew. I think they realized early on that I didn't know anything. If they'd thought differently, I'm sure they would have hurt me. Don't ask me how I know. I could just feel it. There was something about them, some sort of coldness in their eyes, as if they'd done terrible things, or witnessed terrible things." She shivered. "I don't know. I can't explain. They were the kind of people you look away from when they make eye contact."

"What did they want to know about?"

"Where Mr. Clegg was."

"That's all?"

"Yes. I asked them why they wanted to know, but they just said they had important business with him. I'd never seen them before, and I'm sure I'd know if they were new clients."

"Did they leave their names?"

"No."

"What did they look like?"

"Just ordinary businessmen, really. One was black and the other white. They both wore dark suits, white shirts, ties. I can't remember what colours."

"What about their height?"

"Both about the same. Around six foot, I'd say. But the white one was burly. You know, he had thick shoulders and a round chest, like a wrestler or something. He had very fair hair, but he was going bald on top. He tried to disguise it by growing the hair at the side longer and combing it right over, but I just think that looks silly, don't you? The black man was thin and fit looking. More like a runner than a wrestler. He did most of the talking."

Banks got her to describe them in as much detail as she could and took notes. They certainly didn't match Alison Rothwell's description of the two men in black who had tied her up and killed her father. "What about their accents?" he asked.

"Not local. The black one sounded a bit cultured, well educated, and the other didn't speak much. I think he had a slight foreign accent, though I couldn't swear to it and I can't tell you where from."

"You've done fine, Betty."

"I have?"

Banks nodded.

"There's something else," she said. "When I came in this morning, I got the impression that someone had been in the place since then. Again, I can't say why, and I certainly couldn't prove it, but in this job you develop a feel for the way things should be—you know, files, documents, that sort of thing—and you can just tell if something's out of place without knowing what it really is, if you follow my drift."

"Were there any signs of forced entry?"

"No. Nothing obvious, nothing like that. Not that it would be difficult to get in here. It's hardly the Tower of London. I locked myself out once when Mr. Clegg was away on business and I just slipped my Visa card in the door and opened it.'' She put her hand to her mouth. "Oops. I don't suppose I should be telling you that, should I?''

Banks smiled. "It's all right, Betty. I've had to get into my car with a coat-hanger more than once. Was anything missing?''

"Not so far as I can tell. It's pretty secure inside. There's a good, strong safe and it doesn't look as if anyone tried to tamper with it.''

"Could it have been Mr. Clegg?''

"I suppose so. He sometimes comes in on a Sunday if there's something important in progress.'' Then she shook her head. "But no. If it had been Mr. Clegg I'd have known. Things would have looked different. They looked the same, but not quite the same, if you know what I mean.''

"As if someone had messed things up and tried to restore them to the way they were originally?''

"Yes.''

"Do you employ a cleaning lady?''

"Yes, but she comes Thursday evenings. It can't have been her.''

"Did she arrive as usual last Thursday?''

"Yes.''

"May I have a look in the office?''

Betty got up, took a key from her drawer and opened Clegg's door for him. He stood on the threshold and saw a small office with shelves of law books, box files and filing cabinets. Clegg also had a computer and stacks of disks on a desk at right angles to the one on which he did his other paperwork. The window, closed and locked, Banks noticed, looked out over the central square with its neatly cut grass, shady trees and people sitting on benches. The office was hot and stuffy.

Certainly nothing *looked* out of the ordinary. Banks was careful not to disturb anything. Soon, the Fraud Squad would be here to pore over the books and look for whatever the link was between Rothwell and Clegg.

"Better keep it locked," he told Betty on his way out. "There'll be more police here this afternoon, most likely. May I use the phone?"

Betty nodded.

Banks phoned Ken Blackstone at Millgarth and told him briefly what the situation was. Ken said he'd send a car over right away. Next he phoned Superintendent Gristhorpe in Eastvale and reported his findings. Gristhorpe said he'd get in touch with the Fraud Squad and see if they could co-ordinate with West Yorkshire.

He turned back to Betty. "You'll be all right here," he said. "I'll wait until the locals arrive. They'll need you to answer more questions. Just tell them everything you told me. What's your address, in case I need to get in touch?"

She gave him the address of her flat in Burmantofts. "What do you think has happened?" she asked, reaching for her tissue again.

Banks shook his head.

"You don't think anything's happened to him, do you?"

"It's probably nothing," Banks said, without conviction. "Don't worry, we'll get to the bottom of it."

"It's just that Melissa will be so upset."

"Who's Melissa?"

"Oh, didn't you know? It's Mrs. Clegg. His wife."

2

After a hurried bowl of vegetable soup in the Golden Grill, Susan Gay walked out into the street, with its familiar smells and noises: petrol fumes, of course; car horns; fresh coffee; bread from the bakery; a busker playing a flute by the church doors.

In the cobbled market square, she noticed an impromptu evangelist set up his soapbox and start rabbiting on about judgment and sin. It made her feel vaguely guilty just hearing him, and as she went into the station, she contemplated asking one of the uniforms to go out and move him on. There must be a law against it somewhere on the books. Disturbing the peace of an overworked DC?

Charity prevailed, and she went up to her office. It faced the car park out back, so she wouldn't have to listen to him there.

First, she took out the blue file cards she liked to make notes on and pinned them to the cork-board over her desk. It was the same board, she remembered, that Sergeant Hatchley had used for his pin-ups of page-three girls with vacuous smiles and enormous breasts. Now Hatchley was due back any moment. What a thought.

Then, after she had made another appointment to talk to Laurence Pratt, she luxuriated in the empty office, stretching like a cat, feeling as if she were in a deep, warm bubble-bath. Out of the window she could see the maintenance men with their shirtsleeves rolled up washing the patrol cars in the large car park. Sun glinted on their rings and watch-straps and on the shiny chrome they polished; it spread rainbows of oily sheen on the bright windscreens.

One of the men, in particular, caught her eye: well-muscled, but not overbearingly so, with a lock of blond hair that slipped over his eye and bounced as he rubbed the bonnet in long, slow strokes. The telephone broke into her fantasy. She picked it up. "Hello. Eastvale CID. Can I help you?"

"To whom am I speaking?"

"Detective Constable Susan Gay."

"Is the superintendent there?"

"I'm afraid not."

"And Chief Inspector Banks?"

"Out of the office. Can I help you? What's this about?"

"I suppose you'll have to do. My name is Mary Roth-well. I've just had a call from my son, Tom."

"You have? Where is he?"

"He's still in Florida. A hotel in Lido Key, wherever

that is. Apparently the British newspapers are a couple of days late over there, and he's just read about his father's murder. It's only eight in the morning there. He can't get a flight back until this evening. Anyway, he said he should get into Manchester at about seven o'clock tomorrow morning. I'm going to meet him at the airport and bring him home.''

"That's good news, Mrs. Rothwell," Susan said. "You do know we'd like to talk to him?"

"Yes. Though I can't imagine why. You'll pass the message on to the Chief Inspector, will you?"

"Yes."

"Good. And by the way, I've made funeral arrangements for Wednesday. That is still all right, isn't it?"

"Of course."

"Very well."

"Is there anything else, Mrs. Rothwell?"

"No."

"Goodbye, then. We'll be in touch."

Susan hung up and stared into space for a moment, thinking what an odd woman Mary Rothwell was. Imperious, highly strung and businesslike. Probably a real Tartar to live with. But was she a murderess?

Though it would take the Fraud Squad a long time to work out exactly how much Rothwell was worth—and to separate the legal from the illegal money—it was bound to be a fortune. Money worth killing for. The problem was, though Susan could imagine Mary Rothwell being cold-blooded enough to have her husband killed, she could not imagine her having it done in such a bloody, dramatic way.

The image of the kneeling, headless corpse came back to her and she tasted the vegetable soup rise in her throat. No, she thought, if the wife were responsible, Rothwell would have been disposed of in a neat, sanitary way— poison, perhaps—and he certainly wouldn't have made such a mess on the garage floor. What was the phrase? *You don't shit on your own doorstep.* It was too close to home for Mary; it would probably taint Arkbeck Farm for her forever.

Still, there was a lot of money involved. Susan had seen Rothwell's solicitor that morning, and, according to him, Rothwell had owned, or part-owned, about fifteen businesses, from a shipping company registered in the Bahamas to a dry cleaner's in Wigan, not to mention various properties dotted around England, Spain, Portugal and France. Of course, the solicitor assured her, they were all legitimate. She suspected, however, that some had served as fronts for Rothwell's illegal activities.

As Susan was wondering if Robert Calvert's money would now simply get lumped in with Keith Rothwell's, she became aware of a large shadow cast over her desk by a figure in the doorway.

She looked up, startled, right into the smiling face of Detective Sergeant Jim Hatchley. So soon? she thought, with a sinking feeling in the pit of her stomach. Now she knew there really was no God.

"Hello, love," said Hatchley, lighting a cigarette. "I see you've taken my pin-ups down. We'll have to do something about that now I'm back to stay."

3

At one-thirty, the hot, smoky pub was still packed with local clerks and shopkeepers on their lunch break. When Banks had phoned Pamela Jeffreys before leaving for Leeds that morning, she had suggested they meet in the pub across from the hall in West Leeds, where she was rehearsing with a string quartet. There was no beer garden, she said, but the curry of the day was usually excellent. Though he had to admit to feeling excitement at the thought of seeing Pamela again, this wasn't a meeting Banks was looking forward to.

She hadn't arrived yet, so Banks got himself a pint of shandy at the bar—just the thing for a hot day—and man-

aged to grab a small table in the corner by the dartboard,
fortunately not in use. There, he mulled over Daniel
Clegg's disappearance and the mysterious goons Betty
Moorhead had seen.

There was no end of trouble a lawyer could get himself
into, Banks speculated. Especially if he were a bit crooked
to start with. So maybe there was no connection between
Clegg's disappearance and Rothwell's murder. But there
were too many coincidences—the letter, the timing, the
shady accounts—and Banks didn't like coincidences.
Which meant that there were two sets of goons on the
loose: the ones who killed Rothwell, and the ones who
scared Clegg's secretary. But did they work for the same
person?

He was saved from bashing his head against a brick wall
any longer by the arrival of Pamela Jeffreys, looking gorgeous in black leggings and a long white T-shirt with the
Opera North logo on front. She had her hair tied back and
wore black-rimmed glasses. As she sat down, she smiled
at him. "The professional musician's look," she said.
"Keeps my hair out of my eyes so I can read the music."

"Would you like a drink?" Banks asked.

"Just a grapefruit juice with an ice-cube, please, if
they've got any. I have to play through 'Death and the
Maiden' again this afternoon."

While he was at the bar, Banks also ordered two curries
of the day.

"What's been happening?" Pamela asked when he got
back.

"Plenty," said Banks, hoping to avoid the issue of Calvert's identity for as long as possible. "But I've no idea
how it all adds up. First off, have you ever heard of a man
called Daniel Clegg?"

She shook her head. "No, I can't say as I have."

"He's a solicitor."

"He's not mine. Actually, I don't have one."

"Are you sure Robert never mentioned him?"

"No, and I think I'd remember. But I already told you, he never talked about his work, and I never asked. What do I know or care about business?" She looked at him over the top of her glass as she sipped her grapefruit juice, thin black eyebrows raised.

"Did you ever introduce Robert to any of your friends?"

"No. He never seemed really interested in going to parties or having dinner with people or anything, so I never pushed it. They probably wouldn't have got on very well anyway. Most of my friends are young and artsy. Robert's more mature. Why?"

"Did you ever meet anyone he knew when you were out together, say in a restaurant or at the casino?"

"No, not that I can recall."

"So you didn't have much of a social life together?"

"No, we didn't. Just a bit of gambling, the occasional day at the races, then it was mostly concerts or a video and a pizza. That was a bit of a problem, really. Robert was a lot of fun, but he didn't like crowds. I'm a bit more of a social butterfly, myself."

"I don't mean to embarrass you," Banks said slowly, "but did Robert show any interest in pornography? Did he like to take photographs, make videos? Anything like that?"

She looked at him open-mouthed, then burst out laughing. "Sorry, sorry," she said, patting her chest. "You know, most girls might be insulted if you suggested they moonlighted in video nasties, but it's so absurd I can't help but laugh."

"So the answer's no?"

"Don't look so embarrassed. Of course it's no, you silly man. The very thought of it . . ." She laughed again and Banks felt himself blush.

Their curries came and they tucked in. They were, as Pamela had said, delicious: delicately spiced rather than hot, with plenty of chunks of tender beef. They exchanged small talk over the food, edging away from the embarrassing topic Banks had brought up earlier. When they had finished, Pamela went for more drinks and Banks lit a cigarette. Was she going to ask now, he wondered, or was he going to have to bring it up? Maybe she was avoiding the moment, too.

Finally, she asked. "Did you find out anything? You know, about Robert and this Rothwell fellow." Very casual, but Banks could sense the apprehension in her voice.

He scraped the end of his cigarette on the rim of the red metal ashtray and avoided her eyes. A group at the next table burst into laughter at a joke one of them had told.

"Well?"

He looked up. "It looks very much as if Robert Calvert and Keith Rothwell were the same person," he said. "We found fingerprints that matched. I'm sorry."

For a while she said nothing. Banks could see her beautiful almond eyes fill slowly with tears. "Shit," she said, shaking her head and reaching in her bag for a tissue. "Sorry, this is stupid of me. I don't know why I'm crying. We were just friends really. Can we . . . I mean . . ." She gestured around.

"Of course." Banks took her arm and they left the pub. Fifty yards along the main road was a park. Pamela looked at her watch and said, "I've still got a while yet, if you don't mind walking a bit."

"Not at all."

They walked past a playground where children screamed with delight as the swings went higher and higher and the roundabout spun faster and faster. A small wading-pool had been filled with water because of the warm weather and more children played there, splashing one another, squealing and shouting, all under their mother's or father's watchful eyes. Nobody let their kids play out alone these days, as they used to do when he was a child, Banks noticed. Being in his job, knowing what he knew, he didn't blame them.

Pamela seemed lost in her silent grief, head bowed, walk-

ing slowly. "It's crazy," she said at last. "I hardly knew
Robert and things had cooled off between us anyway, and
here I am behaving like this."

Banks could think of nothing to say. He was aware of
the warmth of her arm in his and of her scent: jasmine, he
thought. What the hell did he think he was doing, walking
arm in arm in the park with a beautiful suspect? What if
someone saw him? But what could he do? The contact
seemed to form an important link between Pamela and
something real, something she could hold onto while the
rest of her world shifted under her feet like fine sand. And
he couldn't deny that the touch of her skin meant something
to him, too.

"I was wrong about him, wasn't I?" she went on. "Dead
wrong. He was married, you say? Kids?"

"A son and a daughter."

"I should know. I read it in the paper but it didn't sink
in because I was so *sure* it couldn't have been him. Robert
seemed so . . . such a free spirit."

"Maybe he was."

She glanced sideways at him. "What do you mean?"

They stopped at an ice-cream van and Banks bought two
cornets. "It was a different life he lived with you," he said.
"I can't begin to understand a man like that. It's not that
he had a split personality or anything, just that he was capable of existing in very different ways."

"What ways?" Pamela stuck out her pink tongue and
licked the ice-cream.

"The people in Swainsdale knew him as a quiet, unassuming sort of bloke. Bit of a dry stick really."

"Robert?" she gasped. "A dry stick?"

"Not Robert. Keith Rothwell. The hard-working, clean
living accountant. The man who put his spent matches back
in the box in the opposite direction to the unused ones."

"But Robert was so alive. He was fun to be with. We
laughed a lot. We dreamed. We danced."

Banks smiled sadly. "There you are, then. Keith Rothwell probably had two left feet.''

"Are you saying it *wasn't* the same man?''

"I don't know what I'm saying. Just that your memories of Robert Calvert won't change, shouldn't change. He's who he was to you, what he meant to you. Don't let this poison it for you. On the other hand, I need to know who killed Keith Rothwell, and it looks as if there might be a connection.''

She put her arm in his again and they walked on. There was hardly any breeze at all, but they passed a boy trying to fly a red-and-green kite. He couldn't seem to get it more than about twenty feet off the ground before it came flopping down again.

"What do you mean, a connection?'' Pamela asked, shifting her gaze from the kite back to Banks.

"Maybe something in his life as Robert Calvert spilled over into his life as Keith Rothwell. Are you sure you didn't know he was married, you didn't suspect it?''

She shook her head. "No. I've been a right bloody fool, haven't I? Muggins again.''

"But you were sure he'd found a new girlfriend?''

"Ninety-nine per cent certain, yes.''

"How did you feel about that?''

"What?''

"His new girlfriend. How did you feel about her? On the one hand you tell me you shouldn't be so upset, you hardly knew Robert Calvert, and your relationship had cooled off anyway. On the other hand, it seems to me from what you say and the way you behave that you were extremely fond of him. Maybe in love with him. What's the truth? How did you really feel when someone else came along and stole him from you? Surely you must have felt hurt, angry, jealous?''

Pamela pulled back her arm and stepped aside from him, an expression of pain and anger shadowing her face. She dropped her ice-cream. It splattered on the tarmac path. "What's that got to do with anything? What are you saying? What are you getting at? First you imply that I'm some kind of porn actress, and now you're implying that *I* killed Robert out of jealousy?''

"No," said Banks quickly. "No, nothing like that."

But she was already backing away from him, hands held up, palms out, as if to ward him off.

"Yes, you are. How could you even . . . ? I thought you . . .''

Banks stepped towards her. "That's not what I mean, Pamela. I'm just—"

But she turned and started to run away.

"Wait!" Banks called after her. "Please, stop."

One or two people gave him suspicious looks. As he set off walking quickly after her, a child's coloured ball rolled in front of him, and he had to pull up sharply to avoid knocking into its diminutive owner, whose large father, fast approaching from the nearest bench, didn't seem at all happy about things.

Pamela reached the park exit and dashed across the road, dodging her way through the traffic, back towards the hall. Banks stood there looking after her, the sweat beading on his brow. The remains of his ice-cream had started to melt and drip over the flesh between his thumb and first finger.

"Shit," he cursed under his breath. Then louder, "Shit!"

The little boy looked up, puzzled, and his father loomed closer.

: 7

1

The Merrion Centre was one of the first indoor shopping malls in Britain. Built on the northern edge of Leeds city centre in 1964, it now seems something of an antique, a monument to the heady sixties' days of slum clearance, tower blocks and council estates.

Covered on top, but open to the wind at the sides, it also suffers competition from a number of more recent, fully enclosed, central shopping centres, such as the St. John's Centre, directly across Merrion Street, and the plush dark green and brass luxury of the Schofields Centre, right on The Headrow.

Still, the Merrion Centre does have a large Morrison's supermarket, Le Phonographique discotheque—the longest surviving disco in Leeds—a number of small specialty shops, a couple of pubs, a flea market and the Classical Record Shop, which is how Banks had come to know the place quite well. And on a warm, windless May afternoon it can be pleasant enough.

Banks found Clegg's Wines and Spirits easily enough. He had phoned Melissa Clegg an hour or so earlier, still smarting over his acrimonious parting with Pamela Jeffreys in the park, and she had told him she could spare a little time to talk. It was odd, he thought, that she hadn't seemed overly curious about his call. He had said that it concerned her husband, yet she had asked for no details.

He opened the door and found himself in a small shop cluttered with bottles and cases. There were a couple of bins of specials on the floor by the door—mostly Bulgarian,

Romanian and South African varietals, and some yellow
"marked down" cards on a few of the racks that lined the
walls to his right and left, including a Rioja, a Côtes du
Rhône and a claret.

Banks looked at the racks and thought he might take
something home for dinner, assuming that he and Sandra
ever got the chance to sit down to dinner together again,
and assuming that she wanted to. Perhaps they could have
that wine, candlelight and Chopin evening he had had to
cancel when the Rothwell enquiry got in the way.

Behind the counter ranged the bottles of single malt
Scotch: Knockando, Blair Athol, Talisker, Glendronach.
Evocative names, but he mustn't look too closely. He had
a weakness for single malt that Sandra said hit them too
hard in the pocket. Besides, he still had a drop of Laphroaig
left at home.

The spotty young man behind the counter smiled. "Can
I help you, sir?" He wore a candy-striped shirt with the
sleeves rolled up and his tie loose at the neck, the way
Banks always wore his own when he could get away with
it. His black hair had so much gel or mousse on that it
looked like an oil slick.

"Boss around?" Banks asked, showing his card.

"In the back." He lifted up the counter flap and Banks
went through. Stepping over and around cases of wine, he
walked along a narrow corridor, then saw on his left a tiny
office with the door open. A woman sat at the desk talking
on the phone. It sounded to Banks as if she were complaining over non-delivery of several cases of Hungarian Pinot
Noir.

When she saw him, she waved him in and pointed to a
chair piled high with papers. Banks moved them to the edge
of the desk and she grinned at him over the mouthpiece.
There were no windows, and it was stuffy in the back room,
despite the whirring fan. The office smelled of freshly cut
wood. Banks took his jacket off and hung it over the back

of the chair. He could feel the steady draught of the fan on the left side of his face.

Finally, she put the phone down and rolled her eyes. "Some suppliers . . ."

She was wearing a yellow sun-dress with thin straps that left most of her nicely tanned and freckled shoulders and throat bare. About forty, Banks guessed, she looked as if she watched what she ate and exercised regularly, tennis probably. Her straight blonde hair, parted in the middle, hung just above her shoulders, framing a heart-shaped face with high cheekbones. It was a cheerful face, one to which a smile was no stranger, and the youthful, uneven fringe suited her. But Banks also noticed marks of stress and strain in the wrinkles under her blue-grey eyes and around her slightly puckered mouth. A pair of no-nonsense glasses with tortoiseshell frames dangled on a cord around her neck.

"Your phone call piqued my curiosity," she said, leaning back in her chair and linking her hands behind her head. Banks noticed the shadow of stubble under her arms. "What has Danny-boy been up to now?"

"I'm sorry?" said Banks. "I don't follow."

"Didn't Betty tell you?"

"Tell me what?"

"Oh, God, that woman. Gormless. About Danny and me. We're separated. Have been for about two years now. It was all perfectly amicable, of course."

Of course, Banks thought. How often had he heard that? If it was all so bloody amicable, he wondered, then why aren't you still together? "I didn't know," he said.

"Then I'm sorry you're probably on a wild goose chase." She changed her position, resting her hands on the desk and playing with a rubber band. There were no rings on her fingers. "Anyway, I'm still intrigued," she said. "I am still fond of Danny. I would be concerned if I thought anything had happened to him. It hasn't, has it?"

"Do you still see one another?"

"From time to time."

"When did you last see him?"

"Hmm . . ." She pursed her lips and thought. "A couple of months ago. We had lunch together at Whitelocks."

"How did he seem?"

"Fine." She stretched the rubber band tight. "Look, you've got me worried. All this interest in Danny all of a sudden. First those clients of his. Now you."

Banks pricked up his ears. "What clients?"

"On Saturday. Saturday afternoon. Just a couple of businessmen wondering if I knew where he was."

"Did they know you were separated?"

"Yes. They said it was a long shot and they were sorry to bother me but they'd had an appointment scheduled with him that morning and he hadn't shown up. He'd mentioned me and the shop at some time or other, of course. He often does, by way of sending me business. What a sweetheart. Anyway, they asked if I had any idea where he was, if he'd suddenly decided to go away for the weekend. As if I'd know. It all seemed innocent enough. Is something wrong?"

"What did they look like?"

She described the same two men who had visited Betty Moorhead. It wouldn't have been difficult for them to find out about Melissa's shop—perhaps even Betty had told them—and if they were looking for Clegg, it was reasonable to assume that his ex-wife might know where he was. She must have convinced them quickly that she neither knew nor cared.

The rubber band snapped. "Look," she said, "I've a right to know if something's happened to Danny, haven't I?"

"We don't know if anything has happened to him," Banks said. "He's just gone missing."

She breathed a sigh of relief. "So that's all."

Banks frowned. "His secretary seems worried enough. She says it's unusual."

"Oh, Betty's a nice enough girl, but she is a bit of an alarmist. Danny always did have an eye for the ladies. That's one reason we're no longer together. I should imagine if he's gone missing, then something came up, so to speak." She grinned, showing slightly overlapping front teeth.

"Wouldn't he at least let his secretary know where he was?"

"I'll admit that is a bit unusual. While Danny was never exactly tied to his desk, he didn't like to be too far from the action. You know the type, always on his car phone to the office. Who knows? Maybe he's having a mid-life crisis. Maybe he and his bit of crumpet have gone somewhere where there are no telephones. He's such a romantic, is Danny."

The phone rang and Mrs. Clegg excused herself for a moment. Banks caught her half of the conversation about an order of *méthode champenoise*. A couple of minutes later she put the phone down. "Sorry. Where were we?"

"Mrs. Clegg, we think your husband might have been mixed up in some shady dealings and that might have had something to do with his disappearance."

She laughed. "Shady dealings? That hardly surprises me."

"Do you know anything about his business activities?"

"No. But dishonest in love . . ." She let the thought trail, then shrugged. "Danny never was one of the most ethical, or faithful, of people. Careful, usually, yes, but hardly ethical."

"Would you say he was the type to get mixed up in something illegal?"

She thought for a moment, frowning, then answered. "Yes. Yes, I think so. If he thought the returns were high enough."

"Is he a greedy man?"

"No-o. Not in so many words, no. I wouldn't call him greedy. He just likes to get what he wants. Women. Money.

Whatever. It's more a matter of power, manipulation. He just likes to win.''

"What about the risk?"

She tipped her head to one side. "There's always *some* risk, isn't there, Chief Inspector? If something's worth having. Danny's not a coward, if that's what you mean."

"Did you know Keith Rothwell?"

"Yes. Not well, but I had met him. Poor man. I read about him in the paper. Terrible. You're not suggesting there's any link between his murder and Danny's disappearance, are you?"

She's quicker on the ball than Betty Moorhead, Banks thought. "We don't know. I don't suppose you'd be in a position to enlighten us about their business dealings?"

"Sorry. No. I haven't seen Keith since Danny and I split up. Even then I'd just bump into him at the office now and then, or when he helped with my taxes."

"So you've no idea what kinds of dealings they were involved in?"

"No. As I said, Keith Rothwell did my accounts a couple of times—you know, the wine business—when Dan and I were together, before things became awkward and our personal life got in the way. He was a damn good accountant. He saved me a lot of money from the Inland Revenue—all above board. Now, it doesn't take a Sherlock Holmes to figure out that if the two of them were in business together it probably involved tax havens of one kind or another, and that they both probably did quite well from it.''

"Have you ever heard of a man called Robert Calvert?"

"Calvert? No. I can't say I have. Should I have? Look, I'm really sorry I can't help you, Chief Inspector. And I certainly didn't mean to sound callous at all. But knowing Danny, I'm sure he's popped off to Paris for the weekend with some floozie or other and just got too over-excited to remember to let anyone know. He'll turn up."

Banks stood up. "I hope you're right, Mrs. Clegg. And if he gets in touch, please let us know." He gave her his card. She stood up as he left the office. He turned in the doorway and smiled. "One more thing."

"Yes."

"Could you recommend a decent claret for dinner, not too pricey?"

"Of course. If you're not absolutely stuck on Bordeaux, try a bottle of the Chateau de la Liquière. It's from Faugères, in Languedoc. Very popular region these days. Lots of character." She smiled. "And you can even afford it on a policeman's salary."

After Banks thanked her, he made his way back down the corridor, dodging the wine cases, and bought the bottle she had suggested. Not an entirely wasted visit, he thought. At least he'd got a decent bottle of wine out of it. And then there was the Classical Record Shop just around the corner. He couldn't pass so closely without going in. Besides, he needed balm for his wounds. He was still feeling annoyed with himself after the way he had messed things up with Pamela Jeffreys. The new CD of the Khachaturian Piano Concerto, if they had it, might just help make him feel better.

As he walked outside with his bottle of wine, he felt a large hand clap down on his shoulder.

"Well, if it isn't my old mate, Banksy," a voice said in his ear.

Banks spun round and saw the source of the voice: Detective Superintendent Richard "Dirty Dick" Burgess, from Scotland Yard. What the hell was he doing here?

"I hope you haven't been accepting bribes," Burgess said, pointing to the wine. Then he put his arm around Banks's shoulders. "Come on," he said. "We need to go somewhere and have a little chat."

2

Laurence Pratt was waiting in his office, again with his shirtsleeves rolled up, black-framed glasses about halfway

down his nose, fingers forming a steeple on the neat desk
in front of him. His white shirt was more dazzling than any
Susan had seen in a detergent advert. Susan felt stifled. The
temperature outside was in the twenties, and the window
was closed.

Pratt seemed less easy in his manner this time, Susan
observed, and she guessed it was because he had given too
much away on her last visit. This was going to be a tough
one, she thought, taking her notebook and pen out of her
handbag. They had discovered a lot more about Keith Rothwell since Friday, and this time, she didn't want to give
too much away.

Susan opened her notebook, resisting the impulse to fan
her face with it, and unclipped her pen. "The last time I
talked to you, Mr. Pratt," she began, "you told me you
saw the Rothwells for the last time in March."

"That's right. Carla and I were out to Arkbeck for dinner. Duck *à l'orange*, if I remember correctly."

"And the new kitchen."

"Ah, yes. We all admired the new kitchen."

"Can you be a bit more precise about the date?"

Pratt frowned and pulled at his lower lip. "Not exactly.
It was just after St. Patrick's Day, I think. Hang on a sec."
He fished in his briefcase by the side of the desk and pulled
out a Filofax. "Be lost without it," he grinned. "Even in
the computer age. I mean, you don't want to turn the computer on every time you need an address, do you?" As he
talked, he flipped through the pages. "Ah, there it is." He
held up the open page for Susan to see. "19th March. Dinner with Keith and Mary."

"And you said Tom dropped in to talk about his trip?"

"Yes."

"From where?"

"What? Oh, I see. From his room, I suppose. At least I
think he'd been up there. He just came in to say hello while
we were having cocktails. Is he back from America, by the
way?"

No harm in telling a family friend that, Susan thought. "He's on his way," she said. "What was the atmosphere like between Tom and his father that night?"

"They didn't talk, as I remember."

"Did you notice any antagonism or tension between them?"

"I wouldn't say that, no. I told you before that their relationship was strained because Tom drifted off the course his father had set for him."

"Was anything said about that on the night you were there?"

"No, I'm certain of it. They didn't talk to one another at all. Tom was excited about going to America. I think he'd been upstairs poring over a map, planning his route."

"And Keith Rothwell said nothing during your little chat?"

"No. He just sat there rather po-faced. Now you mention it, that *was* a bit odd. I mean, you'd hardly call old Keith a live wire these days, but he'd usually take a bit more interest than he did that night. Especially as his son was off on a big adventure."

"So his behaviour *was* strange?"

"A little unusual, on reflection, yes."

"What about Tom? Did he say anything to or about his father?"

Pratt shook his head slowly. Susan noticed a few beads of sweat around his temples where his hairline was receding. She could feel her own sweat tickling her ribs as it slid down her side. So much for the expensive extra-dry, long-lasting anti-perspirant she had put on after her morning shower. This didn't happen to the high-powered women executives and airline pilots in the television adverts. On the other hand, *they* didn't have to deal with the return of Sergeant Hatchley. It had taken her a good five minutes to stop shaking after he had left the office.

She asked Pratt to open the window. He complied, but it didn't do much good. The air outside was still and hot.

Even the gargoyles on the upper walls of the community centre looked grumpy and sweaty.

"Did Mr. Rothwell ever express any interest in pornography?"

Pratt raised his eyebrows. "Good lord. How do you mean? As a business venture or for personal consumption?"

"Either."

"Not in my presence. As I said, I don't know about the extent of his business interests, but he always struck me as rather . . . say . . . sexless. When we were younger, of course, we'd chase the lasses, but since his marriage . . ."

"Have you ever met a solicitor called Daniel Clegg?"

"No. The name doesn't sound familiar. Are you sure he practises in Eastvale?"

"You've never met him?"

"I told you, I've never even heard of him. Why do you ask? Is there some—"

"Did Mr. Rothwell ever mention him?"

"Is there some connection?"

"Did Mr. Rothwell ever mention him?"

Pratt stared at Susan for about fifteen long seconds, then said, "No, not that I recall."

Susan ran the back of her hand across her moist brow. She was beginning to feel a little dizzy. "What about Robert Calvert?"

"Never heard of him, either. Is this another business colleague of Keith's? I told you we never talked about his business. He played his cards close to his chest."

"Did he ever mention a woman called Pamela Jeffreys?"

Pratt raised an eyebrow. "A woman? Keith? Another woman? Good lord, no. I told you he didn't strike me as the type. Not these days, anyway. Besides, Mary would have killed him. Oh, my God . . ."

"It's all right, Mr. Pratt," Susan said. "Slip of the tongue. Jealous type, is she?"

He pushed his glasses back up to the bridge of his nose.

"Mary? Well, I'd guess so, yes."

"But you don't know for certain?"

"No. It's just the impression she gives. How everything centred around Keith, the house, the family. If anything came along to jeopardize that, threaten it, then she'd be a formidable enemy. Possessive, selfish, I'd say, definitely. Is that the same thing?"

Susan closed her notebook and stood up. "Thank you, Mr. Pratt. Thank you very much. Again, you've been most helpful." Then she hurried out of the hot, stuffy office before she fainted.

3

They walked down to Stumps, under the museum, and made their way to the bar, where Burgess ordered a pint of McEwan's lager and Banks a pint of bitter. It wasn't Theakston's, but it would have to do.

As it was a warm day, they took their drinks outside and found a free table. There was a broad, tiled area between the museum-library complex and the buses roaring by on The Headrow, and pedestrians hurried back and forth, some heading for the Court Centre or the Town Hall and some taking short-cuts to Calverley Street and the Civic Hall. A group of people stood playing chess with oversize figures on a board drawn on the tiles. Scaffolding covered the front of one of the nineteenth-century buildings across The Headrow, Banks noticed. Another renovation.

Banks felt both puzzled and apprehensive at Burgess's arrival on the scene. The last time they had locked horns was over the killing of a policeman at an anti-government demonstration in Eastvale back in the Thatcher era.

Burgess had fitted in just fine back then. An East Ender, son of a barrow boy, he had fought his way up from the bottom with a fierce mixture of ego, ambition, cunning and a total disregard for the rules most people played by. He also felt no sympathy for those who had been unable to do likewise. Now, at about Banks's age, he was a Detective Superintendent working for a Scotland Yard department that was not quite Special Branch and not quite M15, but close enough to both to give Banks the willies.

In a period when a fully functioning human heart was regarded as a severe disability, he had been one of the new, golden breed of working-class Conservatives, up there in the firmament of the new Britain alongside the bright young things in the City, the insider traders and their like. Cops and criminals: it didn't seem to make a lot of difference, as long as you were successful. But then, it never did to some people.

Nobody could gainsay Burgess's abilities—intelligence and physical courage being foremost among them—but "The end justifies the means" could have been written just for him. The "end" was some vague sort of loyalty to whatever the people in power wanted done for the preservation of order, as long as the people in power weren't liberals or socialists, of course; and as for the "means," the sky was the limit.

Maybe he had changed, Banks wondered. After all the recent inquiries and commissions, a policeman could surely no longer walk into a pub, pick up the first group of Irish people he saw and throw them in jail as terrorists, could he? Or walk down Brixton Road and arrest the first black person he saw running? According to the public-relations people, today's policeman was a cross between Santa Claus and a hotel manager.

On the other hand, perhaps that was only according to the PR people: truth in advertising, *caveat emptor* and the rest. Besides, if there was one thing not likely to make the slightest impression on Burgess's obsidian consciousness, it was political correctness.

Banks lit a cigarette and held out his lighter as Burgess fired up one of his Tom Thumb cigars. He was still in good shape, though filling out a bit around the belly. He had a square jaw and slightly crooked teeth. His black, slicked-back hair was turning silver at the temples and sideboards, and the bags under his seen-it-all grey eyes looked as if they had taken on a bit more weight since Banks had last seen him. About six feet tall, casually dressed in black leather jacket, open-neck shirt and grey cords, he was still handsome enough to turn the heads of a few thirtyish women, and had a reputation as something of a rake. It wasn't entirely unfounded, Banks had discovered the last time they worked together.

Banks reached for his pint. "To what do I owe the honour?" he asked. He had never dignified Burgess with the "sir" his rank demanded, and he was damned if he was about to start now.

Burgess swigged some lager, swished it around his mouth and swallowed.

"Well?" said Banks. "Enough bloody theatrics, for Christ's sake."

"I don't suppose you'd believe me if I said I'd missed you?"

"Get on with it."

"Right. Thought not. Ever heard of a place called St. Corona?"

"Of course. It's a Caribbean island, been in the news a bit lately."

"Clever boy. That's the one. Population about four point eight million. Area about seven thousand square miles. Chief resources, bauxite, limestone, aluminium, sugar cane, plus various fruits and spices, fish and a bit of gold, silver and nickel. A lot of tourism, too, or there used to be."

"So you've been studying *Whitaker's Almanac*," said Banks. "Now what the bloody hell is this all about?"

A tipsy youth bumped into the table and spilled some of Burgess's lager. The youth stopped to apologize, but the look Burgess gave him sent him stumbling off into the bright afternoon sunlight before he could get the words out.

"Fucking lager lout," Burgess muttered, wiping the beer off the table-top with a handkerchief. "Gone to the dogs, this country. Where was I? Oh, yes. St. Corona. Imports just about everything you need to live, including the machinery to make it. Lots of television sets, radios, fridges, washing machines.'' He paused and whistled between his teeth as a young redhead in a mini-skirt walked by. ''Now *that's* not bad,'' he said. ''Which reminds me, have you rogered that young redhead in Eastvale yet? You know, the psychologist.'' He flicked the stub of his cigar towards the gutter; it hit the wall just above with a shower of sparks.

Burgess meant Jenny Fuller, as he knew damn well. Banks managed a smile, remembering what happened the last time those two met. ''St. Corona,'' he said. ''You were saying?''

Burgess pouted. ''You're no fun. Know who the president is?''

''What is this, bloody 'Mastermind'? Martin Churchill. Now, if you've got something to tell me, get it off your chest and let me go home. It's been a long day.''

''Back to that lovely wife of yours, eh? Sandra, isn't it? All right, all right. St. Corona is a republic, and you're right, Martin Churchill is president for life. Good name for the job, don't you think?''

''I've read about him.''

''Yes, well, the poor sod's a bit beleaguered these days, what with the opposition parties raking up the muck and the independence and liberation movements going from strength to strength.'' He sighed. ''I don't know. It seems people just don't believe in a good old benevolent dictatorship any more.''

''Benevolent, my arse,'' said Banks. ''He's been bleeding the country dry for ten years and now they're closing in on him. What am I supposed to do, cry?''

Burgess glared at Banks through squinting eyes. ''Still the bloody pinko, huh? Still the limp-wristed, knee-jerking liberal?'' He sighed. ''Somehow, Banks, I hadn't expected you to change. That's partly why I'm here. Anyway, whatever you or I might think about it, the powers that be decided it was a good idea to have a stable government in that part of the world, someone we could trust. Of course, it doesn't seem quite so important now, with the Russkies swapping their rusty old atomic warheads for turnips, but other threats exist. Anyway, Britain, France, Canada, the States and a few others pumped millions into St. Corona over the years, so you can estimate how important it is to us.''

Banks listened intently. There could be no rushing Burgess; he would get where he was going in his own sweet time.

"Churchill's finished," Burgess went on with a sweeping hand gesture. "It's just a matter of time. Weeks . . . months. He knows it. We know it. The only thing now is for him to get out alive with his family while he still can and take up life in exile.''

"And he wants to come here?''

Burgess looked around at the chess players and The Headrow. "Well, I don't think he's got the north of England in mind specifically, but you're on the right track. Maybe a nice little retirement villa in Devon or Cornwall, the English Riviera. Somewhere where the weather's nice. Cultivate his herbaceous borders. Live out his days in the contemplation of nature. Prepare himself for the life hereafter. Make his peace with the Almighty. That kind of thing. Somewhere he won't do any more harm." Burgess lit another little cigar and spat out a flake of loose tobacco. "The Yanks have said no, but then they've got a good record of turning their backs on their mates. The French are dithering and jabbering and waving their arms about, as usual. They'd probably sneak him in the back door like the good little hypocrites they are, if they had any real incentive left. And the Canadians . . . well, they're just too fucking moral for their own good. The bottom line, Banks, is that there's a lot of pressure on our government to take him in, as quietly as possible, of course.''

"Sneak him in the back door, you mean, like the hypocritical French?"

"If you like."

"His human rights record is appalling," Banks said. "The infant mortality rate in St. Corona is over fifteen per cent, for a start. Life expectancy isn't much more than fifty for a man and sixty for a woman."

"Oh, dear, dear. You've been reading *The Guardian* again, haven't you, Banks?"

"And other papers. The story's the same."

"Well, you should know better than to believe all you read in the papers, shouldn't you?" Burgess looked around conspiratorially and lowered his voice. Nobody seemed in the least bit interested in them. Laughter and fragments of conversation filled the air. "Have you ever wondered," he said, "why women always seem to have a higher life expectancy rate than men? Don't they have as many bad habits as we do? Maybe they just don't work as hard, don't suffer as much stress? Maybe it's all that slimming and aerobics, eh? Maybe there's something in it.

"Anyway, back to Mr Churchill's predicament. And this is classified, by the way. There are some people in power who want him here, who feel we owe him, and there are some who don't, who feel he's a low-life scumbag and deserves to die as slowly and painfully as possible." As usual, Burgess liked to show off his American slang. He went to the States often, on "courses."

"Oh, come off it," said Banks. "If they want him here it's not out of any sense of duty, it's because he's got something they want, or because he's got something on them."

Burgess scratched his cheek. "Cynic," he said. "But you're partly right. He's not a nice man. As far as I can gather he's a glutton, a boor, a murderer and a rapist, sodomy preferred. But that's not the issue at all. The problem is that we educated him, made him what he is. Eton and Cambridge. He read law there. Did you know that? He went through school and university with a lot of important people, Banks. Cabinet ministers, bankers, power brokers, back-room boys. You know how people can behave indiscreetly when they're young? Do things they wouldn't want to come back and haunt them when they're in the public eye? And we're talking about people who have the power to loosen the government purse strings now and then, whenever St. Corona asks for more aid. And rumour has it that he's also got quite a nice little savings account that won't do our economy any harm at all."

"Let me guess," said Banks. "Laundered money?"

Burgess raised his eyebrows. "Well, of course. Which brings me to the murder of Keith Rothwell. You are senior field investigator, I understand?"

"Yes."

"That's why I thought I'd better deal with you in person. I know you, Banks. You're still a pinko liberal, as you've proved time and time again. In fact, as soon as they told me you were on the case, I thought, 'Oh, fuck we're in trouble.' You've no respect for the venerable institutions of government, or for the necessity of secrecy in some of their workings. You've got no respect for tradition and you don't give a toss about preserving the natural order of things. You probably don't even stand up for 'God Save the Queen.' In short, you're a bloody bolshie troublemaker and a menace to national security."

Banks smiled. "Thanks for the compliment," he said. "But I wouldn't go quite *that* far."

Burgess grinned. "Maybe I exaggerate. But you get my point?"

"Loud and clear."

"Good. That's why I'm going to tell you something very, very important and very, very secret, and I'm going to trust you with it. We've been keeping an eye on the St. Corona situation, and anything that could possibly have to do with Martin Churchill gets flagged. Now, we just got a report from your Fraud Squad late yesterday evening that they found something on Keith Rothwell's computer that indicates he may have been laundering money for Martin Churchill. Lots of trips to the Channel Islands and the Caribbean. Some very dodgy bank accounts. Some very dodgy banks, too, for that matter. Anyway, there's a pattern and a time period that matches exactly the sort of thing we've been looking for. We've known this was going on for some time, but until now we hadn't a clue who was doing it. There's no proof it was Rothwell, yet—the Fraud Squad still has a lot of work to do, chasing down transactions and what have you—but if I'm right, then we're talking about a lot of money. Something in the region of thirty or forty million pounds over three or four years. Mostly money that was originally provided as aid by leading western nations. It's the same kind of thing Baby Doc did in Haiti.''

"And you think this might have something to do with Rothwell's murder?"

Burgess shook his head. "I don't really know, but the odds are that there's some kind of connection, don't you think? Especially considering the way he was killed. I mean, it was hardly a domestic, was it?"

"Possibly," Banks agreed. "Do you have any leads on the killers?"

"No more than you. I'm only *suggesting* that Churchill might be behind them."

"And if he is?"

"Watch your back."

Banks thought about that for a moment. He wasn't sure who constituted the greatest threat to his exposed back, Churchill or Burgess. "I must say this is pretty quick work on your part," he said.

Burgess shrugged. "Like I said, orders to flag. When I called your station, Superintendent Gristhorpe told me where you were. I missed you at the solicitor's office, but the secretary told me you were coming here."

"What's Daniel Clegg's connection with all this?"

"We don't know yet. We don't even know if there is

one. I only just found out about his disappearance. It's early days yet.''

"Two other men have been looking for him, too. One black, one white. Are they your lot?''

Burgess frowned. "No, they're nothing to do with me.''

"Know anything about them?''

"No.''

He was lying, Banks was certain. "So why are you here?'' he asked. "What do you want me to do?''

"Nothing. Just carry on as normal. I simply wanted to warn you to tread very carefully, that's all, that things might be more complicated than they appear on the surface. And to let you know there's help available if you want it, of course. Naturally, if you get close to uncovering the killers' identities, I'd be interested in talking to them.''

"Why?''

"Because I'm interested in everything to do with Martin Churchill, as I told you.'' Burgess looked at his watch. "Good lord, is that the time already?'' he said, then knocked back the rest of his pint, winked and stood up. "Got to be off now. Be seeing you.'' And he strutted off over the square towards Park Row.

Banks lit a cigarette and brooded over the meeting as he finished his pint, wondering what the hell the bastard was up to. He didn't trust Burgess as far as he could throw him, and he was convinced that all that stuff about offering help and giving a friendly warning was rubbish. Burgess was up to something.

At a guess, he wanted to be one of the first to get to the killers so he could find a way of hushing them up. The last thing he would want was a big story about Churchill hiring assassins to murder a Yorkshire accountant splashed all over the press. Churchill might well be up to much worse things on St. Corona, but this was England, after all.

Still, no matter what Burgess suspected, and whether or not Martin Churchill was behind it all, Banks still had two killers to find, locals by the sound of them, and he wasn't

going to do that by sitting around in Stumps fretting about
Dirty Dick Burgess.

4

Banks didn't expect to find anything new in Calvert's
Headingley flat, but for some reason he felt the need to
revisit the place after he had picked up the Khachaturian
compact disc.

West Yorkshire police had talked to the other tenants,
who all said they knew nothing about Mr. Calvert or Keith
Rothwell: they never really saw much of him; he was out
a lot; and, yes, now you mention it, there was a resemblance, but it was only a newspaper photo and Mr. Calvert
didn't look quite the same; besides, Calvert wasn't an Eastvale accountant, was he? He lived in Leeds. Couldn't argue
with that. Banks headed upstairs.

The only immediate difference he noticed was the thin
layer of fingerprint powder on surfaces of metal or glass:
around the gas fireplace, on the glass-topped coffee table
and the TV set.

This time, Banks examined the books more closely.
There weren't many, and most of them were the usual best-
seller list paperbacks: Tom Clancy, Clive Cussler, Ken Fol-
lett, Robert Ludlum. There was also some espionage
fiction—Len Deighton, John le Carre, Adam Hall, Ian
Fleming—plus a couple of Agatha Christies and an oddly
out-of-place copy of *Middlemarch*, which looked unread.
Hardly surprising, Banks thought, having given up on even
the television adaptation. The only other books were *Palgrave's Golden Treasury*, the first part of William Manchester's Churchill biography and a *Concise Oxford
Dictionary*.

The small compact disc collection concentrated entirely
on jazz, mostly Kenny Ball, Acker Bilk and a few collec-
tions of big-band music. Banks noticed some decent stuff:
Louis, Bix, Johnny Dodds, Bud Powell. On the whole,

though, judging from the Monet print over the fireplace, the *Palgrave* and the music, Robert Calvert had agreed with Philip Larkin about the evils of Parker, Pound and Picasso.

In the bedroom, all the papers had been removed from the desk, as had the wallet with the Calvert identification and credit card. The Fraud Squad would be working already on Calvert's financial profile, now they knew that he and Rothwell were one and the same. The magazines and coins were still there, the bed still unmade.

Why had Rothwell *needed* Calvert? Banks wondered. Simple escapism? According to what everyone said, he was a different person altogether at Arkbeck Farm and in the wider community of Swainsdale. Most people there spoke of him as a rather dull chap, maybe a bit henpecked.

Then there was Robert Calvert, the dancing, gambling, laughing, fun-loving Lothario and dreamer. The man who had attracted and bedded the beautiful Pamela Jeffreys. The man who squeezed his toothpaste tube in the middle.

So which was the real Keith Rothwell? Both or neither? In a sense, Banks guessed, he needed both worlds. Did that make him a Jekyll and Hyde figure? Did it mean he was mad? Banks didn't think so.

He remembered Susan's account of her interview with Laurence Pratt, in which Pratt had indicated that Rothwell had changed over the years, cut himself off, penned himself in. Perhaps he had once been the kind of person who liked gambling, dancing and drinking. Then he had been pushed into marriage with the boss's daughter, and marriage had changed him. It happened often enough; people settled down. But, for some reason, Rothwell had felt the need for an outlet, one that would not interfere with his family life, or with his local image as a respectable, decent citizen.

Banks could think of one good reason why it was important for Rothwell to maintain this fiction: Rothwell was a crook. He certainly didn't want to draw attention to himself by high living. As Calvert, he could relive his youth as much as he wished and enjoy the proceeds of his money-laundering. Perfect.

Did Mary Rothwell know about her husband's other life? She had probably suspected something was wrong time and time again over the last few years, but denied and repressed the suspicions in order to maintain the illusion of happy, affluent family values in the community. She probably needed to believe in the lies as much as her husband needed to live them.

But you can only maintain an illusion for so long, Banks thought, then cracks appear and the truth seeps in. You can ignore that for a long time, too, but ultimately the wound begins to fester and infect everything. That's when the bad things start to happen. Did Alison know? Or Tom? It would be interesting to meet the lad.

He looked through the wardrobe and dresser drawers again. Most of Calvert's clothes were still there, though the condoms had gone. Genuine scientific testing, Banks wondered, or a Scene-of-Crime Officer with a hot date and no time to get to the chemist's?

He looked under chairs, under the bed, on top of the wardrobe, in the cistern, and in all the usual hiding places before he realized that Vic Manson and his lads had probably already done most of that, even though the flat wasn't a crime scene *per se*, and that he didn't know what he was looking for anyway. He paused by the front window, which looked out onto a tree-lined side-street off Otley Road.

Fool, he told himself. He had been looking for Keith Rothwell in Robert Calvert's flat. But he wasn't there. He wasn't anywhere; he was just a slab of chilled meat waiting for a man with his collar on the wrong way around to chant a few meaningless words that might just ease the living's fear of death until the next time it touched too close to home for comfort.

As he glanced out of the window, he glimpsed two men in suits across the street looking up at him. They were partially obscured by trees, but he could see that one was black, the other white.

He hurried down to the street. When he got there, nobody was about except a young man washing his car three houses down.

Banks approached him and showed his identification. The man wiped the sweat off his brow and looked up at Banks, shielding his eyes from the glare. Sunlight winked on the bubbles in his bucket of soapy water.

"Did you see a couple of blokes in business suits pass by a few minutes ago?" Banks asked.

"Yeah," said the man. "Yeah I did. I thought it was a bit odd the way they stopped and looked up at that house. To be honest, though, the way they were dressed I thought they were probably coppers."

Banks thanked him and went back to the car. So he wasn't getting paranoid. How did the saying go? Just because you think they're out there following you, it doesn't mean they aren't.

: 8

1

Tom Rothwell resembled his father more than his mother, Banks thought, sitting opposite him in the split-level living-room at Arkbeck Farm the following morning. Though his hair was darker and longer, he had the same thin oval face and slightly curved nose and the same grey eyes as Banks had seen in the photograph. His sulky mouth, though, owed more to early Elvis Presley, and was no doubt more a result of artifice than nature.

His light brown hair fell charmingly over one eye and hung in natural waves over his ears and the collar of his blue denim shirt. Both knees of his jeans were torn, and the unlaced white trainers on his feet were scuffed and dirty.

The best of the lot, Cathy Grafton had said, and it wasn't hard to guess why a rather plain girl like her would value a smile and a kind word from a handsome lad like Tom.

But right from the start Banks sensed something else about him, an aura of affected arrogance, as if he were condescending from a great intellectual and moral height to answer such stupid questions as those relating to his father's murder.

It was rebellious youth, in part, and Banks certainly understood that. Also, Tom seemed to exhibit that mix of vanity and over-confidence that Banks had often encountered in the wealthy. In addition there was a hell of a lot of the wariness and subterfuge that he usually associated with someone hiding a guilty secret. Tom's body language said it all: long legs stretched out, crossed at the ankles, arms folded high on his chest, eyes anywhere but on the questioner. Susan Gay sat in the background to take notes. Banks wondered what she thought about Tom.

"Did you have any problems getting a flight?" Banks asked.

"No. But I had to change at some dreary place in Carolina, and then again in New York."

"I know you must be tired. I remember from my trip to Toronto, the jet lag's much worse flying home."

"I'm all right. I slept a little on the plane."

"I can never seem to manage that."

Tom said nothing. Banks wished that Alison and Mary Rothwell weren't flanking Tom on the sofa. And again the room felt dark and cold around him. Though it had windows, they were set or angled in such a way that they didn't let in much natural light. And they were all closed.

"I imagine you're upset about your father, too," he said.

"Naturally."

"We wanted to talk to you so soon," Banks said, "because we hoped you might be able to tell us something about your father, something that might help lead us to his killers."

"How would I know anything? I've been out of the country since the end of March."

"It's possible," Banks said, weighing his words carefully, "that the roots of the crime lie farther back than that."

"That's ridiculous. You lot have far too much imagination for your own good."

"Oh? What do *you* think happened?"

Tom curled his lip and looked at the carpet. "It was clearly a robbery gone wrong. Or a kidnap attempt. Dad was quite well off, you know."

Banks scratched the scar beside his right eye. "Kidnapping, eh? We'd never thought of that. Can you explain?"

"Well, that's your job, isn't it? But it's hardly difficult to see how it could have been a kidnap attempt gone wrong.

My father obviously wouldn't co-operate, so they had to kill him."

"Why not just knock him out and take him away?"

Tom shrugged. "Perhaps the gun went off by accident."

"Then why not take the body and pretend he was still alive till they got the money?"

"How would I know? You're supposed to be the professionals. I only said that's what it *might* have been. I also suggested a bungled robbery."

"Look, Tom, this is a pointless game we're playing. Believe me, we've covered all the possibilities, and it wasn't a kidnap attempt or a bungled burglary. I realize how difficult it is for the family to accept that a member may have been involved in something illegal, but all the evidence points that way."

"Absurd," spat Mary Rothwell. "Keith was an honest businessman, a good person. And if you persist in spreading these vicious rumours, we'll have to contact our solicitor."

"Mrs. Rothwell," Banks said, "I'm trying to talk to your son. I'd appreciate it if you would keep quiet." More than once he had thought about breaking the news that her husband led another existence as Robert Calvert, but he held back. In the first place, it would be cruel, and in the second, Gristhorpe said the Chief Constable wanted it kept from the press and family, if possible, at least until they developed a few more leads on the case.

Mary Rothwell glared at him, lips pressed so tight they were white around the edges.

Banks turned back to Tom. "Were you close to your father?"

"Close enough. He wasn't . . ." Tom turned up his nose. "He wasn't a clinging, emotional sort of person."

"But you were on good terms?"

"Yes, of course."

"Then you might know something that could help us."

"I still don't see how, but if I can be of any use. . . . Ask away."

"Did he ever mention a man called Martin Churchill?"

"Churchill? No."

"Do you know who he is?"

"That chap in the Caribbean?"

"Yes."

"Are you serious?" Tom looked puzzled. "You are, aren't you. The answer's no, of course he didn't. Why would he?"

"Did you ever see your father with two well-dressed men, both about six feet tall, one black, one white?"

Tom frowned. "No. Look, I'm sorry but I don't know what you're talking about."

"Did he ever talk to you about business?"

"No."

"Did you ever meet any of his business associates?"

"Only if they came over to dinner. And even then, I wasn't generally invited." Tom looked at his mother. "I had to find something else to do for the evening. Which usually wasn't much trouble." He glanced over at Susan, and Banks sensed a softening in his expression as he did so. He seemed interested in her presence, curious about her.

The radio had been playing a request programme quietly in the background, and Banks suddenly picked out the haunting chorus of Delibes's "Viens, Mallika . . . Dôme épais," popularized as the "Flower Duet" by a television advert. Even trivialization couldn't mar its beauty and clarity. After pausing for a moment, he went on.

"When did you leave for your holiday?"

"March," he said. "The thirty-first. But I don't see—"

"What about your job?"

"What job?"

"The one in the video shop in Eastvale."

"Oh, that. I packed it in."

"What kind of videos did they deal in?"

"All sorts. Why?"

"Under-the-counter stuff?"

"Oh, come off it, Chief Inspector. Suddenly my father's

a crook and I'm a porn merchant? You should be writing for television.'' Alison looked up from her book and giggled. Tom smiled at her, obviously pleased with his insolence. ''It was called Monster Videos, that place in the arcade by the bus station. Ask them if you don't believe me.''

''Why did you leave?'' Banks pressed on.

''Not that it's any of your business, but it was hardly a fast track to a career.''

''Is that what you want?''

''I'm going to film school in the States.''

''I see.''

''I want to be a movie director.''

''Was that what your father wanted?''

''I don't see that what *he* wanted has anything to do with it.''

It was there, the rancour, Banks thought. Time to push a little harder. ''It's just that I understood you had a falling out over your career choice. I gather he wanted you to become an accountant or a lawyer but he thought you preferred to be an idle, shiftless sod.''

''How dare you?'' Mary Rothwell jumped to her feet.

''It's all right, Mother,'' Tom sneered. ''Sit down. It's all part of their game. They only say things like that to needle you into saying something you'll regret. Just ignore it.'' He looked at Susan again, as if expecting her to defend Banks, but she said nothing. He seemed disappointed.

Mary Rothwell sat down again slowly. Alison, at the other side of Tom, glanced up from *Villette* again for a couple of seconds, raised the corners of her lips in what passed for a smile, then went back to her book.

''Well?'' said Banks.

''Well what?''

''What is it that I might needle you into regretting you said?''

''Clever. It was just a figure of speech.''

"All right. Did you and your father have such an argument?"

"You must know as well as I do," Tom said, "that fathers and sons have their disagreements. Sure, Dad wanted me to follow in his footsteps, but I had my own ideas. He's not big on the arts, isn't Dad, except when it's good for business to get tickets for the opera or the theatre or something to impress his clients."

"Where did you travel in America?"

"All over. New York. Chicago. Los Angeles. San Francisco. Miami. Tampa."

"How did you get around?"

"Plane and car rental. Where is this—"

"Did you visit the Caribbean? St. Corona?"

"No, I didn't."

"How did you finance the trip?"

"What?"

"You heard me. You were over there a month and a half, and you'd still be there now if it weren't for your father's death. All that travelling costs money. You can't have earned that much working in a video shop, especially one that only deals in legal stuff. How could you afford a lengthy trip to America?"

Tom shifted uncomfortably. "My parents helped me out."

Banks noticed a confused look flit across Mary Rothwell's face.

"Did you?" Banks asked her.

"Why, yes, of course."

He could tell from the hesitation that she knew nothing about it. "Do you mean your father helped you?" he asked Tom.

"He was the one with all the money, wasn't he?"

"So your father financed your trip. How?"

"What do you mean?"

"How did he finance it? Cash? Cheque?"

"He got me the ticket, some travellers' cheques and a

supplementary card on his American Express Gold account. You can check the records, if you haven't done already."

Banks whistled between his teeth. "American Express Gold, eh? Not bad." Judging by the look on Mary Rothwell's face, it was news to her. Alison didn't seem to care. She turned a page without looking up. "Why would he do that?" Banks asked.

"I'm his son. It's the kind of thing parents do, isn't it? Why not?"

Banks had never spent so much on Brian and Tracy, but then he had never been able to afford it. "Was he usually so generous?" he asked.

"He was never mean."

Banks paused. When the silence had made Tom restless, he went on. "Just before you went away, you had an argument with your father in which he expressed great disappointment in you. Now, I know why that is. You've just told me you didn't want to follow the career he set out for you. But you also expressed disappointment in him. Why did you do that?"

"I don't remember any argument."

"Come on, Tom. You can do better than that."

Tom looked at Susan again, and Banks noticed a plea for help in his eyes. He looked left and right for support, too, but found none. His mother seemed lost in thought and Alison was still deep in her Charlotte Brontë.

"I'm telling you," Tom said, "I don't know what you're talking about."

"Why were you disappointed in your father, Tom?"

Tom reddened. "I wasn't. I don't know what you mean."

"Did you find out something incriminating about his business dealings?"

"Is *that* what you think?"

"You'd better tell me, Tom. It could help us a lot. What was he up to?"

Tom seemed to relax. "Nothing. *I* don't know. You're way off beam."

"Does the name Aston or Afton mean anything to you?"

Banks was sure he saw a flicker of recognition behind Tom's eyes. Recognition and fear. "No," Tom said. "Never heard of him."

Banks decided they would get nothing more out of this situation, not with the whole family closing ranks. It would be best to leave it for now. No doubt, when Banks and Susan left, the Rothwells would fall into an argument, for Mary Rothwell wasn't looking at all pleased with the return of her prodigal son. Tom could stew over whatever it was that confused him. Plenty of time.

It was a gorgeous morning in the dale. Banks put a Bill Evans solo piano tape in the cassette player as he drove through Fortford, gold and green in the soft, slanting light. To their left, the lush fields of the Leas were full of buttercups, and here and there the fishermen sat, still as statues, lines arcing down into the River Swain.

"What do you think?" he asked Susan.

"He's lying, sir."

"That's obvious enough. But why? What about?"

"I don't know. Everything. I just got a strange feeling."

"Me, too. Next time, I think it might be a good idea if you talked to him alone."

"Maybe I can catch him after the funeral?"

"You were thinking of going? Damn!"

Half a mile before the road widened at the outskirts of Eastvale, a farmer was moving his sheep across from one pasture to another. There was nothing to be done. They simply had to stop until the sheep had gone.

"Stupid creatures," Banks said.

"I think they're rather cute, in a silly way," Susan said. "Anyway, I thought I might go. You never know, the murderers might turn up to pay their respects, like they do in books."

Banks laughed. "Do you know that actually happened to me once?" he said.

"What?"

"It did. Honest. Down in London. There was a feud between two families, the Kinghorns and the Franklins—none of them exactly intellectual giants—been going on for years. Anyway, old man Franklin gets shot in broad daylight, and there's half a dozen witnesses say they saw Billy Kinghorn, the eldest son, do it. Only trouble is, Billy does a bunk. Until the funeral, that is. Then there he is, young Billy, black tie, armband and all, face as long as a wet Sunday, come to pay his last respects."

"What happened?"

"We nabbed him."

Susan laughed. The sheep kept wandering all over the road, despite the ministrations of an inept collie, which looked a bit too long in the tooth for such exacting work.

"I thought there had to be a reason for going," Susan said. "Anyway, I quite like funerals. My Auntie Mavis died when I was six and my mum and dad took me to the funeral. It was very impressive, the hymns, the readings. I couldn't understand a word of it at that age, of course, but it certainly sounded important. Anyway, when we got outside I asked my mum where Auntie Mavis was and she sniffled a bit then said, 'In Heaven.' I asked her where that was and she pointed up at the sky. It was a beautiful blue sky, a bit like today, and there was only one cloud in it, a fluffy white one that looked like a teddy bear. From then on I always thought when people died they became clouds in a perfect blue sky. I don't know . . . it made me feel happy, somehow. I mean, I know funerals are solemn occasions, but I don't seem to mind them so much after that."

The last sheep finally found the gate and scrambled through. The farmer held up his hand in thanks, as if Banks had had any option but to wait, and closed the gate behind him. Banks set off.

"Rather you than me," he said. "I can't stand them.

Anyway, see if you can take young Tom aside, take him
for a drink or something. I've a feeling he really wants to
tell us what he knows. Did you notice the way he kept
looking at you?"

"Yes."

"Think he fancies you?"

"No," Susan said, after a pause for thought. "No.
Somehow, I don't think it was that at all."

2

Banks crunched the last pickled onion of his ploughman's
lunch and swilled it down with a mouthful of Theakston's
bitter, then he lit a cigarette. He would have to resort to a
Polo mint if he found himself interviewing anyone in the
afternoon. Superintendent Gristhorpe sat opposite him in
the Queen's Arms, cradling a half-pint. It was the first time
they had been able to get together since Banks had met
Burgess.

"So," Gristhorpe said, "according to Burgess, Rothwell
was laundering money for Martin Churchill?"

"Looks that way," said Banks. "He said he couldn't be
certain but I don't think he'd come all the way up here if
he wasn't, do you?"

"Knowing how little Burgess thinks of the north, no. But
I still don't think we should overlook the possibility of
Rothwell's involvement in some other kind of organized
crime, most likely drugs, prostitution or porn. Even if he
were laundering money for Churchill, he could have been
into something else dirty too. We can't assume it was the
Churchill link that got him killed until we know a hell of
a lot more."

"I agree," said Banks.

"Better do as Burgess says and watch your back,
though."

"Don't worry, sir, I will."

"Anyway," Gristhorpe went on, "I've just had a meet-

ing with Inspector Macmillan, and he tells me that Daniel
Clegg acted as Robert Calvert's reference for his bank account and his credit card in Leeds. The account has about
twenty thousand in it. Interesting, isn't it?''

"Play money," Banks said.

"Aye. I wouldn't mind that much to play with, myself.
Anyway, according to Inspector Macmillan, the bank em-
ployees didn't recognize Rothwell's picture as Calvert because they hardly saw him. He used a busy branch in the
city centre, and the only person who did make the connection when Macmillan pushed it said Calvert looked and
dressed so differently she wouldn't have known.''

"Thank the lord for Pamela Jeffreys, then.''

"Aye, or we might never have known. What does his
family have to say?''

Banks sighed and put the edge of his hand to his throat.
"I've had it up to here with the bloody Rothwells," he
said. "They give a whole new meaning to 'dysfunctional.'
There's the victim laundering illegal money and leading a
double life just for a hobby. There's the daughter, who'd
rather bury her face in a book than face reality now that
the shock and the tiredness have worn off. There's a son
with more than a few guilty secrets hidden away. And then,
watching over them all, there's the Queen Bee, who just
wants to keep up the usual upper middle-class appearances
and swears the sun shone out of her husband's arse.''

"What do you expect her to do, Alan? Her world's fallen
apart. She must be having a hell of a job just holding things
together. Have a bit more bloody compassion, lad.''

Banks took a drag at his cigarette and blew the smoke
out slowly. "You're right," he said. "I'm sorry. I've just
had it with the bloody Rothwells, that's all. What do they
know? It's hard to tell. I think the wife suspects something
weird was going on, but she doesn't know what and she
doesn't want to know. She denies it, especially to herself.''

"Could they have any involvement?''

"I've thought about it," Banks said, "and I've discussed

it with Susan. In the final analysis, I don't really think so. Mary Rothwell might well hit out at anything that threatens her comfortable world, and if she thought her husband were profiting from porn, for example, I can't just see her sitting still and accepting it.'' He shook his head. ''But not this way. This brings her exactly the kind of attention she *doesn't* want. I don't know how she'd deal with him— Susan guessed poison, maybe, or an accident—but it wouldn't be like this.''

''Hmm. Try this for size,'' said Gristhorpe. ''One: Let's assume that Rothwell and Clegg are in the money-laundering business together, for Martin Churchill or who-ever.''

Banks nodded. ''It makes sense, Clegg being a tax specialist and all.''

''And we'll leave Robert Calvert out of it, as, say, just a personal aberration on Rothwell's part, at least for the moment. A red herring, right?''

''Okay.''

''Something goes wrong. Rothwell finds out something that makes him want to get out of it, so he writes to Clegg ending their association.''

''And,'' said Banks, ''Churchill, or whoever it is they're working for, doesn't like this at all.''

''Makes sense, doesn't it?''

''So far. Keep going.''

''Rothwell gets scared. Either he's been cheating on his masters, and they've found out, or they're afraid he's getting nervous and is going to blow the whistle. So what do they do?''

''Take out a contract.''

''Right. And that's the end of Rothwell.''

Gristhorpe paused as a couple of office-workers on a lunch break brushed past them and sat down at the next table. Cyril's cash register rang up another sale.

''He could have been cheating on them to finance his life as Calvert,'' said Banks. ''I know we were going to leave him out of the equation, but it fits. He had twenty grand in the bank, you say, and he liked to gamble, according to Pamela Jeffreys.''

"True, but let's stick to the simple line. What's important is that Rothwell has become a liability, or a threat, and his masters want him dead. They've got enough money to be able to pay for the privilege without getting their own hands dirty. Which brings us to Mr. Daniel Clegg. The killers had a fair bit of information about Rothwell. They seemed to know that he and his wife would be out celebrating their wedding anniversary, for example. Clegg could probably have told them that. They knew Rothwell had a daughter, too, and that she would be at home. She wasn't 'part of the deal,' remember? And they knew where he lived, the layout, everything.''

"Clegg?"

Gristhorpe nodded. "Let's put it this way. If Rothwell were laundering money for someone, there'd be as little, if any, contact between him and his masters, wouldn't there?''

"That would seem to be one point of a laundering operation," Banks agreed. "Certainly Tom Rothwell seemed genuinely puzzled when I brought up Martin Churchill.''

"Right. And Clegg was the only other person we suspect was involved, and he had information about Rothwell's personal life.''

"So you reckon Clegg was behind it?"

"It's a theory, isn't it? They weren't exactly friends, Alan. Not according to what you've told me. They were business colleagues. Different thing. It was a matter of you scratch my back, I'll scratch yours. Strange bedfellows, maybe. And crooked too. It's an odd thing is a professional gone bad. They talk about bent coppers, but what about bent lawyers, bent accountants, bent doctors? If push came to shove, would you expect one crooked businessman to stick up for another?''

"So you think Clegg was not just involved in the laundering business but in Rothwell's murder, too?''

"Aye. He could be our link."

"And his disappearance?"

"Scarpered. He knew what was coming, knew when. Maybe they paid him well. It doesn't matter whether he was scared of us or them, the result was the same. He took his money and ran, collected two hundred pounds when he passed go, didn't go to jail. Then his bosses couldn't get in touch with him, so they sent their two goons to find him. The timing's right."

"What about this scenario," Banks offered. "Maybe Churchill had Clegg killed, too. With Rothwell gone, Clegg might just be a nuisance who knew too much, a loose cannon on the deck. If Churchill is planning on coming here, maybe he wanted a clean break."

Gristhorpe took a sip of his beer. "Possible, I'll grant you."

"You know, it's just struck me," said Banks, "but do we know if Clegg ever practised criminal law?"

"Seems to be the only kind he practised," replied Gristhorpe, then held up his hand and grinned as Banks groaned. "All right, all right, Alan. I promise. No more bad lawyer jokes. As far as we know he didn't. He's a solicitor, not a barrister, so he didn't represent clients in court. But people might have come to him, and he could have referred them. Why?"

"I was just wondering where a man like Clegg might meet a killer for hire."

"Local Conservative Club, probably," said Gristhorpe. "But I see what you mean. It's a loose end we've got to pursue. If we assume Clegg was involved in arranging for Rothwell's murder, then we can look through his contacts and his activities to find a link with a couple of likely assassins. We've got that and the wadding. Not very much is it?"

"No," said Banks. "What if Clegg's dead?"

"Nothing changes. West Yorkshire police keep looking for a body and we keep nosing around asking questions.

We could get in touch with Interpol, see if he's holed up somewhere in Spain.'' He looked at his watch. "Look, Alan, I'd better get finished and be off. I've got another meeting with the Chief Constable this afternoon.''

"Okay. I'll be over in a minute.''

Gristhorpe nodded and left, but no sooner had Banks started to let his imagination work on Clegg meeting two hired guns in a smoky saloon than the superintendent poked his head around the door again. "They think they've found the killers' car," he said. "Abandoned near Leeds city centre. Ken Blackstone asks if you want to go and have a look.''

Banks nodded. "All roads lead to Leeds," he sighed. "I might as well bloody move there.'' And he followed Gristhorpe out.

: 9

1

A tape of Satie's piano music, especially the "Trois Gymnopédies," kept Banks calm on his way to Leeds, even though the A1 was busy with juggernauts and commercial travellers driving too fast. He found the car park without too much difficulty; it was an old school playground surrounded by the rubble of demolished buildings just north of the city centre.

"Cheers, Alan," said Detective Inspector Ken Blackstone. "You look like a bloody villain with those sunglasses on. How's it going?"

"Can't complain." Banks shook his hand and took off the dark glasses. He had met Blackstone at a number of courses and functions, and the two of them had always got along well enough. "And how's West Yorkshire CID?"

"Overworked, as usual. Bit of a bugger, isn't it?" said Blackstone. "The weather, I mean."

Banks scratched the scar beside his right eye. Sometimes when it itched, it was trying to tell him something; other times, like this, it was just the heat. "I remember an American once told me that all we English do is complain about the weather," he said. "It's either too hot or too cold for us, too wet or too dry."

Blackstone laughed. "True. Still, the station could do with a few of those air-conditioner thingies the Yanks use. It's hotter indoors than out. Sends the crime figures up, you know, a heat wave. Natives get restless."

A light breeze had sprung up from the west, but it did nothing to quell the warmth of the sun. Banks took off his

sports jacket and slung it over his shoulder as they walked
across the soft tarmac to the abandoned car. His tie hung
askew, as usual, and his top shirt button was open so he
could breathe easily. He could feel the sweat sticking his
white cotton shirt to his back. This weather was following
a pattern he recognized; it would get hotter and hazier until
it ended in a storm.

"What have you got?" he asked.

"You'll see in a minute." Despite the weather, Ken
Blackstone looked cool as usual. He wore a lightweight
navy-blue suit with a grey herringbone pattern, a crisp
white shirt with a stiff collar, and a garish silk tie, secured
by a gold tieclip in the shape of a pair of handcuffs. Banks
was willing to bet that his top button was fastened.

Blackstone was tall and slim with light brown hair, thin
on top but curly over the ears, and a pale complexion, definitely not the sun-worshipping kind. His Cupid's bow lips
and wire-rimmed glasses made him look about thirty, when
he was, in fact, closer to Banks's age. He had a long, dour
sort of face and spoke with a local accent tempered by three
years at Bath University, where he had studied art history.

Blackstone had, in fact, become something of an expert
on art fraud after his degree, and he often found himself
called in to help out when something of that nature happened. In addition, he was a fair landscape artist himself,
and his work had been exhibited several times. Banks remembered Blackstone and Sandra getting into a long conversation about the Pre-Raphaelites at a colleague's
wedding once, and remembered the stirrings of jealousy he
had felt. Though he was eager to learn, read, look and listen
as much as his time allowed, Banks was always aware of
his working-class background and his lack of a true formal
education.

They arrived at a car guarded by two hot-looking uniformed constables and Banks stood back to survey it. Ancient, but not old enough to attract attention as an antique,
the light blue Ford Escort was rusted around the bottom of

the chassis and had spider-leg cracks on the passenger side of the windscreen. It matched the description, as far as that went.

"How long's it been here?" Banks asked.

"Don't know," said Blackstone. "Our lads didn't notice it until last night. When they ran the number they found it was stolen."

Banks knelt by the front tire. Flat. There was plenty of soil and gravel lodged in the grooves. They could have it analyzed and at least discover if it came from around Arkbeck Farm. He looked through the grimy window. The beige upholstery was dirty, cracked and split. A McDonald's coffee cup lay crushed on the floor at the driver's side, but apart from that he could see nothing else inside.

"We've looked in the boot," said Blackstone. "Nothing. Not even a jack or a spare tire. I've arranged for it to be taken to our police garage for a thorough forensic examination, but I thought you'd like a look at it *in situ* first."

"Thanks," said Banks. "I don't expect we'll get any prints, if they were pros, but you never know. Who's the lucky owner?"

"Bloke called Ronald Hamilton."

"When did he report it missing?"

Blackstone paused before answering. "Friday morning. Said he left it in the street as usual after he got in about five or six in the evening and it was gone when he went out at ten the next morning. Thought it was maybe kids joy-riding. There's been a lot of it on the estate lately. It's not the safest place in the city. He lives on the Raynville estate in Bramley. Ring any bells?"

Banks shook his head. Pamela Jeffreys lived in Armley, which wasn't far away, and Daniel Clegg lived in Chapel Allerton, a fair distance in both miles and manners. Most likely the killers had picked it at random a good distance from where they lived. "That's four days ago, Ken," said Banks. "And nobody spotted it before last night?"

Again, Blackstone hesitated. "Hamilton's an unemployed labourer,'' he said finally. ''He's got at least one wife and three kids that we know of, and lately he's been having a few problems with the social. He's also got a record. Dealing. Aggravated assault.''

''You thought he'd arranged to have it nicked for the insurance?''

Blackstone smiled. ''Something like that. I wasn't involved personally. I don't know what you lot do, but here in the big city we don't send Detective Inspectors out on routine traffic incidents.''

Banks ignored the sarcasm. It was just Blackstone's manner. ''So your lads didn't exactly put a rush on it?''

''That's right.'' Blackstone glanced towards the horizon and sighed. ''Any idea, Alan, how many car crimes we've got in the city now? You yokels wouldn't believe it. So when some scurvy knave comes on with a story about a beat-up old Escort, you think he'd have to pay somebody to steal that piece of shit. So let the fucking insurance company pay. They can afford it. In the meantime we've got joy-riding kids, real villains and organized gangs of car thieves to deal with. I'm not making excuses, Alan.''

''Yeah, I know.'' Banks leaned against a red Orion. The metal burned through his shirt, so he stood up straight again.

''Didn't you once tell me you came up from the Met for a peaceful time in rural Yorkshire?'' Blackstone asked.

Banks smiled. ''I did.''

''Getting it?''

''I can only suppose it's got proportionately worse down there.''

Blackstone laughed. ''Indeed. Business is booming.''

''Have you talked to Hamilton?''

''Yes. This morning. He knows nothing. Believe me, he's so scared of the police he'd sell his own mother down the tubes if he thought we were after her.'' Blackstone made an expression of distaste. ''You know the type, Alan, belligerent one minute, yelling that you're picking on him because he's black, then arse-licking the next. Makes you want to puke."

"Where's he from?"

"Jamaica. He's legit; we checked. Been here ten years."

"What's his story?"

"Saw nothing, heard nothing, knows nothing. To tell you the truth, I got the impression he'd driven back from the pub after a skinful then settled in front of the telly with a few cans of lager while his wife fed the kiddies and put them to bed. After that he probably passed out. Whole bloody place smelled of shitty nappies and roll-ups and worse. We could probably do him for possession if it was worth our while. At ten the next morning he staggers out to go and sign on, finds his car missing and, bob's your uncle, does the outraged citizen routine on the local bobby, who's got more sense, thank the lord."

Blackstone stood, slightly hunched, with his hands in his pockets, and kicked at small stones on the tarmac. You could see your face in his shoes.

"Do me a favour, Ken, and have another go at him. You said he was done for dealing?"

"Uh-huh. Small stuff. Mostly cannabis, a little coke."

"It's probably just a coincidence that the car used belongs to a drug dealer, but pull his record and have another go at him all the same. Find out who his suppliers are. And see if he has any connections with St. Corona. Friends, family, whatever. There might be a drug connection or a Caribbean connection in Rothwell's murder, and it's a remote possibility that Mr. Hamilton might have done some work for the organization behind it, whoever they are."

"You mean he might have *loaned* his car?"

"It's possible. I doubt it. I think we're dealing with cleverer crooks than that, but we'd look like the rear end of a pantomime horse if we didn't check it out."

"Will do."

"Have you questioned the neighbours?"

"We're doing a house-to-house. Nothing so far. Nobody

sees anything on these estates.''

"So that's that?"

"Looks like it. For the moment, anyway."

"No car-park attendant?"

"No." Blackstone pointed to the rubble. "As you can see, it's just an old schoolyard with weeds growing through the tarmac. The school was knocked down months ago."

Banks looked around. To the south-west he could see the large dome of the Town Hall and the built-up city centre; to the west stood the high white obelisk of the university's Brotherton Library, and the rest of the horizon seemed circled with blocks of flats and crooked terraces of back-to-backs poking through the surrounding rubble like charred vertebrae. "I could use a break on this, Ken," Banks said.

"Aye. We'll give it our best. Hey up, the lads have come to pick up the car."

Banks watched the police tow-team tie a line to the Escort. "I'd better be off," he said. "You'll let me know?"

"Just a minute," said Blackstone. "What are your plans?"

"I'm checking into the Holiday Inn. For tonight, at least. There's a couple of people I want to talk to again in connection with Clegg and Rothwell—Clegg's secretary and his ex-wife, for a start. I'd like to get a clearer idea of their relationship now we've got a bit more to go on."

"Holiday Inn? Well, la-di-dah. Isn't that a bit posh for a humble copper?"

Banks laughed. "I could do with a bit of luxury. Maybe they'll give me the sack when they see my expenses. These days we can't even afford to do half the forensic tests we need."

"Tell me about it. Anyway, if you're going to be sticking around, I'd appreciate it if we could have a chat. There seems to be a lot going on here I don't know about."

"There's a lot I don't know about, too."

"Still . . . I'd appreciate it if you would fill me in."

"No problem."

Blackstone hesitated and shifted from foot to foot. "Look," he said, "I'd like to invite you over for a bit of home-cooking but Connie left a couple of months ago."

"I'm sorry to hear that," said Banks. "I didn't know."

"Yeah, well, it happens, right? Comes with the territory. Still taking care of that lovely wife of yours?"

"You wouldn't think so by the amount of time we've spent together lately."

"I know what you mean. That was one of the problems. She said we were living such separate lives we might as well make it official. Anyway, I'm not much of a cook myself. Besides, Connie got the house and I'm in a rather small bachelor flat for the moment. But there's a decent Indian restaurant on Eastgate, near the station, if you fancy it? It's called the Shabab. About half past six, seven o'clock? We might have something on Hamilton and the car by then, too."

"All right," said Banks. "You're on. Make it seven o'clock."

"And, Alan," said Blackstone as Banks walked away, "you watch yourself. Hotels give married men strange ideas sometimes. I suppose it's the anonymity and the distance from home, if you know what I mean. Anyway, there's some seem to act as if the normal vows of marriage don't apply in hotels."

Banks knew what Blackstone meant, and he felt guilty as an image of Pamela Jeffreys flashed unbidden through his mind.

2

Susan Gay heard Sergeant Hatchley burp before she had even opened the office door after more fruitless interviews with Rothwell's legitimate clients. She felt apprehension churn in her stomach like a badly digested meal. She could not work with Hatchley; she just couldn't.

Hatchley sat at his desk smoking. The small, stifling

room stank of stale beer and pickled onions. The warped
window was open about as far as it would go, but that
didn't help much. If this oppressive weather didn't end
soon, Susan felt she would scream.

And, by God, he's repulsive, she thought. There was his
sheer bulk, for a start—a rugby prop forward gone to fat.
Then there was his face: brick-red complexion, white eyelashes and piggy eyes; straw hair, thinning a bit at the top;
a smattering of freckles over a broad-bridged nose; fleshy
lips; tobacco-stained teeth. To cap it all, he wore a shiny,
wrinkled blue suit, and his red neck bulged over his tight
shirt collar.

From the corner of her eye, Susan noticed the coloured
picture on the cork-board: long blonde hair, exposed skin.
Without even stopping to think, she walked over and pulled
it down so hard the drawing-pin shot right across the room.

"Oy!" said Hatchley. "What the hell do you think
you're playing at?"

"I'm not playing at anything," Susan said, waving the
picture at him. "With all respect, sir, I don't care if you
are my senior officer, I won't bloody well have it!"

A hint of a smile came to Hatchley's eyes. "Calm down,
lass," he said. "You've got steam coming out of your ears.
Maybe you're being a bit hasty?"

"No, I'm not. It's offensive. I don't see why I should
have to work with this kind of thing stuck to the walls. You
might think it's funny, but *I* don't. *Sir.*"

"Susan. Look at it."

"No. Why—"

"Susan!"

Slowly, Susan turned the picture over and looked at it.
There, in all her maternal innocence, Carol Hatchley, with
her long blonde hair hanging over her shoulders, held her
naked, newborn baby to her breast, which was covered well
beyond the point of modesty by a flesh-tone T-shirt. Susan
felt herself blush. All she had seen were the woman's face,
hair, and a lot of skin colour. "I . . . I thought . . ." She

could think of nothing else to say.

"I know what you thought," said Hatchley. "You thought my daughter's head was a tit. You *could* apologize."

Susan felt such a fool she couldn't even bring herself to do that.

"All right," Hatchley said, putting his feet up on the desk, "then you can listen to me. Now, nobody's ever going to convince me that looking at a nice pair of knockers is wrong. Since time immemorial, since our ancestors scratched images on cave walls, men have enjoyed looking at women's tits. They're beautiful things, nothing dirty or pornographic about them at all."

"But they're private," Susan blurted out. "Don't you understand? They're a woman's private parts. You don't see pictures of men's privates all over the place, do you? You wouldn't like people staring at yours, would you?"

"Susan, love, if I thought it would make you happy I'd drop my trousers right now. But that's not the point. What I'm saying is it's my opinion that there's nowt wrong in admiring a nice pair of bristols. A lot of people agree with me, too. But you don't like it." He held up his large hand. "All right, now I might not be the most sensitive bloke in Christendom, and I certainly reserve my right to disagree with you, but I'm not that much of a monster that I'd use my rank to expose you to something you feel offends you day in, day out, however wrongheaded I think you are. I respect your opinion. I don't agree with you, and I never will, but I respect it. I can live without.

"And another thing. I know you're a bugger about smoking. I'll try and cut down on the cigarettes in the office, too. But don't expect miracles, and don't expect it's going to be all bloody give and no take on my part. You don't like my smoke. I don't like your perfume. It makes my nose itch and it's probably rotting my lungs as we speak. But for better or for worse, lass, we've got to work together, and we've got to do it in the same damn little cubby-hole

for the time being. Mebbe one day we'll have separate offices. Myself, I can hardly wait. But for now, let's just keep
the window open and make a bit of an effort to get along,
all right?''

Susan nodded. She felt all the wind go out of her sails.
She swallowed. ''All right. Sorry, sir.''

Hatchley swung his legs to the floor and rubbed his
hands together. ''We'll say no more, then. Now, about that
wadding?''

''Yes, sir?''

Hatchley burped again and put his hamlike hand to his
mouth. ''Shaved pussies. Smooth and shiny as a baby's
bottom.''

''Yes, sir.'' Susan felt herself blush again and hated herself for it. Hatchley smiled at her. He seemed to be enjoying
himself. Her spirits sank. She had thought for a moment
that he might be getting serious about the case, but here he
was simply creating another opportunity to embarrass her.

''Aye. Now, I know that's not a lot to go on, but at least
we know it's not kiddie porn or the bum brigade. And
we've got penetration and a clear image of 'a penis in an
excited state,' as it says in the book, so this is definitely
under-the-counter stuff.''

''True, sir.''

''And as far as I can tell,'' he went on, ''there's no sign
of dogs or cats, either.''

''Sir, can you get to the point?'' Susan couldn't keep the
impatience out of her voice.

''Hold your horses, lass.'' He started to laugh. ''Get that?
No animals. Hold your horses? Never mind. The point is,
shaved pussies aren't exactly ten a penny, though if we'd
come up with something *really* kinky it would have made
my job a lot easier. I mean, there aren't many people sell
photos of Rottweilers bonking thirteen-year-old girls that
we don't know about.''

''I still don't see what you're getting at, sir,'' said Susan,
a little calmer. She should have known that, if anyone was,

Hatchley would be an expert on pornography. "Surely most of that stuff is sent through the mail from abroad, or from London?"

"Not all of it. There's a fair chance it was bought under the counter somewhere. When I did my stint on Vice with West Yorkshire a few years back, I made one or two useful contacts. Now, if we're assuming these lads were at all local, the odds are they're from the city, as there aren't that many killers-for-hire living in rural areas. Too exposed. That means Leeds, Bradford, Manchester, maybe Newcastle or Liverpool at a stretch. Now if the boss thinks this Clegg chap from Leeds was involved, then Leeds is as good a choice as any, agreed?"

Susan nodded. "Yes. The daughter, Alison, thought the man had a Leeds accent. She could be wrong about that, of course. Not everyone's accurate on voices. I don't reckon I could tell the difference. But it looks like they've found the car used for the job there. Anyway, as I've already told you, West Yorkshire's got some men asking around. Have had for days."

"Well, you know how I hate sitting idle," Hatchley said. "Guess where I've been this lunch-time."

"The Queen's Arms, sir?"

Hatchley smiled. "Not far off. We'll make a detective of you yet, lass. I've been having drinks with an old informer of mine in The Oak, that's what." He touched the side of his nose. "Lives in Eastvale now, but he used to live in Leeds. Gone straight. See, I thought I probably remembered a few purveyors of this kind of porn—if they're still around, that is—and it's odds on that some wet-behind-the-ears young pansy DC fresh from university doesn't even know they exist. There aren't as many as you think, you know, at least not selling shaved pussy porn. It *is* something of a specialist taste. Anyway, there's still plenty prefer the friendly old corner shop to the impersonal supermarket, if you get my drift. I'm not talking about sex shops—I imagine they've all been checked already—just

regular newsagents that sell a bit of imported stuff from
under the counter along with their *Woman's Weekly*s and
gardening magazines. Harmless enough. Hardly any reason
for our lads to be interested, really. So I asked my old
friend.''

''And?''

''Yes. They're still in business, still selling the same kind
of stuff to the same old customers. Some of them, anyway.
A couple have retired, some have moved on, and one's
dead. Heart attack. Not business related. The point is, I
knew these blokes were a bit bent, but I left them alone.
In exchange, they'd pass on the odd tip if anyone came
hawking really serious stuff, like kiddie porn or snuff films.
Live and let live. Now, what I propose is that you and me
go to Leeds and ask a few questions of our own.'' He
looked at his watch. ''Tomorrow, of course. Don't worry,
I'll arrange permission from the super and from West Yorkshire CID. Are you game?''

Susan was aware of her jaw dropping. He made sense,
all right, and that was the problem. She was about to go
on a porn hunt with Sergeant Hatchley, she could feel it in
her bones. But it could pay off. If it led to the owner of
the wadding, that would be feathers in both their caps. She
swallowed.

''It's a hell of a long shot,'' she said.

Hatchley shrugged. ''Nothing ventured, nothing gained.
What do you say?''

Susan thought for a moment. ''All right,'' she said. ''But
you've got to convince Superintendent Gristhorpe.''

''Right, lass,'' Hatchley beamed, rubbing his hands together. ''You're on.''

Oh my God, thought Susan, with that sinking feeling. *A
porn hunt.* What have I let myself in for?

3

By the looks of it, the heat had drawn one or two refugees
from the Magistrates Court over to the Park Square. Two

skinheads, stripped to the waist, dozed on the grass under a tree. One, lying on his back, had tattoos up and down his arms and scars criss-crossing his abdomen, old knife wounds by the look of them; the other, on his stomach, boasted a giant butterfly tattoo between his shoulder-blades.

In Clegg's offices, Betty Moorhead was still holding the fort and fighting off her cold.

"Oh, Mr. Banks," she said when he entered the ante-room. "It's nice to see a friendly face. There's been nothing but police coming and going since you were last here, and nobody will tell me anything."

Had she forgotten he was a policeman, too? he wondered. Or was it just that he had been the first to arrive and she had somehow latched onto him as a lifeline?

"Some men in suits took most of his papers," she went on, "and there's been others asking questions all day. They've got someone keeping an eye on the building as well, in case those two men come back. Then there was that man from Scotland Yard. I don't know what's what. They all had identification cards, of course, but I don't know whether I'm coming or going."

Banks smiled. "Don't worry, Betty," he said. "I know it sounds complicated, but we're all working together."

She nodded and pulled a tissue from the box in front of her and blew her nose; it looked red raw from rubbing. "Is there any news of Mr. Clegg?" she asked.

"Nothing yet. We're still looking."

"Did you talk to Melissa?"

"Yes."

"How is she?"

Banks didn't really know what to say. He wasn't used to giving out information, just digging it up, but Betty Moorhead was obviously concerned. "She didn't seem unduly worried," he said. "She's sure he'll turn up."

Betty's expression brightened. "Well, then," she said. "There you are."

"Do you mind if I ask a few more questions?"

"Oh, no. I'd be happy to be of help."

"Good." Banks perched at the edge of her desk and looked around the room. "Sitting here," he said, "you'd see everyone who called on Mr. Clegg, wouldn't you? Everyone who came in and out of his office."

"Yes."

"And if people phoned, you'd speak to them first?"

"Well, yes. But I did tell you Mr. Clegg has a private line."

"Did he receive many calls on it?"

"I can't say, really. I heard it ring once in a while, but I was usually too busy to pay attention. I'm certain he didn't give the number out to just anyone."

"So you didn't unintentionally overhear any of the conversations?"

"I know what you're getting at," she said, "and you can stop right there. I'm not that sort of a secretary."

"What sort?"

"The sort that listens in on her boss's conversations. Besides," she added with a smile, "the walls are too thick. These are old houses, solidly built. You can't hear what's being said in Mr. Clegg's office with the door shut."

"Even if two people are having a conversation in there?"

"Even then."

"Or arguing?"

"Not that it happened often, but you can only hear the raised voices, not what they're saying."

"Did you ever hear Mr. Clegg arguing with Mr. Rothwell?"

"I don't remember. I don't think so. I mean if they ever *did*, it would certainly have been a rarity. Normally they were all cordial and businesslike."

"Mr. Clegg specializes in tax law, doesn't he?"

"Yes."

"How many clients does he have?"

"That's very hard to say. I mean, there are regular clients, and then people you just do a bit of work for now and then.''

"Roughly? Fifty? A hundred?"

"Closer to a hundred, I'd say."

"Any new ones?"

"He's been too busy to take on much new work this year."

"So there's been no new clients in, say, the past three months?"

"Not really, no. He's done a bit of extra work for friends of friends here and there, but nothing major."

"What I'm getting at," Banks said, leaning forward, "is whether there's been anyone new visiting him often or phoning in the past two or three months."

"Not visiting, no. There's been a few funny phone calls, though."

"What do you mean, funny?"

"Well, abrupt. I mean, I know I told you people are sometimes rude and brusque, but usually they at least tell you what they want. Since you were here last, I've been thinking, trying to remember, you know, if there was anything odd. My head's so stuffed up I can hardly think straight, but I remembered the phone calls. I told the other policeman, too."

"That's okay. Tell me. What did this brusque caller say?"

"I don't know if it was the same person each time, and it only happened two or three times. It was about a month ago."

"Over what time period?"

"What? Oh, just a couple of days."

"What did he say? I assume it was a *he?*"

"Yes. He'd just say, 'Clegg?'. And if I said Mr. Clegg was out or busy, he'd hang up."

"I see what you mean. What kind of voice did he have?"

"I couldn't say. That's all I ever heard him say. It just sounded ordinary, but clipped, impatient, in a hurry."

"And this happened two or three times over a couple of days?"

"Yes."

"You never heard the voice again?"

"I never had that sort of call again, if that's what you mean."

"Nobody visited the office who sounded like the man?"

She sneezed, then blew her nose. "No. But I told you I don't think I would recognize it."

"It wasn't anything like one of the men who came around asking questions?"

"I don't know. I don't think so. I'm sorry."

"That's all right."

"What's going on?"

"We don't know," Banks lied. He was testing Gristhorpe's theory about Clegg's involvement in Rothwell's murder, but he didn't want Betty Moorhead to realize he suspected her boss of such a crime. Certainly the odd phone calls *could* have been from someone giving him orders, or from the people he hired to do the job. The timing was about right. "Do you think Mr. Clegg might have given this caller his private number?"

She nodded. "That's what must have happened. The first two times, Mr. Clegg was out or with a client. The third time, I put the caller through, and he never called me again."

"And you're sure you never put a face to the voice?"

"No."

Banks stood up and walked around the small room. Welltended potted plants stood on the shelf by the small window at the back that looked out onto narrow Park Cross Street. Clegg had obviously been careful where Betty Moorhead was concerned. If he had been mixed up with hired killers and Caribbean dictators, he had been careful to keep them at arm's length. He turned back to Betty. "Is there anything else you can tell me about Mr. Clegg?"

"I don't know what you mean."

"How would you describe him as a person?"

"Well, I wouldn't know."

"You never socialized?"

She blushed. "Certainly not."

"Had he been depressed lately?"

"No."

"Did Mr. Clegg have many women calling on him?"

"Not as far as I know. What are you suggesting?"

"Did you ever see or hear mention of a woman called Pamela Jeffreys? An Asian woman."

She looked puzzled. "No. She wasn't a client."

"Did he have a girlfriend?"

"I wouldn't know. He kept his private life private."

Banks decided to give up. Melissa Clegg might know a bit more about her husband's conquests, or Ken Blackstone's men would question his colleagues and perhaps come up with something. It was after five and he was tired of running around in circles. Betty Moorhead clearly didn't know anything else, or if she did she didn't realize its importance. Getting at information like that was like target practice in the dark.

Why not just accept Gristhorpe's theory that Clegg had arranged for Rothwell to be killed, and that they hadn't a hope in hell of finding either Clegg or the killers? And what could they do to Martin Churchill, if indeed he was behind it all? Banks didn't like the feeling of impotence this case was beginning to engender.

On the walk back to his hotel, Banks picked up a half-bottle of Bell's. It would be cheaper than using the minibar in his room. As he threaded his way among the office workers leaving the British Telecom Building for their bus-stops on Wellington Street, Banks wished he could just go home and forget about the whole Clegg-Rothwell-Calvert mess.

After leaving Blackstone at the car park, he had phoned Pamela Jeffreys at home, half-hoping she might be free for a drink that evening, but he had only got her answering machine. She was probably playing with the orchestra or something. He had left a message anyway, telling her which hotel he was staying at, and now he was feeling guilty. He remembered Blackstone's warning about hotels.

On the surface, he wanted to apologize for their misunderstanding yesterday, but if truth be told, he had let himself get a bit too carried away with his fantasies. Would he do anything if he had the chance? If she agreed to come back to his hotel room for a nightcap, would he try to seduce her? Would he make love to her if she were willing? He didn't know.

He remembered his attraction to Jenny Fuller, a professor of psychology who occasionally helped with cases, and wondered what his life would be like now if he had given in to his desires then. Would he have told Sandra? Would they still be together? Would he and Jenny still be friends? No answer came.

Rather glumly, he recalled the bit at the beginning of the Trollope biography he was reading, where Trollope considers the dreary sermons persuading people to turn their backs on worldly pleasure in the hope of heaven to come and asks, if such is really the case, then ''Why are women so lovely?'' That set him thinking again about Pamela's shapely, golden body, her bright personality and her passion for music. Well, at least he had a curry with Ken Blackstone to look forward to, and time for a shower and a rest before that. He thought he might even check out the hotel's Health and Leisure Club, maybe have a swim, take a sauna or a whirlpool.

There were no messages. Banks went straight up to his room, took off his shoes and flopped on the bed. He phoned Sandra, who wasn't in, then called the Eastvale station again and spoke to Susan Gay. Nothing new, except that she sounded depressed.

After a brisk shower, much better than the tepid dribble at home, he poured himself a small Scotch and put the television on while he dried off and dressed. He caught the end of the international news and heard that the St. Corona riots had been put down swiftly and brutally by Martin Churchill's forces. And Burgess wanted to give the man a retirement villa in Cornwall?

After that, he was only half paying attention to the local news, but at one point, he saw a house he recognized and heard the reporter say, ". . . when she failed to report for rehearsals today. Police are still at the scene and so far have refused to comment. . . ."

It was Pamela Jeffreys's house, and outside it stood two patrol cars and an ambulance. Stunned, Banks sat on the side of the bed and tossed back his Scotch, then he got his jacket out of the cupboard and left the room so fast he forgot to turn off the television.

: 10

1

It was hard to imagine that anything terrible could happen on such a fine spring evening, but the activity around the little terrace house in Armley indicated that evil made no allowances for the weather.

Three police cars were parked at angles in front of the house. Beyond the line of white tape, reporters badgered the PCs on guard duty, one of whom jotted down Banks's name and rank before he let him through. Neighbours stood on their doorsteps or by privet hedges and gazed in silence, arms folded, faces grim, and the people working their allotments stopped to watch the spectacle. A small crowd also stood gawping from the steps of the Sikh Temple down the street.

Banks stood on the threshold of the living-room. Whatever had happened here, it had been extremely violent: the glass coffee table had been smashed in two; the three-piece suite had been slashed and the stuffing ripped out; books lay torn all over the carpet, pages reduced to confetti; the glass front of the cocktail cabinet was shattered and the crystalware itself lay in bright shards; the music stand lay on the floor with the splintered pieces and broken bow of Pamela's viola beside it; even the print of Ganesh over the fireplace had been taken from its frame and torn up. Worst of all though, was the broad dark stain on the cream carpet. Blood.

One of the officers cracked a racist joke about Ganesh and another laughed. The elephant god was supposed to be the god of good beginnings, Banks remembered. Upstairs someone was whistling "Lara's Theme" from *Doctor Zhi-vago*.

"Who the hell are you?"

Banks turned to face the plainclothes man coming out of the wreckage of the kitchen.

"Press?" he went on before Banks had time to answer. "You're not allowed in. You ought to bloody well know that. Bugger off." He grabbed Banks's arm and steered him towards the door. "What does that fucking useless PC think he's up to, letting you in? I'll have his bloody balls for Christmas tree decorations."

"Hang on." Banks finally managed to get a word in and jerk his arm free of the man's grasp. He showed his card. The man relaxed.

"Oh. Sorry, sir," he said. "Detective Sergeant Waltham. I wasn't to know." Then he frowned. "What's North York-shire want with this one, if you don't mind my asking?"

He was in his early thirties, perhaps a few pounds over-weight, about three inches taller than Banks, with curly ginger hair. He had a prominent chin, a ruddy complexion and curious catlike green eyes. He wore a dark brown suit, white shirt and plain green tie. Behind him stood a scruffy-looking youth in a leather jacket. Probably his DC, Banks guessed.

"First things first," said Banks. "What happened to the woman who lives here?"

"Pamela Jeffreys. Know her?"

"What happened to her? Is she still alive?"

"Oh, aye, sir. Just. Someone worked her over a treat. Broken ribs, broken nose, broken fingers. Multiple lacera-tions, contusions. In fact, multiple just about everything. And it looks as if she broke her leg when she fell. She was in a coma when we found her. First officer on the scene thought she was dead."

Banks felt a wave of fear and anger surge through his stomach, bringing the bile to his throat. "When did it hap-pen?" he asked.

"We're not sure, sir. There's a clock upstairs was smashed at twenty past nine, but that doesn't necessarily mean anything. A bit too Agatha Christie, if you ask me. Doc thinks last night, but we're still interviewing the neighbours."

"So you think she lay there for nearly twenty-four hours?"

"Could be, sir. The doctor said she'd have bled to death if she hadn't been a good clotter."

Banks swallowed. "Raped?"

Waltham shook his head. "Doc says no signs of sexual assault. When we found her she was fully clothed, no signs of interference. Some consolation, eh?"

"Who found her?"

"One of her musician friends got worried when she didn't show up for rehearsals this morning. Some sort of string quartet or something. Apparently she'd been a bit upset lately. He said she was usually reliable and had never missed a day before. He phoned the house several times during the day and only got her answering machine. After work he drove by and knocked. Still no answer. Then he had a butcher's through the window. After that, he phoned the local police. He's in the clear."

Banks said nothing. DS Waltham leaned against the bannister. The scruffy DC squeezed by them and went upstairs. In the front room, someone laughed out loud again.

Waltham coughed behind his hand. "Er, look, sir, is there something we should know? There'll have to be questions, of course, but we can be as discreet as anyone if we have to be. What with you showing up here and . . ."

"And what, Sergeant?"

"Well, I recognize your voice from her answering machine. It *was* you, wasn't it?"

Banks sighed. "Yes, yes it was. But no, there's nothing you need to be discreet about. There is probably a lot you should know. Shit." He looked at his watch. Almost seven. "Look, Sergeant, I'd clean forgot I'm supposed to be meeting DI Blackstone for dinner.''

"*Our* DI Blackstone, sir?''

"Yes. Know him?''

"Yes, sir.''

"Do you think you can get one of the PCs to page him
or track him down? It's the Shabab on Eastgate.''

Waltham smiled. "I know it. Very popular with the lads
at Millgarth. I'll see to it, sir.''

He went to the door and spoke to one of the uniformed
constables then came back. "He's on his way. Look, sir,
PC O'Brien there just told me there's an old geezer across
the street thinks he might have seen something. Want to
come over?''

"Yes. Very much.'' Banks followed him down the path
and through the small crowd. One or two reporters shouted
for comments, but Waltham just waved them aside. PC
O'Brien stood by the low, dark stone wall that ran by the
allotments, talking to a painfully thin old man wearing a
grubby, collarless shirt. Behind them, other allotment workers stood in a semi-circle, watching, some of them leaning
on shovels or rakes. Very Yorkshire Gothic, Banks thought.

"Mr. Judd, sir,'' O'Brien said, introducing Waltham,
who, in turn, introduced Banks. "He was working his allotment last night just before dark.'' Waltham nodded and
O'Brien walked off. "Keep those bloody reporters at bay,
will you, please, O'Brien?'' Waltham called after him.

Banks sat on the wall and took out his cigarettes. He
offered them around. Waltham declined, but Mr. Judd accepted one. "Might as well, lad,'' he croaked, tapping his
chest. "Too late to worry about my health now.''

He did look ill, Banks thought. Sallow flesh hung off the
bones of his face above his scrawny neck with its turkey-
flaps and puckered skin, like a surgery scar, around his
Adam's apple. The whites of his eyes had a yellow cast,
but the dark blue pupils glinted with intelligence. Mr. Judd,
Banks decided, was a man whose observations he could
trust. He sat by and let Waltham do the questioning.

"What time were you out here?" Waltham asked.

"From seven o'clock till about half past nine," said Judd. "This time of year I always come out of an evening after tea for a bit of peace, weather permitting. The wife likes to watch telly, but I've no patience with it, myself. Nowt but daft buggers acting like daft buggers." He took a deep draw on the cigarette. Banks noticed him flinch with pain.

"Were you the only one working here?" Waltham asked.

"Aye. T'others had all gone home by then."

"Can you tell us what you saw?"

"Aye, well it must have been close to knocking-off time. It were getting dark, I remember that. And this car pulled up outside Miss Jeffreys's house. Dark and shiny, it were. Black."

"Do you know what make?"

"No, sorry, lad. I wouldn't know a Mini from an Aston Martin these days, to tell you the truth, especially since we've been getting all these foreign cars. It weren't a big one, though."

Waltham smiled. "Okay. Go on."

"Well, two men gets out and walks up the path."

"What did they look like?"

"Hard to say, really. They were both wearing suits. And one of them was a darkie, but that's nowt to write home about these days, is it?"

"One of the men was black?"

"Aye."

"What happened next?"

Judd went through a minor coughing fit and spat a ball of red-green phlegm on the earth beside him. "I packed up and went home. The wife needs a bit of help getting up the apples and pears to bed these days. She can't walk as well as she used to."

"Did you see Miss Jeffreys open the door and let the men in?"

"I can't say I was watching that closely. One minute they were on the doorstep, next they were gone. But the car was still there."

"Did you hear anything?"

"No. Too far away." He shrugged. "I thought nothing of it. Insurance men, most like. That's what they looked like. Or maybe those religious folks, Jehovah's Witnesses."

"So you didn't see them leave?"

"No. I'd gone home by then."

"Where do you live?"

Judd pointed across the street. "Over there. Number fourteen." It was five houses down from Pamela Jeffreys's. "Been there forty years or more, now. A right dump it was when we first moved in. Damp walls, no indoor toilets, no bathroom. Had it done up over the years, though, bit by bit."

Waltham paused and looked at Banks, who indicated he would like to ask one or two questions. Waltham, Banks noted, had been a patient interviewer, not pushy, rude and condescending towards the old, like some. Maybe it was because he had a DCI watching over his shoulder. And maybe that was being uncharitable.

"Did you know Miss Jeffreys at all?" Banks asked.

Judd shook his head. "Can't say as I did."

"But you knew her to say hello to?"

"Oh, aye. She was a right nice lass, if you ask me. And a bonny one, too." He winked. "Always said hello if she passed me in the street. Always carrying that violin case. I used to ask her if she were in t'mafia and had a machine-gun in it, just joking, like."

"But you never stopped and chatted?"

"Not apart from that and the odd comment about the weather. What would an old codger like me have to say to a young lass like her? Besides, people round here tend to keep themselves to themselves these days." He coughed and spat again. "It didn't used to be that way, tha knows. When Eunice and I first came here there used to be a com-

munity. We'd have bloody great big bonfires out in the
street on Guy Fawkes night—it were still just cobbles, then,
none of this tarmac—and everyone came out. Eunice would
make parkin and treacle-toffee. We'd wrap taties in foil and
put 'em in t'fire to bake. But it's all changed. People died,
moved away. See that there Sikh Temple?'' He pointed
down the street. ''It used to be a Congregationalist Chapel.
Everyone went there on a Sunday morning. They had Monday whist drives, too, and a youth club, Boys' Brigade and
Girl Guides for the young uns. Pantos at Christmas.

''Oh, aye, it's all changed. People coming and going.
We've got indoor toilets now, but nobody talks to anyone.
Not that I've owt against Pakis, like. As I said, she was a
nice lass. I saw them taking her out on that stretcher an
hour or so back.'' He shook his head slowly. ''Nowadays
you keep your door locked tight. Will she be all right?''

''We don't know,'' Banks said. ''We're keeping our fingers crossed. Did she have many visitors?''

''I didn't keep a look out. I suppose you mean boy-
friends?''

''Anyone. Male or female.''

''I never saw any women call, not by themselves. Her
mum and dad came now and then. At least, I assumed it
was her mum and dad. And there was one bloke used to
visit quite regularly a few months back. Used to park outside our house sometimes. And don't ask me what kind of
car he drove. I can't even remember the colour. But he
stopped coming. Hasn't been anyone since, not that I've
noticed.''

''What did this man look like?''

''Ordinary really. Fair hair, glasses, a bit taller than
thee.''

Keith Rothwell—or Robert Calvert, Banks thought.
''Anyone else?''

Judd shook his head then smiled. ''Only you and that
young woman, t'other day.''

Banks felt Waltham turn and stare at him. If Judd had

seen Banks and Susan visit Pamela Jeffreys on Saturday, then he obviously didn't miss much—morning, afternoon or evening. Banks thanked him.

"We'll get someone to take a statement soon, Mr. Judd," said Waltham.

"All right, son," said the old man, turning back to his allotment. "I won't be going anywhere except my final resting place, and that'll be a few months off, God willing. I only wish I could have been more help."

"You did fine," said Banks.

"What the bloody hell was all that about, sir?" Waltham asked as they walked away. "You didn't tell me you'd been here before."

Banks noticed Ken Blackstone getting out of a dark blue Peugeot opposite the Sikh Temple. "Didn't have time," he said to Waltham, moving away. "Later, Sergeant. I'll explain it all later."

2

Banks and Blackstone sat in an Indian restaurant near Woodhouse Moor, a short drive across the Aire valley from Pamela Jeffreys's house, drinking lager and nibbling at pakoras and onion bhaji as they waited for their main courses. Being close to the university, the place was full of students. The aroma was tantalizing—cumin, coriander, cloves, cinnamon, mingled with other spices Banks couldn't put a name to. "Not exactly the Shabab," Blackstone had said, "but not bad." A Yorkshire compliment.

In the brief time they had been there, Banks had explained as succinctly as he could what the hell was going on—at least to the extent that he understood it himself.

"So why do you think they beat up the girl?" Blackstone asked.

"They must have thought she knew where Daniel Clegg was, or that she was hiding something for him. They ripped her place up pretty thoroughly."

"And you think they're working for Martin Churchill?"

"Burgess thinks so. It's possible."

"Do you think it was the same two who visited Clegg's secretary and his ex-wife?"

"Yes. I'm certain of it."

"But they didn't beat up either of them, or search their places. Why not?"

"I don't know. Maybe they were getting desperate by the time they got to Pamela. Let's face it, they'd found out nothing so far. They must have been frustrated. They felt they'd done enough pussyfooting around and it was time for business. Either that or they phoned their boss and he told them to push harder. They also probably thought she was lying or holding out on them for some reason, maybe something in her manner. I don't know. Perhaps they're just racists."

Banks shook his head, feeling a sudden ache and rage. He couldn't seem to banish the image of Pamela Jeffreys at the hands of her torturers: her terror, her agony, the smashed viola. And would her broken fingers ever heal enough for her to play again? But he didn't know Blackstone well enough to talk openly about his feelings. "They'd been polite but pushy earlier," he said. "Maybe they just ran out of patience."

The main course arrived: a plate of steaming chapatis, chicken bhuna and goat vindaloo, along with a selection of chutneys and raita. They shared out the dishes and started to eat, using the chapatis to shovel mouthfuls of food and mop up the sauce. Blackstone ordered a couple more lagers and a jug of ice water.

"There is another explanation," Blackstone said between mouthfuls.

"What?"

"That she *did* know something. That she was involved in the double-cross, or whatever it was. From the quick look I got at her house, I'd agree there's no doubt they were looking for something. DS Waltham suggested the same thing.''

"Don't think I haven't considered it," Banks said, carefully piling a heap of the hot vindaloo on a scrap of chapati. "But I'm sure she didn't even know Clegg."

"That's only what she told you, remember."

"Nobody else contradicted her, Ken. Not Melissa Clegg, not the secretary, not even Mr. Judd."

"Oh, come on, Alan. The old man can't have seen everything. Nor could the secretary or the ex-wife have *known* everything. Maybe Clegg never visited her at her home. They could have had some clandestine relationship, met in secret."

"Why the need for secrecy? Neither of them was married."

"Perhaps because they were involved in some funny business—not necessarily of a sexual nature—and it wouldn't be good to be seen together. Maybe she was involved in whatever scam Clegg and Rothwell had going?"

Banks shook his head. "Clegg was a lawyer, Rothwell a financial whiz-kid, and Pamela Jeffreys is a classical musician. It just doesn't fit."

"They *could* have had business interests in common, though."

"True. Anything's possible. But remember, Pamela Jeffreys knew *Robert Calvert*. She told me they met by chance in a pub. She'd never heard of Keith Rothwell until after his murder, when his photo appeared in the papers. She had no reason to lie. She was even putting herself in an awkward situation by calling us. She needn't have done so. We hadn't heard of Robert Calvert and might never have done if it weren't for her. Usually people want to stay as far away from a murder investigation as they can get. You know that, Ken. Until we find out differently, we have to assume that Calvert was a persona invented by Rothwell, with Clegg's help, solely for pleasure."

Blackstone swallowed a mouthful of bhuna. "I

sometimes think I could do with one of those myself," he said.

Banks laughed. "Calvert helped Rothwell express another side of his nature, a side he couldn't indulge at home. Or perhaps it helped him be the way he used to be, relive something he'd lost. As Calvert, he'd have fun gambling and womanizing, and probably subsidizing himself with his illicit earnings from the money-laundering. And Pamela Jeffreys wasn't his only conquest, you know. There were no doubt others before her, and she was convinced that he'd met someone else, someone he'd really fallen for."

"That would upset the apple-cart, wouldn't it?" said Blackstone.

Banks stopped chewing for a moment.

"Alan?" Blackstone said. "Alan, are you all right? I know the curry's hot, but . . .''

"What? Oh, yes. It was just something you said, that's all. I'm surprised I never thought of it before."

"What?"

"If *Calvert* really did do it, you know, fall in love, the real thing, with all the bells and whistles, then what would happen to Rothwell?"

"I don't get you. It's the same person, isn't it?"

"Yes and no. What I mean is, how could he go on living his Rothwell life, the one we assumed was his *real* life, at Arkbeck Farm with Mary, Alison and Tom? Forgive me, I'm just thinking out loud, going nowhere. It doesn't matter."

"I do see what you mean," said Blackstone. "It would bugger up everything, wouldn't it?"

"Hmm." Banks finished his meal and washed away some of the spicy heat with a swig of watery lager. His lips still burned, though, and he felt prickles of sweat on his scalp. The signs of a good curry.

"Did the suspects in the Jeffreys beating know about Rothwell?" Blackstone asked.

Banks shook his head. "Don't know. They haven't been

seen locally, and they certainly don't match the daughter's description of his killers.''

''How old is she?''

''Alison? Fifteen.''

''She didn't see their faces. Could she be wrong?''

''It's possible, but not that wrong, I don't think. Nothing matches.''

''Just a thought. I mean, if Rothwell and Clegg were in the laundering business together, and whoever they were working for sent a couple of goons to find Clegg and whatever money he's made off with, you'd think they'd start with Rothwell's family, wouldn't you?''

''Perhaps. But we've been keeping too close a watch. They wouldn't dare show up within twenty miles of Arkbeck Farm.''

''And another thing: if they killed Rothwell, why did they use different people to chase down Clegg? It seems a bit excessive, doesn't it?''

''Again,'' said Banks, ''I can only guess. I think some of what's been happening took them by surprise. It's possible that they asked Clegg to get rid of Rothwell and he hired his own men. As you know, we're looking into what connections he might have had with criminal types.''

Blackstone nodded. ''I see,'' he said. ''Then Clegg became a problem and they had to send their own men?''

''Something like that.''

''Makes sense. Clegg was a bit of a ladies' man, you know, according to my DC who talked to his colleagues,'' Blackstone said.

''Yes. His estranged wife, Melissa, suggested as much. Did he have a girlfriend?''

''Yes. Apparently nothing serious since he split up with his wife. Prefers to play the field. Recently he's been seeing a receptionist from Norwich Insurance. Name of Marci Lapwing, if you can believe that. Aspiring actress. DC Gaitskill had a word with her this morning. Says she's a bit of a bimbo with obvious attractions. But he's a bit of an arsehole himself, is Gaitskill, so I'd take it with a pinch of salt. Anyway, they saw each other the Saturday before Clegg's disappearance. They went for dinner, then to a nightclub in Harehills. She spent the night with him and he took her home—that's Seacroft—after a pub lunch out at the Red Lion in Burnsall on Sunday afternoon. She hasn't seen or heard from him since.''

''Is she telling the truth?''

''Gaitskill says so. I'd trust him on that.''

''Okay. Thanks, Ken.''

''Clegg had a reserved parking space at the back of the Court Centre. According to what we could find out, he used to eat at a little trattoria on The Headrow after work on Thursdays. The waiters there remember him, all right. Nothing odd about his behaviour. He left about six-thirty or a quarter to seven last Thursday, heading west, towards where his car was parked, and that's the last sighting we have.''

''The car?''

''Red Jag. Gone. We've put it out over the PNC along with this.'' Blackstone took a photograph from his briefcase and slid it over the tablecloth. It showed the head and shoulders of a man in his early forties, with determined blue eyes, a slightly crooked nose, fair hair and a mouth that had a cruel twist to its left side.

''Clegg?''

Blackstone nodded and put the photograph back in his briefcase. ''We've also been through Clegg's house in Chapel Allerton. Nothing. Whatever he was up to, he kept it at the office.''

''Anything on Hamilton and the other car?''

''The boffins are still working on the car. I pulled Hamilton's record myself and we had another chat with him at the station this afternoon.'' He shook his head. ''I can't see it, Alan. The man's as thick as two short planks. I don't think he's even *heard* of St. Corona, and he's strictly small fry on the drugs scene. By the time he gets his stuff to sell, it's been stepped on by just about every dealer in the city.''

"It was just a thought. Thanks for giving it a try.''

"No problem. We'll have another shot in a day or two, just in case. And we'll keep a discreet eye on him. Look, back to what I was saying before. How do you think the goons knew about Pamela Jeffreys if she wasn't involved?''

Banks felt the anger flare up inside him again, but he held it in check. "That's all too easy," he said. "Remember, they were also following me around yesterday. I think they started at Clegg's office first thing yesterday morning and one, or both of them, stayed on my tail until I spotted them outside Calvert's flat that evening. They didn't know who the hell I was, and the only other person I met that they hadn't talked to already was Pamela Jeffreys. They must have thought we were in it together. I met her near the hall where she was rehearsing, and either one of them hung around to follow her home, or they found out some other way who she was and where she lived.

"She must have looked like their best lead so far. They thought she had some connection with Clegg and that she knew where he was or was holding something for him. Clegg has obviously got something they want. Most likely money. If he was laundering for their boss, then it looks like he might have skipped with a bundle. Either that or he's got some sort of evidence for blackmail—books, bank account records. And that's probably what they were looking for when they tore her place apart. Back to square one. The goons worked Pamela over because they thought she knew something, or had something of theirs. She didn't. And I blame myself. I should have bloody well known I was putting her at risk.''

"Come off it, Alan. How could you know?''

Banks shrugged and tapped out a cigarette. He was the only smoker in the entire restaurant and had to ask the waiter specially for an ashtray. It was getting like that these days, he noted glumly. He'd have to stop sometime soon; he knew he was only postponing the inevitable. He had thought about getting a nicotine patch, then quickly dismissed the idea. It was the feel of the cigarette between his fingers he wanted, the sharp intake of tobacco smoke into the lungs, not some slow oozing of poison through his skin into his blood. Pity about the health problems.

He felt rather like St. Augustine must have felt when he wrote in his *Confessions:* "Give me chastity and continency—but not yet!"

"You know what really pisses me off?" Banks said after he had lit the cigarette. "Dirty Dick Burgess was following me around that day, too, and it wouldn't surprise me at all if he'd seen them outside Melissa Clegg's shop."

"How would he know who they are?"

"Oh, I think he knows them, all right."

"Even so, what could he have done? They hadn't broken any laws."

Banks shrugged. "I suppose not. It's too bloody late now, anyway," he said. "Let's just hope they don't go back to see Betty Moorhead and Melissa Clegg."

"Don't worry. Charlie Waltham will have them both covered by now. He's a good bloke, Alan. And he'll have descriptions of Mutt and Jeff out, too. They won't get far."

"I hope not," said Banks. "I bloody hope not. I'd like a few minutes alone with them in a quiet cell."

3

Back at the hotel, Banks felt caged. Anger burned inside him like the hot Indian spices, but it would take more than Rennies to quell it. What a bloody fool he'd been to do nothing when he realized he had been followed. He had practically signed Pamela Jeffreys's death warrant, and it was through no virtue of his that she had survived her ordeal. So far.

He poured himself a shot of Bell's and turned on the television. Nothing but a nature programme, a silly comedy, an interview with a has-been politician and an old Dirty

Harry movie. He watched Clint Eastwood for a while. He had never much enjoyed cop films or cop programmes on television, but watching right here and now, he could identify with Dirty Harry tracking down the villains and dealing with them his own way. He had meant what he said to Blackstone. A few minutes alone with Pamela Jeffreys's attackers and they would know what police brutality was all about.

But he hated himself when he felt that way. Luckily, it was rare. After all, policemen are only human, he reminded himself. They have their loyalties, their lusts, their prejudices, their agonies, their tempers. The problem was that they have to keep these emotions in check to do their jobs properly.

"You go home and puke in your own time if you want to get anywhere in this job, lad," one of his early mentors had told him at a grisly crime scene. "You don't do it all over the corpse. And you go home and punch holes in your own wall, not in the child molester's face."

Unable to concentrate, even on Dirty Harry, he turned off the television. He couldn't stand up, couldn't sit down, didn't know what he wanted to do. And all the time, the anger and pain churned inside him, and he couldn't find a way to get them out.

He picked up the phone and dialled the code for Eastvale, then put it down before he started dialling his own number. He wanted to talk to Sandra, but he didn't think he could explain his feelings to her right now, especially the way they'd been drifting apart of late. God knew, under normal circumstances she was an understanding wife, but this would be pushing it a bit far: a woman he had lusted after, fantasized about, gets beaten within a hair's breadth of her life, and he's whipping himself over it. No, he couldn't explain that to Sandra.

And it wasn't just a fantasy. Had things turned out differently, he would have phoned Pamela Jeffreys again and would probably be having dinner or drinks with her right now, plucking up the courage to ask her up to his hotel room, Bell's at the ready. Well, he would never know the outcome now; his virtue hadn't even been put to the test. Hadn't St. Augustine said something about that, too, or was that someone else?

He phoned the hospital, and after a bit of officious rank-pulling, actually got a doctor on the line. Yes, Ms. Jeffreys was stable but still in intensive care . . . no, she was still unconscious . . . there was no way of telling when or if she would come round . . . no idea yet if there was any permanent damage. He didn't feel any better when he hung up.

It was just after nine-thirty. He knocked back the rest of the glass of Scotch, grabbed his sports jacket and went out. Maybe a walk would help, or the anonymous comfort of a crowded pub, not that he expected Leeds city centre on a Tuesday evening to be the West End.

He walked along Wellington Street past the National Express coach station and the tall Royal Mail Building to City Square, which was deserted except for the silent nymphs, who stood bearing their torches around the central statue of the Black Prince on his horse. From somewhere along Boar Lane, a drunk shouted in the night; a bottle smashed and a woman laughed loudly.

Banks crossed City Square. He walked fast, trying to burn off some of his rage, and soon found himself in the empty Bond Street Centre with only his reflection in the shop windows he passed.

His memories of Leeds city centre were vague, but he was sure that somewhere among the jungle of refurbished Victorian arcades and modern shopping centres there were a number of pubs down the dingy back alleys that riddled the heart of the old city centre.

And he was right.

The first one he found was an old brass, mirrors and dark wood Tetley's house with a fair-sized crowd and a jukebox at tolerable volume. He ordered a pint and stood sideways

at the bar, just watching people chat and laugh. It was
mostly a young crowd. Only kids seemed to venture into
the city centres at night these days. Perhaps that was why
their parents and grandparents stayed away. The pubs in
Armley and Bramley, in Headingley and Kirkstall, would
be full of locals of all age groups mixed together.

As he leaned against the bar, drinking and smoking, nobody paid him any attention. Banks had always been
pleased that he didn't stand out as an obvious policeman.
There'd be no mistaking Hatchley or Ken Blackstone no
matter how ''off duty'' they were, but Banks could fit in
almost anywhere without attracting too much attention.
Over the years, he had found it a useful quality. It wasn't
only that he didn't look like a copper, whatever that meant,
but for some reason his presence didn't set off the usual
warning bells. At the same time, he didn't like to sit or
stand with his back to the door, and he didn't miss much.

He finished his pint quickly and ordered another one,
lighting up again. He was smoking too much, he realized,
and he would feel it in the morning. But that was the morning. In the meantime, it gave him something to do with his
hands, which, left to their own devices, curled and hardened
into fists.

His second pint went down easily, too. The ebb and flow
of conversation washed over him. Loudest was a group of
two middle-aged couples sitting behind the engraved
smoked glass and dark wood at the side of the door. The
only people over twenty-five, apart from Banks and the bar
staff, they had all had a bit too much to drink. The men
were on pints of bitter, and the women on oddly coloured
concoctions with umbrellas sticking out of them and bits
of fruit floating around. By the sound of things they were
celebrating the engagement of one couple's daughter, who
wasn't present, and this brought forth all the old, blue jokes
Banks had ever heard in his life.

''There's these three women,'' said one of the men.
''The prostitute, the nymphomaniac and the wife. After sex,

the prostitute says, 'That's it, then,' all businesslike. The nympho says, 'That's *it*?' And the wife says, 'Beige. I think the ceiling should be beige.' ''

They howled with laughter. One of the women, a rather blowsy peroxide blonde, like a late-period Diana Dors, with too much make-up and unfocused eyes, looked over and winked at Banks. He winked back and she nudged her friend. They both started to laugh. A man Banks assumed to be her husband popped his head around the divide and said, ''Tha's welcome to her, lad, but I'll warn thee, she'll have thee worn out in a week. Bloody insatiable, she is.'' She hit him playfully and they all laughed so much they had tears in their eyes. Banks laughed with them, then turned away. The barmaid raised her eyebrows and drew a finger across her throat. Banks drank up and moved on.

Outside, he noticed that the evening had turned a little cooler and dark clouds were fast covering the stars. There was an electric edge to the air that presaged a storm. As if he didn't feel tense and wound up enough already without the bloody weather conspiring against him, too.

The next pub, down another alley off Briggate, was busier. Groups of young people stood about outside leaning against the wall or sitting on the wooden benches. The place danced with long shadows like something out of an old Orson Welles film. Banks took his pint out into the narrow, whitewashed alley and rested it on a ledge at elbow level, like a bar.

He thought of his last meeting with Pamela Jeffreys. She had run off in tears and he had stood there like an idiot in the park watching his ice-cream melt. He had wanted to apologize for treating her feelings so shoddily, but at the same time another part of him, the professional side, knew he had had to ask, and knew an apology would never be completely genuine. Still, he was only human; susceptible to beauty, he found her attractive, and he liked her warm, open personality, her enthusiasm for life and her sense of humour. Her connection with music also excited him. How much of that would she have left when she came out of hospital? If she came out.

Now, slurping his ale in a back alley in Leeds, he considered again what Blackstone had suggested about her involvement in the affair, but he didn't think Pamela Jeffreys was that good an actress. She had liked Calvert; they had had simple fun together, with no demands, no strings attached, no deep commitment. And what was wrong with that? She may have felt hurt when he found someone else—after all, nobody likes rejection—but she had liked him enough to swallow her pride and remain friends. She was young; she had energy enough to deal with a few hard knocks. If she had been jealous enough for murder, she would have killed Robert Calvert, probably in his Leeds flat, and if she had been involved in the laundering operation with Rothwell and Clegg, she wouldn't have phoned the Eastvale station and told them about Calvert.

It was close to eleven; most of the people had gone home. Banks ordered one more for the road, as he would be walking beside it, not driving on it. He was glad he had taken a little time out. The drink had helped douse his anger, or at least dampen it for a while. He was also rational enough to know that tomorrow he would be the professional again and nobody would ever know about his complex, knotted feelings of lust and guilt for Pamela Jeffreys.

He drained his glass, put his cigarettes back in his jacket pocket and set off down the alley. It was long and narrow, rough whitewashed stone on both sides, and lit only by a single high bulb behind wire mesh. When he was a couple of yards from the end, two men walked in from the street and blocked the exit. One of them asked Banks for a light.

Contrary to what one sees on television, detectives rarely find themselves in situations where immediate physical violence is threatened. Banks couldn't remember the last time he had been in a fight, but he didn't stop to try to remember. A number of thoughts flashed through his mind at once, but so quickly that an observer would not have seen him hesitate for a second.

First, he knew that they underestimated him; he was neither as drunk nor as unfit as they probably believed. Secondly, he had learned an important lesson from schoolyard fights: you go in first, fast, dirty and hard. Real violence doesn't take place in slow motion, like a Sam Peckinpah film; it's usually over before anyone realizes it has begun.

Before they could make their move, Banks took a step closer, pretended to fumble for matches, then grabbed the nearest one by his shirt-front and nutted him hard on the bridge of the nose. The man put his hands over his face and went down on his knees groaning as blood dripped down his shirt-front.

The other hesitated a moment to glance down at his friend. Mistake. Banks grabbed him by the arm, whirled him around and slammed him into the wall. Before the man could get his breath back, Banks punched him in the stomach, and as he bent forward in pain brought his knee up into the man's face. He felt cheekbone or teeth smash against his kneecap. The man fell, putting his hands to his mouth to stem the flow of blood and vomit.

His mate had clambered to his feet by now and he threw himself at Banks, knocking him hard into the wall and banging the side of his head against the rough stone. He got in a couple of close body punches, but before he could gain any further advantage, Banks pushed him back far enough to start throwing quick jabs at his already broken nose. In the sickly light of the alley, Banks could see blood smeared over his attacker's face, almost closing one eye and dripping down his chin. The man backed off and slumped against the wall.

By this time, the other was back wobbling on his feet, and Banks went for him. He aimed one sharp blow to the head after the other, splitting an eyebrow, a lip, jarring a tooth loose. The other stumbled away towards the exit. There was no fight left in either of them, but Banks couldn't stop. He kept slugging away at the man in front of him, feeling the anger in him explode and pour out. When the man tried to protect his face with his hands, Banks pummelled his exposed stomach and ribs.

The man backed away, begging Banks to stop hitting him. His friend, swaying at the alley's exit now, yelled, "Come on, Kev, run for it! He's a fucking maniac! He'll fucking kill us both!" And they both staggered off towards Commercial Street.

Banks watched them go. There was no-one else around, thank God. The whole debacle couldn't have taken more than a couple of minutes. When they were out of sight, Banks fell back against the whitewashed wall, shaking, sweating, panting. He took several deep breaths, smoothed his clothes and headed back to the hotel.

: 11

1

The storm broke in the middle of the night. Banks lay in the dark in his strange hotel bed tossing and turning as lightning flashed and thunder first rumbled in the distance then cracked so loudly overhead that the windows rattled.

Once unbound, the shape of his rage was fluid; it could be as easily warped and twisted into fanciful images by sleep as it had been channelled into violence earlier. He kept waking from one nightmare and drifting back into another. Rain lashed against the windows, and in the background something hissed constantly, the way something always hisses in hotel rooms.

In the worst nightmare, the one he remembered the most clearly, he was talking on the telephone to a woman who had dialled his number by mistake. She sounded disoriented, and the longer she spoke the longer the spaces stretched between her words. Finally, silence took over completely. Banks called hello a few times, then hung up. As soon as he had done so, he was stricken by panic. The woman was committing suicide. He knew it. She had taken an overdose of pills and fallen into a coma while she was still on the line. He didn't know her name or her telephone number. If he had kept the line open and not hung up, he would have been able to trace her and save her life.

He awoke feeling guilty and depressed. And it wasn't only his soul that hurt. His head pounded from too much whisky and from the ''Glasgow handshake'' he had given one of his attackers, his chest felt tight from smoking, his knuckles ached, and his side felt sore where he had been slammed into the wall. His mouth tasted as dry as the bottom of a budgie's cage and as sour as month-old milk. When he got up to go to the toilet, he felt a stabbing pain shoot through his kneecap and found himself limping. He felt about ninety. He took three extra-strength Panadols from his traveller's survival kit and washed them down with two glasses of cold water.

It was four twenty-three A.M. by the red square numbers of the digital clock. Cars hissed by through the puddles in the road. Around the edges of the curtains, he could see the sickly amber glow of the street-lights and the occasional flash of distant lightning as the storm passed over to the north.

He didn't want to be awake, but he couldn't seem to get back to sleep. All he could do was lie there feeling sorry for himself, remembering what a bloody fool he had been. What had started as a simple bit of childish self-indulgence, drowning his sorrows in drink, had turned into a full-blown exhibition of idiocy, and both his skinned knuckles and the empty Scotch bottle on the bedside table were evidence enough of that.

After the fracas, he had dashed back to the hotel and hurried straight up to his room before anyone could notice his bloody knuckles or torn jacket. Once safe inside, he had poured himself a stiff drink to stop the shakes. Lying on the bed watching television until the programmes ended for the night, he had poured another, then another. Soon, the halfbottle was empty and he had fallen asleep. Now it was time to pay. He had heard once that guilt and shame contributed to the pain of hangovers, and at four thirty-two that morning, he certainly believed it.

Christ, it was so bloody easy to slide down one's thoughts into the pit of misery and self-recrimination at four thirty-two A.M. At four thirty-two, if you feel ill, you just *know* you have cancer; at four thirty-two, if you feel depressed, suicide seems the only way out. Four thirty-two is the perfect time for fear and self-loathing, the time of the dark night of the soul.

But it wouldn't do, he told himself. Feeling sorry for himself just wouldn't bloody well do. So he wasn't perfect. He had contemplated committing adultery. So what? He wasn't the first and he wouldn't be the last. He felt responsible for Pamela Jeffreys's injuries. Maybe, just *maybe*, he should have acted differently when he knew he was being followed—put a guard on everyone he had talked to—but it was a big maybe. He wasn't God almighty; he couldn't anticipate everything.

Most detective work was pissing about in the dark, anyway, waiting for the light to grow slowly, as it was doing now outside. On rare occasions, the truth hit you quick as a lightning flash. But they were very rare occasions indeed. Even then, before the lightning hit you, you had spent months looking for the right place to stand.

So last night, in the alley, he had lost it. So what? Two yobbos had tried to mug him and he had gone wild on them, plastered them all over the walls. Most of it was a blur now, but he remembered enough to embarrass him.

They had just been kids, really, early twenties at most, out looking for aggro. But one had been black and one white, like the men who had put Pamela Jeffreys in hospital. Banks knew in his mind that they weren't the same ones, but when the bubble of his anger burst and the fury unleashed itself, when the blood started to flow, they were the ones he was lashing out at. No wonder they ran away shitting bricks. There was nothing rational about it; blinded by rage, he had thought he was hurting the people he really wanted to hurt. He had taken out his anger on two unwary substitutes. They had simply been in the wrong place at the wrong time.

Still, he told himself, they bloody well deserved it, bleeding amateurs. At least he might have discouraged two apprentice muggers from their chosen career. And nobody would ever know what happened. *They* certainly wouldn't

say anything. After all, he *hadn't* killed them; they had
managed to run away and lick their wounds. They would
survive to fight again another day, if they got back the
bottle. It wasn't the worst thing he had ever done. And
soon, surely, that feeling of being a total fucking idiot
would go away and he could get on with his life.

He dozed briefly and woke again at five forty-one. Not
quite as bad as four thirty-two, he thought, at first glance.
He got up and looked outside at the grey morning. The
road and pavement were still awash with puddles. Green
double-decker buses were already running people to work,
splashing up the water where it had collected in the gutters.
Banks was on the fifth floor, and he could see the grey sky
streaked with blood and milk behind the majestic dome of
the Town Hall. Already, dim shadows were shuffling out
of the Salvation Army shelter opposite.

Banks made a cup of instant coffee with the electric kettle and sachet provided and took it back to bed with him.
He turned on the bedside light and picked up the copy of
Evelyn Waugh's *Sword of Honour* trilogy he had brought
with him. Guy Crouchback's misadventures should cheer
him up a bit. At least he didn't have *that* much misfortune.

He would put last night behind him, he decided, sipping
the weak Nescafé. A man was allowed his mistakes; he had
just better not cling to them or they would drag him down
to the bottom of the abyss.

2

At nine o'clock that morning, Susan Gay sat alone on the
second pew from the back of the small non-denominational
chapel at Eastvale Crematorium. It was cool inside, thanks
to a large fan below the western stained-glass window, and
the lighting was suitably dimmed. The place smelled of
shoepolish, not the usual musty hymn-books she associated
with chapels.

The service went briskly enough. The rent-a-vicar said a

few words about Keith Rothwell's devotion to his family
and his dedication to hard work, then he read Psalm 51.
Susan thought it particularly apt, all that guff about being
cleansed of sin. ''Bloodguiltiness'' was a word she hadn't
heard before, and it made her give a little shudder without
knowing why. The mention of ''burnt offering'' brought
the unwelcome image of Rothwell's corpse, the head a
black mess, as if it had indeed been burned, but ''Wash
me; and I shall be whiter than snow'' almost made her
laugh out loud. It brought to mind an old television advert
for detergent, then Rothwell's money-laundering.

After the vicar read a bit from ''Revelation'' about a new
heaven and a new earth and all sorrow pain and death disappearing, it was all over.

The Rothwells, all suitably dressed in shades of black for
the occasion, sat on the front row. Throughout the ceremony, Mary sat stiffly, Alison kept glancing around her at
the stained-glass and the font, and Tom sat hunched over.
As far as Susan could tell from behind, nobody reached for
a handkerchief.

When she watched them walk out into the sunlight, she
could tell she was right: dry eyes; not a tear in sight; Mary
Rothwell doing her stiff-upper-lip routine, bearing her loss
and grief with dignity.

Everyone ignored Susan except Tom, who approached
her and said, ''You're the detective who was at our house
when I got back from the States, aren't you?''

''Yes. DC Susan Gay, in case you've forgotten.''

''I hadn't forgotten. What are you doing here?''

''I'd like a word with you, if you can spare a few
minutes.''

Tom took a silver pocket-watch from his waistcoat and
looked at it. Susan saw it was attached by a chain to one
of his belt loops. Somehow, it seemed like a very affected
gesture in one so young. Maybe it had impressed the Americans. He slipped it back in his pocket. ''All right,'' he said.
''But I can't come just now. Everyone's going back to Mr.

Pratt's for coffee and cake. I'll have to show up."

"Of course. How about an hour?"

"Okay."

"Look, it's a fine morning," Susan said. "How about that café by the river, the one near the pre-Roman site?"

"I know it."

Susan busied herself with paperwork back at the station for three quarters of an hour, then set off to keep her appointment.

The River Swain was flowing swiftly, still high after the spring thaw. On the grass by the bank, the owner of the small café had stuck a couple of rickety white tables and chairs. Susan bought a tin of Coke for Tom and a pot of tea for herself and they sat by the water. Two weeping willows framed the rolling farmland beyond. Right across, in the centre of the view, was a field of bright yellow rapeseed.

Flies buzzed around her head, and Susan kept fanning them away. "How was it?" she asked.

Tom shrugged. "I hate those kinds of social gatherings," he said. "And Laurence Pratt gets on my nerves."

Susan smiled. At least they had something in common. She let the silence stretch as she looked closely at the youth sitting opposite her. Wavy brown hair fell over his ears about halfway down his neck. He was tanned, slender, handsome, and he looked as good now in his mourning suit as he had in torn jeans and a denim shirt. The more she let herself simply feel his presence, the more she was sure she was right about him.

He shifted in his chair. "Look," he said, "I'm sorry about the other day. I was rude, I know. But I was tired, upset."

"I understand," Susan said. "It's just that I got the impression there was something you wanted to tell me."

Tom looked away over the river. His face was scrunched up in a frown, or maybe the sun was in his eyes. "You know, don't you?" he asked. "You can tell."

"That you're homosexual? I have a strong suspicion, yes."

"Am I that obvious?"

Susan laughed. "Maybe not to everyone. Remember, I'm a detective."

Tom managed a weak smile. "Funny thing, that, isn't it?" he said. "You'd think it would be men who'd guess."

"I don't know. Women are used to responding to men in certain ways. They can tell when something's . . ."

"Wrong?"

"I was going to say missing, but even that's not right."

"Different, then?"

"That'll do. Look, I'm not judging you, Tom. You mustn't think that. It's really none of my business, unless your sexual preference connects somehow with your father's murder."

"I can't see how it does."

"You're probably right. Tell me about this Aston, or Afton, then. When Chief Inspector Banks mentioned the name, you assumed it was a man. Why?"

"Because I didn't assume. I know damn well who he is. His name's Ashton. Bloody Clive Ashton. How could I forget?"

"Who is he?"

"He's the son of one of my father's clients—Lionel Ashton. We were at a party together once. I made a mistake."

"You made advances towards him?"

"Yes."

"And they weren't welcome?"

Tom gave a dry laugh. "Obviously not. He told his father."

"And?"

"And his father told my father. And my father told me I was disgusting, sick, *queer*, and that I should see about getting myself cured. That's the exact word he used, *cured*. He said it would kill Mum if she ever found out."

"And he suggested you take off to America for a while, at his expense?"

"Yes. But that came a bit later. First we let it lie while we figured out what was best."

"What did you do in the meantime?"

Tom looked at her, tilted his tin back and finished his Coke. His Adam's apple bobbed up and down. Susan turned away and watched a family of ducks drift by on the Swain. Tom wiped his lips with the back of his hand, then said, "I followed him."

She turned back towards him. "You followed your father? Why?"

"Because I thought he was up to something. He was away so often. He was always so remote, like he wasn't really with us even when he was at home. I thought he was doing damage to the family."

"He wasn't always like that?"

Tom shook his head. "No. Believe it or not, Dad used to have a bit of life about him. I'm sorry, I didn't intend to make a bad joke."

"I know. How long had he been behaving this way?"

"Hard to say. It was gradual, like. But this past couple of years it was getting worse. You could hardly talk to him." He shrugged.

"Was that the only reason you followed him, because you thought he was up to something?"

"I don't know. Maybe I wanted to get something on *him*. Revenge, I don't know. Find out what *his* guilty secret was."

"And did you?"

Tom took a deep breath, held it for a moment, then let it out loudly with a nervous laugh. "This is harder than I thought. Okay. Here goes. Yes. I saw my father with another woman." He said it fast, staccato-style. "There, that's it. I said it."

Susan paused a moment to take the information in, then asked, "When?"

"Sometime in February."

"Where?"

"Leeds. In a pub. They were sitting together at a table in the Guildford, on The Headrow. They were holding hands. Christ." His eyes were glassy with gathering tears. He rubbed the backs of his hands over them and collected himself. "Do you know what that feels like?" he asked. "Seeing your old man with another woman. No, of course you don't. It was like a kick in the balls. Sorry."

"That's all right. Did your father see you?"

"No. I kept myself well enough hidden. Not that they had eyes for anyone but each other."

"What happened next?"

"Nothing. I left. I was so upset I just got in the van and drove around the countryside for a while. I remember stopping somewhere and walking by a river. It was very cold."

"Was the woman dark-skinned? Indian or Pakistani?"

Tom looked surprised. "No."

Susan took her notepad and pen out. "What did she look like?"

Tom closed his eyes. "I can see her now," he said, "just as clearly as I could then. She was young, much younger than Dad. Probably in her mid-twenties, I'd guess. Not much older than me. She was sitting down, so I couldn't really see her figure properly, but I'd say it was good. I mean, she didn't look fat or anything. She looked nicely proportioned. She was wearing a blouse made of some shiny white material and a scarf sort of thing, more like a shawl, really, over her shoulders, all in blues, whites and reds. It looked like one of those Liberty patterns. She had long fingers. I noticed them for some reason. Am I going too fast?"

"No," said Susan. "I've got my own kind of shorthand. Carry on."

"Long, tapered fingers. No nail varnish, but her nails looked well kept, not bitten or anything. She had blonde hair. No, that's not quite accurate. It was a kind of reddish blonde. It was piled and twisted on top with some strands falling loose over her cheeks and shoulders. You know the kind of look? Sort of messy but ordered.''

Susan nodded. Hairstyles like that cost a fortune.

"She was extraordinarily good-looking,'' Tom went on. "Very fine, pale skin. A flawless complexion, like marble, sort of translucent. The kind where you can just about see the blue veins underneath. And her features could have been cut by a fine sculptor. High cheekbones, small, straight nose. Her eyes were an unusual shade of blue. They may have been contact lenses, but they were sort of light but very bright blue. Cobalt, I guess. Is that it?''

"It'll do. Go on.''

"That's about all really. No beauty spots or anything. She was wearing long dangly earrings, too. Lapis lazuli. No rings, I don't think.''

"That's a very good description, Tom. Do you think you could work with a police artist on this? I think we'd like to have a talk with this woman, and your description might help us find her.''

Tom nodded. "No problem. I could paint her myself from memory if I had the talent.''

"Good. We'll arrange something, then. Maybe this evening.''

Tom took his watch out again. "I suppose I'd better be going home. Mum and Alison need my support.''

"Did you ever challenge your father about what you saw?'' Susan asked.

Tom shook his head. "I came close once, when he kept going on about how disappointed he was in me, how sick I was. I told him I was disappointed in him, too, but I wouldn't tell him why.''

"What did he say?''

"Nothing. Just carried on as if I hadn't spoken.''

"Does your mother know?''

He shook his head. "No. She doesn't know. I'm sure of it.''

"Do you think she suspects?"

"Maybe. Who knows? She's been living in a bit of a dream world. I'm worried about her, actually. Sometimes I get the feeling that underneath all the lies she knows the truth but she just won't admit it to herself. Do you know what I mean?"

"Yes. What about Alison?"

"Alison's a sweet thing really, but she hasn't got a clue. Lives in her books. She's Brontë mad, is Alison, you know. Reads nothing but. And she's got notebooks full of her own stories, all in tiny handwriting like the Brontës did when they were kids. Made up her own world. I keep thinking she'll grow out of it, but . . . I don't know . . . she seems even worse since . . . since Dad . . ." He shook his head slowly. "No, she doesn't know. I wouldn't confide in her. I kept it all to myself. Can you imagine that? I still do. You're the first person I've told." He stood up. "Look, I really must be off."

"We'll be in touch about the artist, then."

"Yes. Okay. And . . ."

"Yes?"

"Thanks," he said, then turned abruptly and hurried off.

Susan watched him go down the path, hands in pockets, shoulders slumped. She poured herself another cup of tea, stewed though it was, and looked out at the river. A beautiful insect with iridescent wings hovered a few feet above the water. Suddenly, a chaffinch shot out from one of the trees and took the insect in its beak in mid-air. Susan left her lukewarm tea and headed off to meet Sergeant Hatchley. The porn hunt awaited.

3

After Banks had gone for a swim in the hotel pool, taken a long sauna, and put away three cups of freshly brewed coffee and a plateful of bacon and eggs, courtesy of room service, he was feeling much better.

As he made a few phone calls, he tried to remember something that had been nagging away at him since the early hours, something he should do, but he failed miserably. At about the same time that Susan Gay was talking to Tom Rothwell, he went out for his first appointment, with Melissa Clegg.

The morning sun had burned off most of the rain, and the pavements had absorbed the rest, leaving them the colour of sandstone, with small puddles catching the light here and there. As wind ruffled the water's surface, golden light danced inside the puddles.

It wasn't as warm as it had been, Banks noticed. He had left his torn sports jacket at the hotel. All he wore on top was a light blue, open-neck shirt. He carried his notebook, wallet, keys and cigarettes in his briefcase.

A cool wind whispered through the streets, and there were plenty of dark, heavy clouds now lurking on the northern horizon behind the Town Hall. It looked like the region was in for some ''changeable'' weather, as the forecasters called it: sunny with cloudy periods, or cloudy with sunny periods.

He could drive to his appointment, he knew, but the one-way system was a nightmare. Besides, the city centre wasn't all that big, and the fresh air would help blow away the cobwebs that still clung to his brain.

Banks had grown quite fond of Leeds since he had been living in Yorkshire. It had an honest, slightly shabby charm about it that appealed to him, despite the new ''Leeds-look'' architecture—redbrick revival with royal blue trim—that had sprouted up everywhere, and despite the modern shopping centres and the yuppie developments down by the River Aire. Leeds was a scruff by nature; it wouldn't look comfortable in fancy dress, no matter what the price. And then there was Opera North, of course.

Avoiding City Square and the scene of the previous evening's debacle, he cut up King Street instead, walked past the recently restored Metropole Hotel, all redbrick and gold sandstone masonry, and along East Parade through the business section of banks and insurance buildings in all their jumbled glory. Here, Victorian Gothic rubbed shoulders with Georgian classicism and sixties concrete and glass. As in many cities, you had to look up, above eye level, to see the interesting details on the tops of the buildings: surprising gables where pigeons nested, gargoyles, balconies, caryatids.

As he walked along The Headrow past Stumps and the art gallery, he became aware again of the sharp pain in his knee, with which he had probably chipped a cheekbone or broken a jaw the previous evening.

He arrived at the Merrion Centre a couple of minutes early. Melissa Clegg had told him on the phone that she had a very busy day planned. She was expecting a number of important deliveries and had appointments with her suppliers. She could, however, allow him half an hour. There was a quiet coffee bar with outside tables, she told him, on the second level, up the steps over the entrance to Le Phonographique. She would meet him there at half past ten.

Banks found the coffee bar, and an empty table, with no trouble. At that time on a Wednesday morning, the Merrion Centre was practically deserted: especially the upper level, which seemed to have nothing but small offices and hairdressers.

Melissa Clegg arrived on time with all the flurry of the busy executive. When she sat down, she tucked her hair behind her ears. Today, she wore a pink dress cut square at her throat and shoulders.

The last thing on earth Banks felt he needed was another cup of coffee, but he took an espresso just to have something in front of him. Also, by the feel of his chest, he didn't need a cigarette, either, but he lit one nonetheless. The first few drags made him a bit dizzy, then it tasted fine.

"You look a bit the worse for wear," Melissa observed.

"You should have seen the other two," Banks said. He could tell by the way she laughed that she didn't believe him, just as he had expected. But he had also noticed the angry contusion high on his left cheek, just to the side of his eye, when he shaved that morning. Another result of his crash into the alley wall. He tried to keep his skinned knuckles out of sight, which made drinking coffee difficult.

"What can I do for you this time, Inspector, or Chief Inspector, is it?"

"Chief Inspector. I don't suppose you've heard anything from your husband?"

"Ex. Well, near as. No, I haven't. But he's hardly likely to get in touch with me. I still don't know why you're so worried. I'm sure he'll turn up."

"I don't think so, Mrs. Clegg. Remember last time we met I asked you if you knew a Robert Calvert?"

"Yes. I said I didn't and I still don't."

"I'd appreciate it if you would keep this quiet for the moment, but we believe that Robert Calvert was also Keith Rothwell."

"I don't understand. Do you mean he had a false name, an alias?"

"Something like that. More, actually. He lived in Leeds, had a flat in the name of Robert Calvert. A whole other life. Mary Rothwell doesn't know, so—"

"Don't worry, I won't say anything. You've got me puzzled."

"We were, too. But the reason I'm telling you this is that your husband acted as a reference for Robert Calvert in the matter of his bank account and credit card. Also, ironically enough, Calvert listed his employer as Keith Rothwell."

"Curiouser and curiouser," said Melissa. "Daniel must have known about this double life, then?"

"It looks that way."

"Well, I certainly knew nothing about it. As I told you before, I haven't seen Keith Rothwell since Danny and I split up two years ago." She frowned. "I must say it surprises me that Daniel would risk doing something so obviously dishonest as that. Not that dishonesty is beneath him, but it seems too much of a risk for no return.''

"We don't know what the returns were," Banks said. "How close are you and Daniel?"

"What do you mean?"

"Did he ever mention a woman called Marci Lapwing to you?"

"God, what a name. No. Who is she? His girlfriend?"

"Someone he's been seeing lately."

"Well, he wouldn't tell me about her, would he?"

"Why not?"

She shrugged. "He never does. Maybe he thinks I'd be jealous.''

"Would you?"

"Look, I don't see what it has to do with anything, but no. It's over. O. V. E. R. We made our choices."

"Is there someone else?"

She blushed a little but met his gaze with steady eyes as she fingered the top of her dress over her freckled collarbone. "As a matter of fact there is. But I won't tell you anything more. I don't want him dragged into this. It's none of your business, anyway. Danny's probably run off with his bimbo.''

"No. Marci Lapwing is still around. Never mind. Let's move on. How do you explain the two men who visited you?''

"I don't know. Perhaps her husband sent them?"

"Whose husband?"

"The bimbo's. Marci whatever-her-name-is."

"She's not married. Since we last talked," Banks said, lowering his voice, "things have taken several turns for the worse. We're talking about very serious matters indeed. It looks as if your husband might be implicated in murder, money-laundering, theft and fraud, and that he may be partly responsible for the savage beating of a young woman.''

"My God . . . I . . .''

"I know. You didn't take all this seriously. Nor did you want to. Now will you?"

She began to fidget with her coffee-spoon. "Yes. Yes, of course. I assume you're talking about Keith Rothwell's murder?"

"Yes."

"And who has been beaten?"

"A friend of Mr. Rothwell's. The way it looks, both Keith Rothwell and your husband were laundering money for a Mr. X. We think we know his identity, but I'm afraid I can't reveal it to you. Rothwell was either stealing or threatening to talk, or both, and Mr. X asked your husband to get rid of him."

She shook her head. "Danny? No. I don't believe it. He couldn't kill anyone."

"Hear me out, Mrs. Clegg. He did as he was asked. Maybe his own life was threatened, we don't know. Immediately after he arranged to get rid of Keith Rothwell, he either became a threat himself, or he made off with a lot of illegal money, so Mr. X sent two goons to track him down. Maybe he'd seen it coming and anticipated what they would do. At this point, there's a lot we can only speculate about."

"And that explains the two men?"

"Yes." Banks leaned forward and rested his arms on the table. "They visited your ex-husband's office, they visited you, then they visited a girl they saw me talking to. She was the one they beat up. Now tell me again, Mrs. Clegg, have you ever seen or heard of a woman called Pamela Jeffreys? She was born here in Yorkshire, but her family came originally from Pakistan. She's about five foot four, slender figure, with almond eyes and long black hair that she sometimes wears tied back. She has a smooth, dark gold complexion and a gold stud through her left nostril. She's a classical musician, a violist with the Northern Philharmonia."

Banks watched Melissa's face as he described Pamela

Jeffreys. When he had finished, she shook her head. "Honestly," she said, "I've never seen her, and Danny never mentioned anyone like that. She sounds impressive, but he doesn't go for that type."

"What type?"

"Bright women. Career women. It scared him to death when I started to make a success of the wine business. At first he could just look down on it as my little hobby. You said she was a classical musician?"

"Yes."

"He doesn't like classical music. All he likes is that bloody awful trad jazz. A woman like the one you describe would bore Danny to death. Besides, she sounds so gorgeous, I'm sure I'd remember her."

A gentle gust of wind blew through the centre, carrying the smells of espresso and fried bacon from the café. "Two more things," Banks said. "First, in the time you lived with your husband, did you ever come across any acquaintances, say, or clients of his whom you'd describe as shady?"

She laughed. "Oh, a tax lawyer has plenty of shady clients, Chief Inspector. That's what keeps him in business. But I assume you mean something other than that?"

"Yes. If Daniel did have anything to do with Keith Rothwell's death, he certainly didn't commit the murder himself, as you pointed out."

"That's true. The Daniel I know wouldn't have had the stomach for it."

"So he must have hired someone. You don't usually just walk into your local and say, 'Look chaps, I need a couple of killers. Do you think you could help me out?'"

Melissa smiled. "You might try it at a Law Society banquet. I'm sure you'd get a few takers. But I see what you mean."

"So he might have known someone who would consider the task, and it might have been someone he met through his practice. I doubt very much that the two of you socialized with hit-men, but there might be someone who struck you as dangerous, perhaps?''

''Who knows who we socialized with?'' Melissa said. ''Who knows anything about anyone, when it comes right down to it? No-one immediately springs to mind, but I'll think about it, if I may.''

''Okay.'' Banks passed on Alison Rothwell's vague description of the two men, especially the one with the puppy-dog eyes, the only distinguishing feature. ''I'll be at the Holiday Inn here for the next day or so, or you can leave a message with Detective Inspector Blackstone at Millgarth.''

''Is he the one who came over last night with my bodyguard?''

''No, that's Detective Sergeant Waltham. I don't honestly believe you're in any danger, Mrs. Clegg—I think they're probably miles from here by now—but it's best to be on the safe side. Are you happy with the arrangement?''

''I didn't really understand all the fuss at first, but after what you've just told me I'll sleep easier tonight for knowing there's someone out there watching over me.'' She looked at her watch. ''Sorry, Mr. Banks. Time's pressing. You said you had two things to ask.''

''Yes. The other is a bit more personal.''

Melissa raised her eyebrows. ''Yes?''

''I mean personal in the true sense, not necessarily embarrassing.''

She frowned, still looking at him. It was a strong, attractive face with its reddish tan and freckles over the nose and upper cheeks; every little wrinkle around her grey-blue eyes looked as if it had been earned.

''We think Daniel Clegg has probably done a bunk with a lot of money,'' Banks began. ''Enough to set him up for life, otherwise these goons wouldn't be so keen on finding him. But it's a bloody big world if you don't know where to look. The two of you shared your dreams at one stage, I suppose, like most married couples. Where do you think he would go? Where did he dream of living?''

Melissa continued to frown. "I see what you mean," she murmured. "That's an interesting question. Where's Danny's Shangri-la, his Eldorado?"

"Yes. We all have one, don't we?"

"Well, Danny wasn't much of a dreamer, to tell you the truth. He didn't have a lot of imagination. But whenever he talked of winning the pools and packing it all in, it was always Tahiti."

"Tahiti?"

"Yes. He was a big fan of *Mutiny on the Bounty*. Had every version on video. I think he liked the idea of those barebreasted native girls serving him long, cool drinks in coconut shells." She laughed and looked at her watch again. "Look, Mr. Banks, I'm sorry, but I really *do* have to go now. I've got a hell of a day ahead." She pushed her chair back and stood up.

Banks stood with her. "Of course," he said, shaking her hand.

"But if I can be any more help, I'll get in touch. I mean it. I never thought Danny was capable of real evil, but if what you say is true . . ." She shrugged. "Anyway, I'll give what you said some thought. I . . . just a minute."

Her brow furrowed and she turned her eyes up, as if inspecting her eyelashes. She looked at her watch again, bit her lip, then perched on the edge of the chair, knees together, clutching her briefcase to her chest. "There *was* someone. I really can't stay. I'm going to be late. I can't think of the name, but I might be able to remember if you give me a bit of time. He did have those sort of sad eyes, like a puppy, now I think of it."

Banks sat forward. "What were the circumstances?"

"I told you Danny doesn't do criminal work, but he is a solicitor, and apparently he was the only one this chap knew. According to Danny, they met in a pub, had a few drinks, got talking. You know how it is. This chap had been in the army or something, over in Northern Ireland. When he got himself arrested, Danny was the only one he knew to call on.''

''What happened?''

''Danny referred him to someone else. I only remember because he came round to the house once. He wasn't too happy about the solicitor Danny passed him on to for some reason. I think it might have been the fee or something like that. They argued a bit, then Danny managed to calm him down. They had a drink, then the man left. I never saw or heard of him again. I'm sorry, I didn't really hear what was going on. Not that I'd remember now.''

''How long ago was it?''

''A little over two years. Shortly before we separated.''

''And you remember nothing more about this man?''

''No. Not off-hand.''

''What pub did they meet in?''

''I can't remember. Isn't that odd? You mentioning about meeting a killer in a pub? What if it was him?''

''What was he arrested for?''

''It was something to do with assault, I think. A fight. I know it wasn't really serious. Certainly not murder or anything. Look, I really must go. I'll try and remember more, I promise.''

''Just one thing,'' Banks said. ''Can you remember the name of the solicitor your husband referred him to? We might be able to trace him through our records.''

She compressed her lips in thought for a moment, then said, ''Atkins. Of course, it would have been Harvey Atkins. He and Danny are good friends, and Harvey does a fair bit of criminal work.''

''Thank you,'' Banks said, but she was already dashing away.

''I'll be in touch,'' she called over her shoulder.

Banks headed for the staircase. While he had been talking with Melissa Clegg, he had remembered what it was that had been nagging at him all morning. He decided to satisfy his curiosity before meeting Ken Blackstone. Things were moving fast.

: 12

"Take the scenic route," said Sergeant Hatchley. "We're not in a hurry."

Instead of going east to the A1 at the roundabout by the Red Lion Hotel, Susan headed south-west along the edge of the Dales through Masham, Ripon and Harrogate.

Hatchley didn't smoke at all during the journey, though he insisted she stop once at a café in Harrogate for a cup of coffee, during which he chain-smoked three cigarettes. It was very different from travelling with Banks. For a start, Banks liked to drive, and with him there was always music, sometimes tolerable, sometimes execrable. Hatchley preferred to sit with his arms crossed and look out of the window at the passing scenery, no doubt with visions of bare breasts flashing through what passed for his mind.

She wished she didn't have to work with men all the time. One crying jag or sharp response, and it was PMT; a day off for any reason meant it was "that time of the month." She had to put up with it without complaint, just take it all in her stride.

Maybe she was being unfair, though. Hatchley aside, the men she worked with were mostly okay. Phil Richmond, with whom she spent the most time, was a sweetheart. But Phil was leaving soon.

Superintendent Gristhorpe frightened her a little, perhaps because he made her think of her father, and she always felt like a silly little girl when he was around.

Banks, though, was like an older brother. And, like a brother, he teased her too much, especially about music when they were in the car. She was sure he played some terrible things just to make her uncomfortable. Right now, though, as she approached the busy Leeds Ring Road, she would have welcomed something soothing to listen to.

Susan was building up a nice collection of classical music. Every month, she bought a magazine that gave away a free CD of bits and pieces of the works reviewed. It provided a breakdown of what to listen for at what points of time—like "6:25: The warm and sunny feeling of the spring day returns," or "4:57: Second theme emerges from interplay of brass and woodwinds." Susan found it very helpful, and if she liked the part she heard, she would buy the complete work, unless it was a lengthy and expensive opera. At the moment her favourite piece was Beethoven's "Pastoral" Symphony. She knew Banks would approve, but she was too embarrassed to tell him.

Susan went on to think about her talk with Tom Rothwell by the river, and about the agonies he must be going through. It was hard enough being homosexual anywhere, she imagined, but it would be especially tough in Yorkshire, where men prided themselves on their masculinity and women were supposed to know their place and stick to it.

There was a prime example of Yorkshire manhood sitting right next to her, she thought, all Rugby League, roast beef and pints of bitter. And she couldn't imagine what he could find offensive about her perfume. It certainly smelled pleasant enough to her, and she used it sparingly.

The traffic snarled up on the Ring Road, and Hatchley sat there with the tattered Leeds and Bradford *A to Z* on his lap squinting at signs. He was the kind of navigator who shouted, "Turn here!" just as you passed by the turning. After several misdirections and a couple of hair-raising U-turns, they pulled up outside candidate number one, a newsagent's shop at the edge of a rundown council estate in Gipton.

Two scruffy kids swaggered out as Susan and Hatchley

went in. The girl behind the counter couldn't have been more than fifteen or sixteen. She was pale as a ghost and skinny as a rake. Her hair, brown streaked with silver, red and green, teetered untidily on top of her head, and unruly strands snaked down over her white neck and face, partly covering one over-mascaraed eye.

She looked as if she had a small, pretty mouth underneath the full and pouting one she had superimposed with brownish purple lipstick. Susan also noticed a pungent scent, which she immediately classified as cheap, not at all like her own. The girl rested her ring-laden fingers with the long crimson nails on the counter and slanted her bony shoulders towards them, head tilted to one side. She wore a baggy white T-shirt with "SCREW YOU" written in black across her flat chest.

"Mr. Drake around, love?" Hatchley asked.

She moved her head a fraction; the hair danced like Medusa's snakes. "In the back," she said, without breaking the rhythm of her chewing.

He moved towards the counter and lifted the flap.

"Hey!" she said. "You can't just walk through like that."

"Can't I, love? Do you mean I have to be announced all formally, like?" Hatchley took out his identification and held it close to her eyes. She squinted as she read. "Maybe you'd like to get out your salver?" he went on. "Then I can put my calling card on it and you can take it through to Mr. Drake and inform him that a gentleman wishes to call on him?"

"Sod off, clever arse," she said, slouching aside to let them pass. "You're no fucking gentleman. And don't call me love."

"Who have we got here, then?" Hatchley stopped and said. "Glenda Slagg, feminist?"

"Piss off."

They went through without further ceremony into the

back room, an office of sorts, and Susan saw Mr. Drake sitting at his desk.

Below the greasy black hair was the lumpiest face Susan had ever seen. He had a bulbous forehead, a potato nose, and a carbuncular chin, over all of which his oily, red skin, pitted with blackheads, stretched tight, and out of which looked a pair of beady black eyes, darting about like tiny fish in an aquarium. His belly was so big he could hardly get close enough to the desk to write. A smell of burned bacon hung in the stale air, and Susan noticed a hotplate with a frying-pan on it in one corner.

When they walked in, he pushed his chair back and grunted, "Who let you in? What do you want?"

"Remember me, Jack?" said Hatchley.

Drake screwed up his eyes. They disappeared into folds of fat. "Is it . . . ? Well, bugger me if it isn't Jim Hatchley."

He floundered to his feet and stuck out his hand, first wiping it on the side of his trousers. Hatchley leaned forward and shook it.

"Who's the crumpet?" Drake asked, nodding towards Susan.

"The 'crumpet,' as you so crudely put it, Jack, is Detective Constable Susan Gay. And show a bit of respect."

"Sorry, lass," said Drake, executing a little bow for Susan. She found it hard to hold back her laughter. She knew that old-fashioned sexism was alive and well and living in Yorkshire, but it felt strange to have Sergeant Hatchley defending her honour. Drake turned back to Hatchley. "Now what is it you want, Jim? You're not still working these parts, are you?"

"I am today."

Drake held his hands out, palms open. "Well, I've done nowt to be ashamed of."

"Jack, old lad," said Hatchley heavily, "you ought be ashamed of being born, but we'll leave that aside for now. Girlie magazines."

"Eh? What about 'em?"

"Still in business?"

Drake shifted from one foot to the other and cast a beady eye on Susan, guilty as the day is long. "You know I don't go in for owt illegal, Jim."

"Believe it or not, at the moment I couldn't care less. It's not you I'm after. And it's *Sergeant* Hatchley to you."

"Sorry. What's up, then?"

Hatchley asked him about the masked killer with the puppy-dog eyes. Drake was shaking his head before he had finished.

"Sure?" Hatchley asked.

"Aye. Swear on my mother's grave."

Hatchley laughed. "You'd swear night was day on your mother's grave if you thought it would get me off your back, wouldn't you, Jack? Nonetheless, I'll believe you, this time. Any ideas where we might try?"

"What have you got?"

"Shaved pussies, excited penises. Right up your alley, I'd've thought."

Drake turned up his misshapen nose in disgust. "Shaved pussies? Why, that's pretty much straight stuff. Nay, Jim, times have changed. They're all into the arse-bandit stuff or whips and chains these days."

"I'm not just talking about the local MPs, Jack."

"Ha-ha. Very funny. Even so."

Hatchley sighed. "Benny still in business?"

Drake nodded. "Far as I know. But he deals mostly in body-piercing now. Very specialized taste." He looked at Susan. "You know, love—pierced nipples, labia, foreskins, that kind of thing."

Susan repressed a shudder.

"Bert Oldham?" Hatchley went on. "Mario Nelson? Henry Talbot?"

"Aye. But you can practically sell the stuff over the counter, these days, Ji—Sergeant."

"It's the 'practically' that interests me, Jack. You know

what the law says: no penetration, no oral sex, and no hard-ons. Anyway, if you get a whiff of him, phone this number." He handed Drake a card.

"I'll do that," said Drake, dropping back into his chair again. Susan thought the legs would break, but, miraculously, they held.

The girl didn't look up from her magazine as they went out. "Better give that reading a rest, love," said Hatchley. "It must be hell on your lips."

"Fuck off," she said, chewing gum at the same time.

Shit, thought Susan, it's going to be one of those days.

2

Banks was right, he saw, as he stood on the threshold of Robert Calvert's flat and surveyed the wreckage. The only difference between this and Pamela Jeffreys's flat was that there had been no human being hurt and no prized possessions utterly destroyed. Stuffing from the sofa lay strewn over the carpet, which had been partly rolled up to expose the bare floorboards. In places, wallpaper had been ripped down, and the television screen had been shattered.

So they had come back. It supported his theory. They obviously didn't know that Banks was a policeman, didn't know that Calvert's flat had already been thoroughly searched by professionals. If they had known, they would never have come here.

It was as he had suspected. They had started following him when he left Clegg's Park Square office on Monday morning. They must have seen the police arrive first, but from their point of view, the police arrived sometime *after* Banks, and he left alone, so there was no reason to make a connection, certainly none to suspect that *he* was a policeman. For all they knew, he could have been a friend of Betty Moorhead's, or a colleague of Clegg's.

Still looking for clues to Clegg's whereabouts, they had trailed him on his lunch date with Pamela and noted where she was rehearsing. One of them must have found out where she lived. They didn't know about the Calvert flat until Banks led them there, and they must have thought the place had something to do with Clegg. Finally, when Banks saw them from the window, they ran off, only to come back later and search the place when the coast was clear.

Where were they now? Already, their descriptions had been sent to other police forces, to the airports and ports. If the men had any sense, they would lie low for a while before trying to leave the country. But criminals don't always have sense, Banks knew. In fact, more often than not, they were plain stupid.

And what about Rothwell's killers? If the man Melissa Clegg remembered was involved—and it was a big if—then he was local. Was he the kind to stay put or run? And what about his partner?

No-one else was at home in the building, and there was no point looking over the rest of the flat. From the box at the corner of the street, Banks went through the motions of calling the local police to report the break-in, but he knew there was nothing they could do. He had no doubts as to *who* had done it; he just had to find them. Dirty Dick Burgess knew something, Banks believed, but he would talk only when he wanted and tell only as little as he needed.

When Banks had finished the call, he took a bus to Millgarth at the bottom of Eastgate. Over the road, on the site of the demolished Quarry Hill flats, stood the new West Yorkshire Playhouse with its "City of Drama" sign. It seemed uncannily appropriate, Banks thought, given the events of the past couple of days. Beyond the theatre, high on a hill, was Quarry House, new home of the Department of Health and Social Security, and already nicknamed "The Kremlin" by locals.

Ken Blackstone was in his office bent over a stack of paperwork. He pushed the pile aside and gestured for Banks to sit opposite him.

"No earth-shattering developments to report, before you

get your hopes up," he said. "We're still no closer to finding Clegg or Rothwell's killers, but there's a couple of interesting points. First off, you might like to know that the lab boys say the dirt and gravel on the tires of Ronald Hamilton's Escort match that around Arkbeck Farm. They said a lot of other things about phosphates and sulphides or whatever, which I didn't understand, but it looks like the car the killers used. Rest of it was clean as a whistle. And airport security at Heathrow have found Clegg's red Jag in the long-stay car park."

"Surprise, surprise," said Banks.

"Indeed. Coffee?"

Banks's stomach was already grumbling from too much caffeine, so he declined. Blackstone went and poured himself a mug from a machine in the open-plan office and returned to his screened-off corner. There was a buzz of constant noise around them—telephones, computer printers, fax machines, doors opening and closing, and the general banter of a section CID department—but Blackstone seemed to have carved himself a small corner of reasonably quiet calm.

Banks told him about Calvert's flat.

"Interesting," said Blackstone. "When do you think that happened?"

"I'd say before they went to Pamela's," Banks said. "Finding nothing there would put them in a fine mood for hurting someone. Is there any news from the hospital?"

Blackstone shook his head. "No change. She's stable, at least." He frowned at Banks and touched the side of his own cheek. "What about you? And I noticed you limping a bit when you came in."

"Slipped in the shower. Look, Ken, I might have a lead on one of Rothwell's killers." He went on quickly to tell Blackstone what Melissa Clegg had said about the mysterious client with the puppy-dog eyes that Clegg had passed on to Harvey Atkins.

Blackstone put the tip of a yellow pencil to his lower lip.

"Hmm . . ." he said. "We're already running a check on all Clegg's contacts and clients. We can certainly check the court records. At least we've got the brief's name, which helps a bit. Harvey Atkins is certainly no stranger around here. He's not a bad bloke, as lawyers go. It's a bit vague, though, isn't it? About two years ago, she says, something to do with assault, maybe? Do we know if the bloke was convicted?"

Banks shook his head. "I'm afraid we'll have to depend on the kindness of microchips."

Blackstone scowled. "Hang on a minute." He made a quick phone call and set the inquiry in motion. "They say it could take a while," he said. "It might be a long list."

Banks nodded. "What do you know about Tahiti?" he asked.

"Tahiti? That's where Captain Bligh's men deserted in the film. It's part of French Polynesia now, isn't it?"

"I think so. It's in the South Pacific at any rate. And Gauguin painted there."

"Why are you interested?"

Banks told him what Melissa Clegg had said.

"Hmm," said Blackstone. "It wouldn't do any harm to put a few inquiries in motion, check on flights, would it? Especially now we've found the car at Heathrow. A relative newcomer might stand out there. I'll see what I can do."

"Thanks. Anything else?"

"We finished the house-to-house in Pamela Jeffreys's street. Nothing really, except I think we've fixed the time. One neighbour remembered hearing some noise at about nine-fifteen Monday evening, which fits with what the doc said, and with Mr. Judd's statement."

Banks nodded.

"The people on the other side were out."

"These neighbours," said Banks, "they said they just heard *some noise*?"

"Yes."

"Ken, imagine how much noise it must have made when

they smashed that stuff. Imagine how Pamela Jeffreys must have screamed for help when she realized what was happening.''

"I know, I know." Blackstone shook his head and sighed. "I suppose they would have gagged her."

"Still . . ."

"Look, Alan, according to DC Hyatt, who talked to them, they said they thought it was the television at first. He asked them if she usually played her television set so loud, and they said no. Then they said they thought she was having a fight with her boyfriend. He asked them if that was a regular occurrence, too, and again they said no. Then they said, or implied, that dark-skinned people have odd forms of entertaining themselves and that we white folks had best leave them to it.''

"They really said that?"

Blackstone nodded. "Words to that effect. They're the sort of people who wouldn't cross the street to piss on an Asian if she was on fire. And they don't want to get involved.''

"And that's it?"

"Afraid so." Blackstone looked at his watch. "I don't know about you, but I'm a bit peckish. What do you say about lunch, on me?"

Banks didn't feel especially hungry, but he knew he ought to try to eat something if he were to keep going all day. "All right, you're on," he said. "But no curries."

3

The other shops were not much different from the first: usually with the windows barred or covered in mesh, and usually close to dilapidated, graffiti-scarred corporation estates or surviving pre-war terraces of back-to-backs in areas like Hunslet, Holbeck, Beeston and Kirkstall. One moment the sun was out, the next it looked like rain. Around and around they drove, Hatchley flipping through the *A to Z*, which had now become so well-thumbed that the pages were falling out, missing turnings, looking for obscure streets. It was all depressing enough to Susan, and a far cry from the nice big semi at the top of the hill in Sheffield where she grew up.

But Hatchley, she noticed, seemed to relish the task, even though after another three visits they had got nowhere. His reputation for laziness, she was beginning to realize, might be unfounded. He certainly didn't like to waste energy, and usually took the line of least resistance, but he was hardly alone in that.

Susan had known truly lazy policemen—some of them had even made detective sergeant—but none of them were like Hatchley. They simply put in the time until the end of their shift, generally trying to stay out of the way of any situation that might generate paperwork. Hatchley was determined. When he was after something, he didn't let go until he got it.

The fifth shop was larger and more modern than the others, a kind of mini-market-cum-off-licence that sold milk, tinned foods, bread and all sorts of odds and ends as well as booze, newspapers and magazines. It was on Beeston Road, not far from Elland Road, where Leeds United played, and it was run, Hatchley said, by a man called Mario Nelson, who, as his name suggested, had an Italian mother and an English father.

It was immediately clear to Susan that Mario took after his father. She knew there were blond-haired Italians in the north of the country, but they didn't look as downright Nordic as Mario. Tall, slim, wearing a white smock, he looked far too elegant to be running a shop. In his early fifties, Susan guessed, he was handsome in a Robert Redford sort of way, and he looked as if he would be more comfortable being interviewed on a film set than unpacking a box of mushroom soup, which is what he was doing when they entered. When he saw Hatchley, a look of caution came to his ice-blue eyes. There was nobody else in the shop.

"Mario, old mate," said Hatchley. "Long time no see."

"Not long enough for me," muttered Mario, putting the box aside. "What can I do for you?"

"No need to be so surly. How's business?" Hatchley took out a cigarette and lit up.

"There's no smoking in here."

Hatchley ignored him. "I asked how's business?"

Mario stared at him for a moment, then broke off eye contact. "Fair to middling."

"Doing much special trade?"

"Don't know what you mean. Look, if you've just come to chat, I'm a busy man."

Hatchley looked exaggeratedly around the shop. "Doesn't look that way to me, Mario."

"There's more to running a shop than serving customers."

"Well, soon as you've answered our questions, you can get back to it." He described the man in the balaclava. "Ever seen anyone like that in here? Is he on your list?"

"It's a bit of a vague description."

"True, but concentrate on the eyes. They'd just about come up to your chin. Poor misguided bloke has an appetite for shaved pussy magazines, and I know you supply them."

"You've never proved that."

"Come off it! The only reason you're still in business is that you've done me a few favours over the years. Remember that. You're a filth-peddler. You know I don't like filth-peddlers, Mario. You know I rank them a bit below a dollop of dog-shit on my shoe."

Hatchley made some very interesting distinctions, Susan thought, some delicate moral judgments. Simple display of naked flesh was fine with him, obviously, but anything more was pornographic. Bit of a puritan, really, when it came down to it.

She watched Mario shift from foot to foot, and she saw

something in his eyes other than wariness; she saw that he recognized Hatchley's description, or thought he did. Hatchley noticed it, too. And she saw fear.

Hatchley dropped his cigarette on the floor and ground it out. "Susan," he said, "would you go put up the 'Closed' sign, please?"

"You can't do that," said Mario, coming out from behind the counter and moving to stop Susan. Hatchley got in the way. He was about the same height and two stones heavier. Mario stopped. Susan went to the door and turned the sign over.

"Might as well drop the latch and pull the blinds down, too," said Hatchley, "seeing as it's such a quiet time."

Susan did as he said.

"Right." Hatchley turned to face Mario. "What's his name?"

"Whose name? I don't know what you're on about."

"We're not gormless, Susan and I. We're detectives. That means we detect. And I detect that you're lying. What's his name?"

Mario looked pale. Beads of sweat formed on his brow. Susan almost felt sorry for him. Almost. "Honest, Mr. Hatchley, I don't know what you mean," he said. "I run an honest business here. I—"

But before he could finish, Hatchley had grabbed him by the lapels of his shop-coat and pushed him against the shelves. A jar of instant coffee fell to the floor and smashed; tins dropped and rolled all over; a packet of spaghetti noodles burst open.

"Watch what you're doing!" Mario cried. "That stuff costs money."

Hatchley pushed him up harder against the shelving, twisting the lapels. Mario's face turned red. Susan was worried he was going to have a heart attack or something. She wished she hadn't become part of this. Gristhorpe would find out, she knew, and she would be thrown off the force in shame. Outside, she heard somebody rattle the door. Do something, her inner voice screamed. "Sir," she said levelly. "Maybe Mr. Nelson wants to tell us something, and he's having difficulty speaking."

Hatchley looked at Nelson and relaxed his grasp. "Is that so, Mario?"

Mario nodded as best he could under the circumstances. Hatchley let him go. A jar of pickled onions rolled off the shelf and smashed, infusing the air with the acrid smell of vinegar.

"Who is he?" asked Hatchley.

Mario massaged his throat and gasped for breath. "You ...shouldn't . . . have ... done ... that," he wheezed. "Could have k-k-killed me. Weak heart. I c-c-could report you."

"But we both know you won't, don't we? Imagine trying to run an honest business with the local police breathing down your neck day and night. Come on, give us the name, Mario."

"I ... I don't know his name. J-just that he's been in occasionally."

"For your under-the-counter stuff? Shaved pussies?"
Mario nodded.

Hatchley shook his head. "I wouldn't believe it if I hadn't seen it with my own eyes," he said, "but you're lying again. After all this." He reached out for Mario's lapels.

"No!" Mario jumped back, dislodging a few more tins from the shelf. A bottle of gin fell and smashed. He put his hands out. "No!"

"Come on, then," said Hatchley. "Give."

"Jameson. Mr. Jameson. That's all I know," said Mario, still rubbing his throat.

"I want his address, too. He's on one of your paper routes, isn't he? I'll bet one of your lads delivers his papers, maybe with a special colour supplement on Sundays, eh? Come on."

"No. I don't know."

"Be reasonable, Mario. It's no skin off your nose, is it? And it'll put you in good stead with the local bobbies. What's his address?"

Mario paused a moment, then went behind the counter and looked in the ledger where he kept the addresses for newspaper deliveries. "Forty-seven Bridgeport Road," he said. "But you won't find him there."

"Oh?"

"Cancelled his papers."

"How long for?"

"Three weeks."

"Since when?"

"Last Friday."

"Where's he gone?"

"I've no idea, have I? Off on his holidays, maybe."

"Don't come the clever bugger with me."

"I'm not. Honest."

"Is that all you know?" Hatchley moved forward and Mario backed off.

"I swear it. We're not mates or anything. He's just a customer. And do me a favour—when you do find him, don't tell him you found out from me."

"Scared of him?"

"He's got a bit of a reputation for scrapping, that's all. When he's had a few, like. I don't think he'd take kindly."

"Aye, all right, then," said Hatchley. "Susan, would you do the honours?"

Susan went over and unlocked the door. A red-faced old woman bustled in. "What's going on here? I've been waiting five minutes. My poor Marmaduke is going to starve to death if you—" She stopped talking, looked at the mess on the floor, then back at the three of them.

"Slight accident, Mrs. Bagshot," said Mario, straightening his tie and smiling. "Nothing serious."

Hatchley bent down and grabbed a pickled onion. After a cursory check to make sure there was no broken glass

clinging to it, he popped it in his mouth, smiled at Mrs.
Bagshot, and left.

4

After a light lunch in the police canteen with Ken Blackstone—a toasted cheese sandwich and a plastic container
of orange juice—Banks set off back to the hotel. The
weather was the same, fast-moving cloud on the wind, sun
in and out casting shadows over the streets and buildings.
He would have to do something about his jacket, he realized as he walked past the Corn Exchange. Maybe he could
get it fixed this afternoon. The hotel should be able to help.
Or maybe he should buy a new one.

He wasn't looking forward to explaining his adventures
to Sandra, either. He hadn't phoned her last night, and she
would probably be out until this evening. He could phone
the gallery, he knew, but she would be busy. Besides, it
would only worry her if he told her about the fight over
the telephone. He might get his jacket fixed, but there
would be no hiding the skinned knuckles and bruised
cheekbone from Sandra, let alone the bruises that would
soon show up on his side.

All he had to say was that two kids had tried to mug
him, simple as that. It might not be the complete truth, but
it certainly wasn't a lie. On the other hand, he wondered
who he was trying to fool. If he couldn't talk to Sandra
about what had happened, who could he talk to? Right now,
he just didn't know.

A local train must have just come in, judging from the
hordes issuing from the station and heading for the bus
stops around City Square and Boar Lane. Banks picked up
a *Yorkshire Evening Post* from the aged vendor, who was
shouting out a headline that sounded like ''TURKLE AN
HONEST LIAR'' but which, on reading, turned out to be
''TWO KILLED IN HUNSLET FIRE.'' Banks refused the

free packet of Old El Paso Taco Shells he was offered with his newspaper.

At the hotel, he found three messages: one to call Melissa Clegg at the wine shop; one to meet Sergeant Hatchley and Susan Gay at The Victoria, behind the Town Hall, as soon as possible; and one to call Ken Blackstone at Millgarth. First, he went to his room and phoned Melissa Clegg.

"Oh, Mr. Banks," she said. "I didn't want to get your hopes up, but I've remembered his name, the man Daniel met in the pub."

"Yes?"

"Well, I knew there was something funny about it. After I left you I just couldn't get it out of my mind. Then I was filling some orders and I saw it written down. It came to me, just like that."

"Yes?"

"Irish whiskey. Funny how the mind works, isn't it?"

"Irish whiskey?"

"His name. It was Jameson. I'm sure of it."

Banks thanked her and called Ken Blackstone.

"Alan, we've got some names for you," Blackstone said. "Quite a lot, I'm afraid."

"Never mind," said Banks. "Is Jameson among them?"

Banks heard Blackstone muttering to himself as he went through the list. "Yes. Yes, there he is. Bloke called Arthur Jameson. Alan, what—"

"I can't talk now, Ken. Can you pull his file and meet me at The Victoria in about fifteen minutes? I assume you know where it is?"

"The Vic? Sure. But—"

"Fifteen minutes, then." Banks hung up.

: 13

1

It was foolish, Susan knew, but she couldn't help feeling butterflies in her stomach as she turned the corner where Courtney Terrace intersected Bridgeport Road at number thirty-five. It was mid-afternoon; there was no-one about. She felt completely alone, and the click of her heels, which seemed to echo from every building, was the only sound breaking the blanket of silence. Her instructions were simple: find out what you can about Arthur Jameson and his whereabouts.

In her blue jacket and matching skirt, carrying a briefcase and clipboard, she looked like a market researcher. A light breeze ruffled her tight blonde curls and a sudden burst of sun through the clouds dazzled her. She could smell rain in the air.

We know he's not at home, she repeated to herself. He has cancelled his papers for three weeks and gone on a long holiday on the proceeds earned from killing Keith Rothwell. He doesn't answer his telephone, and the two men observing the house over the past hour or so have seen no signs of occupation. So there's nothing to worry about.

But still she worried. She remembered Keith Rothwell kneeling there on the garage floor in his suit, his head blown to a pulp. She remembered the tattered pieces of the girlie magazine, ripped images of women's bodies, as if the killer had intended some kind of sick joke.

And she remembered what Ken Blackstone had told her about Jameson at the makeshift briefing in The Victoria. He had been kicked out of the army for rushing half-

cocked, against orders, into an ambush that had killed two
innocent teenage girls as well as one suspected IRA trigger-
man. After that, he had drifted around Africa and South
America as a mercenary. Then, back home, he had beaten
an Irishman senseless in a pub because the man's Belfast
accent hit a raw nerve. Since the GBH, he hadn't done
much except work on building sites and, perhaps, the occasional hit, though there was no evidence of this. He had
four A-levels and an incomplete degree in Engineering
from the University of Birmingham.

Susan looked around her as she walked. Bridgeport Road
was a drab street of dirty terrace houses with no front gardens. From each house, two small steps led right onto the
worn pavement, and the tarmac road surface was in poor
repair. At the back, she knew, each house had a small
bricked-in backyard, complete with privy, full of weeds,
and each row faced an identical row across an alley. A
peculiar smell hung in the air, a mix of raw sewage and
brewery malt, Susan thought, wrinkling her nose.

Outside one or two houses, lines of washing propped up
by high poles hung out to dry right across the street. A
woman came out of her house with a bucket and knelt on
the pavement to scour her front steps. She glanced at Susan
without much interest, then started scrubbing. If Jameson
really is our man, Susan thought, he'll probably be looking
for somewhere a bit more upmarket to live after he has laid
low for a while.

There was nobody at home in the first two houses; the
timid woman at number thirty-nine said she knew nothing
about anyone else in the street; the man at number forty-
one didn't speak English; the West Indian couple at number
forty-three had just moved into the area and didn't know
anyone. Number forty-five was out. Susan felt her heart
beat faster as she lifted the brass lion's head knocker of
number forty-seven, Jameson's house. She was sure the
whole street could hear her heart and the knocker thumping
in concert, echoing from the walls.

She had it all rehearsed. If the man with the puppy-dog eyes answered the door, she was going to lift up her clipboard and tell him she was doing market research on neighbourhood shopping habits: how often did he use the local supermarket, that kind of thing. Under no circumstances, Banks had said, was she to enter the house. As if she would. As her mother used to say, she wasn't as green as she was cabbage-looking.

But the heavy knocks just echoed in the silence. She listened. Nothing stirred inside. All her instincts told her the house was empty. She relaxed and moved on to number forty-nine.

"Yes?" An old lady with dry, wrinkled skin opened the door, but kept it on the chain.

Susan kept her voice down, even though she was sure Jameson wasn't home. She showed her card. "DC Susan Gay, North Yorkshire Police. I'd like to talk to you about your neighbour Mr. Jameson, if I may."

"He's not at home."

"I know. Do you know where he is?"

The face looked at Susan for some time. She couldn't help but be reminded of reptile skin with slit lizard eyes peeping out of the dry folds.

The door shut, the chain rattled, and the door opened again. "Come in," the woman said.

Susan walked straight into the small living-room, which smelled of mothballs and peppermint tea. Everything was in shades of dark brown: the wallpaper, the wood around the fireplace, the three-piece suite. And in the fireplace stood an electric fire with fake coals lit by red bulbs. All three elements blazed away. There might be a chilly breeze outside, but the temperature was still in the mid-teens. The room was stifling, worse than Pratt's office. As the door closed, Susan suddenly felt claustrophobic panic, though she had never suffered from claustrophobia in her life. A heavy brown curtain hung from a brass rail at the top of the door; it swept along the floor with a long hissing sound as the door closed.

"What's Arthur been up to now?" the woman asked.

"Will you tell me your name first?"

"Gardiner. Martha Gardiner. What's he been up to? Here, sit down. Can I get you a cup of tea?"

Susan remained by the door. "No, thank you," she said. "I can't stop. It's very important we find out where Mr. Jameson is."

"He's gone on his holidays, that's where. Has he done anything wrong?"

"Why do you keep asking me that, Mrs. Gardiner? Would it surprise you?"

She chuckled. "Surprise me? Nowt much surprises me these days, lass. That one especially. But he's a good enough neighbour. When my lumbago plays me up he'll go to the shops for me. He keeps an eye on me, too, just in case I drop dead one of these days. It happens with us old folk, you know." She grabbed Susan's arm with a scrawny talon and hissed in her ear. "But I know he's been in jail. And I saw him with a gun once."

"A gun?"

"Oh, aye. A shotgun." She let go. "I know a shotgun when I see one, young lady. My Eric used to have one when we lived in the country, bless his soul. Young Arthur doesn't think I know about it, but I saw him cleaning it through the back window once. Still, he's always polite to me. Gives me the odd pint of milk and never asks for owt. Who am I to judge? If he likes to go off shooting God's innocent creatures, then he's no worse than many a gentleman, is he? Ducks, grouse, whatever. Even though he says he's one of that *green* lot."

"How long ago did you see him with the shotgun?"

"Couldn't say for certain. Time has a funny way of moving when you're my age. Couple of months, perhaps. Are you going to arrest him? What are you going to arrest him for? Who'll do my shopping?"

"Mrs. Gardiner, first we've got to find him. Have you any idea where he went?"

"How would I know? On his holidays, that's what he said."

"Abroad?"

She snorted. "Shouldn't think so. Doesn't like foreigners, doesn't Arthur. You should hear him go on about the way this country's gone downhill since the war, all because of foreigners taking our jobs, imposing their ways. No, he's been abroad, he said, and had enough of foreigners to last him a lifetime. Hates 'em all. 'Foreigners begin at Calais, Mrs. Gardiner, just you remember that.' That's what he says. As if I needed reminding. My Eric was in the war. In Burma. Never the same, after. England for the English, that's what Mr. Jameson always says, and I can't say I disagree."

Susan gritted her teeth. "And all he told you was that he was going on holiday?"

"Aye, that's what he told me. Likes to drive around the English countryside. At least that's what he's done before. Sent me a postcard from the Lake District once. He wished me well and asked me to keep an eye on his place. You know, in case somebody broke in. There's a lot of that these days." She snorted. "Foreigners again, if you ask me."

"I don't suppose he left you a key, did he?"

She shook her head. "Just asked me to keep an eye out. You know, check the windows, try the door every now and then, make sure it's still locked."

"When did he leave?"

"Late Thursday afternoon."

"When did you last see him?"

"Just before he went. About four o'clock."

"Was he driving?"

"Of course he was."

"What kind of car does he drive?"

"A grey one."

"Did he take his shotgun with him?"

"I didn't see it, but he might have. I don't know. I imagine he'd want to shoot a few animals if he's on holiday, wouldn't he?"

Susan could feel the sweat itching behind her ears and under her arms. Her breathing was becoming shallow. She couldn't take much more of Mrs. Gardiner's hothouse atmosphere. But there were other things she needed to know.

"What make was the car?"

"A Ford Granada. I know because he told me when he bought it."

"I don't suppose you know the number?"

"No. It's new, though. He only got it last year."

That would make it an "M" registration, Susan noted. "How was he dressed?" she asked.

"Dressed. Just casual. Jeans. A short-sleeved shirt. Green, I think it was. Or blue. I've always been a bit colour blind. One of those anoraks—red or orange, I think it was."

"And he drove off at about four o'clock on Thursday."

"Yes, I told you."

"Was he alone?"

"Aye."

"Do you have any idea where he was heading first?"

"He didn't say."

Susan needed to know about any friends Jameson might have entertained, but she knew if she stayed in the house a moment longer she would faint. She opened the door. The welcome draught of fresh air almost made her dizzy. Banks would want to question Mrs. Gardiner further, anyway. They would need an official statement. Any other questions could wait. They had enough.

"Thank you, Mrs. Gardiner," she said, edging out of the door. "Thank you very much. Someone else will be along to see you soon to take a statement."

And she hurried off down the street, heels clicking in the silence, to where Banks and the rest waited in their cars in the Tesco car park off the main road.

2

It took the locksmith all of forty-five seconds to open Arthur Jameson's door for Banks and Blackstone to get in. As it wasn't often that four detectives and two patrol cars appeared in Bridgeport Road, and as it was still a nice enough day, despite the occasional clouds, everyone who happened to be home at the time stood out watching, gathered on doorsteps, swapping explanations. The consensus of opinion very quickly became that Mr. Jameson was a child molester, and it just went to show you should never trust anyone with eyes like a dog. And, some added, this kind of thing wouldn't happen if the authorities kept them locked up where they belonged, or fed them bromide with their cornflakes, or, better still, castrated them.

Like Mrs. Gardiner's, Jameson's front door opened directly into the living-room. But unlike the gloomy number forty-nine, this room had cream wallpaper patterned with poppies and cornflowers twined around a trellis. Banks opened the curtains and the daylight gave the place a cheery enough aspect. It smelled a little musty, but that was to be expected of a house that had been empty for almost six days.

Jameson's mug shot and a description of his car had already gone out to police all over the country. They had got the Granada's number quickly enough from the central Driver and Vehicle Licensing Centre in Swansea. Local police were warned *not* to approach him under any circumstances, simply to observe and report.

Hatchley and Susan Gay were taking a statement from the woman next door, whom they had managed to persuade, at Susan's insistence, to accompany them to the local station. Mrs. Gardiner had, in fact, been quite thrilled to be asked to "come down to the station," just like on television, and had managed a regal wave to all the neighbours, who had whistled and whooped their encouragement as she got in the car. Things were on the move.

In the living-room, Banks and Blackstone examined a small bookcase filled with books on nature, the English heritage and the environment: rain forests, ozone layers, whaling, oil spills, seal-clubbing, the whole green spectrum. Jameson had a healthy selection on birds, flowers and wildlife in general, including Gilbert White's *Natural History of Selborne* and Kilvert's diaries. There were also a few large picture books on stately homes and listed buildings.

Blackstone whistled. "Probably a member of Greenpeace and the National Trust, as well," he said. "There'll be trouble if we arrest this one, Alan. Loves Britain's heritage, likes furry little animals and wants to save the seals. They'll be calling him the Green Killer, just you wait and see."

Banks laughed. "It's not every murderer you meet has a social conscience, is it?" he said. "I suppose we should take it as an encouraging sign. Loves animals and plants but has no regard for human life." He pulled a girlie magazine from down the side of a battered armchair. "Yes, it looks like we've got a real nature boy here."

After the living-room, they went into the kitchen. Everything was clean, neat and tidy: dishes washed, dried and put away, surfaces scrubbed clean of grease. The only sign of neglect was a piece of cheddar, well past its sell-by date, going green in the fridge. The six cans of Tetleys Bitter on the shelf above it would last for a long time yet.

As he looked in the oven, Banks remembered a story he had heard from Superintendent Gristhorpe's nephew in Toronto about a Texan who hid his loaded handgun in the oven when he went to Canada to visit his daughter and son-in-law, Canadian gun laws being much stricter than those in the USA. He forgot about it when he got back, until his wife started to heat up the oven for dinner the first night. After that, he always kept it in the fridge. Jameson didn't keep his shotgun in the oven or the fridge.

The first bedroom was practically empty except for a few cardboard boxes of small household appliances: an electric kettle, a Teasmade, a clock radio. They looked too old and well used to be stolen property. More likely things that had broken, things he hadn't got around to fixing or tossing out. There were also an ironing board and a yellow plastic laundry basket.

The other bedroom, clearly the one Jameson slept in, was untidy but basically clean. The sheets lay twisted on the bed, and a pile of clothes lay on the floor under the window. A small television stood on top of the dresser-drawers opposite the bed. All the cupboard held was clothes and shoes. Perhaps the soil expert might be able to find something on the shoes linking Jameson to Arkbeck Farm and its immediate area. After all, he had succeeded with the car. The only reading material on his bedside table was a British National Party pamphlet.

There was a small attic, reached through a hatch in the landing ceiling. Banks stood on a chair and looked around. He saw nothing but rafters and beams; it hadn't been converted for use at all.

Next, they opened the cistern and managed to get the side of the bath off, but Jameson had avoided those common hiding places.

Which left the cellar.

Banks never had liked cellars very much, or any underground places, for that matter. He always expected to find something gruesome in them, and he often had when he worked in London. At their very best, they were dark, dank, dirty and smelly places, and this one was no exception. The chill air gripped them as soon as they got down the winding steps and Banks smelled mould and damp coal dust. It must have been there for years, he thought, because the area was a smoke-free zone now, like most of the country. Thank the Lord there was an electric light.

The first thing they saw was a bicycle lying in parts on the floor next to a workbench and a number of planks of wood leaning against the wall. Next to them hung a World War II gas mask and helmet.

Dark, stained brick walls enclosed a number of smaller storage areas, like the ones used for coal in the old days. Now they were empty. The only thing of interest was Jameson's workbench, complete with vice and expensive tool-box. On the bench lay a box of loose shot and a ripped and crumpled page from a magazine. When Banks rubbed his latex-covered index finger over the rough surface wood, he could feel grains of powder. He lifted up the finger and sniffed. Gunpowder.

There was a drawer under the bench and Banks pulled it open. Inside, among a random collection of screws, nails, electrical tape, fuse wire and used sandpaper, he found a half-empty box of ammunition for a 9mm handgun.

"Right, Ken," he said. "I think we've got the bastard, National Trust or not. Time to call in the SOCOs."

3

Banks cadged a lift with Blackstone back to Millgarth, where Susan and Hatchley were just about to take Mrs. Gardiner home before returning to Eastvale. They had found out nothing more from her, Hatchley said as they stood at the doors ready to leave. It seemed that Jameson was a bit of a loner. He had had no frequent visitors, male or female, and she had seen no-one answering the vague description of his partner. Neither had the other neighbours, according to the results of the house-to-house.

Banks asked about Pamela Jeffreys's condition and was told there had been some improvement but that she was still in intensive care.

Christ, Banks thought, as he sat opposite Blackstone, it had been a long day. He felt shagged out, especially given his previous night's folly, which seemed light years ago now. He looked at his watch: ten to six. He wanted to go home, but knew he might not be able to make it tonight, depending on the developments of the next few hours. At least he could go back to the hotel and have a long bath,

phone Sandra, listen to Classic FM and read the army and
probation officer's reports on Jameson while he waited
around. If nothing happened by, say, eight o'clock, then he
would perhaps go back to Eastvale for the night.

He slipped the reports into his briefcase and again decided to walk back to the hotel. It was that twilight hour
between the evening rush-hour and going-out-on-the-town
time. The city centre was practically deserted; the shops
had closed, workers had gone home, and only a few people
lingered in the few cafés and restaurants still open in the
arcades and pedestrian precincts off Vicar Lane and Briggate. The sun had at last won its day-long battle with cloud;
it lay in proud gold pools on the dusty streets and
pavements, where last night's rain was a dim memory; it
cast black shadows that crept slowly up the sides of buildings; it reflected harshly in shop windows and glittered on
the specks of quartz embedded in stone surfaces.

Back at the hotel, he picked up his jacket, which he had
handed over to be mended before leaving for The Vic.
There was one message for him: "Please come to Room
408 as soon as you get back, where you will find out some
useful information." It wasn't signed.

That was odd. Informers didn't usually operate this way.
They certainly didn't book rooms in hotels to pass along
their information.

"Who's staying in room 408?" Banks asked, slipping
his jacket on. After the obligatory refusal to give out such
information on the part of the clerk, and the showing of a
warrant card on the part of Banks, he discovered that the
occupant of said room was a Mr. Wilson. Very odd indeed.
It was a common enough name, but Banks couldn't remember, offhand, any Mr. Wilson.

He was tempted to ignore the message and carry on with
what he planned, but curiosity got the better of him, as it
always did.

When the lift stopped at the fourth floor, he poked his
head through the doors first to see if there was anyone in

the corridor. It was empty. He followed the arrow to room 408, took a deep breath and knocked. He debated whether to stand aside, but decided it was only in American films that people shot holes through hotel doors. Still, he found himself edging away a little, so he couldn't be seen through the peep-hole.

The door opened abruptly. Banks tensed, then let out his breath. Before him stood Dirty Dick Burgess.

"You again? What the hell?" Banks gasped. But before he could even enter the room Burgess had put on a leather jacket and taken him by the elbow.

"About bloody time, Banks," he said. "I'm sick of being cooped up in here. There's been developments. Come on, let's go get a drink."

: 14

Despite Burgess's protest that it would be full of commercial travellers and visiting rugby teams, Banks insisted on
their drinking in the Holiday Inn's idea of a traditional En-

1

Despite Burgess's protest that it would be full of commercial travellers and visiting rugby teams, Banks insisted on
their drinking in the Holiday Inn's idea of a traditional English pub, the Wig and Pen. He did this because his car
was nearby and he still held hopes of getting back to Eastvale that evening. As it turned out, Burgess seemed to take
a shine to the place.

He sat at the table opposite Banks with his pint of
McEwan's lager, lit a Tom Thumb and looked around the
quiet pub. "Not bad," he said, tapping his cigar on the rim
of the ashtray. "Not bad at all. I never did like those places
with beams across the ceiling and bedpans on the walls."

"Bed warmers," Banks corrected him.

"Whatever. Anyway, what do you think of those two
over there as a couple of potential bed warmers? Do you
think they fancy us?"

Banks looked over and saw two attractive women in their
late twenties or early thirties who, judging by their clothes,
had dropped by for a drink after working late at one of the
many Wellington Street office buildings. There was no
doubt about it, the one with the short black hair and the
good legs did give Burgess the eye and whisper something
in her friend's ear.

"I think they do," said Burgess.

"Didn't you say something about developments?"

"What? Oh, yes." Burgess looked away from the
women and leaned forward, lowering his voice. "For a
start, Fraud Squad think they've found definite evidence in

Daniel Clegg's books and records that Clegg and Rothwell were laundering money for Martin Churchill.''

''That hardly counts as a development,'' Banks said. ''We were already working on that assumption.''

''Ah, but now it's more than an assumption, isn't it? You've got to hand it to those Fraud Squad boys, boring little fuckers that they are, they've been burning the candle at both ends on this one.''

''Have you any idea why Churchill would use a couple of provincials like Rothwell and Clegg?''

''Good point,'' said Burgess. ''As it happens, yes, I do know. Daniel Clegg and Martin Churchill were at Cambridge together, reading law. Simple as that. The old boy network. I'd reckon the one knew the other was crooked right from the start.''

''Did they keep in touch over the years?''

''Obviously. Remember, Clegg's a tax lawyer. He's been using St. Corona as a tax shelter for his clients for years. It must have seemed a natural step to call on him when Churchill needed expert help. You can launder money from just about anywhere, you know. Baby Doc used a Swiss lawyer and did a lot of his business in Canada. You can take it out or bring it into Heathrow or Gatwick by the suitcase-load, using couriers, or you can run it through foreign exchange, wire services, whatever. Governments keep coming up with new restrictive measures, but it's like plugging holes in a sieve. It's easy if you know how, and a tax lawyer and a financial consultant with a strong background in accounting certainly knew how.''

''What made Clegg choose Rothwell as his partner?''

''How would I know? You can't expect me to do your job for you, Banks, now can you? But they clearly knew one another somehow. Clegg must have known that Rothwell was exceptionally good with finances and none too concerned about their source. Takes one to know one, as they say.''

Burgess looked over at the two women, who had got

another round of drinks, and smiled. The black-haired one crossed her long legs and smiled back shyly; the other put her hand over her mouth and giggled.

"My lucky night, I think," Burgess said, clapping his hands and showering cigar ash over his stomach. He had a disconcerting habit of sitting still for ages then making a sudden, jerky movement. "I'll say one thing for the north," he went on, "you've got some damned accommodating women up here. *Damned* accommodating. Look, why don't you get a couple more pints in, then I'll tell you something else that might interest you? And mine's lager, remember, not that pissy real ale stuff."

Banks thought about it. Two pints. Yes, he would be fine for driving back to Eastvale, if he got the chance. "All right," he said, and went to the bar.

"Okay," said Burgess, after his first sip. "The two men, the white one and the darkie who were following you around?"

Banks lit a cigarette. "You know who they are?"

"I've got to admit, I wasn't entirely truthful with you last time we met."

"When have you ever been?"

"Unfair."

"So you knew who they were last time we talked?"

"Suspected. Now we've got confirmation. They're Mickey Lanois and Gregory Jackson, two of Churchill's top enforcers. They came into Heathrow last Friday. The way it looks is that Churchill asked Clegg to get rid of Rothwell, and after he did it he took off with a lot of money, probably figuring that he might be next. Churchill heard about Clegg's scarpering pretty quickly and sent his goons to do some damage control. You know what their favourite torture is, Banks?"

Banks shook his head. He didn't want to know, but he knew Burgess would tell him anyway.

"They get a handful of those little glass tubes the doctors use to keep liquid in. What do you call them, phials, right?

Really thin glass, anyway. And they put them in the victim's mouth, lots of them. Then they tape the mouth shut securely and beat him a bit about the face. Or her. Churchill himself thought that up. He likes to watch. Think about it.''

Banks thought, swallowed and felt his throat constrict. "Been letting you practise it at the Yard, have they?'' he asked.

Burgess laughed. "No, not yet. They're still running tests in Belfast. Anyway, the point is that we know who they are.''

"No, that's not entirely the point,'' said Banks. "The point is where are they now and what are you going to do about them?''

Burgess shook his head. "That's a whole different ball game. We're talking about international politics here, politically sensitive issues. It's out of your hands, Banks. Accept that. All you need to know is that we know who they are and we're keeping tabs.''

"Don't give me that politically sensitive crap,'' said Banks, stabbing out his cigarette so hard that sparks flew out of the ashtray. "These two men damn near killed a woman here a few days ago. You say they like to go around stuffing people's mouths full of glass, then you tell me to trust you, you're keeping tabs. Well, bollocks, that's what I say.''

Burgess sighed. "Somehow, I knew you were going to be difficult, Banks, I just knew it. Can't you leave it be? They won't get away with it, don't worry.''

"Do you know where they are now?''

"They won't get away with it,'' Burgess repeated.

Banks took a sip of his beer and held back his rage. There was something in Burgess's tone that hinted he had something up his sleeve. "What are you telling me?'' Banks asked.

"That we'll get them. Or somebody will. But they'll go down quietly, no fuss, no publicity.''

Banks thought for a moment. He still didn't trust Burgess. "Can I talk to them?" he asked, aware he was speaking through clenched teeth, still keeping his anger in check.

Burgess narrowed his eyes. "Got to you, did it? What they did to the girl? I've seen pictures of her, before and after. Nasty. I'll bet you fancied her, didn't you, Banks? Nice dusky piece of crumpet, touch of the tarbrush, probably knew a lot of those *Kama Sutra* tricks. Just your type. Tasty."

Banks felt his hand tighten on the pint glass. Why did he always let Burgess get to him this way? The bastard had a knack of touching on exactly the right raw nerve. Did it every time. "I'd just like to be there when you question them, that's all," he said quietly.

Burgess shrugged. "No problem. If it's possible, I'll arrange it. All I'm saying is no publicity on the Churchill matter, okay? Let your liberal humanist sentiments fuck this one up and you'll be in deep doo-doo, Banks, very deep doo-doo indeed."

"What about the press?"

"They can be dealt with. Have you ever considered that for every scandal you read about how many you don't? Do you think it's all left to chance? Don't be so bloody naïve."

"Come off it. You might be able to tape a few mouths shut, but even you can't guarantee that no hotshot investigative reporters aren't going to be all over this one like flies around shit."

Burgess shrugged. "Maybe they'll hear Churchill's been killed in a coup. Maybe they'll even see the body."

"Maybe it'd be best for everyone if he did get killed in a coup. Less embarrassing all round."

Burgess remained silent for a moment, glass in hand. Then he said, slowly, "And maybe he's got life insurance."

"Well, I suppose you'd know. Let's hope there's a good plastic surgeon on St. Corona."

"Look," Burgess said, "let's stop pissing around. What I want from you is a promise that you won't talk to the press about the Churchill angle."

Banks lit another cigarette. What could he do? If Burgess were telling the truth, Mickey Lanois and Gregory Jackson would be caught and punished for their crimes. He could live with that. He would have to. Burgess certainly had a better chance of catching them than Banks did, by the sound of things. Perhaps they were even in custody already.

Also, with luck, Arthur Jameson and his accomplice would go down for the murder of Keith Rothwell. But was Burgess telling the full truth? Banks didn't know. All he knew was that he couldn't trust the bastard. It all sounded too easy. But what choice did he have?

"All right," he said.

Burgess reached over and patted his arm. "Good," he said. "Good. I knew I could depend on you to keep shut when it counts."

Banks jerked his arm away. "Don't push it. And if I find out you've been buggering me around on this one, my promise is null and void, okay?"

Burgess held up his hands in mock surrender. "Okay, okay."

"There is another thing."

"What's that?"

"Rothwell's killers. Lanois and Jackson didn't do that."

Burgess shook his head. "I'm not interested in them. They're not in my brief."

"So what happens when we catch Jameson, if we catch him?"

"Jameson?"

"Arthur Jameson. One of Rothwell's killers."

"I don't give a monkey's toss. That's up to you. I'm not interested. It's unlikely that this Jameson, whoever he is, knows anything about Churchill's part in the matter. He was probably just a hired killer working for Clegg, who has conveniently disappeared with a shitload of cash."

"Any ideas where?"

Burgess shook his head then jabbed his finger in the air close to Banks's chest. "But I can tell you one thing.

Wherever he is, he won't be there for long. Churchill has the memory of an elephant, the reach of a giraffe and the tenacity of a bloody pit bull. He didn't get to bleed an entire country dry for nothing. It takes a special talent. Don't underestimate the man just because he's a butcher.''

"So we write off Clegg?''

"I think he's already written himself off by double-crossing Churchill.''

"And Jameson?''

"*If* he goes to trial, and *if* he talks—both big ifs, by the way—all he can say is that Clegg hired him to kill Rothwell. I doubt that Clegg would tell him the real reason. He might be a crooked lawyer, but I'm sure he still knows the value of confidentiality. He wouldn't want to let his hired killers know exactly how much money was involved, would he? It would make him too vulnerable by half. Anyway, I trust you'll have enough physical evidence to prosecute this Jameson when the time comes. If not, maybe we can fabricate some for you. Always happy to oblige.'' He held his hand up. "Only kidding. My little joke.''

Burgess glanced over at the two women, who had got yet another round of drinks and seemed to be laughing quite tipsily. "Look,'' he said, "if I don't strike soon they'll be past it. Are you sure you won't join me? It'll be a laugh, and the wife need never know.''

"No,'' said Banks. "No, thanks. I'm going home.''

"Suit yourself.'' Burgess stretched back his shoulders and sucked in his gut. "Anything to liven up a miserable evening in Leeds,'' he said. "Once more unto the breach.'' And with that, he strutted over to their table, smiling, pint in hand. Banks watched them make room for him, then shook his head, drank up and left.

2

"What on earth happened to you?'' asked Sandra when Banks walked into the living-room at about ten o'clock that evening.

"I had a slight disagreement with a couple of would-be muggers," Banks said. "Don't worry, I'm okay." And he left it at that. Sandra raised her dark eyebrows but didn't pursue it. He knew she wouldn't. She wasn't the mothering type, and she rarely gave him much sympathy when he whimpered through flu or moaned through a bad cold.

Banks walked over to the cocktail cabinet and poured a stiff shot of Laphroaig single malt whisky. Sandra said she'd have a Drambuie. A good sign. After that, he put on his new CD of Khachaturian's piano concerto and flopped onto the sofa.

As he listened to the music, he looked at Sandra's framed photograph over the fireplace: a misty sunset in Hawes, taken from the daleside above the town, all subdued grey and orange with a couple of thin streaks of vermilion. The unusual church tower, square with a turret attached to one corner, dominated the grey slate roofs, and smoke curled up from some of the chimneys. Banks sipped the peaty malt whisky and smacked his lips.

Sandra sat beside him. "What are you thinking?" she asked.

Banks told her about his meetings with Dirty Dick Burgess. "There's always some sort of hidden agenda with him," he said. "I'm not sure what he's up to this time, but there's not a hell of a lot I can do about it except wait and see. That's about all we can do now, wait."

" 'They also serve . . . ' "

"I was thinking about the Rothwells on the drive home, too. How could a man lead an entire other life, away from his family, under another name?"

"Is that what happened?"

"Yes." Banks explained about Robert Calvert and his flat in Leeds, his fondness for gambling, women and dancing. "And Pamela Jeffreys said she was sure he wasn't a married man. She said she'd have been able to tell."

"Did she? Who's Pamela Jeffreys?"

"His girlfriend. It doesn't matter."

Sandra sipped her drink and thought it over. "It's probably not as difficult as you think for two people who live together on the surface to lead completely separate lives, one unknown to the other. Lord knows, so many couples have drifted so far apart anyway that they don't communicate any more."

Banks felt his chest tighten. "Are you talking about us?" he asked, remembering what Ken Blackstone had said about *his* marriage.

"Is that what you think?"

"I don't know."

Sandra shrugged. "I don't know, either. It was just a comment. But if the cap fits . . . Think about it, Alan. The amount we see each other, talk to each other, we could both be living other lives. Mostly, we just meet in passing. Let's face it, you could be up to anything most of the time. How would I know?"

"Most of the time I'm working."

"Just like this Rothwell was?"

"That's different. He was away a lot."

"What about the last couple of nights? You didn't phone, did you?"

Banks sat forward. "Oh, come on! I tried. You weren't home."

"You could have left a message on the machine."

"You know how I hate those things. Anyway, it's not as if you didn't know where I was. You could easily have checked up on me. And it's not that often I'm away from home for a night or more."

"Secret lives don't always have to be lived at night."

"This is ridiculous."

"Is it? Probably. All I'm saying is we don't talk enough to know."

Banks slumped back and sipped his drink. "I suppose so," he said. "Is it my fault? You always seemed to handle my absences so well before. You understand the *Job* better than any other copper's wife I've met."

"I don't know," Sandra said "Maybe it just took longer for the strain to work its way through. Or maybe it's just worse because *I'm* busy a lot now, too."

He put his arm around her. "I don't know what's been happening to us lately, either," he said, "but maybe we'll go away when this is all over."

He felt Sandra stiffen beside him. "Promises," she said. "You've been saying that for years."

"Have I?"

"You know you have. We haven't had a bloody holiday since we moved to Eastvale."

"Well, dust off your camera. I've got a bit of leave due and I might just surprise you this time."

"How long do you think the case will last?"

"Hard to say."

"There you are, then."

He stroked her shoulder. "Tell me you'll think about it."

"I'll think about it. Tracy comes back on Sunday."

"I know."

"Won't you be pleased to see her? Will you even be around to meet her at the airport?"

"Of course I will."

Sandra relaxed a little and moved closer. A very good sign. The Drambuie was clearly working. "You'd better," she said. "She phoned earlier tonight. She sends her love."

"How's she getting on?"

Sandra laughed. "She said it's not quite like *A Year in Provence* down there, but she likes it anyway. She hasn't bumped into John Thaw yet."

"Who?"

"John Thaw. You know, the actor who was in *A Year in Provence* on television? I liked him better as Morse."

"Who?"

She elbowed him in the ribs. "You know quite well who I'm talking about. I know you liked Morse. He used to be in *The Sweeney*, too, years ago, and you used to watch that down in London. Remember, in your old macho days?

Didn't you even go drinking with him once?''

"What do you mean, 'old'?'' Banks flexed his biceps.

Sandra laughed and moved closer. "I don't want to fight,'' she said. "Honest, I don't. Not since we've seen so little of one another.''

"Me neither,'' said Banks.

"I just think we've got a few problems to deal with, that's all. We need to communicate better.''

"And we will. How about a truce.'' He tightened his arm around her shoulder.

"Mmm. All right.''

"I'll have to call the station and see if there's been any developments,'' he said.

But he didn't move. He felt too comfortable. His limbs felt pleasantly heavy and weary, and the warmth of the malt whisky flowed through his veins. The slow second movement started in its haunting, erotic way. Soon, the eerie flexatone entered and sent shivers up and down his spine. A cheap effect, perhaps, but sometimes effective if you happened to be in the right mood.

Banks drained his glass and put it on the table by the sofa. Sandra let her head rest between his shoulder and chest. Definitely a good sign. "Remember that silly film we saw on TV a while back?'' he said. "The one where the couple has sex listening to Ravel's *Bolero*?''

"Hmm. It's called *10*. Dudley Moore and Bo Derek. And I don't think they were really listening. More like using it as background music.''

"Well, I've never really liked *Bolero*. It's far too ordered and mechanical. It's got a kind of inevitability about it that's too predictable for my taste. I've always thought this Khachaturian piece would be a lot better to make love to. Much better. Wanders all over the place. You never really know where it's going next. Slow and dreamy at the start, with plenty of great climaxes later on.''

"Sounds good to me. Have you ever tried it?''

"No.''

Sandra moved her head up until she was facing him, her lips about two inches away. He swept back a strand of hair from her cheek and let his fingers rest on her cool skin. "I thought you had to call the station?" she said.

"Later," he said, stroking her cheek. "Later. Are the curtains closed?"

3

Boredom. They never told you about that down at the recruitment drives, thought PC Grant Everett as he rolled down the window of the patrol car and lit a cigarette. His partner, PC Barry Miller, was good about the smoking. He didn't indulge, himself, but he understood Grant's need to light up every now and then, especially on a quiet night like this one.

They were parked in a lay-by between Princes Risborough and High Wycombe. To the south, through the rearview mirror, Grant could see the faint glow of the nearest town, while to the north only isolated lights twinkled from scattered farms and cottages. All around them spread the dark, rolling landscape of the Chilterns. It was an attractive spot on a nice day, especially in spring with the bluebells and cherry blossom out, but in the dark it seemed somehow forbidding, inhospitable.

A light breeze swirled the smoke out of the car. Grant inhaled deeply. It had just stopped raining and he loved the way the scent of rain seemed to blend with the tobacco and make it taste so much better. It was at moments like this when he understood why he smoked, despite all the health warnings. On the other hand, he never quite understood it when he got up after a night's chain-smoking in the pub and coughed his guts up for half an hour.

Next to him, Barry was munching on a Mars bar. Grant smiled to himself. Six foot two and sixteen stone already and the silly bugger still needed to feed his face with chocolate bars. Who am I to talk? Grant thought, sucking on his cigarette again. To each his own poison.

Grant felt sleepy and the cigarette helped keep him awake. He had never got used to shift work; his biological rhythms, or whatever they were, had never adapted. When he lay down his head in the morning as the neighbour's kids were going to school, the postman was doing his rounds and everyone else was off to work, he could never get to sleep. Especially if the sun were shining. And then there was Janet, bless her soul, doing her best, trying hard to be as quiet as she could around the house, and Sarah, only six months, crying for feeding and nappy-changing. And the bills to pay, and . . . Christ, he wasn't going to think about that. At least the job got him out of the house, away from all that for a while.

A lorry rumbled by. Grant flicked the stub of his cigarette out of the window and heard it sizzle as it hit a puddle. Occasionally, voices cut through the static on the police radio, but the messages weren't for them.

"Shall we belt up and bugger off, then?" said Barry. He screwed up the wrapper of his Mars bar and put it in his pocket. Ever the careful one, Grant thought, with an affectionate smile. Wouldn't even be caught littering, wouldn't Barry.

"Might as well." Grant reached for his belt. Then they heard the squealing sound of rubber on wet tarmac. "What the fuck was that?"

On the main road, a north-bound car skidded as it turned the bend too fast, then righted itself.

"Shall we?" said Barry.

"My pleasure."

Grant loved it when the lights were flashing and the siren screaming. First he was pushed back in the seat by the force when he put his foot down, and then he felt as if he were taking off, seeming somehow to be magically freed from all the restraints of the road: not just the man-made rules, but the laws of nature. Sometimes, Grant even felt as if they were really taking off, wheels no longer on the ground.

But there was no chase to be had here; it was over before
it began. The car was about two hundred yards ahead of
them when its driver seemed to realize they meant business.
He slowed down as they caught up and pulled over to the
side of the road, spraying up water from the hedgerow. His
number-plate was too muddy to read.

Grant pulled up behind him, and Barry got out to approach the car.

It wasn't likely to be much, Grant thought as he sniffed
the fresh night air through the open window—maybe a
drunk, maybe a few outstanding parking tickets—but at
least it was *something* to relieve the boredom for a few
minutes.

He could hear perfectly clearly when Barry asked the
driver to turn off his ignition and present his driving documents. The driver did as he was told. Barry looked at the
papers and passed them back. Next, he asked the man if he
had been drinking. Grant couldn't hear the man's reply, but
it seemed to satisfy Barry. Grant knew he would be listening for slurred words and sniffing for booze on the driver's
breath.

After that, Barry asked the man where he had been and
where he was going. Grant thought he heard the man mention Princes Risborough.

No other cars passed. The night was quiet and Grant
caught a whiff of beech leaves and cherry wood on the
damp air. He thought he heard some cows low in the distance and, farther still, a nightingale.

Then Barry asked the man to get out of the car and clean
off his number-plate. Grant heard him explain patiently that
it was an offence to drive with a number-plate that is ''not
easily distinguishable'' and smiled to himself at the stilted,
textbook phrase. But the man would get off with a caution
this time; Barry seemed satisfied with his behaviour.

The man got back in the car and Grant heard Barry speak
over his personal radio.

''465 to Control.''

"465 go ahead."

"Ten nine vehicle check please."

The voices crackled unnaturally over the country night air.

"Pass your number."

"Mike four, three, seven, Tango Zulu Delta."

"Stand by."

Grant knew it would take three or four minutes for the operator to check the number on the computer, then, all being well, they could be on their way.

Barry and the driver seemed to be chatting amiably enough as they waited. Grant looked at the newly cleaned number-plate and reached idly for the briefing-sheet beside him. There seemed to be *something* familiar about it, something he ought to remember.

He ran his finger down the list of stolen cars. No, not there. He wouldn't remember any of those numbers; there were always too many of them. It had to be something more important: a vehicle used in a robbery, perhaps? Then he found it: M437 TZD, grey Granada.

Suddenly, he felt cold. The owner was wanted in connection with a murder in North Yorkshire. Possibly armed and dangerous. Shit. All of a sudden, Barry seemed to be taking a hell of a long time out there.

A number of thoughts passed quickly through Grant's mind, the first of which was regret that they didn't do things the American way. Get the guy out of the vehicle, hands stretched on the roof, legs apart, pat him down. "Assume the position, asshole!" Why pretend they were still living in a peaceful society where the local bobby was your best friend? Christ, how Grant wished he had a gun.

Should he go out and try to get Barry to the car, use some excuse? He could say they'd been called to an emergency. Could he trust himself to walk without stumbling, to speak without stuttering? His legs felt like jelly and his throat was tight. But he felt so impotent, just watching. All he could hope was that the radio operator would understand

Barry's predicament and give the guy a clean bill of health. According to the information on the sheet, the man, Arthur Jameson, didn't even *know* he was wanted.

The radio crackled back into life.

"Control to 465."

"Go ahead, over."

"Er . . . Mike four, three, seven, Tango Zulu Delta . . . No reports stolen. Er . . . Do you require keeper details over?"

"Affirmative."

More static. Grant tensed in his seat, hand on the door-handle. Too many pauses.

"Keeper is Arthur Jameson, 47 Bridgeport Avenue, Leeds. Er . . . is keeper with you over?"

"Affirmative. Any problem?"

She was blowing it, Grant sensed. Someone, probably the super, was standing over her trying to help her calmly get Barry back to the car and the driver on his way, but she was nervous, halting. It was all taking far too long, and if the suspect couldn't sense there was something wrong over the radio, then he was an idiot.

"No reports stolen."

"You already told me that, love," said Barry. "Is something wrong?"

"Sorry . . . er . . . 465 . . . Stand by."

Grant tightened his grip on the door-handle. This was it. He wasn't going to stand around and let his partner, who had probably dozed off at the briefing and to whom the number obviously meant bugger-all, just stand there and take it.

But before he got the door half open, he saw Barry, all sixteen stone and six foot two of him, drop to the wet road clutching the side of his neck, from which a dark spray of blood fountained high and arced to the ground. Then he heard the shots, two dull cracks echoing through the dark countryside.

Left foot still in the car, right foot on the road, Grant

hesitated. Mistake. His last thought was that it was so bloody unfair and pointless and miserable to die like this by a roadside outside High Wycombe. Then a bullet shattered the windscreen and took him full in the face, scattering blood, teeth and bone fragments all over the car. After its echo had faded, the Granada revved up and sped off into the night, and the nightingale sang again into the vacuum of silence the car left behind.

: 15

1

The sky was a sheet of grey shale, smeared here and there by dirty rags of cloud fluttering over the wooded hillsides on a cool wind. Rooks and crows gathered noisily in the roadside trees like shards of darkness refusing to dispel. Even the green of the dense beech forests looked black.

Banks and Sergeant Hatchley, who had driven through the night at breakneck speed from Eastvale, stood and looked in silence at the patrol car with the shattered windscreen and at the outline of the body on the tarmac about six or seven feet ahead, near which dark blood had coagulated in shallow puddles on the road surface. Close by, Detective Superintendent Jarrell from the Thames Valley Police paced up and down, shabby beige raincoat flapping around his legs.

The road had been cordoned off, and several patrol cars, lights circling like demented lighthouses, guarded the edges of the scene, where the SOCOs still worked. Local traffic had been diverted.

"It was a cock-up," Superintendent Jarrell growled, glaring at the two men from Yorkshire the minute they got out of Banks's Cortina and walked over to him. "A monumental cock-up."

Jarrell was clearly looking for somewhere to place the blame, and it irritated the hell out of him that no matter how hard he tried, it fell squarely on his own shoulders. The two PCs might have made a mistake in not tattooing the Granada's number on their memories, and the radio operator had certainly screwed up royally, but in the police force, as in other hierarchical structures, when an underling screws up, the responsibility goes to the top. You don't blame the foot-soldiers, you blame the general, and *everybody* gets a good bollocking, from the top down.

Banks knew that Ken Blackstone at West Yorkshire had followed correct procedure in getting a photograph, description and details about Arthur Jameson out to all divisions. And the point he had most emphasized was, "May be armed. Observe only. UNDER NO CIRCUMSTANCES ATTEMPT TO APPREHEND."

Jarrell's was one of those unfortunate faces in which the individual features fail to harmonize: long nose, small, beady eyes, bushy brows, a thin slit of a mouth, prominent cheekbones, receding chin, mottled complexion. Somehow, though, it didn't dissolve into total chaos; there was an underlying unity about the man himself that, like a magnetic field, drew it all together.

"Any update on the injured officer, sir?" Banks asked.

"What? Oh." Jarrell stopped pacing for a moment and faced Banks. He had an erect, military bearing. Suddenly the fury seemed to bleed out of him like air from a tire. "Miller was killed outright, as you know." He gestured at the outline and the surrounding, stained tarmac with his whole arm, as if indicating a cornucopia. "There's about seven pints of his blood here. Everett's still hanging on. Just. The bullet went in through his upper lip, just under the nose, and it seems to have been slowed down or deflected by cartilage and bone. Anyway, it didn't get a chance to do serious brain damage, so the doc says he's got a good chance. Bloody fool."

"If you don't mind my saying so, sir," Banks said, "it looks like they got into a situation they couldn't get out of. We had no reason to think Jameson knew we were onto him. Nor had we any reason to think he was a likely spree killer. We want him for a job he was hired to do cold-bloodedly. He must have panicked. I know it doesn't help the situation, sir, but the men *were* inexperienced. I doubt they'd handled much but traffic duty, had they?"

Jarrell ran his hand through his hair. "You're right, of course. They pulled him over on a routine traffic check. When Miller called in the vehicle number, the radio operator called the senior officer on the shift. He tried to talk her through it calmly, but . . . Hell, she was new to the job. She was scared to death. It wasn't her fault."

Banks nodded and rubbed his eyes. Beside him, Hatchley's gaze seemed fixed on the bloody tarmac. When Banks had got the call close to two A.M.—his first night at home in days—he had first thought of taking Susan Gay, then, not without malice entirely, though affectionate malice, he had decided that it was time Sergeant Hatchley got his feet wet. He knew how Hatchley loved his sleep. Consequently, they hadn't said much on the way down. Banks had played Mitsuko Uchida's live versions of the Mozart piano sonatas, and Hatchley had seemed content to doze in the passenger seat, snoring occasionally.

Most chief inspectors, Banks knew, would have had someone else drive, but he was using his own car, the old Cortina, no longer produced now and practically an antique. And, damn it, he *liked* driving it himself.

"Seen enough here?" Jarrell asked.

"I think so."

"Me, too. Let's go."

Jarrell drove them down the road. "Believe it or not," he said, "this is very pretty countryside under the right circumstances."

About a mile along the road, towards Princes Risborough, Jarrell turned left onto a muddy farm track and bumped along until they got to a gate on the right, where he pulled up. A hedgerow interspersed with hawthorns shielded the field and its fence from view. Cows mooed in the next field.

The gate stood open, and as Banks and Hatchley followed Jarrell through, they both sank almost to their ankles in mud. Too late, Banks realized, he hadn't brought the right gear. He should have known to bring the wellingtons he always carried in the boot of his car. Like most police-men, he took pride in keeping his shoes well polished; now they were covered in mud and probably worse, judging by the prevalence of cows. He cursed and Jarrell laughed. Hatchley stood holding onto the gatepost trying to wipe most of it off on the few tufts of grass there. Banks looked at the muddy field dotted with cowpats and didn't bother. They'd only get dirty again.

In the field, a group of men in white boiler suits and black wellington boots worked around a car that stood bogged down in the mud with its doors open. The air was sharp with the tang of cow-clap.

One of the men had propped a radio on a stone by the hedgerow, and it was tuned to the local breakfast show, at the moment featuring a golden oldie: Cilla Black singing "Anyone Who Had a Heart." One of the SOCOs sang along with it as he worked. The cows mooed even louder, demonstrating remarkably good taste, Banks thought. They weren't so far away after all. They were, in fact, all lying down in a group just across the field. Cows lying down. That meant it was going to rain, his mother always said. But it had rained already. Did that mean they'd been in the same position for hours? That it was going to rain again?

Giving up on folk wisdom, Banks turned instead to look at the abandoned Granada, the bottom of its chassis streaked with mud and cow-shit. It had been found, Jarrell said, just over an hour ago, while Banks and Hatchley had been in transit.

"Anything?" Jarrell shouted over to the team.

One of the men in white shook his head. "Nothing but the usual rubbish, sir," he said. "Sweet wrappers, old road maps, that sort of thing. He must have taken everything of use or value. No sign of any weapons."

Jarrell grunted and turned away.

"He'd hardly have left his guns, would he?" said Banks, "not now he's officially on the run. I'd guess he probably had a rucksack or something with him in the car. Look, sir, you know the landscape around here better than I do. If you were him, where would you go?''

Jarrell looked up at the louring sky for a moment, as if for inspiration, then rubbed at the inside corner of his right eye with his index finger. "He has a couple of choices," he said. "Either head immediately for the nearest town, get to London and take the first boat or plane out of the country, or simply lie low." He pointed towards the hills. "A man could hide himself there for a good while, if he knew how to survive."

"We'd better cover both possibilities," Banks said. "He's spent time in the army, so he's probably been on survival courses. And if he heads for London, he'll likely know someone who can help him."

"Whatever he does, I'd say he'll most likely go across country first," said Jarrell. "He'd be smart enough to know that stealing a car or walking by the roadside would be too risky." He looked at his watch. "The shooting occurred at about half past twelve. It's half past six now. That gives him a six-hour start."

"How far could he get, do you reckon?"

"I'd give him about three miles an hour in this terrain, under these conditions," Jarrell went on. "Maybe a bit less."

"Where's the nearest station?"

"That's the problem," said Jarrell slowly. "This is close to prime commuter country. There's Princes Risborough, Saunderton and High Wycombe on the Chiltern Line, all nearby. If he heads east, he can get to the Northampton Line at Tring, Berkhamsted or Hemel Hempstead. If he heads for Amersham, he can even get on the underground, the Metropolitan Line. Unfortunately for us, there's no shortage of trains to London around here, and they start running early."

"Let's say he's managed about sixteen or seventeen miles," said Banks. "What's his best bet?"

''Probably the Chiltern Line. Plenty of trains and an easy connection with the underground. He could even be in London by now.''

They started walking back to the car. ''I can tell you one thing,'' said Banks. ''Wherever he is, his shoes will be bloody muddy.''

2

If. If. If. Such were Banks's thoughts as he followed Superintendent Jarrell into Jameson's rented cottage an hour or so later. *If* Everett and Miller hadn't stopped Jameson last night. *If* Jameson hadn't panicked and shot them. *If.*

In an ideal world, they would have tracked Jameson to this cottage through a cheque stub or a circled address in an accommodation guide. Quietly, they would have surrounded the place when they were certain Jameson was inside, then arrested him, perhaps as he walked out to his car, unsuspecting, without a shot being fired. For he hadn't known. That was the stinger; he *hadn't known* they were after him. Now, though, things were different. Now he was a dangerous man on the run.

As it turned out, they discovered that Jameson was renting a cottage just to the east of Princes Risborough through an Aylesbury estate agent shortly after the office opened at eight-thirty that Friday morning. Policemen were showing Jameson's photograph around and asking the same questions in every estate agent's, hotel and bed and breakfast establishment in Buckinghamshire, and the pair of DCs given the Aylesbury estate agents just happened to get lucky. Like Everett and Miller got unlucky. Swings and roundabouts. That was often the way things happened.

Jameson had simply driven off from Leeds on his holidays. Being a lover of nature, he had headed for the countryside. Why the Chilterns? It was anyone's guess. It could just as easily have been the Cotswolds or the Malverns, Banks supposed.

According to the estate agent, the man had simply dropped in one afternoon and asked after rental cottages in the area. He had paid a cash deposit and moved in. There was no need for subterfuge or secrecy. Arthur Jameson had nothing to fear from anyone. Or he wouldn't have had, were it not for a weakness for pornography, a fleeting contact with Daniel Clegg's estranged wife, Melissa, and Sergeant Hatchley's network of informers. He had either been careless about the wadding, or he thought it was a joke; they didn't know which yet. It hadn't shown up as a trademark in any other jobs over the past few years.

Last night he had probably gone into High Wycombe for a bite to eat, lingered over his dessert and coffee, maybe celebrated his new-found wealth with a large cognac, then headed back for the rented cottage, taking the bend a little too fast.

The cottage was certainly isolated. It stood just off a winding lane about two miles long, opposite a small, perfectly rounded tor. The lane carried on, passed another farmhouse about a mile further on, then meandered back to the main road.

From the mud on the floor, it looked very much as if Jameson had been there after the shooting. A bit of a risk, maybe, but the cottage wasn't far from his abandoned car. In the kitchen, yesterday's lunch dishes soaked in cold water, and breadcrumbs, cheese shavings and tiny florets of yellowed broccoli dotted the counter.

In the living-room, Jameson had left the contents of his suitcase strewn around, including a number of local wildlife guides beside a girlie magazine on the table. Hatchley picked up the magazine and flipped through it quickly, tilting the centrefold to get a better look. Then they all followed the mud trail upstairs.

At the bottom of the wardrobe, hardly hidden at all by the spare blankets Jameson had obviously used to cover them, lay a twelve-gauge shotgun wrapped in an oil-stained cloth, and a small canvas bag. Carefully, Banks leaned forward and opened the flap of the bag with the tip of a Biro. It was empty, but on the floor by the blankets lay a few used ten-pound notes. Banks visualized the hunted man hurriedly stuffing the notes into his pockets until they spilled over on the floor. The shotgun was obviously too big and awkward for him to take with him, but he was still armed with the handgun.

Banks pointed to the shotgun and the canvas bag. "Can we get this stuff to your lab?" he asked Jarrell. "That shotgun's probably evidence in a murder case."

Jarrell nodded. "No problem."

As Hatchley bent to pick up the shotgun, careful to handle only the material it was wrapped in, and as Banks reached for the canvas bag, a message for Jarrell crackled through on his personal radio.

"Jarrell here. Over."

"HQ, sir. Subject, Arthur Jameson, spotted at Aylesbury railway station at nine fifty-three a.m. Subject bought London ticket. Now standing on platform. Locals await instructions. Over."

"Has he spotted them?"

"They say not, sir."

"Tell them to keep their distance." Jarrell looked at his watch. It was ten o'clock. "When's the next train?" he asked.

"Twelve minutes past ten, sir."

"Which route?"

"Marylebone via Amersham."

"Thank you. Stand by." Jarrell turned to Banks and Hatchley. "We can pick up that train at Great Missenden or Amersham if you want," he said.

Banks looked first at Hatchley, then back at Jarrell. "Come on, then," he said. "Let's do it."

3

Banks and Hatchley boarded the train separately at Amersham at ten thirty-two. Reluctantly, Superintendent Jarrell, being the local man, had agreed to stay behind and coordinate the Thames Valley end of the operation.

Neither Banks nor Hatchley looked much like a policeman that morning. Waking miserably to the middle-of-the-night phone call, Banks had put on jeans, a light cotton shirt and a tan sports jacket. Over this, he had thrown on his Columbo raincoat. Even though he had done his best to clean the mud off his shoes with a damp rag, it still showed.

Sergeant Hatchley wore his shiny blue suit, white shirt and no tie; he looked as if he had been dragged through a hedge backwards, but there was nothing unusual in that.

They had been told by the Transport Police, who had spotted Jameson, that the suspect still resembled his photograph except that he had about two days' growth around his chin and cheeks. He looked like a rambler. He was wearing grey trousers of some light material tucked into walking boots at the ankles, a green open-neck shirt and an orange anorak. Nice of him, Banks thought, dressing so easy to spot. He was also carrying a heavy rucksack, which no doubt held his gun and money, amongst other things.

The train rattled out of the station. Banks managed to find a seat next to a young woman who smiled at him briefly as he sat down, then went back to reading her copy of *PC Magazine*. Banks had his battered brown leather briefcase with him, and its chief contents were his omnibus paperback copy of Waugh's *Sword of Honour* and his Walkman. He opened the book at the marker and started to read, but every so often he glanced at the man in the green short-sleeve shirt who sat about four seats down, over to his left. The rucksack and the orange anorak lay on the luggage rack above.

The train moved in a comforting rhythm, but Banks couldn't help feeling tense. He left the Walkman in his briefcase because he was too distracted to listen to music.

They could probably take Jameson right now, he thought. He and Jim Hatchley. Just approach quietly from behind like anyone going to the toilet and grab an arm each. The gun, surely, was up in the rucksack on the luggage rack.

But it wasn't worth the risk. Something could go wrong. Jameson could hold the entire coach hostage. It didn't bear thinking about. This way was far safer and would, with a little patience, skill and luck, guarantee success.

Banks and Hatchley had got on the train simply to keep an eye on Jameson. At the station, Superintendent Jarrell had talked to the Yard, who promised that there would be a number of plainclothes officers waiting at Marylebone, mixed in with the crowds. These men were experts at surveillance, and they would keep Jameson in sight, no matter how he travelled, without being spotted, until he arrived at his final destination, be it hotel or house.

Some were posing as taxi-drivers, and, with luck, Jameson would get into one of their cabs. Banks had every intention of trying to keep up with the chase, but it was comforting to know that if he lost sight of Jameson, someone else would have him. There were plainclothes officers at all the stops on the way, too, in case he got off, but Jameson had bought a ticket for London and it was almost certain that was where he was heading. Given his past, he would likely know someone there who could help get him out of the country. What Banks hoped—and this was one of the main reasons for letting their quarry go to ground—was that Jameson would lead them to his accomplice in the Rothwell murder.

As the train rattled out of Rickmansworth, Jameson got up and walked past Banks on his way to the toilet. Banks looked down at his book, not registering the words his eyes passed over. While Jameson was gone, he stared at the khaki rucksack and held himself back. How easy it would be, he thought, just to take it, then grab Jameson when he came back. But he had to keep thinking like a policeman, not give in to the maverick instinct, however strong. This way, with a little patience, the catch might be bigger.

And there was another reason. The gun might not be in

the rucksack. Jameson's trousers were of the bulky, many-pocketed kind favoured by ramblers. Banks had glanced quickly as he went by and hadn't been able to discern the weight or outline of a gun, but it *could* be there, and there were too many civilians present to make the risk worthwhile. Best wait. He thought of how much money there might be in the rucksack and smiled at how ironic it would be if someone snatched it while Jameson was having a piss.

Jameson came back. They passed Harrow and entered a landscape of factory yards, piles of tires and orange oil drums, pallets, warehouses, schoolyards full of screaming kids, bleak housing estates, concrete overpasses. Before long, the people in the carriage were standing up to get their jackets and bags as the train rumbled slowly into Marylebone station, all anxious to be first off.

Banks spotted Hatchley ahead of him, his head above most people in the crowd that shuffled through the ticket gate. Jameson had his anorak on now and was easy to keep in sight. Banks noticed him look around and lick his lips every now and then, sad, cruel puppy-dog eyes scanning the station forecourt.

But there was nothing to see. Nothing out of the ordinary. The uniformed Transport Police went about their business as usual, people leafed through magazines at the bookstall or headed for the buffet, checked the schedule displays, ran for trains. Carts of luggage and mail threaded in and out of the crowds, announcements about forthcoming departures came over the public-address system in the usual monotone echoing from the roof, where pigeons nested. To Banks, the station smelled of diesel oil and soot, though the age of steam was long gone.

Jameson made his way through the exit and managed to get a taxi. That was their first stroke of good fortune. If things went according to plan, the driver would be a DC; if not, then a taxi crawling through London traffic was easy enough for even a one-legged septuagenarian on foot to follow.

Banks opened the door of the next taxi, Hatchley beside him now. Banks was dying to jump in and say, "Follow that taxi!" but the driver didn't want to let them in. He leaned over and tried to pull the door shut, holding up a police ID card. "Sorry, mate," he said. "Police business. There's another one behind." Just in time, Banks managed to get his own card out. "Snap," he said. "Now open the fucking door."

"Sorry, sir," said the driver, eyes on the road, following Jameson's cab through the thick traffic on Marylebone Road. "I wasn't to know. They never said to expect a DCI jumping in the cab."

"Forget it," said Banks. "I'm assuming it's one of your men driving in the taxi ahead?"

"Yes, sir. DC Formby. He's a good bloke. Don't worry, we're not going to lose the bastard."

With excruciating slowness, the taxis edged their way south towards Kensington, along the busy High Street and down a side street of five- or six-storey white buildings with black metal railings at the front. Jameson's taxi stopped outside one that announced itself a HOTEL on the smoked glass over the huge shiny black doors. Across the street came the sound of drilling where workmen stood on scaffolding renovating the building opposite. The air was dry with drifting stone dust and thick with exhaust fumes. Jameson got out, looked around quickly, and went into the hotel. His taxi drove off.

"Right," said Banks. "Looks like we've run the bastard to earth. Now we wait for the reinforcements."

4

For grey, the hotel manager could have given John Major a good run for his money. His suit was grey; his hair was grey; his voice was grey. He also had one of those faces—receding chin, goofy teeth, stick-out ears—that attract such abusive and bullying attention at school. At the moment, his face was grey, too.

He reminded Banks of Parkinson, a rather unpleasant large-nosed boy who had been the butt of ridicule and recipient of the occasional thump in the fourth form. Banks had always felt sorry for Parkinson—had even defended him once or twice—until he had met him later in life, fully transformed into a self-serving, arrogant and humourless Labour MP. Then he felt Parkinson probably hadn't been thumped enough.

The manager had obviously never seen so many rough-looking, badly dressed coppers gathered in one place since they stopped showing repeats of *The Sweeney*. Jeans abounded, as did leather jackets, anoraks, blousons, T-shirts and grubby trainers. There wasn't a uniform, a tie or a well-polished shoe in sight, and the only suit was Sergeant Hatchley's blue polyester one, which was so shiny you could see your face in it.

It was also obvious that a number of the officers were armed and that two of them wore bullet-proof vests over their T-shirts.

Short of the SAS, Police Support Units or half a dozen Armed Response Vehicles, none of which the police authorities wanted the public to see mounting a major offensive on a quiet Kensington hotel on a Thursday lunch-time, these two were probably the best you could get. Vest One, the tallest, was called Spike, probably because of his hair, and his smaller, more hirsute associate was called Shandy. Spike was doing all the talking.

"See, squire," he said to the wide-eyed hotel manager, "our boss tells us we don't want a lot of fuss about this. None of this evacuating the area bollocks you see on telly. We go in, we disarm him nice and quiet, then bob's your uncle, we're out of your hair for good. Okay? No problems for us and no bad publicity for the hotel."

The manager, clearly not used to being called "squire," swallowed, bobbing an oversize Adam's apple, and nodded.

"But what we do need to do," Spike went on, "is to clear the floor. Now, is there anyone else up there apart from this Jameson?"

The manager looked at the keys. "Only room 316," he said. "It's lunch-time. People usually go out for lunch."

"What about the chambermaids?"

"Finished."

"Good," said Spike, then turned to one of the others in trainers, jeans and leather jacket. "Smiffy, go get number 316 out quietly, okay?"

"Right, boss," said Smiffy, and headed for the stairs.

Spike tapped his long fingers on the desk and turned to Banks. "You know this bloke, this Jameson, right, sir?" he said.

Banks was surprised he had remembered the honorific. "Not personally," he said, and filled Spike in.

"He's shot a policeman, right?"

"Yes. Two of them. One's dead and the other's still in the operating room waiting to find out if he's got a brain left."

Spike slipped a stick of Wrigley's spearmint gum from its wrapper and popped it in his mouth. "What do you suggest?" he asked between chews.

Banks didn't know if Spike was being polite or deferential in asking an opinion, but he didn't get a chance to find out. As Smiffy came down the stairs with a rather dazed old dear clutching a pink dressing-gown around her throat, the phone rang at the desk. The manager answered it, turned even more grey as he listened, then said, "Yes, sir. Of course, sir. At once, sir."

"Well?" Spike asked when the manager had put the phone down. "What's put the wind up you?"

"It was *him*. The man in room 324."

"What's he want?"

"He wants a roast beef sandwich and a bottle of beer sent up to his room."

"How'd he sound?"

"Sound?"

"Yeah. You know, did he seem suspicious, nervous?"

"Oh. No, just ordinary."

"Right on," said Spike, grinning at Banks. "Opportunity knocks." He turned back to the manager. "Do the doors up there have those peep-hole things, so you can see who's knocking?"

"No."

"Chains?"

"Yes."

"No problem. Right," said Spike. "Come with me, Shandy. The rest of you stay here and make sure no-one gets in or out. We got the back covered?"

"Yes, sir," one of the blousons answered.

"Fire escape?"

"That, too, sir."

"Good." Spike looked at Banks. "I don't suppose you're armed?"

Banks shook his head. "No time."

Spike frowned. "Better stay down here then, sir. Sorry, but I can't take the responsibility. You probably know the rules better than I do."

Banks nodded. He gave Spike and Shandy a floor's start, then turned to Sergeant Hatchley. "Stay here, Jim," he said. "I don't want to lead you astray."

Without waiting for an answer, he slipped into the stairwell. One of the Yard men in the lobby noticed but made no move to stop him. At the first-floor landing, Banks heard someone wheezing behind him and turned.

"Don't worry, I'm not deaf," said Hatchley. "I just thought you might like some company anyway."

Banks grinned.

"Mind if I ask you what we're doing this for?" Hatchley whispered as they climbed the next flight.

"To find out what happens," said Banks. "I've got a funny feeling about this. Something Spike said."

"You know what curiosity did."

They reached the third floor. Banks peeked around the stairwell and put his arm out to hold Hatchley back.

Glancing again, Banks saw Spike point at his watch and mouth something to Shandy. Shandy nodded. They drew their weapons and walked slowly along the corridor towards Jameson's room.

The worn carpet that covered the floor couldn't stop the old boards creaking with each footstep. Banks saw Spike knock on the door and heard a muffled grunt from inside.

"Room service," said Spike.

The door rattled open—on a chain, by the sound of it. Someone—Spike or Jameson—swore loudly, then Banks saw Shandy rear back like a wild horse and kick the door open. The chain snapped. Spike and Shandy charged inside and Banks heard two shots in close succession, then, after a pause of three or four seconds, another shot, not quite as loud.

Banks and Hatchley waited where they were for a minute, out of sight. Then, when Banks saw Spike come out of the room and lean against the door jamb, he and Hatchley walked into the corridor. Spike saw them coming and said, "It's all over. You can go in now, if you like. Silly bugger had to try it on, didn't he?"

They walked into the room. Banks could smell cordite from the gunfire. Jameson had fallen backwards against the wall and slid down into a perfect sitting position on the floor, legs splayed, leaving a thick red snail's trail of blood smeared on the wallpaper. His puppy-dog eyes were open. His face bore no expression. The front of his green shirt, over the heart, was a tangle of dark red rag and tissue, spreading fast, and there was a similar stain slightly above it, near his shoulder. His hands lay at his side, one of them holding his gun. Another dark wet patch spread between his legs. Urine.

Banks thought of the chair at Arkbeck Farm, where this man had scared Alison Rothwell so much that she had wet herself. "Jesus Christ," he whispered.

"We'd no choice," Spike said behind him. "He had his gun in his hand when he came to the door. You can see for yourself. He fired first."

Two shots, in close succession, followed by another, sounding slightly different. Two patches of spreading blood. "Our boss tells us we don't want a lot of fuss about this."

Banks looked at the two policemen, sighed and said, "Give my regards to Dirty Dick."

Shandy came back with a not very convincing, "Who's that?"

Spike grinned, rubbed the barrel of his gun against his upper thigh, and said, "Will do, sir."

: 16

1

Banks had always hated hospitals: the antiseptic smells, the starched uniforms, the mysterious and unsettling pieces of shiny equipment around every corner—things that looked like modern sculpture or instruments of torture made of articulated chrome. They all gave him the creeps. Worst of all, though, was the way the doctors and nurses seemed to huddle in corridors and doorways and whisper about death, or so he imagined.

It was Saturday afternoon, 21st May, just over a week since Rothwell's murder and two days after Jameson's shooting, when Banks walked into Leeds Infirmary.

He had spent Thursday night in London, then headed back to Amersham for his car the next morning. After spending a little time with Superintendent Jarrell, Banks and Hatchley had driven back to Eastvale that Friday evening and arrived a little after nine.

On Saturday morning, he had to go into Leeds to consult with Ken Blackstone and wrap things up. After their pub lunch, he had taken a little time off to go and buy some more compact discs at the Classical Record Shop and pay a sick visit before heading back to Eastvale for Richmond's farewell bash. Sandra was off with the Camera Club photographing rock formations at Brimham Rocks, so he was left to his own devices for the day.

Banks paused and looked at the signs, then turned left. At last, he found the right corridor. Pamela Jeffreys shared a room with one other person, who happened to be down in X-ray when Banks called. He pulled up a chair by the side of the bed and put down the brown paper package he'd brought on the table. Pamela looked at it with her one good eye. The other was covered in bandages.

"Grapes," said Banks, feeling embarrassed. "It's what you bring when you visit people in hospital, isn't it?"

Pamela smiled, then decided it hurt too much and let her face relax.

"And," Banks said, pulling a cassette from his pocket, "I made you a tape of some Mozart piano concertos. Thought they might cheer you up. Got a Walkman?"

"Wouldn't go anywhere without it," Pamela said out of the side of her mouth. "It's a bit difficult to get the headphones on with one hand, though." She directed his gaze to where her bandaged right hand lay on the sheets.

He set the cassette on the bedside table beside the grapes. "The doctor says you're going to be okay," he said.

"Hm-mm," murmured Pamela. "So they tell me." It came out muffled, but Banks could tell what she said.

"He said you'll be playing the viola again in no time."

"Hmph. It might take a bit longer than that."

"But you *will* play again."

She uttered a sound that could have been a laugh or a sob. "They broke two fingers on my right hand," she said. "My bowing hand. It's a good thing they know bugger all about musical technique. If they'd broken my wrist that might really have put an end to my career."

"People like that aren't chosen for their intelligence, as a rule," said Banks. "But the important thing is that there's no permanent damage to your fingers, or to your eye."

"I know, I know," she said. "I ought to think myself lucky."

"Well?"

"Oh, I'm okay, I suppose. Mostly just bored. There's the tapes and the radio, but you can't listen to music all day. There's nothing else to do but watch telly, and I can stomach even less of that. Reading still hurts too much with just one good eye. And the food's awful."

"I'm sorry," Banks said. "And I'm sorry about that day in the park."

She moved her head slowly from side to side. "No. My fault. You had to ask. I overreacted. Is this an official visit? Have you come about the men? The men who hurt me?"

"No. But we know who they are. They won't get away with it."

"Why have you come?"

"I . . . that's a good question." Banks laughed nervously and looked away, out of the window at the swaying tree-tops. "To see you, I suppose," he said. "To bring you some grapes and some Mozart. I just happened to be in the area, you know, buying CDs."

"What did you get?"

Banks showed her: Keith Jarrett playing Shostakovitch's 24 preludes and fugues; Nobuko Imai playing Walton's viola concerto. She raised her eyebrow. "Interesting." Then she tapped the Walton. "It's beautiful if you get it right," she said. "But so difficult. She's very good."

"It says in the notes that the viola is an introvert of an instrument, a poet-philosopher. Does that describe you?"

"My teacher told me I had to be careful not to get over-whelmed by the orchestra. That tends to happen to violas, you know. But I manage to hold my own."

"How long are they going to keep you here?"

"Who knows? Another week or so. I'd get up and go home right now but I think my leg's broken."

"It is. The right one."

"Damn. The prettiest."

Banks laughed.

"Did you catch the men who killed Robert?" she asked. "Was it the same ones?"

Banks gave her the gist of what had happened with Jameson, avoiding the more lurid details.

"So one got away?" she said.

"So far."

"That's not bad going."

"Not bad," Banks agreed. "Fifty per cent success rate. It's better than the police average."

"Will you get a promotion out of it?"

He laughed. "I doubt it."

"Don't look so worried," she said, resting her bandaged hand on his. "I'll be all right. And don't blame yourself . . . you know . . . for what happened to me."

"Right. I'll try not to." Banks felt his eyes burn. He could see her name bracelet and the tube attached to the vein in her wrist. It made him feel squeamish, even more so than seeing Jameson's body against the wall in the hotel room. It didn't make sense: he could take a murder scene in his stride, but a simple intravenous drip in a hospital made him queasy.

Pamela was right. She would be fine. Her wounds would heal; her beauty would regenerate. In less than a year she would be as good as new. But would she ever recover fully inside? How would she handle being alone in the house? Would she ever again be able to hear someone walking up the garden path without that twinge of fear and panic? He didn't know. The psyche regenerates itself, too, sometimes. We're often a damn sight more resilient than we'd imagine.

"Will you come and see me again?" she asked. "I mean, when it's all over and I'm home. Will you come and see me?"

"Sure I will," said Banks, thinking guiltily of the feelings he had had for Pamela, not sure at all.

"Do you mean it?"

He looked into her almond eye and saw the black shape of fear at its centre. He swallowed. "Of course I mean it," he said. And he did. He leaned forward and brushed his lips against her good cheek. "I'd better go now."

2

Why was he born so beautiful?
Why was he born so tall?

He's no bloody use to anyone,
He's no bloody use at all.

Richmond took the Yorkshire compliment, delivered in
shaky harmonies by Sergeant Hatchley and an assorted
cat's choir of PCs, very well, Banks thought, especially for
someone who listened to music that sounded like Zamfir
on Valium.

"Speech! Speech!" Hatchley shouted.

Embarrassed, Richmond gave a sideways glance at Ra-
chel, his fiancée, then stood up, cleared his throat and said,
"Thank you. Thank you all very much. And thanks specially for the CD-ROM. You know I'm not much at giving
speeches like this, but I'd just like to say it's been a pleasure working with you all. I know you all probably think
I'm a traitor, going off down south—" Here, a chorus of
boos interrupted his speech. "But as soon as I've got that
lot down there sorted out," he went on, "I'll be back, and
you buggers had better make sure you know a hard drive
from a hole in the ground. Thank you."

He sat down again, and people went over to pat him on
the back and say farewell. Everyone cheered when Susan
Gay leaned forward and gave him a chaste kiss on the
cheek. She blushed when Richmond responded by giving
her a bear-hug.

They were in the back room of the Queen's Arms on
Saturday night, and Banks leaned against the polished bar,
pint of Theakston's in his hand, with Sandra on one side
and Gristhorpe on the other. Someone had hung balloons
from the ceiling. Cyril had hooked up the old jukebox for
the occasion, and Gerry and the Pacemakers were singing
"Ferry Across the Mersey."

Banks knew he should have been happier to see the
end of the Rothwell case, but he just couldn't seem to get
rid of a niggling feeling, like an itch he couldn't reach.
Jameson had killed Rothwell. True. Now Jameson was

dead. Justice had been done, after a fashion. An eye for an eye. So forget it.

But he couldn't. The two men who had beaten Pamela Jeffreys hadn't been caught yet. Along with Jameson's accomplice, that left three on the loose. Only a twenty-five per cent success rate. Not satisfactory at all.

But it wasn't just that. Somehow, it was all too neat. All too neat and ready for Martin Churchill to slip into the country one night with a new face and a clean, colossal bank account and retire quietly to Cornwall, guarding the secrets of those in power to the grave. Which might not be far off. Banks wouldn't be surprised if someone from MI6 or wherever slipped into Cornwall one night and both Mr. Churchill *and* his insurance had a nasty accident.

Susan Gay walked over from Richmond's table and indicated she'd like a word. Banks excused himself from Sandra and they found a quiet corner.

"Sorry for dragging you away from the festivities, sir," Susan said, "but I haven't had a chance to talk to you since you got back. There's a couple of things you might be interested in."

"I'm listening."

Susan told him about her talk with Tom Rothwell after the funeral, about his homosexuality and what he had seen his father do that day he followed him into Leeds. "The artist came in on Wednesday evening, sir, and we managed to get the impression in the papers on Thursday, while you were down south."

"Any luck?"

"Well, yes and no."

"Come on, then. Don't keep me in suspense."

"We've found out who she is. Her name's Julia Marshall and she lives in Adel. That's in north Leeds. She's a schoolteacher. We got a couple of phone calls from colleagues. Apparently, she was a quiet person, shy and private."

"Was?"

"Well, I shouldn't say that, really, sir, but it's just that she's disappeared. That's all we know so far. I just think we should find her, that's all," she said. "Talk to her friends. I don't really know why. It's just a feeling. She might know something."

"I think you're right," said Banks. "It's a loose end I'd like to see tied up as well. There are too many bloody disappearances in this case for my liking. Is there anything else?"

"No. But it's not over yet, is it, sir?"

"No, Susan, I don't think it is. Thanks for telling me. We'll follow up on it first thing tomorrow. For now, we'd better get back to the party or Phil will think we don't love him."

Banks walked back to the bar and lit a cigarette. The music had changed; now it was the Swinging Blue Jeans doing "Hippy, Hippy Shake" and some of the younger members of the department were dancing.

Banks thought about Tom Rothwell and his father. Susan had been sharp to pick up on that. It didn't make sense, given Rothwell's *other* interests, that he should be so genuinely upset that his son didn't want to be an accountant or a lawyer. On the other hand, perhaps nothing was more of an anathema, an insult, to a confirmed heterosexual philanderer than a gay son.

"Penny for them?" Sandra said.

"What? Oh, nothing. Just thinking, that's all."

"It's over, Alan. Leave it be. It's another feather in your cap. You can't solve the whole world's problems."

"It feels more like a lead weight than a feather. I think I'll have another drink." He turned and ordered another pint. Sandra had a gin and tonic. "You're right, of course," he said, standing the drink on the bar. "We've done the best we can."

"You've done *all* you can. It's being pipped at the post by Dirty Dick that really gets your goat, isn't it?" Sandra taunted. "You two have got some kind of macho personal vendetta going, haven't you?"

"Maybe. I don't know. I won't say it's a good feeling, knowing the bastard's got his way."

"You did what you could, didn't you?"

"Yes."

"But you still think Burgess has won this time, and it pisses you off, doesn't it?"

"Maybe. Yes. Yes, it bloody well does. Sandra, the man had someone *shot*."

"A cold-blooded murderer. Besides, you don't know that."

"You mean I can't prove it. And we're not here to play vigilantes. If Burgess had Jameson shot, you can be damn sure it wasn't just an eye for an eye. He was making certain he didn't talk."

"*Men*," said Sandra, turning to her drink with a long-suffering sigh. Gristhorpe, who had been listening from the other side, laughed and nudged Banks in the ribs. "Better listen to her," he said. "I can understand how you feel, but there's no more you can do, and there's no point making some kind of competition out of it."

"I know that. It's not that. It's . . . oh, maybe Sandra's right and it is macho stuff. I don't know."

At that moment, Sergeant Rowe, who had been manning the front desk across the street, pushed through the crowd of drinkers and said to Banks, "Phone call, sir. He says it's important. Must talk to you in person."

Banks put his pint glass back on the bar. "Shit. Did he say who?"

"No."

"All right." He turned to Sandra and pointed at his pint. "Guard that drink with your life. Back in a few minutes."

He couldn't ignore the call; it might be an informer with important information. Irritated, nonetheless, he crossed Market Street and went into the Tudor-fronted police station.

"You can take it in here, sir," said Rowe, pointing to an empty ground-floor office.

Banks went in and picked up the receiver. "Hello. Banks here."

"Ah, Banks," said the familiar voice. "It's Superintendent Burgess here. Remember me? What do you want first, the good news or the bad?"

Speak of the devil. Banks felt his jaw clench and his stomach start to churn. "Just tell me," he said as calmly as he could.

"Okay. You know those two goons, the ones that beat up the tart of colour?"

"Yes. Have you got them?"

"We-ell, not exactly."

"What then?"

"They got away, slipped through our net. That's the bad news."

"Where did they go?"

"Back home, of course. St. Corona. That's the good news."

"What's so good about that?"

"Seems they didn't realize they'd become *persona non grata* there, or whatever the plural of that is."

"And?"

"Well, I have it on good authority that they've both been eating glass."

"They're dead?"

"Of course they're bloody dead. I doubt they'd survive a diet like that."

"How do you know this?"

"I told you. Good authority. It's the real McCoy. No reason to doubt the source."

"Why?"

"Ours is not to reason why, Banks. Let's just say that their bungling around England drawing attention to themselves didn't help much. Things are in a delicate balance."

"Did you know in advance that they were out of favour? Did you let them slip out of the country, knowing what would happen? Did you even try to find them?"

"Oh, Banks. You disappoint me. How could you even think something like that of me?"

"Easy. The same way I think you sent Spike and Shandy down to Kensington to make damn sure Arthur Jameson didn't survive to say anything embarrassing in court."

"I told you, Jameson wasn't in my brief."

"I know what you told me. I also know what happened in that hotel room. They shot the bastard down, Burgess, and you're responsible."

"*Superintendent* Burgess, to you. And he shot first is what I heard. That's the official version, at any rate, and I don't see any reason not to believe it. As our cousins over the pond would say, it was a 'righteous shoot.' "

"Bollocks. They shot him twice then fired off a round from his gun to make it look like he fired first. Apart from the shots, do you know what gave them away?"

"No, but I'm sure you're going to tell me."

"They left the gun in his hand for me to see. Procedure is that you disarm a suspect *first thing*, whether you think he's dead or not."

"Well, hurray for you, Sherlock. Don't you think they might have got careless in the heat of the moment?"

"No. Not with their training."

"But it doesn't matter does it? You weren't there, officially, were you? In fact you were ordered to stay on the ground floor. Anyway I don't think we need to go into all that tiresome stuff do we? Do you really want me to have to pull rank? Believe it or not, I *like* you, Banks. Life would be a lot duller without you. I wouldn't want to see you throw your career down the tubes over this. Take my word for it, *nobody* will take kindly to your rocking the boat. The official verdict is the only one that counts."

"Not to me."

"Leave it alone, Banks. It's over."

"Why does everyone keep telling me that?"

"Because it's true. One more thing. And don't interrupt me. We found an address book in Jameson's stuff and it led us to an old ex-army crony of his called Donald Pembroke. Ring any bells?''

"No.''

"Anyway, it seems this Pembroke just inherited a lot of money according to his neighbour. The first thing he did was buy a fast sports car, cash down according to the salesman. Two days later he lost control on a B road in Kent—doing eighty or ninety by all accounts—and ran it into a tree.''

"And?''

"And he's dead isn't he? What's more there's no way you can put it down to me. So don't say there's no justice in the world, Banks. Goodbye. Have a good life.'' Burgess hung up abruptly, leaving Banks to glare into the receiver. He slammed it down so hard that Sergeant Rowe popped his head around the door. "Everything all right, sir?''

"Yes, fine,'' said Banks. He took a deep breath and ran his hand through his short hair. "Everything's just bloody fine and dandy.'' He sat in the empty office gaining control of his breathing. Susan's words echoed in his mind. *"It's not over yet, is it, sir?"* No, it bloody well wasn't.

: 17

1.

Banks sat at a *tavérna* by the quayside sipping an ice-cold Beck's and smoking a duty-free Benson and Hedges Special Mild. When he had finished his cigarette, he popped a *dolmáde* into his mouth and followed it with a black olive. One or two of the locals, mostly mustachioed and sun-leathered fishermen, occasionally glanced his way during a pause in their conversation.

It was a small island, just one village built up the central hillside, and though it got its share of tourists in season, none of the big cruise ships came. Banks had arrived half an hour ago on a regular ferry service from Piraeus and he needed a while to collect his thoughts and get his land-legs back again. He had a difficult interview ahead of him, he suspected. He had already contacted the Greek police. Help had been offered, and the legal machinery was ready to grind into action at a word. But Banks had something else he wanted to try first.

By Christ, it was hot, even in the shade. The sun beat down from a clear sky, a more intense, more saturated blue than Banks had ever seen, especially in contrast to the white houses, shops and *tavérnas* along the quayside. A couple of sailboats and a few fishing craft were moored in the small harbour, bobbing gently on the calm water. It was hard to describe the sea's colour; certainly there were shades of green and blue in it, aquamarine, ultramarine, but in places it was a kind of inky blue, too, almost purple. Maybe Homer was right when he called it "wine-dark," Banks thought, remembering his conversation with Super-

intendent Gristhorpe before the trip. Banks had never read
The Odyssey, but he probably would when he got back.

He paid for his food and drink and walked out into the
sun. On his way, he popped into the local police station in
the square near the harbour, as promised, then set off along
the dirt track up the hill.

The main street itself was narrow enough, but every few
yards a side-street branched off, narrower still, all white,
cubist, flat-roofed houses with painted shutters, mostly blue.
Some of the houses had red pantile roofs, like the ones in
Whitby. Many people had put hanging baskets of flowers
out on the small balconies, a profusion of purple, pink, red
and blue, and lines of washing hung over the narrow streets.
By the roadside were poppies and delicate lavender flowers
that looked like morning glories.

Mingled with the scents of the flowers were the smells
of tobacco and wild herbs. Banks thought he recognized
thyme and rosemary. Insects with red bodies and transparent wings flew around him. The sun beat relentlessly. Before Banks had walked twenty yards, his white cotton shirt
stuck to his back. He wished he had worn shorts instead of
jeans.

Banks looked ahead. Where the white houses ended halfway up the hillside, scrub and rocky outcrops took over.
The house he wanted, he had been told, was on his right,
a large one with a high-gated white wall and a shaded
courtyard. It wasn't difficult to spot, now about fifty yards
ahead, almost three-quarters of the length of the road.

He finally made it. The ochre gate was unlocked, and
beyond it, Banks found a courtyard full of saplings, pots
of herbs and hanging plants by a *krokalia* pathway of black
and white pebbles winding up to the door. Expensive, definitely. The door was slightly ajar, and he could hear voices
inside. By the plummy tones, it sounded like the BBC
World Service news. He paused a moment for breath, then
walked up to the door and knocked.

He heard a movement inside, the voices stopped, and in

a few seconds someone opened the door. Banks looked into
the face that he had thought for so long had been blown to
smithereens.

"Mr. Rothwell?" he said, slipping his card out of his
wallet and holding it up. "Mr. Keith Rothwell?"

2

"You've come, then?" Rothwell said simply.

"Yes."

He looked over Banks's shoulder. "Alone?"

"Yes."

"You'd better come in."

Banks followed Rothwell into a bright room where a
ceiling fan spun and a light breeze blew through the open
blue shutters. It was sparsely furnished. The walls were
plastered white, the floor was flagged, covered here and
there by rugs, and the ceiling was panelled with dark wood.
Outside, he could hear birds singing; he didn't know what
kind.

He sat down in the wicker chair Rothwell offered, surprised to be able to see the sea down below through the
window. Now he was at the end of his journey, he felt bone
weary and more than a little dizzy. It had been a long way
from Eastvale and a long uphill walk in the sun. Sweat
dribbled from his eyebrows into his eyes and made them
sting. He wiped it away with his forearm. At least it was
cooler inside the room.

Rothwell noticed his discomfort. "Hot, isn't it?" he said.
"Can I get you something?"

Banks nodded. "Thanks. Anything as long as it's cold."

Rothwell went to the kitchen door and turned, with a
smile, just as he opened it. "Don't worry," he said. "I
won't run away."

"There's nowhere to run," replied Banks.

A minute or so later he came back with a glass of ice
water and a bottle of Grölsch lager. "I'd drink the water

first," he advised. "You look a bit dehydrated."

Banks drained the glass then opened the metal gizmo on the beer. It tasted good. Imported, of course. But Rothwell could afford it. Banks looked at him. The receding sandy hair, forming a slight widow's peak, had bleached in the sun. He had a good tan for such a fair-skinned person. Behind wire-rimmed glasses, his steady grey eyes looked out calmly, not giving away any indication as to his state of mind. He had a slightly prissy mouth, a girl's mouth, and his lips were pale pink. He looked nothing at all like the photograph of Daniel Clegg.

He wore a peach short-sleeve shirt, white shorts and brown leather sandals. His toenails needed cutting. He was an inch or so taller than Banks, slim and in good shape—about all he did have in common with Clegg, apart from the colour of his hair, his blood group and the appendicitis scar. When he went to get the drinks, Banks noticed, he moved with an athlete's grace and economy. There was nothing of the sedentary penpusher about his bearing.

"Anyone else here?" Banks asked.

"Julia's gone to the shops," he said, glancing at his watch. "She shouldn't be long."

"I'd like to meet her."

"How did you find me?" Rothwell asked, sitting opposite, opening a tin of Pepsi. The gas hissed out and liquid frothed over the edge. Rothwell held it at arm's length until it had stopped fizzing, then wiped the tin with a tissue from a box on the table beside him.

"It wasn't that difficult," said Banks. "Once I knew who I was looking for. We found you partly through Julia." He shrugged. "After that it was a matter of routine police work, mostly boring footwork. We checked travel agents, then we contacted the local police through Interpol. It didn't take that long to get word back about two English strangers who resembled your descriptions taking a lease on a captain's house here. Did you really believe we wouldn't find you eventually?"

"I suppose I must have," said Rothwell. "Foolish of me, but there it is. There are always variables, loose ends, but I thought I'd left enough red herrings and covered my tracks pretty well. I planned it all very carefully."

"Do you have any idea what you've done to your family?"

Rothwell's lips tightened. "It wasn't a family. It was a sham. A lie. A façade. We played at happy families. I couldn't stand it any more. There was no love in the house. Mary and I hadn't slept together in years and Tom . . . well . . ."

Banks let Tom pass for the moment. "Why not get a divorce like anyone else? Why this elaborate scheme?"

"I assume, seeing as you're here, you know most of it?"

"Humour me."

Rothwell squinted at Banks. "Look," he said. "I can't see where you'd have any room to hide one, but you're not 'wired' as the Americans say, are you?"

Banks shook his head. "You have my word on that."

"This is just between you and me? Off the record?"

"For the moment. I am here officially, though."

Rothwell sipped some Pepsi then rubbed the can between his palms. "I might have asked Mary for a divorce eventually," he said, "but it was still all very new to me, the freedom, the taste of another life. I'm not even sure she would have let me go that easily. The way things turned out, though, I had to appear dead. If he thinks I'm alive, there'll be no peace, no escape anywhere."

"Martin Churchill?"

"Yes. He found out I was taking rather more than I was entitled to."

"How did you find out he knew?"

"A close source. When you play the kind of games I did, Mr. Banks, it pays to have as much information as you can get. Let's say someone on the island tipped me that Churchill knew and that he was pressuring Daniel Clegg to do something about it."

"Is that how it happened?"

"Yes. And it made sense. I'd noticed that Daniel had been behaving oddly lately. He was nervous about something. Wouldn't look me in the eye. Now I had an explanation. The bastard was planning to have me executed."

"So you had him killed instead?"

Rothwell gazed out of the window at the sea and the mountainside in silence for a moment. "Yes. It was him or me. I beat him to it, that's all. Someone had to die violently, someone who could pass for me under certain circumstances. We looked enough alike."

"Without a face, you mean?"

"I . . . I didn't look . . . in the garage . . . I couldn't."

"I'll bet you couldn't. Go on."

"We were about the same age and build, same hair colour. I knew he'd had his appendix out. I even knew his blood group was 'O,' the same as mine."

"How did you know that?"

"He told me. We were talking once about blood tainted by the HIV virus. He wondered if he had a greater chance of catching it from a transfusion because he shared his blood group with over forty per cent of the male population."

"What did you do once you had the idea of passing him off as you?"

"There was this man we'd both met in the Eagle a couple of times, down there for the Ed O'Donnell Band on a Sunday lunch-time, and he'd boasted about being a mercenary and doing anything for money. Arthur Jameson was his name. He was a walking mass of contradictions. He loved animals and nature, but he liked hunting and duck-shooting, and he didn't seem to give a damn for human life. I found him fascinating. Fascinating and a little frightening.

"It was perfect. Daniel knew him, too, of course, and he told me that Jameson had even approached him for some legal help once, shortly after we met. I thought if you found out anything, that would be it. He might have had something in his files. You know how lawyers hoard every scrap of paper. But there was nothing linking Jameson to *me*. It would only reinforce what you suspected already, that Daniel had had *me* killed instead of the other way round. You weren't to know that I was with Daniel the day we met Jameson, or that I'd chatted with Jameson on a number of subsequent occasions.''

"So you and Clegg were pals? Socialized together, did you?''

Rothwell paused. A muscle by his jaw twitched. "No. It wasn't quite like that," he said quietly. "Daniel had a hold over me, but sometimes he seemed to want to play at being boozing buddies. I didn't understand it, but at least for a while we could bury our differences and have a good time. The next day it would usually be back to cold formality. At bottom, Daniel was a terrible snob. Been to Cambridge, you know.''

"How much did you pay Jameson?''

"Fifty thousand pounds and a plane ticket to Rio. I know it's a lot, but I thought the more I paid him the more likely he'd be to disappear for good with it and not get caught.''

"First mistake.''

"How did it happen?''

Banks told him about the wadding and about Jameson's attitude to the world beyond Calais. Rothwell laughed, then stared at the sea again. "I knew it was a risk," he said. "I suppose I should have known, the way he used to go on about the Irish and the Frogs sometimes. But if you have a dream you have to take risks for it, pay a price, don't you?''

"You needn't try to justify your actions to me," said Banks, finally feeling steady and cool enough to light a cigarette. He offered one to Rothwell, who accepted. "I was the one left to clean up your mess. And Jameson killed one policeman and seriously wounded another trying to escape." The fan drew their smoke up to it, then pushed it towards the windows.

"I'm sorry."

"I'll bet you are."

"It wasn't my fault, what Jameson did, was it? You can't blame me."

"Can't I? Let's get back to your relationship with Daniel Clegg. How did you get involved?"

"We met in the George Hotel, on Great George Street. It was about four years ago. A year or so after I left Hatchard and Pratt, anyway. Expenses were high, what with renovations to Arkbeck and everything else, and business wasn't exactly booming, though I wasn't doing too badly. They have jazz at the George on Thursdays, and as I was in Leeds on business, I thought I'd drop by rather than watch television in the hotel room. It turns out we were both jazz fans. We just got talking, that's all.

"I didn't tell him very much at first, except that I was a freelance financial consultant. He seemed interested. Anyway, we exchanged business cards and he put a bit of work my way, off-shore banking, that sort of thing. Turns out some of it was a bit shady, though I wasn't aware at the time—not that I mightn't have done it, anyway, mind you—and he brought that up later, in conversation."

"He put pressure on you?"

"Oh, yes." Rothwell paused and looked Banks in the eye. "A smooth blackmailer, was Danny-boy. I suppose you know about my bit of bad luck at Hatchard and Pratt's, don't you?"

"Yes."

"That was five years ago. We'd just moved into Arkbeck then and we couldn't really afford it. Not that the mortgage itself was so high, but the place had been neglected for so long. There was so much needed doing, and I'm no DIY expert. But Mary wanted to live there, so live there we did. The upshot was that I had to pad the expenses a little. If I hadn't been married to the boss's daughter, and if Laurence

Pratt hadn't been a good friend, things could have gone very badly for me at the firm then. As it was, after I left I didn't have a lot of work at first, and Mary . . . well, that's another story. Let's just say she doesn't have a forgiving nature. One night, in my cups, I hinted to Daniel about what had happened, how I had parted company with Hatchard and Pratt.

"Anyway, later, Daniel used what he knew about me as leverage to get me involved when his old college friend Martin Churchill first made enquiries about rearranging his finances. That was a little over three years back. See, he knew he couldn't handle the task by himself, that he needed my expertise. He told me he could still report me to the board, that it wasn't too late. Well, maybe they would have listened to him, and maybe they wouldn't. Who knows now? Quite frankly, I didn't care. I already knew a bit about money-laundering, and it looked to me like a licence to print money. Why wouldn't I want in? I think Daniel just enjoyed manipulating people, having power over them, so I didn't spoil his illusion. But he really wasn't terribly bright, wasn't Danny-boy, despite Cambridge.''

"A bit like Frankenstein and the monster, isn't it?''

Rothwell smiled. "Yes, perhaps. And I suppose you'd have to say that the monster far outstripped his creator, though you could hardly say the good doctor himself was without sin.''

"How did you arrange it all? The murder, the escape?''

Rothwell emptied his tin, put it on the table and leaned back. The chair creaked. Outside, gulls cried as they circled the harbour looking for fish. "Another Grölsch?'' he asked.

There was still an inch left in the bottle. "No,'' said Banks. "Not yet.''

Rothwell sighed. "You have to go back about eighteen months to understand, to when I first started using the Robert Calvert identity. Daniel and I were doing fine laundering Churchill's money, and he allowed us a decent percentage for doing so. I was getting rich quick. I suppose I should have been happy, but I wasn't. I don't know exactly when I first became aware of it, but life just seemed to have lost its savour, its sweetness. Things started to oppress me. I felt like I was shrivelling up inside, dying, old before my time. Call it mid-life crisis, I suppose, but I couldn't see the *point* of all that bloody money.

"All Mary wanted was her bridge club, more renovations, additions to the house, jewelry, expensive holidays. Christ, I should have known better than to marry the boss's daughter, even if I did get her pregnant. One simple mistake, that and my own bloody weakness. What was it the philosopher said about the erect penis knowing no conscience? That may be so, but it certainly understands penitence, regret, remorse. One bloody miserable, uncomfortable screw in the back of an Escort halfway up Crow Scar set me on a course straight to hell. I'm not exaggerating. Twenty-one years. After that long, my wife hated me, my children hated me, and I was beginning to hate myself."

Banks noticed that Rothwell had picked up the empty Pepsi tin and started to squeeze until it buckled in his grip.

"Then I realized I was handling millions of pounds—literally, millions—and that my job was essentially to clean it and hide it ready for future use. It wasn't difficult to find a few hiding places of my own. Small amounts at first, then, when no-one seemed to miss it, more and more. Shell companies, numbered accounts, dummy corporations, property. I liked what I was doing. The manipulation of large sums of money intrigued me and excited me like nothing else, or almost nothing else. Just for the sake of it, much of the time. Like art for art's sake.

"I began to spend more time away from home on 'business.' Nobody cared one way or another. They never asked me where I'd been. They only asked for more money for a new kitchen or a sun-porch or a bloody gazebo. When I was home, I walked around like a zombie—the dull, boring accountant, I suppose—and mostly kept to my office or nipped out to the pub for a smoke and a jar occasionally. I had plenty of time to look back on my life, and though I didn't like a lot of what I saw, I remembered I hadn't always been so bloody bored or boring. I used to go dancing, believe it or not. I used to like a flutter on the horses now and then. I had friends. Once in a while, I liked to have too much to drink with the lads and stagger home singing, happy as a lark. That was before life came to resemble an accounts ledger—debits and credits, profit and loss, with far too much on the loss side." He sighed. "Are you sure you wouldn't like another beer?"

"Go on, then," Banks said. His bottle was empty now.

Rothwell brought back a Pepsi for himself and another Grölsch for Banks. His glasses had slipped down over the bridge of his nose and he pushed them back.

"So I invented Robert Calvert," Rothwell said after a sip of Pepsi.

"Where did you get the name?"

"Picked it from a magazine I was reading at the time. With a pin. *The Economist*, I believe."

"Go on."

"I rented the flat, bought new clothes, more casual. God, you've no idea how strange it felt at first. Good, but strange. There were moments when I really did believe I was going mad, turning into a split personality. It became a kind of compulsion, an addiction, like smoking. I'd go to the bookie's and put bets on, spend a day at the races, go listen to trad jazz in smoky pubs—the Adelphi, the George, the Duck and Drake—something I hadn't done since my early twenties. I'd go around in jeans and sweatshirts. And nobody back at Arkbeck Farm ever asked where I'd been, what I'd been doing, as long I turned up every now and then in my business suit and the money kept coming in for a new freezer, a first edition Brontë, a Christmas trip to Hawaii. After a while I realized I wasn't going mad, I was just becoming myself, returning to the way I was before I let life grind me down.

"And, sure enough, the money kept coming in. I had tapped into an endless supply, or so I thought. So I played the family role part of the time, and I started exploring my real self as Robert Calvert. I had no idea where it would lead, not then. I was just trying out ways of escape. I told Daniel Clegg one night when we'd had a few, and he thought it was a wild idea. I had to tell someone and I couldn't tell my family or Pratt or anyone local, so why not tell my blackmailer, my confidant? He helped me get a bank account and credit card as Calvert, which he thought gave him an even stronger hold over me. He could always claim he'd been deceived, you see."

"What about the escape?"

"You're jumping ahead a bit, but as I'd already created Robert Calvert successfully enough, it wasn't very difficult to go on from there and create a third identity: David Norcliffe. As you no doubt know, seeing as you're here. Rothwell was dead, and I couldn't go as Calvert. I had to leave him behind; that was part of the plan. So I shuffled more money into various bank accounts in various places over a period of several weeks. After all, that's what I do best. I've laundered and hidden millions for Churchill and his wife."

"How much for yourself?"

"Three or four million," he said with a shrug. "I don't know exactly. Enough, anyway, to last us our lifetime. And there was plenty left in Eastvale for my family. They're well provided for in the will and by the life insurance. I made sure of that. Believe me, they'll be better off without me."

"What about Daniel Clegg? What about Pamela Jeffreys?"

"Pamela? What about her?"

Banks told him.

He put his head in his hands. "Oh, my God," he said. "I would never have hurt Pamela . . . It wasn't meant to be like that."

"How did you meet her?"

Rothwell sipped some more Pepsi and rubbed the back of his hand across his brow. "I told you the Calvert thing felt very strange at first. Mostly, I just used to walk around Leeds in my jeans and sweatshirt. I'd drop in at a pub now and then and enjoy being someone else. Occasionally, I got chatting to people, the way you do in pubs. I'll never forget how frightening and how exciting it was the first time someone asked me my name and I said 'Robert Calvert.' I knew it was still me—you have to understand that—we're not really talking about a split personality here. I was Keith Rothwell, all right, just playing a part, or trying to find himself, perhaps. It gave me an exhilarating sense of freedom.

"Anyway, as I said, I used to drop in at pubs now and then, mostly in the city centre or up in Headingley, near the flat. One night I saw Pamela in The Boulevard—you know, the tarted-up Jubilee Hotel on The Headrow. It seemed a likely place to meet women. They stay open till midnight on weekends and they've got a small dance-floor. Pamela was with some friends. They'd been doing something at the Town Hall, a Handel oratorio, or something like that. Anyway, something happened, some spark. We caught one another's eye.

"She wasn't with anyone in particular. I mean, she didn't seem to have a boyfriend with her. The next time she was at the bar, I made sure I got there, too, next to her, and we got chatting. I wasn't a great fan of classical music, but Pamela's a down-to-earth sort of person, not a highbrow snob or anything. I asked her to dance. She said yes. We just got on, that's all. We slept together now and then, but both of us knew it was just a casual relationship really. I don't mean to denigrate it by saying that. We had a wonderful time. I was astounded she fancied me. Flattered. It was the first time in my entire marriage that I'd been with another woman, and the hell of it was that I didn't feel guilty at all. She was fun to be with, and we had a great time, but we weren't in love.''

''What came between you?''

''What? Well, we stayed friends, really. At least, I like to think we did. There was her work, of course. It's very demanding and between us we couldn't always be sure we could make time to get together. And Pamela was more outgoing. She wanted more of a social life. She wanted me to meet her friends, and she wanted to meet mine.''

''But you didn't have any?''

''Exactly. And I didn't want to get too well known around the place. It was a risk, playing Calvert, always a risk.''

''Go on. What happened next?''

''I met Julia.''

''How?''

''We met on a bus, would you believe? It had been raining, one of those sudden showers, and I was out walking without an umbrella. So I jumped on a bus into town. Then the rain stopped and the sun came out. I'd been looking at her out of the corner of my eye. She was so beautiful, like a model, such delicate, fragile, sculpted features. I imagined she was probably stuck-up and wouldn't talk to the likes of me. Anyway, she left her umbrella. I saw it, grabbed it, and dashed after her. When I caught her up she seemed startled at first, then I gave it to her and she blushed. She seemed flustered, so I asked her if she wanted to go for a coffee. She said yes. She was very shy. It was hard to get her talking at first, but slowly I found out she was a teacher and she lived in Adel and she adored Greek history and literature.

''Do you believe in love at first sight, Mr. Banks? Do you? Because that's what this is all about, really. It's not just about money. It's not just about leaving my old life behind and seeking novelty. I fell in love with Julia the moment I saw her, and that's the truth. It might sound foolish and sentimental to you, but I have never in my life felt that way before. Bells ringing, earth moving, all the cliches.

And it's mutual. She's everything I've ever wanted. When I met Julia, nothing else mattered. I knew we had to get away, find our Eden, if you like, our paradise. I had to get a new life, a new identity. Everything was in such a mess, falling apart. No-one was supposed to get hurt.''

"Except Daniel Clegg.''

Rothwell banged on his chair arm with his fist. "I told you! That wasn't my fault. I had to appear to have been violently murdered. By Daniel himself, or by someone he'd hired. And that's exactly the way it would have been, too, if I hadn't been tipped off and made other plans. But Julia knew nothing of that. She's a complete innocent. She knows nothing of the things we've just been talking about.''

"So you invited Clegg over to the Calvert flat to get his fingerprints there? Am I right?''

"Yes. On the Monday. I said I had some business to discuss that couldn't wait and he came over. I showed him around, had him touch things. I'd cleaned the place thoroughly. Daniel was a touchy-feely kind of person. Anything he saw, he'd pick it up and have a look: compact discs, wallet, credit cards in Calvert's name, coins, books, you name it. He'd even let his fingers rest on surfaces as if he were claiming them or something. He handled just about everything in the place. I was much more careful to make mine blurred.'' Rothwell laughed quietly. "He really was a fool, you know. Every time I got him to help me with something illegal, like setting up the Calvert bank account and credit card, for example, *he* thought he was getting more power over *me*.''

"So you must have known we'd find out about the Calvert identity, about Pamela, about Clegg and the money-laundering?''

"Of course. As I said earlier, I had to leave Calvert behind. It was part of my plan that you should find out about him. Another dead end. But please believe me, Pamela wasn't meant to be a part of it, except maybe to confirm the Calvert identity. I mean, I thought she might get in touch with the police if she saw my picture in the papers. Or someone else might, someone who thought they recognized me. It was meant to confuse you, that's all. I left a careful trail for you. I thought it led the wrong way. I knew the police would be able to unlock and interpret the data on my computer eventually, that they would realize I'd been laundering money for Martin Churchill. I also left a letter for Daniel Clegg in a locked file. I knew you'd get at that eventually, too."

"That was one of the things that bothered me," Banks said. "In retrospect, it was all too easy. And we never found a copy of the letter among his papers. He could have destroyed it, of course, but it was just one of those little niggling details. Lawyers tend to hang onto things."

"I never sent it," said Rothwell. "I just created the file so you'd get onto Daniel if you hadn't already. It was a way of telling you his name, but I couldn't make it *too* easy. Then you'd assume he'd had me killed and disappeared with the money."

"Oh, we did," said Banks. "We did."

"Then why are you here?"

"Because I'm a persistent bastard, among other things. There were too many loose ends. They worried me. Two different sets of thugs roaming the country, for a start. They could be explained, of course, but it still seemed odd. And we couldn't find any trace of Clegg, no matter how hard we tried. His ex-wife said he fancied Tahiti, but we had no luck there. We had no luck anywhere else, either. Of course we didn't. We were looking for the wrong person. But mostly, I think, it was the connection with Julia that really did you in."

"How did you find out about her?"

"Pamela Jeffreys mentioned her first. She said she thought you were in love. Just a feeling she had, you understand. Then I began to wonder how it would upset the apple-cart if you fell in love as *Robert Calvert*. How would you handle it? Then Tom came back from America for your funeral.''

"Ah, Tom. My Achilles heel.''

"Oh, he didn't realize the significance of it. But you made him angry. He followed you to Leeds once. He saw you have lunch with a woman. Julia Marshall. You didn't know that, did you? But Tom couldn't imagine the scale of your plans. He's just a kid who caught his father with another woman. He was already angry, mixed up and confused at the way you treated him. He was after getting his own back, but what he saw upset him so much that all he could do was keep it to himself.''

"Christ," he muttered. "I didn't know that. He didn't tell Mary?''

"No. He wanted to protect her.''

"My God." Rothwell ran his hand over the side of his face. "Maybe you think I reacted too harshly, Chief Inspector? I know we're living in liberal times, where anything goes. I know it's old-fashioned of me, but I still happen to believe that homosexuality is an aberration, an abomination of nature, and not just an 'alternative lifestyle,' as the liberals would have it. And to find out that *my* own son . . .''

"So you decided it would be best to send Tom away?''

"Yes. It seemed best for both of us if he went away, a long way away. He was well provided for. As it turned out, he wanted to go travelling in America and try to get into film school there. By then I knew I had to get away, too, so it seemed best to let him go. At least he had a good chance. I might have abhorred his homosexuality, but I'm not a tyrant. He was still my son, after all.''

"Tom gave us an accurate description of Julia," Banks went on. "He's a very observant young man. We ran the artist's impression in the *Yorkshire Post* and a woman called Barbara Ledward came forward, a colleague of Julia's, then Julia's family. Nobody lives in a vacuum. When we followed up on their phone calls, we found out that Julia had resigned from her teaching job suddenly and told everyone she was going away, that she had a once-in-a-lifetime opportunity abroad but couldn't divulge the details. She said she'd be in touch, then she simply disappeared about three days before your apparent murder. Her family and friends were worried about her. She didn't usually behave so irresponsibly. But they didn't report her as a missing person because she had *told* them she was going away.

"We might have been a bit slow on the uptake, but we're not stupid. All Julia's friends and colleagues mentioned how fascinated she was by the ancient Greeks. She even tried to teach the kids about the classics at school, though I'm told it didn't go down well with the head. He wanted them to study computers and car maintenance instead. We had to assume you didn't think we'd find out about Julia. Oh, you might have suspected we'd find out there was *someone*, but you didn't think we'd try to find her, did you?"

"No," said Rothwell. "After all, why should you want to? No more than I thought you would waste time and money doing tests to see if it really was *my* body in the garage. Another risk. I was clearly dead, executed because of my involvement in international crime. What did it matter if I, or Calvert, had a girlfriend? I never thought for a moment you'd look very closely at the rest of my private life."

"Then you shouldn't have revealed the Calvert identity to us," Banks said. "If it hadn't been for that, we might have gone on thinking you were a dull, mild-mannered accountant who just happened to get into something beyond his depth. But Calvert showed imagination. Calvert showed a dimension to your character I had to take into account. And I had to ask myself, what if Calvert fell in love?"

"I couldn't get rid of Calvert," said Rothwell. "You know that. I didn't have time. Too many people had seen him. I had to figure out a way to make him work to my advantage quickly. I thought he'd be a dead end."

"Your mistake. Poor judgment."

"Obviously. But I had no choice. What else could I do?"

"So how did you handle the killing?"

"Another drink?"

"Please."

Banks stared out over the pink and purple flowers in the window box at the barren hillside and the blue sea below. Rothwell's mention of the forensic tests galled him. He knew they should have tried to establish the identity of the deceased beyond doubt. Forensics should have reconstructed the teeth and checked dental records. That was an oversight. It was understandable, given the way Rothwell had apparently been assassinated, and given the state the teeth were in, but it was an oversight, nevertheless.

Of course, the lab had been as burdened with work as usual, and tests cost money. Then, when the fingerprints at Calvert's flat matched the corpse's, they didn't think they needed to look any further. After all, they had the pasta meal, the appendix scar and the right blood group, and Mary Rothwell had identified the dead man's clothing, watch and pocket contents.

A red flying insect settled on his bare arm. He brushed it off gently. When Rothwell came back with a Grölsch and a Pepsi, he was not moving with quite the same confidence and grace as he had before.

"I gave Jameson instructions to hold Alison until we got back," he began, "but *not* to harm her in any way."

"That's considerate of you. He didn't. What about his accomplice, Donald Pembroke?"

Rothwell shook his head. He held the Pepsi against his shorts. The tin was beaded with moisture and Banks watched the damp patch spread through the white cotton. "I never met him. That was Jameson's business. He said he needed someone to help and I left it to him, getting guarantees of discretion, of course. I never even knew the man's name, and that's the truth. Pembroke, you say? What happened to him?"

Banks told him.

Rothwell sighed. "I suppose fate catches up with us all in the end, doesn't it? What is it the eastern religions call it? Karma?"

"Back to the murder."

Rothwell paused a moment, then went on. "They held Alison, then when Mary and I got home, they tied her up, too, and took me out to the garage. They had instructions to pick Clegg up after dinner. I knew he didn't like to cook for himself and on Thursdays he always dropped by a trattoria near the office for a quick pasta before going home. That's why I chose that day. I knew Mary and I would be going out for the annual anniversary dinner, and I arranged for us to eat at Mario's. You see, I thought of everything. Even the stomach contents would match.

"They'd already knocked Clegg out and secured him earlier. I even made sure to tell Jameson to use loose handcuffs to avoid rope burns on Clegg's wrists. We got him into my clothes as quickly as possible. He was starting to come round. He was on his hands and knees, I remember, shaking his head as if he was groggy, just waking up, then Jameson put the shotgun to the back of his head. I . . . I turned away. There was a terrible explosion and a smell. Then we went through the woods and they drove me to Leeds. I drove Clegg's Jaguar to Heathrow, wearing gloves, of course. Then I left the country as David Norcliffe. I already had a passport and bank accounts set up in that name. I joined Julia here. It was all pre-arranged. It had to be so elaborate because I was supposed to be murdered. I'd read about a similar murder in the papers a while back and it seemed one worth imitating."

"Well, you know what the poet said. 'The best laid plans . . . ' "

"But you can't prove anything," said Rothwell.

"Don't be an idiot. Of course we can. We can prove that you're alive and Daniel Clegg was murdered in your garage."

"But you can't prove I was there. It's only your word against mine. I could say they were taking me out to kill both of us. I managed to get away and I ran and hid here. They killed Daniel, but I escaped."

"They killed him in *your* clothes?" Banks shook his head slowly. "It won't wash, Keith."

"But it's all circumstantial. Jameson and Pembroke are both dead. A good lawyer could get me off, and you know it."

"You're dreaming. Say you do beat the murder conspiracy charge, which I think is unlikely, there's still the money-laundering and the rest."

Rothwell looked around the room, mouth set firmly. "I'm not going back," he said. "You can't make me. I know there are European extradition treaties. Procedures to follow. They take time. You can't just take me in like some bounty hunter."

"Of course I can't," said Banks. "That was never my intention." He heard the gate open and walked over to the window.

A pale, beautiful woman in a yellow sun-dress, red-blonde hair piled and knotted high on her head, had walked into the courtyard and paused to check on the flowers and potted plants. She carried a basket of fresh bread and other foodstuffs in the crook of her arm. She put out her free hand and bent to hold a purple blossom gently between her fingers for a moment, then inspected the herbs. The sun brought out the blonde highlights in her hair. "It looks like Julia's back," Banks said. "Doesn't tan well, does she?"

Rothwell jumped up and looked out. "Julia knows nothing," he said quickly, speaking quietly so she couldn't hear him. "You have to believe that. I told her I had business problems, that I had to burn a lot of bridges if we were to be together, that we'd be well set up for life but we couldn't go back. Ever. She agreed. I don't know if you can understand this or not, but I *love her*, Banks, more than anyone or anything I've ever loved in my life. I mean it. It's the

first time I've ever . . . I already told you. I love her. She
knows nothing. You can do what you want with me, but
leave her alone.''

Banks kept quiet.

''You'll never be able to prove anything,'' Rothwell
added.

''Maybe I don't even want to take that risk,'' said Banks.
By now they could both see Julia and hear her humming
softly as she rubbed the leaves on a pot of basil and sniffed
her fingers. ''Maybe I'd rather you made a clean breast of
it,'' he went on, keeping his voice low. ''A confession. It
might even go in your favour, you never know. Especially
the love bit. Juries love lovers.''

Julia stood up. Some of her piled tresses had come loose
and trailed over her cheeks. She was flushed from the walk
and some of the hairs stuck to her face, dampened with
sweat.

''You must be mad if you think I'd give all this up will-
ingly,'' Rothwell said.

''You can't buy paradise with blood, Keith,'' said Banks.
''Come on home. Tell us everything about Martin Churchill's finances, everything you know about the bastard.
Let's go public, make plenty of noise, sing louder than a
male-voice choir. We can make sure he never sets foot in
the country even if he turns up looking like Mr. Bean. We
could offer you protection, then perhaps another identity,
another new life. You'd do some time, of course, but I'm
willing to bet that by the time you got out, Martin Churchill
would be just another of history's unpleasant footnotes, and
Julia would be still waiting.''

''You're insane, do you know that? I'd kill you before
I'd do what you're suggesting.''

''No, you wouldn't, Keith. Besides, there'd be others after me.''

Rothwell paused on his way to the door and stared at
Banks, eyes wide open and wild, no longer calm and
steady. ''Do you know what will happen if I go home?''

"It might not be half as bad as what will happen if I let Churchill know you're still alive," said Banks. "They say he has a long reach and a nasty line in revenge." Julia had almost reached the door. "It wouldn't stop at you," Banks said.

Rothwell froze. "You wouldn't. No. Not even *you* would do a thing like that."

At that moment, Banks hated himself probably more than at any other time in his life. He felt sorry for Rothwell, and he found himself on the verge of relenting.

Then he remembered Mary Rothwell, living in a haze of tranquillizers; Alison, burying her head deep in her books and fast losing touch with the real world; and Tom, flailing around in his own private mire of guilt and confusion. Rothwell could have helped these people. Then he thought of Pamela Jeffreys, just out of hospital, physically okay, but still afraid of every knock at her door and unsure whether she would get back the confidence to play her viola again.

For this man's gamble on paradise, Daniel Clegg lay in his grave with his head blown off, Barry Miller had died on a wet road at midnight, and Grant Everett might have to spend the next few years of his life relearning how to walk and talk. Even Arthur Jameson and Donald Pembroke were Rothwell's victims, in a way.

And, much further away but no less implicated, was a dictator who got fat while his people starved, a man who liked to watch people eat glass, a man who, now, if Banks could help it, would never enjoy a peaceful retirement in the English countryside, no matter what he had on some powerful members of the establishment.

And the more Banks thought about these people, victims and predators alike, the less able he was to feel sorry for the fallen lovers.

"Try me," he said.

Rothwell glared at him, then all the life seemed to drain out of him until he resembled nothing more than a tired,

middle-aged accountant. Banks still felt dirty and miserable, and despite his resolve, he wasn't certain he could go
through with his threat. But Rothwell believed him now,
and that was all that mattered. This bastard had caused
enough trouble already. There was no more room for pity.
Banks felt his pulse race, his jaw clench. Then the door
opened and Julia drifted in, all blonde and yellow, with a
big smile for Rothwell.

"Hello, darling! Oh," she said, noticing Banks. "We've
got company. How nice."

Here's a special excerpt from the next Inspector Banks Mystery by Peter Robinson . . .

INNOCENT GRAVES

. . . available in hardcover From Berkley Prime Crime

The night it all began, a thick fog rolled down the dale and enfolded the town of Eastvale in its shroud. Fog in the market square, creeping in the cracks between the cobbles; fog muffling the sound of laughter from the Queen's Arms and muting the light through its red and amber panes; fog rubbing and licking against cool glass in curtained windows and insinuating its way through tiny gaps under doors.

And the fog seemed at its thickest in the graveyard of St Mary's Church, where a beautiful woman with long auburn hair wandered barefoot and drunk, a wineglass full of Pinot Noir held precariously in her hand.

She weaved her way between the squat, gnarled yews, over the unkempt grass, across gravel and cinder paths between crooked grey stones stained green and black with moss and lichen. Sometimes she thought she saw ghosts, grey, translucent shapes flitting among the tombs ahead, but they didn't frighten her.

And she came to the Inchcliffe Mausoleum.

It loomed ahead out of the fog, massive and magnificent: classical lines formed in marble, steps overgrown with weeds leading down to the heavy oak door.

But it was the angel she had come to see. She liked the angel. Its eyes were fixed on heaven, as if nothing earthly mattered, and its hands were clasped together in prayer. Though it was solid marble, she often fancied it was so insubstantial she could pass her hand right through it.

She swayed slightly, raised her glass to the angel and drained half the wine at one gulp. She could feel the cold, damp earth and grass under her feet.

"Hello, Gabriel," she said, voice a little slurred. "I'm sorry but I've sinned again." She hiccupped and put her hand to her mouth. " 'Scuse me, but I just can't seem to—"

Then she saw something, a black-and-white shape, sticking out behind the mausoleum. Curious, she squinted and stumbled towards it. Only when she was about a yard away did she realize it was a black shoe and a white sock. With a foot still in it.

She tottered back, hand to her mouth, then circled around the back of the tomb. All she could make out were the pale legs, the fair hair, the open satchel and the maroon uniform of St Mary's School for Girls.

She screamed and dropped her glass. It shattered on a stone.

Then Rebecca Charters, wife of the vicar of St Mary's, fell to her knees on the broken glass and started to vomit.

2

The fog tasted of ashes, thought Detective Chief Inspector Alan Banks as he pulled up his raincoat collar and hurried down the tarmac path towards the faint, gauzy light. Or perhaps he was being fanciful. Even though he hadn't seen the body yet, he felt that familiar clenching in his stomach that murder always brought.

When he reached the scene, just off a narrow gravel path past the shrubbery, he saw the blurred silhouette of Dr. Glendenning through the canvas screen, bent over a vague shape lying on the ground, like a dumb-show in a Jacobean drama.

Fog had played havoc with the usual order of arrival. Banks himself had been at a senior officers' meeting in Northallerton when he got the call, and he was consequently almost the last person to arrive. Peter Darby, crime-scene photographer, was there already, and so was Detective Inspector Barry Stott, who, for reasons clear to anyone who saw him, was more commonly known as "Jugears." Stott, who had recently been transferred from Salford upon his promotion from detective sergeant, was a temporary replacement for DS Philip Richmond, who had gone to Scotland Yard to join a special computer unit.

Banks took a deep breath and walked behind the screen. Dr. Glendenning looked up, cigarette dangling from his mouth, its smoke indistinguishable from the fog that surrounded them.

"Ah, Banks . . ." he said in his lilting Edinburgh accent, then he shook his head slowly.

Banks looked down at the body. In all his years in Eastvale, he hadn't had to deal with a crime like this. He had seen worse in London, of course, which was part of the reason he had left the Met and transferred up north. But you clearly couldn't hide from it any more now. Not anywhere. George Orwell was right about the decline of the English murder, and this was exactly the kind of thing it had declined into.

The girl, about fifteen or sixteen by the look of her, lay on her back in the long grass behind a huge Victorian sepulchre, upon which stood a marble statue of an angel. The angel had its back turned to her, and through the fog Banks could make out the chipped feathers of its wings.

Her eyes stared into the fog, her long blonde hair lay fanned out around her head like a halo, and her face had a reddish-purple hue. There was a little cut by her left eye and some discolouration around her neck. A trickle of blood the shape of a large teardrop ran out of her left nostril.

Her maroon school blazer lay bunched up on the ground beside her, and her white blouse had been ripped open at the front; her bra had then been removed—roughly, by the looks of it.

Banks felt the urge to cover her. In his job, he had al-

ready seen far more than a man should, and it was little
things like this that sometimes affected him more than the
blood and guts. The girl looked so vulnerable, so callously
violated. He could imagine her shame at being exposed this
way, how she would blush and hurry to cover herself if she
were alive. But she was beyond shame now.

Below her waist, someone had pulled her skirt up to reveal her thighs and pubic region. Her long legs lay open at
a forty-five-degree angle. Her white socks were down
around her ankles. She wore shiny black shoes with buckles
fastened at the sides.

Lying beside her was an open satchel. The strap had
come free of the metal ring at one end. Using his pen,
Banks pushed back the flap and read the neatly inked address:

Miss Deborah Catherine Harrison
28 Hawthorn Close
Eastvale
North Yorkshire
England
United Kingdom of Great Britain and Northern Ireland
European Community
Earth
Solar System
Milky Way
The Universe.

He smiled sadly to himself. It was a typical teenager's sense
of playfulness, exactly the same thing he had done at
school.

Hawthorn Close meant money, as did St Mary's in general. It was an area of large, mostly detached houses, each
with an acre or two of garden, long drives and croquet
lawns shaded by copper beeches. To live there, you had to
make enough money to employ a gardener, at the very
least. St Mary's School required money, too—about £1200

per term. Banks had checked when he first arrived in town, but soon found he couldn't afford to send his daughter, Tracy, there.

Banks cadged some evidence bags from one of the SO-COs and, holding the satchel by its edges, tipped the contents inside one of them. All he found were a couple of exercise books with the name "Deborah Catherine Harrison" written on the cover, a portable chess set, a few cosmetic items and three loose tampons in cellophane wrappers. But why had the satchel been open? he wondered. The buckles seemed strong enough, so he doubted it came open during a struggle. Had someone been looking for something?

Glendenning directed one of his underlings to take oral, vaginal and anal swabs and comb the pubic hair. Then he groaned and got to his feet. "I'm getting old, Banks," he said, massaging his knees. "Too old for this sort of thing." He jerked his head towards the body. Tall and white-haired, with a nicotine-stained moustache, the doctor was probably in his late fifties, Banks guessed.

They moved away, letting the screen block their view of the victim. Every so often, Peter Darby's flash exploded, creating a strobe-light effect in the fog. Banks accepted one of Glendenning's Senior Service. Normally he smoked Silk Cut tipped, but he had cut down drastically on his smoking over the last few months and wasn't even carrying a packet with him. Well, he thought, as Glendenning proffered a gold, initialled lighter, cutting down had been easy enough to do in a lazy summer with no murders to investigate. Now it was November and there was a body at his feet. He lit up and coughed.

"Ought to get that cough seen to, laddie," said Glendenning. "Might be a touch of lung cancer, you know."

"It's nothing. I'm just getting a cold, that's all."

"Aye . . . Well, I don't suppose you dragged me out here on a mucky night like this just to talk about your health, did you?"

"No," said Banks. "What do you make of it?"

"I can't tell you much yet, but judging by her colour and the marks on her throat, I'd say asphyxia due to ligature strangulation."

"Any sign of the ligature?"

"Off the record, that satchel strap fits the bill pretty nicely."

"What about time of death?"

"Oh, come off it, laddie."

"Vaguely?"

"Not more than two or three hours ago. But don't quote me on that."

Banks looked at his watch. Eight o'clock. Which meant she was probably killed between five and six. Not on her way home from school, then. At least not directly.

"Was she killed here?"

"Aye. Almost certainly. Hypostasis is entirely consistent with the position of the body."

"Any sign of the rest of her underwear?"

Glendenning shook his head. "Only the brassiere."

"When can you get her on the table?"

"First thing in the morning. Coming?"

Banks swallowed; the fog scratched his throat. "Wouldn't miss it for the world."

"Fine. I'll reserve you the best seat in the house. I'm off home. You can get her to the mortuary now."

And with that, Glendenning turned and faded into the fog.

Banks stood alone for a moment trying to forget the girl he had just seen spread-eagled so cruelly before him, trying desperately not to see Tracy in her place. He stubbed out his cigarette carefully on the side of the Inchcliffe Mausoleum and pocketed the butt. No point leaving red herrings at the crime scene.

A couple of yards away, he noticed a dark patch on the grass. He walked over and squatted to get a closer look. It looked and smelled as if someone had been sick. He could also make out the stem and fragments of a wineglass, which seemed to have smashed on the stone edging of a grave. He picked up one of the slivers carefully between thumb and forefinger. It was stained with blood or wine; he couldn't be certain which.

He saw DI Stott within hearing range and called him over.

"Know anything about this?" he asked.

Stott looked at the glass and vomit. "Rebecca Charters. Woman who discovered the body," he said. "Bit of an oddball. She's in the vicarage. WPC Kemp is with her."

"Okay. I'll talk to her later." Banks pointed to the mausoleum. "Anyone had a look in there yet?"

"Not yet. I sent PC Aiken to see if he could come up with a key from the vicar."

Banks nodded. "Look, Barry, someone's got to break the news to the girl's parents."

"And seeing as I'm the new lad on the block . . ."

"That's not what I meant. If you're not comfortable with the job, then get someone else to do it. But get it done."

"Sorry," said Stott, taking his glasses off and wiping them on a white handkerchief. "I'm a bit . . ." He gestured towards the body. "Of course I'll go."

"Sure?"

"Yes."

"Okay. I'll join you there soon. Before you go, call in DC Gay and DS Hatchley and tell them to get down here. Someone might have to drag Jim out of The Oak."

Stott raised his eyebrows. Banks noticed his little moue of distaste at the mention of Detective Sergeant Hatchley. Well, he thought, that's *his* cross to bear.

"And get as many officers out on the streets as you can. I want every house in the area canvassed as soon as possible. It's going to be a long, busy night, but we'd better work fast. People forget quickly. Besides, by tomorrow the vultures will be here."

"Vultures?"

"Press, TV people, sightseers. It's going to be a circus, Barry. Prepare yourself."

Stott nodded. PC Aiken turned up with the key to the mausoleum. Banks borrowed a torch from one of the search team, and he and Stott trod carefully down the weed-covered steps.

The heavy wooden door opened after a brief struggle with the key, and they found themselves in the dark with the dead; six sturdy coffins rested on trestles. A few tentacles of fog slid down the stairs and through the door after them, wreathing around their feet.

The small tomb didn't smell of death, only of earth and mould. Fortunately, there were no fresh Inchcliffes buried there; the family had left Eastvale fifty years ago.

All Banks could see on his first glance around were the spiderwebs that seemed to be spun in the very air itself. He gave a little shudder and shone his torch over the floor. There, in the corner furthest from the entrance, were two empty vodka bottles and a pile of cigarette ends. It was hard to tell how recent they were, but they certainly weren't fifty years old.

They found nothing else of interest down there, and it was with great relief that Banks emerged into the open air again; foggy as it was, it felt like a clear night after the inside of the tomb. Banks asked the SOCOs to bag the empty bottles and cigarette ends and search the place thoroughly.

"We'll need a murder room set up at the station," he said, turning to Stott again, "and a van parked near the scene; make it easy for people to come forward. Exhibits Officer, phone lines, civilian staff, the usual thing. Get Susan Gay to see to it. Better inform the Chief Constable, too," Banks added with a sinking feeling.

At the moment, Banks was senior man in Eastvale CID, as Detective Superintendent Gristhorpe had broken his leg while fixing his drystone wall. Technically, Detective Chief Superintendent Jack Wormsley, from North Yorkshire Regional HQ at Northallerton, was supposed to be in charge of a murder investigation. However, Banks knew from experience not to expect much beyond the occasional phone call from DCS Wormsley; he was rumoured to be far too close to finishing his scale matchstick model of the Taj Mahal to be bothered with a mere murder. If it came from anywhere, Banks knew, the main hindrance would come from the new chief constable: Jeremiah "Jimmy" Riddle, a high-flier of the pushy, breathe-down-your-neck school of police management.

"We'll also need a thorough ground-search of the graveyard," Banks went on, "but we might be better doing that in daylight, especially if this fog disperses a bit during the night. Anyway, make sure the place is well secured." Banks looked around. "How many entrances are there?"

"Two. One off North Market Street and one off Kendal Road, just by bridge."

"Should be easy to secure, then. The wall looks high enough to deter any interlopers, but we'd better have a couple of men on perimeter patrol, just to make sure. The last thing we need is some intrepid reporter splashing crime-scene photos all over the morning papers. Is there any access from the riverside?"

Stott shook his head. "The wall's higher there, too, and it's topped with broken glass."

"Welcoming sort of place, isn't it?"

"I understand they've had a bit of vandalism."

Banks peered through the fog at the lights in the vicarage. They looked like disembodied eyes. "You're a bit of a churchman, aren't you, Barry?"

Stott nodded. "Yes. St Cuthbert's, though, not St Mary's."

Banks nodded towards the vicarage. "Do you know who the vicar is here?"

"Father Daniel Charters."

Banks raised his eyebrows. "I thought so. I don't know

all the details, but isn't he the one who's been in the news a bit lately?"

"He is," Stott said through gritted teeth.

"Interesting," said Banks, "Very interesting." And he wandered off towards the vicarage.